C PLAN 21   13/10/04   X

Joss   ed
by   up
and   om
scho   ne
him   gly
com   ats
Alv   ot
only   yll
can   to
con   ig,
beco   th
the   is
crur   ie
Batt   in
love   ic
cons   lls
far   id
heat   ns
are s

TITLE The Burning Blue

THE BURNING BLUE

James Holland

WINDSOR
PARAGON

First published 2004
by
William Heinemann
This Large Print edition published 2004
by
BBC Audiobooks Ltd
by arrangement with
The Random House Group Ltd

ISBN 0 7540 9513 4 (Windsor Hardcover)
ISBN 0 7540 9404 9 (Paragon Softcover)

British Library Cataloguing in Publication Data available

Printed and bound in Great Britain by
Antony Rowe Ltd., Chippenham, Wiltshire

For Ned

High Flight

Oh, I have slipped the surly bonds of earth
And danced the skies on laughter-silvered wings
Sunward I've climbed, and joined the tumbling
    mirth
Of sun-split clouds—
and done a hundred things
You have not dreamed of—wheeled and soared
    and swung
High in the sunlit silence. Hov'ring there,
I've chased the shouting wind along, and flung
My eager craft through footless halls of air.
Up, up the long, delirious, burning blue
I've topped the wind-swept heights with easy grace
Where never lark or even eagle flew—
And, while with silent lifting mind I've trod
The high untrespassed sanctity of space,
Put out my hand and touched the face of God.

— John Gillespie Magee, Jr. 1922–1941

THE BURNING BLUE

North Africa—July, 1942

Although the enemy has lost a great many of his fighter aircraft during the last two months, there has been so far no apparent sign of a decrease in flying ability or combat performance. Combat effectiveness has been maintained, and indeed increased.

Memorandum from General von Waldau,
Fliegerführer Afrika, 25th July 1942

A little after four that afternoon, Joss Lambert left his tent and strode towards his plane in a line of others on the far side of the landing ground. He was twenty-two, unshaven, with blond hair which had thickened with dirt and sand. The last time he'd looked in a mirror he'd noticed a new line that ran from the side of his nose to his mouth; no longer such a baby face.

It was hot again, really hot, but very still and quiet, so that the only sound was of his boots crunching across the desert grit.

He was conscious of very little going on around him. For weeks now, he'd felt an increasing detachment from the job in hand. In part, this was deliberate, a necessary means of dealing with the desperateness of his situation. His life was more bearable if he did not think too much about what it was he was doing. Then perhaps one day—*one day*—he might be allowed to return home to her.

But now—well, now, there was nothing. He'd read her letter a dozen times, but it was as though his brain had simply shut down, refused to absorb

1

the meaning of those words. Instead he had become numb, unable to think about anything other than the task ahead: a German land recce unit to bomb and strafe. More enemy to kill. Sweat glistened on his temples and ran, like a spider, down his back. He brought his upper lip to his sleeve and looked at the wet imprint of a moustache outlined on the material.

Bradshaw, his rigger, was giving the windscreen and canopy a final clean as Joss grabbed the parachute off the plane's wing. Feet first, then arms through the canvas straps and all brought together into the single fastener. He paused, ran his tongue around his gums, and then spat, as he always did in a vain attempt to rid his mouth of sand before a flight. He'd been the first to reach his plane. Ten battered Curtis Kittyhawks, all gently baking in the sun. The metal was too hot to touch, so hot they'd once fried corned beef on one of the wings. Joss put on his gloves, then hoisted himself onto the wing and into the cockpit, his parachute pack thumping against the back of his legs. The other pilots were reaching their planes. Prior, the squadron leader, walked round his, touching it, examining the underside of the wings and rudder. Everyone had their own routines.

'That's as clean as I'm going to get her,' said Bradshaw, leaning back to give the Perspex one last inspection. He glanced up at Joss. 'You all right, sir?'

Joss looked up, forced a fleeting smile.

'Well, she's all ready for you,' said Bradshaw, and slid off the wing.

Out in the open, there was something about the vastness of the desert that muffled the occasional clang or shout. But in the narrow space of the plane, the quietness was close and contained, even with the hood pushed right back: sounds were amplified and tinny so that he was conscious of his breaths, of the squeak of pedals being pushed up and down, and the strapping of his flying helmet; sounds that emphasized the routine of the pre-flight checks.

Without meaning to, his gloved hand felt for the letter in his shirt pocket, and as it did so his mind flooded with the crushing weight of despair. *Stella,* he thought, *how could you do this?* He lifted his arm to rub the sweat off his forehead and saw his hand was shaking.

When the ground crew gave him the signal, he began to manipulate the hand pumps and starter buttons. The airscrew began to turn, silently at first, then chugging, until the exhaust stubs vomited blue flame and black smoke and the whole airframe began to shudder and clank as the Allison engine erupted into life. Moments later, the other nine planes joined him, a deafening roar tearing apart the quiet.

Pulling the hood close, he lowered his goggles. Christ, it was hot. Even his arms and legs were glistening now. *Come on, come on.* Any longer and both he and the plane would be dead from overheating. He felt in his pocket, then realized he'd left his tiny wooden lion behind. *Damn.* Still, it was too late to worry about it now. *Put it out of mind,* he told himself, *put everything out of mind.*

At last, Prior, at Red One, moved off, followed by Reds Two and Three. A new low whining began, then it was his turn, at Blue One, to open the throttle and start trundling into position. Swathes

3

of sand and dust whipped the airframe. It was bad enough taxiing with an enormous engine cowling for a view, but with the man-made sandstorm it was like night-flying without the lights. A further complication—and there always was one—was the way the Kittyhawk tended to veer to the right. He had developed a method of taking a compass bearing and hoping for the best, but with everything juddering—including his legs on the rudder pedals and the arrows on the dials it wasn't easy. And on the ground there was always time to worry. Like the fact that his plane was full to bursting with high-octane fuel and a 500lb bomb.

Sand and grit battered the Perspex. So much for Bradshaw's cleaning efforts. Opening the throttle further, he felt the plane surge forward. A sudden jolt as a wheel went over a large stone and the stick bolted in his hand momentarily, knocking his elbow against the side of the cockpit and numbing his arm. He cursed and corrected the yaw of the plane. The rattling and noise increased with the speed, until with a sigh of relief from both the pilot and machine, Joss pulled back, the stick biting and firming up, his grip tightening, as though controlling a strong dog on a lead. The shaking stopped as he and his plane, strapped together, emerged into the big wide blue. From sand cloud to glaring brightness, he thought, squinting through the goggles at the sun that was now gleaming off the Perspex of the machine in front. He glanced behind him, back at their airfield. One of the planes was still on the ground, its propeller slowing. *That song—Blue Skies.* She'd always sung it wrong— wrong words, wrong tune half the time too.

The target was a wadi some forty miles south of

Mersa Matruh and the coast, full of tanks and other vehicles, and more importantly, ammunition, fuel dumps and several hundred men. These dried river beds were hard to spot from the otherwise flat desert floor, but from the air offered rich pickings, as Prior had cheerfully pointed out. But no one had been fooled by his bravado; such a base would be dense with anti-aircraft flak and machine guns. It was a basic equation: the richer the pickings, the smaller the chances of making it back.

They crossed down into the Qattara Depression, the huge escarpment marking its northern edge clearly visible, then headed west, eighty miles behind enemy lines before looping up north so they could attack low, fast and out of the sun. Surprise was the key. They had to pray no one saw them before they dropped height into the bomb run. At twenty miles from the target, Prior brought the squadron into line astern. An old RAF attack formation, but then again, Prior, *was* a Cranwell man. Joss had tried suggesting they attack in lines of three astern, but it had fallen on deaf ears. 'Doesn't give us enough room for manoeuvre,' Prior had told him, 'and makes us a bigger target.' And that had been that. This was fine on a single run, but when there were two circuits to be made—the bombing, then the strafe—the odds were shortened even further for those at the end of the line.

As they approached the wadi, Joss lifted his goggles onto his forehead. They were low enough now for him to see a burnt-out bomber, crumpled and alone among the sand and stone away to his left. With his thumb, he flicked off the gun safety catch. He had been on the receiving end of such

5

attacks on many occasions. From the ground, the attackers seemed to hold all the advantages, but this was of little comfort. Strapped into the tiny cockpit, so narrow his elbows brushed the sides and his head the canopy roof, he wondered how he ever made it through. A deep breath, the target rushing towards him. Lines of orange and green tracer were already criss-crossing the sky in front of him, despite the advantage of surprise and coming from out of the sun. Arcing lazily at first, they accelerated as they flashed past his plane.

Joss pushed the stick over hard right then left, half-rolling his plane from side to side, stomach lurching as the blue horizon swivelled. On the ground, men fell flat at the roar of nine Allison engines belting past so low. He corrected himself, dropped his bomb, and not waiting to see where it had hit, sped on through the encampment. Explosion after explosion thundered behind him, and one massive fire-ball pitched orange flames and black smoke like a geyser into the sky. Someone had scored well. Tracer followed him out into the desert as he circled, black puffs of smoke filling the sky, ahead, below and to the side. They were way off, but it wouldn't be long now. He glanced round. They'd all made it through the first run, but then that was the easy bit. Now for the strafing. No surprise any more, and the guns would be ready. The puffs of smoke intensified, and the plane jolted. Closer now. Joss gripped the stick tighter, breath quickening. Another crash, the plane shuddered again and tiny shards of shrapnel showered the airframe. *Jesus that was close.* He saw Prior turning in for his second run, followed by Reds Two and Three. Then his turn.

6

One, he counted. The camp looked a mess. Thick oily smoke belching into the sky, but there was no let-up from the flak batteries. More splinters rained across the airframe. *Two,* lines of tracer looking as though they would hit him square between the eyes, but somehow hurrying past and over. The stick jolted and shook with the plane. Joss gripped it with both hands. Sweat poured down his cheeks and back. *Three.* Over 300 miles an hour into a sky raining bullets and debris and pieces of jagged metal. Finger on the firing button. *Four.* More men down below, leaping face-first onto the ground as his bullets sprayed across them. *Five.* Another massive explosion—not flak, not a bomb, but one of their Kittyhawks disintegrating in mid-air. The planes ahead disappeared into a cloud of smoke, then Red Three emerged again, a spectral silhouette, hardly real at all. *Six.* He whipped on through the burning gust. The tracer still pursued him, flashing doggedly over his canopy as he rolled once more, before running out of steam and dropping away.

Six seconds. That was all it took, and then he was away, blind through the smoke wall at fifty feet, and then racing over the desert. The whole attack completed in just over a minute. Joss started to gulp deep breaths of air, realizing he'd stopped breathing again as he'd counted through the strafing run. Looking behind, the puffs of flak and tracer disappeared into the distance, until all he could see was the smoke cloud caused by their sixty seconds of destruction.

Spared again.

*　　　*　　　*

Prior led them back up to 10,000 feet before breaking radio silence. Two pilots killed: one blown up, the other by ploughing straight into the ground (causing as much damage as any 500-pounder). Most of the others had taken some kind of punishment, although no one else was injured and the planes were still flying, still keeping up with the CO.

'Well done everyone,' said Prior, 'but keep a sharp look out. We're not out of the woods yet.' Predictable, routine words.

Sixteen months before, when Joss had first arrived in the desert, he'd been surprised to find his shoulders bleeding after his first sortie. The combination of sand and wearing only a thin shirt rather than a thick jacket or Irvin had caused the straps to chafe as he kept turning his head to scan the sky. His skin had hardened since. He'd also lined both his parachute and the cockpit straps with padding, but even this minor irritation had made him realize there were a number of differences between flying over home and the desert. Another was the lack of cloud cover. Flying over England, they'd cursed when there was little cloud; in North Africa, there simply were *no* clouds. Just a vast, burning blue, with only the sun's glare for cover.

Goggles lowered once more, he continued to search the wide desert sky, although his mind had now begun to drift. He could do that, fly and keep a look out without really concentrating. He'd often thought it was a bit like driving a car. He might indicate, overtake or change down a gear, but without being conscious of it, thoughts on something else entirely.

8

But now the dull nauseous sensation in his stomach had returned. *No,* he thought, *this cannot be happening, not now, not after all this.* 'It can't, it can't,' he said out loud. There had been a time when he'd believed Tommy—that war promised honour, excitement and fellowship—but this place, this *fucking awful* desert, with its freezing nights and scorching days, its sand and its millions of flies and fleas, had soon put paid to that. But he'd persevered, borne it because there'd been the hope of a future worth having; a future with her. *Stella* had made it all bearable, only Stella.

Bob Carter at Red Three was wavering up and down before him. Damage somewhere. Rudder or aileron, maybe. Further ahead was Prior with Brian Scott flying at his side. Christ, but what a bunch they'd become. Sun-bruised faces, uncombed, bony, barely a decent uniform between them. Joss had begun by trying to keep himself presentable, but on a canteen of water a day it was impossible. He'd rather have a glug of water on his return from a sortie than enough to wash in properly. They were all exhausted. They smelled too, of sweat mixed with oil and grease, although it was only when someone came back from leave that anyone noticed. The little round pills the medical officer sometimes issued helped keep them going, but they were no substitute for leave. And leave in Cairo was no substitute for going home.

No wonder lines were appearing on his face.

He looked down: wide, flat and unrelenting, a sprawling, sandy grey desert which disappeared at the horizon into a strip of haze that merged with the sky. He was unable to make out details: without woods or snaking river valleys it all looked the same to him, a barren, lifeless plain that meant nothing. No towns or villages, just sand and rock. A hellish landscape.

The churning throb of the engine had become a neutral background that had evolved into a heavy kind of silence. He could no longer understand why he was still alive. Why was someone playing such a cruel trick on him? He was, he supposed, an above-average fighter pilot with an above-average combat record, but even the greatest aces usually came down eventually: Mannon, Richtofen, Ball; Molders, Wick; even Bader and Tuck were in POW camps now. The chances of his surviving over two years of almost continual active service (bar three months instructing in the Sudanese desert) were virtually nil. But he'd always been lucky; it had been something of a joke. Strange coincidences, or flukes of nature, had followed him from England to North Africa. He had been shot down three times, crash-landed more often than he could count on one hand, been bombed, strafed and nearly died, of all things, from an infection just a few weeks after arriving in the desert. Yet here he still was.

There had been another fortunate escape the previous evening. After dinner, Denis Carr had asked him for a game of cards. At first Joss refused, but Denis was persistent.

'What are we playing for?'

'Cigarettes,' said Denis.

They'd all been running low, and getting quite irritable about it too, but Calloway, the adjutant, had told Joss they were expecting a supply plane the following morning—with plenty more cigarettes on board. Clearly Denis didn't know.

'Not money?'

'No—just fags. More valuable at the moment.'
Joss relented.

In the desert, where so much chipped away the nerves, Joss had soon realized that it was ever more important that everyone got on. After all, there was no escape, no pub and even the beer had usually gone off by the time it reached their mess tent. Any arguments tended to be short-lived affairs: one might see two pilots at each other's throats one night but exchanging jokes the following morning. And he did like most of them well enough—he was just not as close to them as he had been to the squadron in the old days; he'd learnt his lesson the hard way. Only a week before, Laurie Collins had gone missing. The previous day, Joss and Denis had finally packed up his things. Denis had never said anything about it—it wasn't done—but he and Laurie had been close. They all needed distractions, and Joss—who had only recently started smoking—could afford to lose a few smokes.

It was dark and already freezing, so they had sat in Denis's tent with thick jumpers and overcoats on, clutching their cards, Joss blowing into his cupped hands. He'd already lost three cigarettes when they heard, faintly, the whirr of engines.

'Jesus fucking Christ,' said Denis, 'sneaky bastards.'

In no time at all—only the time to pause, look at each other, then realize it was Italian Macchi 202s—they heard the first crack of machine-gun fire, and immediately dived into Denis's slit-trench of a bunk.

The Italian planes were gone as quickly as they'd arrived.

But when Joss checked his tent, he found a neat line of bullet holes that crossed one side to the other. Inside, the fold-away table at which he wrote his letters was cut in two, and his sleeping bag still smoking. Denis had followed, and at the time Joss had turned to him and thanked him for bullying him into playing poker. And God for watching over him again.

Denis hadn't returned that afternoon. His was the Kittyhawk that blew up.

The supply plane—a Whitley—*had* brought more cigarettes.

'You *knew*,' Denis had said that morning. And he'd whacked his cap against Joss's arm. Denis: small, wiry, his almost-black hair sticking up on end, and grinning a gap-toothed smile. Now scattered across that German camp.

What a sham. And the letter had arrived on the same plane. Some of the pilots were sent books and magazines, which were then passed around. Out of date newspapers and copies of *Crusader*, the Eighth Army magazine, were also delivered regularly, and although most of the articles tended to be little more than morale-boosting pep talks, it was at least something new to read. The mail had been one of the first things to be brought out from the plane. Calloway had riffled through the assorted post, reading out names and waiting for them to be snatched from his hand.

Joss had recognized the handwriting immediately, but only once he was in his tent, out of sight from anyone else, did he tear open the seal.

Alvesdon Farm
28ᵗʰ April 1942

Dear Joss,

I don't know how to say this to you, but Philip Mornay has asked me to marry him and I've accepted. I'm so sorry, but I cannot go on like this, worrying about you constantly, not knowing whether you are alive or dead. It's eating me away. I thought I was stronger; thought I would somehow be able to cope. But I can't. Are you still the same Joss? Or someone very different? I don't know where you are, or what you are doing. I can see your face, but I can barely remember the sound of your voice, except that I loved it. I always felt we would be punished, that there would be a price to pay. To expect you to come back to me is tempting fate too much. I can't help feeling that if I wait any longer, God will snatch you from me. That sounds stupid, I'm sure, but I feel it; I've dreamt it countless times. If I release us both, then perhaps we have a chance. I don't expect you to understand, but hope that one day you might forgive me.

I will always love you and those precious months we had together,
Stella.

Oh Stella, no. He'd stayed there, reading and re-reading it, his body frozen with shock. An hour later he was called back to the mess for the mission briefing. Then he'd gone to his plane.

In the past, he'd believed he'd been spared because of her; that the losses they'd suffered, and the torment of being parted for so long were nothing more than tests that had to be endured,

13

and which would make the ultimate reward more wondrous. He thought about some of the pilots who'd come and gone: some had had wives and children back home, others adoring parents who sent regular packages, lovingly wrapped; a few had showed the promise of doing something brilliant in later life. All dead. But he, with only Stella, had survived. He had endured the scraping, abrasive, sand getting *everywhere*, wearing away the skin of his joints, chafing his feet, working its way into every orifice, scratching his eyes. He had helped clear the base after the *khamsin* had crept upon them, bringing with it a vindictive, swirling sandstorm that covered everything, choking engines and half-burying the camp sandpapering their planes to death.

Christ, but what was the point of this torture if not for her? What was the point of being constantly persecuted by the hordes of flies that made their lives a misery? He even had two in his cockpit now, buzzing around, then settling on his back or bare knee. He tried opening the canopy, but they insisted on remaining. Desert flies were different, nothing like the house flies Joss knew back home. The desert fly was smaller but hardier and more aggressive, attracted by sweat to exposed flesh. Especially irritating was when they buzzed around an ear, or swarmed at mealtimes. Eating became a skilled art, done one handed, the other saved to brush away the hordes. Even so, it was still impossible to complete a meal without a sizeable portion of desert fly. Laurie Collins once spent a morning trapping flies in an old tin, which he then doused with petrol and lit. Everyone enjoyed this brief moment of revenge until they were overwhelmed by the powerful, yet familiar stench. With horror, they realized that the flies must have been feeding on rotten flesh. Burnt, rotten, human flesh. There were some who could not eat for several days after. But not Joss; *he* had a reason to keep going. Another irony: by some glitch, her letter had taken three months to reach him. Twelve weeks passing between ship and aeroplane, crossing oceans and continents, denying the truth. He wondered whether she had read the letters he'd sent her in the meantime: letters of love, of hope.

Urgent shouting cut across the air, and out of nowhere bullets and tracer jabbered across his wings. Joss's time for brooding was over. Prior had warned them to be vigilant, but that hadn't prevented them from being bounced again, and out of the sun *again.* Germans this time, in Messerschmitt 109s.

Without thinking, Joss pushed the stick forward, diving then turning in towards the enemy, the horizon rising and rolling before him. His insides churned and an invisible weight thrust him back against his seat, but the tracer was already curving wide behind him. There wasn't much he could say in favour of the Kittyhawk: it had a slow rate of climb, slower even than a Hurricane, and none of the visibility of a Spitfire; nor could the shark teeth painted onto the underside of the engine cowling have been very intimidating. But at least it could out-dive and out-turn a 109.

The firing stopped and Joss glanced back to see that his pursuer had broken off. He turned round to find another 109 heading straight for him, guns spitting bullets and cannon shells. *Shit—where had he come from?* A loud crack and his mirror

15

disappeared. Another, and the plane juddered. Screaming in his ears—a pilot burning. Frank? Hard to tell: one man's screams sounded much the same as another's. But *his* plane kept going, hurtling towards the 109. Joss tensed, closed his eyes.

He opened them again as the 109 flashed its underbelly just feet above him, vulnerable and silvery as a trout, a brief moment before exploding, tearing in half like paper. The blast jolted the stick from Joss's hand and knocked his head against the side of the canopy. A wing cartwheeled through the air, the black cross spinning. The engine and half the fuselage fell in flames. Debris fluttered in every direction, and as Joss turned he saw blood streaked across the outside of his canopy. He retched. For those few seconds he *had* thought they were going to collide.

The pedals kicked his feet. The rudder. He looked round quickly and saw nothing, then another Messerschmitt lurching into view. More sparkling tracer. Something whipped across his right arm, searing, and Joss thrust the stick forward and dived again. The needle on his oil gauge was rising and the whole airframe juddered. He clenched his teeth, both hands gripping the stick. The engine whined, screeching in his ears, then for a second, maybe two, his vision dimmed, on the point of blackout. Only when he was sure the tracer had stopped following him, did he pull back the control column. Down to 1,000 feet. *My arm. Jesus.* Blood was spreading in a widening stain across his shirtsleeve, and dripped from his elbow. He yelled out loud; in unison the engine coughed, spluttered, then stopped. Silence, apart from a

16

gentle whistling. The propellers slowly wound down to a halt, one of them chopped in half.

He was gliding, alone. Four of the nine, himself included, would not be making it back today. Almost half the flight. A bad day by anyone's standards. Blood drained from his head as his energy ebbed. His teeth began to chatter.

Flames were flickering around the engine cowling, and wafts of smoke streaming over the wings. Joss wondered whether he should try and turn the plane and jump out, but he was already almost too low to bale out. If he stuck with it, they might just smash into the ground, and that would be it. Over, once and for all. He realized he didn't mind; in fact, he welcomed it.

Another part of his brain took over, ordering his hands and feet to try and control the plane so that it drifted downwards in a gentle trajectory. The undercarriage was trapped, but everything else seemed to work: the ailerons, flaps, and even the rudder. The eventual landing was almost graceful. Initial contact with the desert floor jolted him enough to wind him, and he gasped with the terrible scraping of metal on stone, but after a short while, the machine ran out of steam and ground, creaking, to a halt.

The flames were growing. In seconds, they were scorching his legs and singeing his bare arms. He thought of the screams, screams he'd heard countless times before. He never, ever wanted to suffer that kind of pain. His right arm had numbed, but from somewhere deep within him, a primeval desire for survival urged him out of the cockpit. Sliding off the wing, he staggered thirty yards and collapsed.

Joss lay on the desert, spread-eagled, dipping in and out of consciousness. The smell, this time not of other men's burnt flesh, but his own, was rich and cloying; and this time he vomited. He clutched his right arm and heard himself cry out. His hand covered in blood, his forearms red and white, blistering and swollen. Such a mess. He dropped his head back onto the ground, the sun bearing down on his closed eyelids, creating a luminous kind of orange glow. They were advised not to wear shorts or rolled-up sleeves: clothing was another layer of protection against fire. But the advisers weren't the ones flying the things in the middle of the day in stultifying heat.

He began thinking about Dick. His voice, very clear, came back to him. 'I knew if I stayed where I was, I would be a dead man, so I started walking.' Twenty-four hours after his crash, Dick had stumbled back into camp. But he'd had some chocolate, plenty of water, a map, a compass, and crucially, had known pretty much where he'd crashed. It hadn't done him much good anyway. He'd been shot down again a day later. No one saw it, but he'd been missing for two weeks, and after a few initial jokes, everyone had agreed even Dick couldn't survive in the desert for that long.

Joss's canteen was still in the plane. Now the whole cockpit was gently burning, the smell of burnt rubber, paint and oil mingling with the stench of his own burns. Without water, and with the loss of blood, he couldn't last long.

*   *   *

He'd been dreaming about being in the belly of a

18

great ship, surging back to England, the pitching and yawing of the boat thrusting him up and down, the roar of the massive pistons drowning out all the other noise. Then voices, English voices. *So then, still alive.* He opened his eyes.

'Don't worry mate, it's going to be all right. You take it easy.'

It was dark in the back of the truck, but there was that smell of metal and oil, familiar to all machinery. Lying flat on his back, occasionally jolted as the truck passed over a bump or a stone in the sand, Joss was watched by the two men. They wore British Army tin hats and khaki drill, but the white armbands and red crosses stood out in the dim light.

'You're going to be just fine,' said one of them. 'Get you back to a nice hospital in no time.'

Joss murmured.

'Watched your plane come down. And saw you charge at that Jerry. Death wish haven't you?'

Maybe then, he thought, but now he wasn't so sure. He moved his lips again, but the words weren't there.

'You were only twenty-odd miles behind the southern section of the front line,' the other man said. 'We were looking for a bomber crew but couldn't find them. Saw you instead. Still, you were lucky. Another few miles further south and you'd have hit the Depression. Then you'd have been well and truly fucked.'

So they're dead and I'm alive.

'All the same,' said the first medic, 'don't reckon you'd have lasted too long where you were on your own. Someone's watching out for you all right.'

'Yes,' Joss managed, and closed his eyes.

19

Cairo—August, 1942

A tall, elegant woman in a light blue dress and bright red lipstick was touring the wards of the 9th Scottish General Hospital with an Egyptian in tow struggling with a large bag. They were a comic pair: she towering above him, her voice sharp and crisp, he at her side, clutching the bag.

'Now, what about you?' She paused in front of Joss's bed. 'Can I get you anything? A magazine? Or a book? Or perhaps you'd like to try some embroidery?' She delved into the bag and produced a set of needles and bundles of brightly coloured threads. She looked at him, ready for his reply—*nothing wrong with men doing embroidery too, you know*. Well, he wasn't interested.

'I'd love to see what novels you have,' he replied. He was sitting up on his bed, his pyjama sleeves and trousers rolled up to allow his arms and legs to breathe.

The lady put the threads and needles back in the bag, told the Egyptian to stand still and then brought out a handful of books.

'Let's see,' she said, peering at them in turn at arm's length. 'Jeffery Farnol, P.G. Wodehouse, Mazo de la Roche and *Twelfth Night.*' She paused, looked at Joss and said, 'Any of these take your fancy? I think there's some others in the bag.'

Joss took a Jeffery Farnol and the Shakespeare. He was prepared to try anything that might distract him from thinking about Stella. The lady moved past the next bed (the occupant had lost both his arms but was also asleep), pausing by the other five

20

in turn, her helper obediently keeping to heel.

The windows were open and Joss could hear the city outside. Car horns, occasional shouts, then the muezzin all stood out above the general murmur coming from the mass of people, animals and machines that shared the streets around the hospital. The heat was unbearable. The fans that wobbled and whirred from the ceiling tried hard but provided only faint relief. Most of his fellow patients had burns of some kind, and most much worse than his. There had been one man who'd screamed continually throughout the night. They were just about to move him when he died. Joss had been relieved, then disgusted with himself for not feeling more pity. And the groans continued; morphine always wore off. The ward smelled too. Burnt flesh hung heavy in the air. A nurse told Joss that it was always worse in summer. He noticed it most whenever he first woke, although he was aware the stench had become more acute the more he recovered. Perhaps he'd have been better off being among the ranks in a much larger ward. It had to be an improvement on their foetid little room.

Where had those medics come from? They'd arrived in the desert from nowhere, like guardian angels.

Why him?

He had begun dreaming too. Lately, it had been the same each night. He was in the hull of the ship once more, the massive pistons of the engines pounding in his head, surging towards England with great urgency. Seamlessly, the ship's engines merged into that of a Merlin. He was sitting in the cockpit of a Spitfire, flying through thick cloud. A

21

moment of exhilaration as he emerged from the cloud to see the English coast beneath him. Home at last, and its familiarity bringing a soothing sense of calm. But in moments, the engine began to whine and Joss was spinning and diving, his vision blocked by blood sprayed across the Perspex. Helpless and out of control, he awoke just as the plane crashed into the ground.

He never used to have nightmares at all in the desert. He supposed he'd become anaesthetized, worn down like the engines in their Kittyhawks.

*   *   *

One of the patients next to him had been discharged that morning, but beds never went spare for long. Joss had only just started reading *Twelfth Night* and had managed to pass over five minutes without thinking of her, when another man was brought in to fill the gap. Putting down the book, he watched the two orderlies lift the man from the trolley while a nurse and doctor hovered behind. The man's face was wrapped in bandages, one side padded with extra wadding. He turned towards Joss and, with his one uncovered eye, blinked or winked—Joss wasn't sure which.

'Is that comfortable for you?' asked the nurse, once the man was safely laid on the bed.

The doctor said, 'Now just lie as still as you can and take it easy and we'll soon have you on your feet again.' Joss had been there long enough to know what that meant.

The nurse turned and approached his bed. 'Everything all right, Joss?'

'Fine, thank you. Who's my new neighbour?'

'A cavalry officer. A lieutenant. Had half his face torn away by some shrapnel.' Quiet, matter of fact; that was their way.

Joss nodded. 'His name?'

'Carter. Alex Carter. Read to him if you like. It might help to keep his mind off the pain. I'll bring you a chair and then you could sit by him and read that novel. Do you good to be out of bed a bit.'

'All right,' Joss agreed, but he was suddenly faltering once more. His throat tightened, aching with the effort not to cry, his mouth dry. It was the smallest thing: the thick, dark hair sprouting the top of Alex Carter's bandages, but it reminded him so much of Guy. *Guy*, thought Joss, remembering. Something within him had been unlocked. He felt tears at the corners of his eyes, so he looked down, not wanting anyone to see. He understood now. He hadn't been favoured at all. He'd been cursed.

An orderly brought over a chair. Joss waited a few moments, breathed in heavily a couple of times, then swivelled his legs over the edge of the bed. Clutching the iron frame for support, he lowered his weight onto his feet. The doctors had told him he was recovering well; his burns and the hole in his arm were healing, even though he would keep the scars. But they hurt enough, and any pressure on his legs sent waves of pain shooting up his spine.

He eased himself into the chair.

'The nurse thought you might like me to read something to you,' he said at length. His new companion turned his head towards him once more. Another blink of that single, pale grey eye and a faint nod. Joss wondered whether Alex

23

Carter was thinking as he was, of a time long ago.

He cleared his throat, then began. *'The Broad Highway* by Jeffery Farnol.'

But he was in no mood for reading, least of all highwayman adventures. Before he'd finished two pages, he put the book down again.

'I'm sorry,' said Joss. 'I'm finding it hard to concentrate. You've reminded me of a friend, you see—a great friend. I haven't seen him for a while, but—' He stopped, then said, 'I'm sorry—I can't stop thinking about before the war.' He glanced up again, but the man with half a face was now lying back, staring up at the ceiling and the slowly rotating fan.

Joss leant back against his pillow, remembering. A house and its landscape. He thought about how the one had become inextricably linked to the other. The land there had been farmed for thousands of years—you only had to look at the two domed barrows on the top of the hill to understand that. And if it had been farmed, then there must have been dwellings there too. There were also the occasional discoveries—bits of old pottery unearthed by a plough, and once even a few coins. Yet for all the changes brought by the centuries—invasions, wars, religious upheaval, revolution—nothing had stopped generation upon generation farming that spot. Joss knew the place in all its seasons: in springtime, with the first hint of green flecking the hedgerows; in high summer, and in winter with snow on the ground and the trees so black and skeletal that he wondered how they could ever be full and bursting again. Yet whatever the time, whatever the year, the curve of the hill above, almost half-encircling the farm in its

24

protective sweep, remained unchangeable. And below, equally resolute, lay the farmhouse, so that it might just as well have been a solid granite outcrop rather than a building made of brick and plaster and timber. Joss could not imagine the landscape *ever* changing, not for all the destruction wrought by war.

But as he thought of it now, it was as it was in summer, the August sun gently feathering his face—a summer before the war. For a moment, the sticky heat of the ward and the flies spinning in their deranged manner above him were almost forgotten.

England—August, 1938

At Grateley, a large bearded man joined the otherwise empty compartment and sat down opposite Joss, sinking heavily onto the grey-blue plush. Joss leant forward, his elbows on his knees and tapped his fingers together. *Next stop.* The train went into a cutting, the open fields either side of the track replaced by sheer walls of white. *Chalk*—the same chalk of the hills above Alvesdon Farm. He glanced at his watch, then stood up to lift his cases and coat from the luggage rack. A button on his coat caught in the string webbing.

'There's still a little way to Salisbury,' said the man, as Joss pulled his coat free.

'I know,' he said, turning, his cheeks flushing. He was about to explain, then realized he would sound foolish. 'Thank you,' he said, placing his battered cases on the empty seat next to him. He'd never been challenged about this routine before. The man smiled, and pulled a tobacco pouch from his pocket.

Sitting down again, Joss pressed his head against the window, the glass already warm now that the sun had appeared. Outside, he saw the field with the dilapidated barn. It had scaffolding around one side, as though repairs were about to be made, but for some reason, the work had never started. He'd once worked out it marked the halfway point on the final stretch to Salisbury. Last time he'd seen the field it had been green, full of newly-sprouting wheat. Now it was being harvested, the crop almost cut.

The man began to fill his pipe, pressing the tobacco into the bowl from a pouch in his jacket pocket. He lit it, cupping the match in his chubby hands, and Joss turned his head to watch the smoke as it was sucked out of the open window.

He thought about the house, as he'd done many times since he'd last been there at Easter. Through the front door with its ornate portico of Chilmark stone, and into the hallway. The black marble slab at the foot of the stairs with the crack across it; and the round table at the centre of the hallway with the silver letter tray and the bowl, never emptied of its eclectic contents: the lone green woollen glove, the frayed cricket ball and giant fir cone would still be there. And that smell, unique to Alvesdon Farm. What was it? Dog, wax polish but some other ingredient too. Then there was the corridor that led to the drawing room. The rug still sometimes skidded beneath him on the parquet floor. And the main staircase hanging with portraits of Liddells dating back 300 years.

Through another cutting, then there, stretching

26

away from him, was the long curve of the hill that shielded the eastern edges of Salisbury. He thought of a trip he and Guy had once made on their bicycles to Clarendon, the far side of the hill. There, overgrown and far from any houses, lay the remains of Henry II's royal palace—mounds, ditches, odd bits of stonework; eerie and quite unlike any other ruin. Guy had crept away and hidden, leaving Joss standing alone. He smiled to himself, remembering how Guy had reappeared after a short while. 'You were supposed to be scared,' he'd said. But he hadn't been at all; quite the opposite in fact. After everything he'd left behind in London, he'd enjoyed the isolation that strange place provided.

Joss stood up again and leant out of the window, the wind making his eyes water and minute particles of soot flecking his face. Ahead was the spire, looming skywards, dwarfing the rest of the city. In the clear light that had followed the rain, it gleamed like a giant stalagmite. *Nearly there.* Houses now—the edge of the city—and a string of allotments, men bent over, spending their Saturday tending their small plot of soil.

The brakes screeched and the train jolted, and Joss almost lost his footing and fell backwards. They entered the tunnel and the carriage was plunged into darkness, so that for a moment the only light was the red glow from the man's pipe. The whistle blew, loud and shrill, resounding down the tight tunnel walls.

Daylight once more, out of the cutting and past the sidings; the train inched into Salisbury station and into the steam of another locomotive about to depart. Joss looked out for Guy and then saw him

27

emerge through the steam, standing there, his thick dark hair unkempt, face and arms tanned from spending time out of doors, and wearing a dark blue short-sleeved shirt, cream flannels and a thick jumper tied round his waist. He was craning his neck at every carriage until he spotted Joss, then, waving with both hands high, he strode towards the carriage.

'Thank God you're here at long last,' said Guy as they clasped hands. 'I've been beginning to feel really bored the last couple of weeks.'

'Guy, that *is* terrible for you. How hard it must have been.'

Guy laughed. 'It was pretty tough.'

'All that lying in the sun, being idle. I got your letters.'

Guy clapped a hand on Joss's back. 'Well, you're here now. No more teaching, no more being cooped up with your mother.' They walked out of the station. 'Roger's home for the party too.'

'How did he manage that?'

'Apparently even in these times the army still get their August leave. He's off again next Monday—more manoeuvres in Scotland or something—but means he's here all this week.'

'Perfect.'

'He thought he was going to have to miss the whole thing. The parents were distraught. Mum saying, "But Roger, you've *never* missed it. Surely if you explained to the Colonel or whoever?" And Dad snapping, "He's not at bloody school now, Celia." '

Joss laughed. 'Thank God the army saw sense.'

'My thoughts exactly.' He pointed to the car, a small open four-seat tourer.

'Stella's here,' said Joss. He realized as soon as he said it that Guy had caught the alarm in his voice.

'Sorry—you don't mind do you?'

'No, why should I?'

Guy paused, then grinned. 'Good. She's learning to drive, which is terrifying. And if it rains again we'll have to stop and quickly put up the hood.'

Joss had never told a soul about his feelings for Stella, least of all Guy. Even when he'd first met her some four years before, he'd discovered his heart began to quicken fretfully whenever she was near him. It was exciting, but a strange form of agony too: he could hardly bear to be near her, yet all the while cherished the times when she spoke to him or showed him any kind of attention.

He supposed her looks had much to do with it. Like Guy, Stella had dark, almost black, hair and pale grey eyes, and although they were alike, they were quite different too. Whereas Guy had a full face like their father, Stella's was narrower and gentler, her skin pale with a scattering of freckles on her nose. Her eyebrows arced in two neat lines, and long eyelashes framed her eyes. Even when he'd first known her as a girl of fourteen, Joss had thought her beautiful. Now, at eighteen, her allure was even greater; while he and Guy remained boyish still, everything about Stella, from her clothes to her hair to the way she walked, proclaimed she had evolved into a grown woman.

Yet Joss's love for her—he assumed it must be that—was not based on looks alone. Like Guy, she was bright and quick-witted, and funny too. Over countless mealtimes at Alvesdon Farm, she and Guy had entertained everyone else from start to finish, a double-act that Joss could only sit back and watch, however much he may have wished to have been a part of it. She was so close to her brother—the sheer number of letters he wrote to her from school alone were testimony to that—and as twins, there was an exclusivity about their relationship to which no one else, not even the beloved Roger, had access. Yet Joss was aware that his own shyness in her presence was as much to blame for her indifference towards him as anything. When Stella was around, the conversation he found so easy with Guy, and that Guy clearly found so effortless with his sister, seemed to dry up. It had caused him much anguish, especially as he knew his feelings for her could never be returned. At least neither Stella nor the other Liddells seemed to suspect anything: he was sure they assumed his reticence in her company was due to nothing more than adolescent shyness. Had they thought otherwise, he was certain Guy would have mentioned it. And in any case, over the past couple of years he had seen considerably less of her, even though he still thought of her often. She had been away a lot of the time, at finishing school abroad and latterly in London; her absence had in many ways been something of a relief. Nor had Guy and Stella ever been part of the same crowd socially. Joss had once asked him whether he liked Stella's friends. 'Not particularly. They're her friends,' he'd replied, 'and they're nearly all girls.'

But now here she was, sitting in the driving seat, fingering a triple-string of pearls, her head resting in the other hand. She was wearing a pale blue dress with a simple open-collar, short sleeves and a narrow belt. As Joss and Guy approached, she looked up, and Joss felt a renewed twist of excitement and anxiety in his stomach.

'There you are,' she said. 'How are you Joss?'

'Hello Stella—fine, thank you.'

She was looking in the mirror, rubbing an invisible mark on her cheek. 'How's London?' she asked as Joss put his case on the back seat.

'Glad to be away from it for a bit. How are you getting on up there?'

'All right,' she said. For the past month she'd been at secretarial training with her friend Charlotte Padfield, and living at the Padfields' house in Kensington.

'She's having a ball,' said Guy. 'She's forgotten all about us. It's a miracle she's managed to drag herself away for the party.'

'Don't be so ridiculous,' she snapped at her brother. 'Anyway, you could always come up too. There is a world beyond school and home, you know.'

'No thanks,' said Guy. 'All those people and smog. I'm quite happy lazing at home and doing very little.'

Stella rolled her eyes—*he's impossible*—then said, 'Well, come on, get in and let's get going.'

'Stella, stop being so strident,' said Guy, as Joss clambered into the back.

'Why am I being strident?'

'You know perfectly well. Anyway, just concentrate on getting us back home.'

'Guy, I'm perfectly capable of driving and holding a conversation at the same time,' she said pulling the starter. The engine turned and caught immediately, but the car groaned as she wrenched it into gear with both hands. Oblivious to any

31

misuse, she looked around, then released the brake, and they lurched out of the station. 'Anyway, I had your interests at heart—the sooner we get going the more chance we have of avoiding the rain. I'm sure you don't particularly want to get soaked.'

Guy, one arm across the back of his seat, smirked.

'What?' said Stella.

'I didn't say anything.'

'Stop making faces.'

'I'm not,' said Guy. 'Just keep your eyes on the road.'

'You're lucky I don't make you get out and walk.'

Guy said something that Joss couldn't catch and Stella burst out laughing. 'I don't know how you can dare say that!' she said.

Joss caught Stella's eye in the mirror. She smiled at him, and he felt a flicker of excitement; almost gratitude.

'Stop that,' said Guy.

'What?' said Stella.

'Flirting with Joss.'

'I was not!'

Joss, his cheeks flushing, said, 'Guy, please—'

Stella cut him off. 'Really, Guy—stop being so over-protective. Anyone would think you were being jealous.' She slapped him on the thigh then began whistling.

'And you can stop that whistling too,' said Guy, but as his sister continued, it was now his turn to laugh. 'Stop making me laugh Stella—if I hear that tune one more time, I'll go mad.'

'Do you think I look like him too?' asked Stella.

'Oh definitely. Grow a moustache and thin your

hair a bit and you'd be a dead ringer.'

Stella puffed out her cheeks. 'I can do the fat face bit,' she said.

Still laughing, Guy turned to Joss. 'Sorry—it's this chap who's been helping Mum. He's—well, you've got to see him, he's hilarious.'

Joss smiled, and Stella began whistling again.

'Stop it Stella, my sides hurt,' said Guy, who turned to Joss once more and said, 'So, how was your mother?'

Joss shrugged. 'All right. We tried to avoid each other as much as possible.'

But Guy had already started sniggering again. 'Stella!' he said, 'stop it! Sorry, Joss.'

'I'll tell you about it later,' said Joss.

At Wilton, Stella ground the gears of the Morris again, the car shuddered, but then they were on their way once more, speeding through the town square lined with lime trees, and on out to the villages that lay along the foot of the downs, Guy and Stella bickering then laughing, then bickering once more, although with the wind and the noise of the engine Joss found it hard to hear what the other was saying. So he gave up trying and leant back instead, his arms stretched out along the back seat, his face tilted to the sun.

Without warning, Stella swung the car off the main road.

'For God's sake Stella!' shouted Guy, clutching his door with both hands.

'Oh stop fussing,' said Stella. 'It's fine.'

They were on a narrow road that led high over the chalk. The Morris almost stalled as they inched round the hairpin bend halfway up, but after spluttering in too high a gear, the car lumbered on, powering them on up over the crest of the hill. On they went, gathering speed again. Sunlight flashed through the gaps in a line of trees, dazzling off the chrome around the windscreen, the shadows of the beeches flickering across them, fat stripes sliding off the bonnet. Outlined along the ridge ahead, Joss saw the clump of trees the Liddells called the Mouse, with its hedgerow following behind resembling a tail.

'Almost there,' said Guy as they turned right onto the valley road. 'Thank God.'

Stella hit him on the leg, swerved slightly, then looked into the mirror at Joss. 'My driving's been perfectly all right, hasn't it Joss?'

'Perfectly.'

Stella gave him a conspiratorial glance in the mirror.

'See?' she said to Guy. 'So stop being so annoying.'

At the bottom of the other side of the hill, they turned into the village, past a row of cottages, then the butcher's shop, newly built with pebble-dash walls and a brick-tiled roof after a fire had destroyed the old thatched one a few years before. Then the pub, the blue paint on the sign peeling badly to reveal dry pale wood beneath; across the road was the post office which now doubled up as a grocery—boxes of vegetables were set out on a table outside. Past the church and the war memorial, scrubbed and clean as though it had been built only the week before; then past the track leading to the cricket ground. A linear village, conforming to much the same pattern as it had in medieval times. Joss watched a woman with a basket hurrying in the direction of the butcher, then an old man wobbling on a bicycle. He did not know their names, but he knew their faces. *Nothing changes.*

Just after they passed the last houses in the village, Stella turned the car onto a track and on under an arcade of low-lying beech and elm. The drive curved round a shallow hill, then straightened. At the end of the long avenue were the old stables of lilac brick with their tired-looking clock-tower, the white wood long since ravaged by green lichen.

The track took them not into the stable courtyard, but left, round the edge of the outbuildings with their moss-encrusted roofs and cobwebbed windows, and onto a circle of gravel at the front of the house.

Alvesdon Farm and the Liddells had grown together. For 400 years they had farmed the surrounding land, each generation following the other in seamless continuity. From his first visit, Joss had been fascinated by the watchful eyes of past Liddells hanging from the walls. No matter where he stood, they always seemed to be staring straight at him. Some kind, some severe, but all saying the same thing. *We live here still you know, part of the fabric.* There was a portrait of David too, painted some years before, during the last war. Guy's father had been a young man when it had been painted: dressed in khaki, silver buttons shining.

'Why are you so fascinated by all my dead relations?' Guy had once asked Joss.

'I'm intrigued,' he'd replied. 'When you don't have much of a family yourself, other people's are very interesting. Anyway, aren't you?'

35

'No, not really. I love the place for what it is now, not what it was like when some bullying great-great-great uncle lived here.'

But David was only too happy to talk about Alvesdon's past. One time, he took Joss to his office. There, in his den below the clock-tower, David kept all the records of the farm. In large leather-bound books, they looked at the handwriting of those Liddells that still breathed life into the house. David showed him the original deeds of 1661, handing over the land to John Liddell, a yeoman of the parish, signed and sealed by Charles II himself in gratitude for help given to the Royalist cause in the Civil War, and then later during the Restoration. During the early eighteenth century, Josiah Liddell, grown prosperous through a judicious marriage and with a keener and more aesthetic eye, had knocked down most of the first house and started again. The account books still survived. There, in neat columns of scratchy black writing, were the precise sums paid to builders, stonemasons and carpenters.

'That's why his painting hangs pride of place in the hall,' David told Joss. 'Without him, Alvesdon would look very different. Would probably have crumbled around us—the previous house was very old. There long before any Liddells.'

A panoramic painting of the farm from the 1750s hung in the drawing room and showed how little the place had changed. Perhaps it was a little barer then: there were certainly no trees along the track leading to the house. It was not a large house, however, although bigger than those in the village, even the rectory. A manor house of sorts, but as David always said, it was a comfortable home rather than a statement of grandeur and wealth. Made with the same lilac brick as the stables, the house was almost square with twin brick-tiled roofs. The large and delicate windows were framed with grey stone; and on all corners of the parapet stood ornate urns. Lawns spread away down to the stream, full and gushing in winter, but barely a trickle in summer, as it was now. Protected by downs on either side and hidden from the rest of the village by the low hill at the beginning of the drive, Alvesdon Farm provided a secret landscape.

Stella brought the car to a standstill, and yanked the handbrake.

Ah, back at last.

The front door opened and then scrunching gravel: two spaniels bounding towards them, followed by Celia, who came towards the car, arms extended in welcome. Slender like Stella, her dark hair now flecked with grey, she was wearing, as always, her silver brooch with the amethyst pinned to a long, pale green cardigan.

'Joss—here you are at last! We've missed you,' she said, embracing him as Stella walked on into the house.

'Where's Dad?' said Guy.

'In the office. You know what he's like.' She turned to Joss. 'I'm afraid he's terribly depressed by all this war talk. I mean, I suppose we all are, especially with Roger . . .' She let the sentence trail, then quickly added, 'but he's got into the habit of retreating there once the papers arrive and listening to every news broadcast on the wireless. He'll emerge at lunch.' She paused to look up at the sky. 'I do so want to eat outside now that it's such a lovely day. What do you both think? Is it

37

going to rain again?'

'I don't know,' said Guy. 'There's still plenty of cloud about. Ask Dad, he's the one who listens to the weather forecast every morning.'

Celia looked towards the clouds gathering to the south. 'Perhaps we'd better not risk it then.' She gripped Joss's arm and said, 'But please let it be all right on Saturday.'

'I think this year we should all worry about the weather too,' said Joss. 'It's unfair leaving you with all that anxiety. Perhaps we should share it out a bit.'

'Great idea,' said Guy, smiling. 'Ease your load, Mum.'

'You are mean to me,' said Celia. 'I know I'm always the butt of all your jokes, but I *do* worry about the rain.' She released her grip and looped her arm through Joss's. 'Anyway, it's lovely to have you here Joss, even if you have started teasing me already.'

'Where's Roger?' asked Guy.

'He's gone to see how the harvest's going. It's the harvesters I really feel sorry for in this odd weather.'

'Is David worried about it?' asked Joss.

'No, I don't think so,' said Celia. 'We seem to have missed a lot of the rain. He's more concerned about everything else.'

They went into the house. Joss paused, first to look up at the portrait of Josiah. *Hello once again.* Gun in one hand, partridge in the other. Long crimson coat, raffish smile. A quick glance in the bowl—*yes, cricket ball and cone still there.*

He was put in his usual room. Next to Guy, at the back of the house overlooking the walled rose-

38

garden, the downs rising up behind. The wash stand in the corner, the picture of the Devon valley painted by a Liddell uncle in the Nineties; the row of battered books on top of the chest of drawers— G.A. Henty, Jeffery Farnol, Thomas Hardy. He'd read them all. Everything the same as ever. Joss sat on the bed, then fell back for a moment. In the garden below, he could hear Celia and Stella talking. One of the dogs barked. A bird flew into the faded wisteria on the wall outside his window. Joss smiled to himself then stood up to change.

*   *   *

The Liddells had always gathered together in the drawing room before meals, even when the children had been young. 'Otherwise they would have grown up without us ever really knowing them,' Celia had once explained. But when Joss walked in before lunch, there was still no sign of either Stella or David.

Roger got up, shook hands and cuffed Joss lightly on the head.

'Drink?'

'Please.'

'Hope you're feeling in form for the match,' he said, pouring out a whisky and squirting in some soda from the sideboard. 'We're a bit low on batting.' Unlike Stella and Guy, Roger was a mixture of both his parents. He had developed David's build, but with a leaner face like Celia. Both David and Celia had been opposed to Roger's decision to join up, but he had been resolute: he didn't want to go to university; he wanted to see something of the world—via a short-service commission—and then come back and take over the running of the farm. A straightforward ambition, and one David finally accepted, because the second part of the plan was something he wanted too. There'd been no secret about that. Roger only had a year left to serve.

Stella wandered in and kissed Roger, then sat down.

'Don't I get one?' said Guy.

'Not a chance after the way you carried on in the car. Anyway, I haven't seen Rog all day and I've had quite enough of you already.'

'How was the driving then, little sis?' asked Roger.

'She was dreadful,' said Guy.

'I was rather good, actually.'

'Apart from the gear changing, sudden swerves and total disregard for everyone else on the road.'

'Joss thought my driving was fine.'

'Of course he said that—he's a guest and was being polite.'

'Joss a guest?' said Stella. 'Rubbish. Joss virtually lives here and is quite capable of telling the truth. Aren't you Joss?'

Joss lifted slightly on his seat.

'Joss, I absolutely insist you tell the truth,' said Guy, 'anything else I will consider a gross betrayal.'

They all turned to him. 'Stella's driving was very good,' he said looking away from Guy, and at Roger instead.

'Ha!' said Stella.

'You traitor! I can't believe you said that!' shouted Guy.

Emboldened, Joss said, 'Well, you're not so brilliant at driving. Last time I was down you nearly

40

killed us both driving back from Salisbury.' He glanced at Stella. She smiled at him.

'Whose side are you on, Joss?' said Guy. 'Honestly, that's the last time you ever get a lift from me.'

'Joss is only telling you a few home truths,' said Stella. Roger laughed, Stella pinched Guy, Guy yelled in pain and began trying to pinch her back, and Joss began laughing too.

'Guy, leave Stella—please,' said Celia. 'Honestly, you're eighteen now, not twelve.'

'Yes, grow up Guy, I'm trying to have my drink,' said Stella.

Guy was still smoothing down his ruffled hair when David finally appeared. He made straight for the drinks, his eyebrows knotted together and his moustache twisted. As usual, his collar looked as though it had barely made it round his thick neck.

'Hello David,' said Joss, standing up.

David turned abruptly and his face lit up at once. 'Joss, forgive me, my dear fellow. Welcome back.' He spoke with a gentle, soft voice, at odds with his appearance. Celia called him 'Bear'—never in public; it was a private name, although they all knew it and sometimes referred to him that way too; it was so apt. Clutching Joss's arm, he shook hands vigorously, and then sat down in an armchair before standing up again, muttering something and shuffling out of the room. Celia shrugged—*he's like that these days.*

David reappeared at lunch, but remained quiet, apart from the conversation going on about him.

'Tell us about the teaching, Joss,' said Celia, finally lifting her knife and fork once everyone had been served. It was just a light lunch: cold meats

41

followed by cheese.

'I can't believe anyone would let you loose on their children,' said Roger. 'What a frightening thought.'

'Hear, hear,' said Guy, 'they must be mad.'

'Better than you sitting on your arse doing nothing all summer,' said David, looking at Guy. Everyone turned. Joss stopped chewing.

'Darling, really,' said Celia, after a short pause.

'Dad, I was joking,' said Guy, reddening.

'Don't be cross with Guy, Dad,' said Stella. She looked anxiously at her brother then at her father. But David was looking down, his knife and fork scraping against his plate, oblivious to the silence around him.

It was left to Roger to rescue the situation. 'Well, come on Joss,' he said. 'Tell us all about it. How was it?'

Joss glanced at David, then said, 'All right, actually. Not as bad as I'd thought.'

'What did you have to teach?' asked Stella.

'Everything, really,' Joss told them. 'History, English, Latin, French and Maths. I felt a bit sorry for them really—John and Michael that is—only eight and ten and having to spend their summer holidays doing extra lessons.' Each morning he'd walked to the underground station at Pimlico and boarded a train along with all the other commuters until he reached South Kensington. From there he walked again to Ranelagh Gardens where the Derrisons had their house. He hardly ever saw Mr Derrison, although his wife would sometimes pause for a chat. Usually though, their butler took him straight upstairs to the top floor where the two boys' old playroom had been converted into a schoolroom.

'Did you have a blackboard?' asked Guy.

'Absolutely. And an old canvas map of the world.'

'Of course,' said Roger.

'And they were very obedient. Never had any trouble at all. I'd been bracing myself for the worst, but I think Mr Derrison must have been quite strict.'

'Well good for you Joss,' said Celia.

'Don't think that's an end to working though,' said Roger. 'Mum's lining up a mountain of jobs for us before the party, aren't you mother?'

'Yes, but it's easy work and all part of the fun of the party. Isn't it?' Amused glances across the table.

'Definitely,' said Roger. 'If only *the weather holds.*' Stella and Guy sniggered.

'Oh, I hope it does. What do you think David? Will we be all right?'

'He's teasing you,' said David.

'Are you Roger? I suppose I should be used to it by now. You are mean to me all of you.'

But the mood around the table had lightened.

The Liddells had held their annual party every last weekend in August since 1919, the first summer after the war, and the anniversary of David's arrival back home after being wounded on the western front. And every year, they followed the same pattern: the cricket match against Marleycombe village on Saturday afternoon, a fancy-dress party in the evening, and then the picnic on the downs for the survivors the following day. Friends and relations, from the village, from further afield and beyond, were all invited. Most usually came.

David and Celia had decided on the theme for the 1938 party as soon as they'd toasted in the New Year. Walking out towards the stream at the end of the garden, Celia had kissed her husband and said, 'What shall we call the party this year?' And without a pause, David had said, 'Restoration.'

'Perfect,' Celia had told him, forgoing their usual argument. It seemed so appropriate: 1937 had seen the abdication crisis, and now there was a new king; and after a hard few years it was only right they should remind everyone that England could still be merry. And finally, as David pointed out, Alvesdon Farm had the Restoration of 1660 to thank for its origins. Celia had been making plans ever since.

Now, with just a week to go, she sat at the table, and as the main course was cleared, sighed and clasped her hands together. 'Well, I don't care if I am the butt of all your jokes,' she said. 'I'm just glad to have everyone here again. And that means you too, Joss. It wouldn't be the same without you.'

'I can't tell you how good it is to be here,' he told her, smiling happily.

She lifted her glass. 'I think we should drink to that, don't you?'

Everyone followed. Joss looked at them all, the family together; Guy chinked his glass with the others, his father's slight forgotten, then grinned at Joss. Even David was beaming too, although there was something strange and unfamiliar about the way he looked. Something that Joss, at that moment, was unable to fathom.

Joss lay back on his bed and closed his eyes. It was impossible to sleep properly with the racket that went on every night; and with the heat. He might doze for a while, then wake up, his back drenched. If he wiped his fingers down his spine there would be droplets on his fingers. So he was tired during the day, and even though he was supposed to be making a good recovery, it often didn't seem like that to him. His eyes stung and he was suffering from an acute headache. During the day the heat was worse, turning the place into a putrid sweatshop. Even now, lying dead still, the perspiration was building up on his temples and upper lip, then running down the side of his face. He could feel the blood pulsating through his head.

A sudden commotion started up beyond the ward doors, and he sat up again, leaning on stiff arms. The swing doors crashed open and Colin Parker hurried through on his wheelchair. He was younger than Joss, probably only eighteen or nineteen—possibly younger—and had lost most of one leg. He'd been increasingly active over the past week and had appointed himself as the ward news reporter.

'Have you heard?' he said looking round the ward, his face lit up with excitement. A rhetorical question; the scoop was his and he knew it. 'Churchill's sacked Auchinleck and replaced him with Alexander, and Montgomery's taking over the Eighth Army.'

'Is that good?' said Joss.

45

Colin paused by his bed—*are you mad?* 'Course it is.'

Joss lay back down again. So that was the big news. Another commander gone, another one in. Two days before, Colin had been given word that Churchill was in town for meetings with his commanders and to bolster the morale of the troops. Then he heard a rumour that the Prime Minister was even going to be touring the wards; but nothing had come of it, and now he was gone. Joss suspected the prospect would have probably upset him too much.

Funny though, but Colin reminded him of someone. For ages he'd been trying to think who. It was that expression of happy excitement. He dozed again.

The boy who'd held the catch. Joss remembered now. The cricket match; the Liddells' party weekend. That was another thing he missed about home: cricket. Was it really only four years ago? It could have been another lifetime. Joss turned over on his side, thinking about it. Remembering the ground: the field on the far end of the village, the little wooden pavilion and the row of horse chestnuts that lined one side, the church and churchyard providing the far boundary. Roger had captained the Liddell XI that day, only for the second time, and everyone had been looking at him knowingly and making comments about the future of Alvesdon Farm. The line would remain unbroken.

And he remembered what David had said at teatime, as they paused between innings, stuffing themselves with tea and cakes and sandwiches and strawberries. He was leaning up against one of the

46

horse chestnuts, more jovial than he'd been all week, and he'd said this: that the best thing about cricket was that it encouraged the very English trait of combining individual with team effort. 'Any player might shine alone,' he'd said, 'but ultimately his success or failure is not his, but the team's.'

It was true. Joss smiled, thinking about the sixty runs he'd scored that day, and still the Liddells had lost. With only ten runs needed but with no one else left to bat, that young boy had held onto the catch. Joss had hit it hard, but somehow it stuck in the lad's hand. There'd been stunned surprise at first, but then had come that look of gleeful excitement and the knowledge that in that one moment, he had won his team the match. A catch held in a village game of cricket, and a new commander of an entire army. Joss began to laugh.

England—August, 1938

In the week that led up to the party, Celia's plans were finally made reality. The focal point was the field behind the stables and farm buildings. They had tried the front lawn once but afterwards David had insisted they hold it in the field. There was, he said, no point in ruining a good lawn when they could use any damn piece of land around about and do what they wanted to it.

The tent arrived on Tuesday, on a lorry from Shaftesbury. The men never rushed, pausing for thick sandwiches and beer brought out to them on Celia's orders while she hovered, watching the gradual transformation of a folded square of canvas and lengths of wood into a taut and outstretched marquee. First the canvas was dragged onto the grass and unfolded; then the poles were screwed together; guy ropes were unknotted, wooden mallets and a sack of thick wooden pegs laid out. Eventually, some while later, came the magic moment when everyone heaved and pulled and the twin posts hoisted skywards.

'I love the smell, don't you Joss?' said Celia as the workers began to pull out one side of the marquee. 'The canvas and the grass and the guy ropes. Such a strong association with the party.'

Everyone had to pitch in and help, and that meant *every*one: maids, cook, gardener, husband, daughter, sons, family friend. Overseeing the operation, in a manner halfway between a military exercise and a theatre production, was Celia. But Joss was glad his presence there was taken for granted. No one else outside Alvesdon was ever asked—or *expected*—to help.

For once Celia's anxieties about the weather were justified, but everyone kept to their tasks and made the most of the sun when it did come out. A maypole was erected a little way away from the marquee. Extra braziers were moved in, and flowers and bunting strewn between the tent posts. Trestle tables were set up in a large horseshoe; Joss and Guy were sent to paint an old phaeton stored in one of the barns, and after covering themselves and the old carriage in whitewash, they wheeled it round in triumph to the courtyard.

Some priorities still overrode everything else: work stopped for the latest cricket scores on the radio, especially since England were winning— actually *thrashing* the Australians. Even Celia

48

began joining in as they gathered round the set in David's office. Records were tumbling—Hutton passed one hundred, then two hundred, then even three hundred. England made their highest innings score ever. Then further drama: Bradman, the Australian ace, fractured his tibia and was out of the running. By Wednesday, England had won.

'At least there's something to smile about,' said David. 'Cheerier than hearing about Hitler running roughshod over the Czechs.'

The evolving European crisis was barely mentioned, but on Thursday, as Guy, Roger and Joss were pausing for coffee, the prospect of war did finally come up. Outside, the rain was streaming down again, clattering above them on the studio roof. Guy was reading the previous day's *Times*.

'Listen to this: there's a letter here from "Brigadier General H.W.Studd"—whoever he might be—quoting Haig in the last war. Apparently he thought planes would never be much use for reconnaissance. Believed the best way to gather information was the Napoleonic method of using cavalry. Can you believe it? No wonder it took us four years.'

'Don't think he'd agree with that now,' said Roger.

'No,' said Guy, laying down the paper.

'Let's see,' said Joss. Guy passed it over, and Joss began glancing through the pages. Admiral Horthy was in Germany inspecting the naval fortress of Heligoland. There was concern about the year's harvest and some figures about the drop in the number of regular farm labourers. And pictures of a triumphant Len Hutton. 'Well, *The Times* doesn't seem too worried,' said Joss. 'They're far too excited about the cricket to worry about the Sudetenland.'

'Listen,' said Guy.

'What?' said Joss.

'Shh.'

Nothing; then a faint drone, gradually getting louder. A plane burst over the trees by the end of the stable courtyard.

'Christ that's low,' said Joss.

'Probably trying to keep out of the cloud,' suggested Roger.

'Is that a Fury?' said Guy, the blue and red roundels visible on the wings.

'It's a Tiger Moth, you idiot,' said Roger.

The plane was gone again. They were silent for a moment, then Guy said, 'Roger, are you worried?'

'No, course not.'

Joss picked at his thumbnail, then glanced at Guy. 'There can't be another war,' he said. 'They won't let it.'

'Exactly,' said Roger.

'Is that what you're told? In the army, I mean?' said Guy.

'No. Can't say anyone really ever mentions it. Look, there's far more things to worry about at the moment. Like whether it really *is* going to rain on Saturday.'

*   *   *

To begin with, it did. Over breakfast, Celia repeatedly stood up and peered out of the windows at the grey sky and light drizzle. Nothing anyone said could placate her, until David came in and

50

slapped the newspaper down in front of her.

'There,' he said, pointing his finger on the weather map. 'A large ridge of high pressure.'

'But that's not much use to me now is it? It's still pouring down outside.'

'Celia, it's *drizzling*, and it's soon going to disappear completely and turn into a beautiful summer's day. So please stop worrying. All this anxiety is giving me a headache.'

'I just want everything to be all right.'

'It will be. The ground might be a bit damp but that hardly matters.'

David had forecast correctly. By mid-morning the last of the cloud had gone, leaving everything to glisten in bright sunshine. Guests started to appear, in buses specially hired to collect people from the station, or in cars, all trundling up the drive. Helen, the parlourmaid, and Elsie, the housemaid, scurried between the guests' rooms and the kitchen, their duties having temporarily merged; and Celia flitted between the twin tasks of welcoming everyone and overseeing final arrangements.

By two o'clock everybody had moved down to the cricket ground. With large rugs and squares of tarpaulin laid down around the boundary, they soon forgot it had been raining at all.

The sun continued to shine in that wide blue cloudless sky. Guy badly bruised a finger fielding and made a great fuss, grimacing and pretending to be brave until Roger told him to stop being feeble and get on with it; and although Joss scored his half-century (he had looked to see if Stella had seen the moment, and was delighted to see her stand up and clap), the Liddells still lost. David said that apart from damaged Liddell pride, it didn't matter at all: cricket had been the winner, and now it was time to move on to the main event.

The fine weather continued and the evening party got underway as the sun began to set. Cricket whites and summer dresses made way for wigs, long waistcoats and shimmering dresses. Dancers cavorted round the makeshift maypole, accompanied by clapping and yells of encouragement. The braziers burned, sending fountains of sparks into the sky as more wood was added. A band, all the way from Bournemouth, played at one end of the tent. Waiters dressed in long aprons and breeches served gargantuan amounts of food: game pies and cold meats, pickles, vegetables, sausages and a spit-roasted pig. Then came bowls bursting with fruit and cream. Punches, wine and beer followed the champagne; David toasted Celia; and everywhere Joss looked, people were smiling and laughing.

The first pale hint of dawn had begun to light up the eastern sky, when Guy suggested to Joss that they climb the downs and watch the sun rise. Tired and drunk, and still dressed in their costumes, they began walking in silence up the track, the bare chalk a luminous guide. The dawn chorus had begun, shrill and clear in the windless morning air. Behind, they saw the faint glow from the braziers and the studio; otherwise the house was still.

At the top, they paused and leant against a gate. Away to their right, the first golden tip of sun burst out over the top of the downs shielding one end of the valley.

'Do you think it's going to be all right?' said Guy.

'I'm sure.'

'I mean, if there's a war?'

'There won't be.'

Guy paused and lit a cigarette. 'No, I suppose not.'

Joss watched the white smoke rise and drift on the morning air. His feet were sodden with dew and it was cold, but Guy noticed neither of these things. The sky was deep and dark above them, stars still shining, but away to the east, the narrow band of pink and pale blue stretched upwards, bringing faint colour to the top of the downs. So quiet, he could hear the paper and tobacco burning as Guy drew on his cigarette.

He had been right: nothing could touch this immovable, unchanging landscape.

England—September, 1938

Stella had gone back to London with Philip Mornay on the Sunday after the picnic, in his two-seater Lagonda. Philip had been attentive to her all weekend: from the moment of his arrival, Joss had barely spoken to her again. The first faint glimmer of intimacy he had known between him and Stella had gone. Some years older than her, Philip oozed the kind of urbanity Joss hoped he might share one day, but which for the moment he resented. Philip was rich too: his was a world of Mayfair flats and St James's clubs, of weekends in the country and summers on the Côte d'Azur, of Jermyn Street tailors and nightclubs where he was known personally by the doormen. And it was a world Stella was relishing, and of which Joss knew nothing. He had been both saddened and relieved to see her go. They'd all come out onto the drive to wave her off, and she'd kissed everyone in turn, even Joss—or rather, offered her cheek and pursed her lips to the air. Then Guy had walked over to the car with her. 'Bye darling brother,' she'd said, then added, 'I'll miss you. Make sure you write.'

On the Monday morning it had been Roger's turn to go. Outside, the rain had returned, so they gathered in the hall to say goodbye. In his uniform, with polished belt and buttons, Roger looked transformed; almost a different person altogether.

'I can't get used to you in that uniform,' said Celia, 'you look so grown up.'

Roger smiled. 'I am twenty-two, Mum.'

'I know, Roger, I'm sorry. Very handsome though.'

'I hardly recognize you, Rog,' said Guy.

Roger turned to his brother. 'Don't become too much of a drunken reprobate at Cambridge. Joss, I'm relying on you to keep him under control.' He shook hands with Joss, then Guy, then his father. Finally he turned to Celia. 'Bye Mum.'

'Goodbye darling,' she said, holding him tightly, 'do be careful.'

'You're creasing my jacket,' he said, laughing. He kissed her. 'I'll be fine. Honestly.'

Outside the car was waiting. Roger turned, waved, then dashed across the gravel. It was at that moment that Joss saw David and Celia glance at each other with silent understanding: Celia, her eyes wide, uncertain; David, unable to provide the assurance she craved.

*   *   *

The party weekend proved to be the last gasp of summer; by the time Roger had gone, it was well and truly over. September brought with it cooler days, less sunshine, and longer periods of overcast grey and showers, mirroring the air of gloom and anticlimax that shrouded the house. David, having briefly regained his good humour, became taciturn and withdrawn once more, spending his days wandering the farm or holed up in his office, reading the paper and listening to the news, or supervising the end of the harvest. Even Celia appeared distant and distracted, without direction now that the party was over and the house almost empty.

One morning Joss wandered into the drawing room and found only Celia there. She was sitting at her writing desk in the corner, looking at the photograph of Michael, their second son. It was approaching his birthday and Joss knew she tended to become withdrawn around this time—it was something Guy had warned him about long before.

'Joss,' she said, turning. 'Come in.'

'Sorry,' said Joss, 'I was looking for Guy.'

'Well you've found me. Come here and talk to me,' she said, beckoning him over. 'I was just— well, a chat would be rather nice. It keeps one's mind off things. I always feel depressed after the party: the end of the summer and everything. It used to mean the children were about to go off to school, but now it means university, the army— much more serious things.' She smiled.

'I know what you mean,' said Joss. 'I hate the end of summer. No more cricket, the evenings getting shorter.'

'Yes, that too,' she said. 'And soon you and Guy

55

will be off as well. Now you're all growing up, I never know when I'm going to see you again.'

'But Guy and Stella will be back for Christmas.' He regretted it as soon as he'd spoken. *But what about Roger?*

'Yes,' said Celia, 'yes, they will.' She paused a moment and then said, 'I just don't feel I dare plan anything at the moment. Life seems so uncertain.'

Joss glanced at the photograph: a smiling baby boy, sitting up, fat fingers clutching a silver rattle, his face lit with contentment.

'At least he was spared another war,' said Celia, following his eyes. Joss saw her eyes glistening, then she stared at him, her hand to her mouth. 'I can't believe I said that. What a terrible thing to say.'

'No, not at all. It's understandable,' Joss muttered, unable to look her in the eye.

She sat up. 'No it's not. We must be brave in such times. Pull ourselves together. Anyway,' she pulled the sleeves of her cardigan and patted her hair, 'perhaps there will be a miracle.'

Joss nodded, ashamed at his inability to offer her any words of comfort. He wanted to reassure her; he wanted to reassure David too, to tell them that war wouldn't happen, that somehow the furore would blow over. Until now, it had always been them who'd offered advice and assurances about life to him. Their anxiety had revealed a vulnerability he'd never seen before.

*   *   *

When the weather was fair, Guy and Joss played croquet, or went to help with the harvest. Drooping sheaves of wheat dotted the fields and hillsides; as soon as they were dry enough, there was a rush to gather and add them to the ricks growing behind the barns. But when it rained, the two of them stayed indoors, working on a large jigsaw and reading in the drawing room. Or they went to the pub in the village. Both avoided the radio. Neither had any desire to discuss the escalating international situation.

'I'm going to have to go back to London soon,' said Joss one evening. 'A few things to sort out with my mother. And I need to pick up some kit before we head up to Cambridge.'

They were sitting in a corner of the Blue Lion, the pub in the village, Joss leaning against a high-backed bench, plucking loose strands of tobacco from a cigarette, Guy rocking back on his stool. There were only a few other drinkers there; a quiet night, the tick of the clock soothing and unhurried. *Nothing disturbs us here.* A small fire flickered gently.

'We've still got over two weeks, Joss.'

'I know, but I really should be heading back to town.'

'Nonsense. You don't want to do that. Stay down, please.'

'I don't know. I just don't want to outstay my welcome—not now, with everything that's going on.'

'Don't be ridiculous, they want you here. They love having us around, especially since Roger and Stella are away.'

'Maybe.'

'Stop being so sensitive. You're staying put and that's that. My express orders.'

Joss eyed him. 'All right then. As long as you're sure.'

'Joss, what is this? Of course I'm sure. I really don't know what's got into you.'

Joss lit his cigarette then said, 'Do you know, I've hardly given my mother a thought since I came down.'

Guy looked at him—*yes?* Joss had been avoiding this conversation, but now, without really knowing why, he could keep it at the back of his mind no longer. That sinking feeling—he couldn't help it. Theirs had always been a patchy relationship, which for Joss's part had meant moments of great affection interspersed with longer periods of frustration, anger and above all, hurt. 'I don't suppose she's thought about me much either,' he said. He knew he sounded self-pitying, but couldn't help himself.

'Come on Joss, I'm sure—'

'Well, I haven't noticed any letters or calls have you?'

'She knows you're having fun down here. Have you written to her?'

'No, but that's hardly the point, is it? I can't imagine Celia ever being like that. I bet you'll have heard from her within a week of being at Cambridge. I mean, how often has she written to Roger, or telephoned Stella? That's what a normal, loving mother would do, Guy. But not Diana.'

'She's just different. Come on.'

Joss snorted. 'You can say that again.' He drummed his fingers on the table.

'Come on Joss,' Guy said again. 'She's not that bad. At least she doesn't fuss. Lets you pretty much do what you want.'

58

Joss nodded, drank from his glass. 'She fusses over money, Guy.'

'And is she still being difficult about Cambridge?'

'Yes. Trying to make me feel guilty for wanting to go. She suggested I joined the army instead. She'd probably rather have me killed off and out of the way. Much more convenient.' He looked up sharply. 'Sorry Guy,' he said. 'I didn't mean— Roger will be fine, I'm sure.'

'Look,' said Guy, leaning forward on the table, 'you've got your scholarship money and what you made from tutoring. What's the problem?'

It wasn't enough, that was the problem. Sixty pounds a year from Queens' College and six weeks' teaching pay and he was still way off. It had been all right when his mother had been married to his stepfather George because he was well off and paid the school fees. But she was on her own now— divorced—and scared that she was nearly forty and that her looks might fade and she would be left with no one and nothing.

He began to say this to Guy. 'I just thought that after all that has happened, she would feel she owed me this, at least.' He stopped. 'Oh, this is pointless,' he said, then after a moment added, 'Look, I expect I'll work it out with her eventually.'

'Tell her a degree will help you make your fortune. Then she can live out the rest of her days in style.'

'Yes, perhaps I will,' said Joss. 'Anyway, let's not talk about it any more.' He lifted his glass of beer. 'I think we should toast two more weeks of being idle instead.'

Guy raised his glass too. 'All right,' he said, 'to being idle. They can't get you down here you know.'

'I know.' Joss smiled.

*   *   *

But Joss's resolve to ignore the German situation began to falter. By the time of Chamberlain's second visit to see the Führer and with the German demands increasing daily, it was hard to escape the panic gripping the country. Only a month before, there had been the diversion of record-breaking cricket scores, and before that, record-breaking high-speed locomotives, and even record-breaking wet harvests. Now the papers were full of wartalk, and maps of Czechoslovakia and pictures of Sudeten Germans hastily formed into a militia marching down a road, still wearing their caps and suits. In addition to the daily news programmes, regular bulletins burst onto the radio with the latest reports on the build-up of troop movements by the Czech border, or from Bad Godesberg where Chamberlain, an old man in the lion's den, was struggling to contain the crisis.

The last weekend of September Stella came home. Guy was overjoyed, and for the first half an hour after her arrival, disappeared with her to her room to talk to her while she unpacked. Joss sat downstairs in the drawing room trying to read, once again torn by his desire to be near her and his frustration at his own inadequacy in her presence.

They both reappeared later when Celia called them down for some tea. David had emerged too, and asked her about London.

'I hear they're frantically preparing defences,' he said.

'My God!' she said. 'You wouldn't believe what's going on. Trenches are being dug all over Hyde Park, there're soldiers *everywhere* and whenever I look up there seem to be more barrage balloons dotting the sky—huge, fat, bulbous- looking things floating about like giant grey fish. Charlotte's parents have had their basement requisitioned as an air-raid shelter. Dad, do you really think there's going to be a war?'

No one had directly asked David this before.

'We must pray to God there won't be,' he said.

'Yes, but if everyone's behaving like this in London it means they must believe it's going to happen.'

'It's just panic,' said David.

*   *   *

'Joss,' said Guy, coming into his room a little while later, 'are you all right?'

'Fine. What about you? It must be hard for you all with Roger away.'

'I suppose I do worry about him a bit, but I'm sure everything will work out. I mean, after the last time, they couldn't let it happen again, could they? Especially not over Czechoslovakia. I mean who the hell are the Czechs anyway?'

Joss nodded.

'It's like Dad said, just panic, isn't it?'

'I'm sure that's the case,' agreed Joss.

If only everyone would stop talking about it; Joss wanted to push it to one side, ignore it, hope the problem melted away. But it was getting harder by the day. And the situation was about to worsen.

A few days later—a Sunday—they had gathered

again in the drawing room for their pre-dinner drink, when Colonel Goddard, a retired army engineer who lived in Shaftesbury, appeared.

Tall and stiff, with thinning white hair, the colonel apologized for bursting in on them unexpectedly.

'Not at all,' said David, 'will you have a drink? Sit down, please.'

The colonel thanked him and asked for Scotch.

'So,' said David, as the colonel eased himself into an armchair.

'Yes,' he said, glancing around the assembled party. They were all looking at him, waiting. It was clear he'd been expecting to talk to David on his own. 'I've come to ask something of you actually,' he said looking at David. 'The Air Raid Precautions services have been launched today. And it really is that, you understand—a precaution. Chamberlain's been around a long time and he's not going to let us get into a fight with Germany over the Czechs.' David nodded. 'But,' the old man continued, 'we must prepare for the worst all the same. Be *ready,* just in case bombers do appear.'

'About time,' said David.

'Quite. Anyway, we want you to chair a meeting here in Marleycombe and, um . . .' he paused, lifted a hand to his mouth and swallowed. 'Well, you see, we've got thirty-eight million gas masks to dish out.'

'Oh my God,' exclaimed Celia. 'Gas? Do you really think we're going to be gassed?' The colour had drained from her face.

'No, no,' said the Colonel. 'Very unlikely, but as I said, we just want to be *prepared.*'

'How long is it going to take to make all those?'

asked David.

'They're almost done actually. Your lot should be ready for collection Tuesday morning.'

'Of course we'll arrange to pick them up. Where from?'

'Wilton. If you pick them up then, and arrange for everyone to gather some time that evening, you could issue them and show everyone how to use them then. I'll arrange for an ARP officer to come along too. Think that can be done?'

'Of course,' said David. 'We can start telling everyone tonight.'

Dinner that night was perfunctory and subdued. Afterwards, David folded his napkin and said to Guy and Joss, 'Come on, you two can come with me.' He said nothing further as they drove into the village. His face was set, jaw clenched.

'Who are we going to see?' asked Guy.

'Dr Chawley,' grunted David, 'the vicar, Mr Lewis—'

'The baker, the candlestick maker.'

'And the Blue Lion.' David glanced at his son. 'For God's sake,' he muttered.

*   *   *

The 27th of September was windy and showery. The horse chestnuts looked thinner, the leaves orange and old. At ten o'clock Guy and Joss went to Wilton in the farm lorry with Sam Hicks, one of the farm workers, to collect the gas masks. There had been increasingly hysterical bulletins on the radio, and now a procession of self-conscious-looking men were parading in the market square.

'Jesus,' said Sam, 'just look at that.' In his early

63

thirties, Sam lived in one of the tenant cottages in the village. He was married and had two small girls. 'They're not catching me joining in with that lot.'

'Nor me if I can help it,' said Guy.

They drove on to the army headquarters, where they were directed to a large dull green warehouse and issued with boxes of gas masks. Other trucks waited their turn.

'Funny how much Charlie Chaplin looks like Hitler. Have you noticed that?' said Sam after they'd signed for their allocation and loaded them into the truck.

'It used to be the other way round though, didn't it?' said Guy. 'We *used* to say Hitler looked like Charlie Chaplin.'

'I hadn't thought of it like that,' said Sam. 'Christ, what a bloody mess, eh?'

In the back, the boxes—containing 500 brand-new gas masks—jolted in unison as they drove over a pot-hole in the road.

*   *   *

It had been announced on the radio that Chamberlain was going to address the nation that evening, so David insisted they should take the large set down with them to the village hall. They had read the instructions that came with the masks, and had practised putting them on. Celia had begun to cry. 'They're horrible,' she said, 'obscene.'

'Yes, but they work,' said David. He'd become even more brusque since Colonel Goddard's visit. 'Come on darling, get a grip.'

'I know, David, I'm sorry,' said Celia, 'but it's all so unbelievable. And we don't look like real people

64

any more.'

'They smell disgusting,' said Stella. 'Makes my stomach churn.'

'They're not supposed to be fashionable Stella,' said Guy.

'No, I can see that,' she said.

'So you might have to put style and beauty to one side in the interest of safety.'

'The box that comes with it will be handy, though.'

Even Celia managed to laugh at that.

*   *   *

By seven o'clock, the village hall was packed. On the stage sat David, the vicar, Dr Chawley and Mr Peters, the ARP officer. The radio was positioned to one side on a table on the stage. Joss and the other Liddells sat on the front row of fold-away wooden chairs. The last time Joss had been in the hall had been for the village amateur dramatic club's version of *A Christmas Carol* the previous Christmas; Dr Chawley had played Scrooge. Now they were on the brink of war.

The low, quiet murmur vanished to silence as the Prime Minister's dry voice filled the room:

'How horrible, fantastic, incredible, it is that we should be digging trenches and trying on gas masks here because of a quarrel in a faraway country between people of whom we know nothing.'

No call to arms, no trumpeting or beating of drums. *He won't let it happen. Can't let it happen,* thought Joss. He bit his nails. And yet, here they were, the villagers of Marleycombe, gathered at this moment because of a national crisis, their faces

65

taut with worry and fear.

After it was over, David switched off the radio. The hall remained silent. To the side of the stage, the thick gold curtains hung limp and dusty. Behind, dismantled scenery from last year's Christmas play lay stacked against the back wall.

The vicar stood up and said some prayers and then David introduced Mr Peters who, clutching his notes, delivered a terse lecture on the variety of poison gases and explained that while every man, woman and child would be issued with a gas mask, there were none, as yet, for babies. Angry cries were thrown at him, until David diffused the situation by outlining methods for gas-proofing the home, and pointing out that for the moment, it would be wise not take a baby far from the front door.

'Amazing,' said David to Joss once the speeches were over and the fitting and issuing of the masks had begun in the adjoining anteroom. 'Out of the four hundred-plus people that live here, three hundred and twenty have come out in the pouring rain at the appointed time, even though the message was largely passed by word of mouth. Makes you realize what a strong little community we are.'

* * *

At half-past eleven that night, Joss was sitting next to David at one end of the dining-room table. The others had already gone to bed; Celia and Stella as soon as their dinner had been cleared; Guy, a few moments before. He'd thought about leaving at the same time, but seeing David make no sign of moving himself, had felt he should remain too. It had been a long and difficult day; especially so for David. Joss sensed he wanted company; and was glad to have an opportunity to provide it.

'Another drink?' said David, picking up the decanter and pouring wine into the glass before Joss could answer.

'Thank you.'

David sighed and rubbed his forehead, which was just beginning to glisten.

'I thought Chamberlain's speech was good,' said Joss after a few moments.

'I suppose so,' muttered David. 'But it's all just a bit bloody late. We may be cut off from things down here, but I read the papers, and I listen to the news, and to me it's clear as day what's going on even if the bloody politicians seem to be blind. Hitler's been in power five years now. Five whole years, while we've sat back on our arses and done nothing, just let him build up his armies and tramp all over whoever he pleases. What was the point of Versailles if all we were going to do was let it crumble into a few meaningless signatures fifteen years later? You know, every year, at the appointed hour, on the appointed day, we stand in silence and remember—not just those who died, but that it should never happen again. But just standing there *thinking* about it isn't enough. That lunatic was right—the one who started shouting at the Cenotaph last year—we have all been bloody hypocrites. So busy saying it must never happen again, but not actually bothering to look up and see what was going on around us.'

Joss fingered his glass, not knowing what to say.

'Even if Chamberlain manages to avoid war this

time,' he continued, 'it'll only be a stay of execution. And I must say, I think it's going to be hard to avoid now. And even if he does, what happens the next time?'

'How do you mean?'

'The next time Hitler decides he wants another country. Poland for example, or Hungary? What then? Do we just let him get away with it?' He poured himself another glass. 'They could have done something about it a few years ago. He was thought a joke to start off with.'

'Not a very funny joke,' suggested Joss.

'No.' He paused again, sat back in his chair, fingers resting on the stem of his smudged glass. He reached for the decanter. 'Top up.' A statement, not a question. Taking a large sip from his own glass, David winced as he swallowed the wine.

'You all right?' asked Joss.

'Bit of indigestion.' He sighed again. 'You know, it's a terrible thing to see history repeat itself like this. I see the faces looking down at me in this house, and realize that most of them fought in wars at some time or other. The men at any rate. A way of life, really. But the last war ... everyone said afterwards that it had been the war to end all wars. Had to be. And I believed it too. So many people dead and maimed. Blown to smithereens. Unimaginable destruction.' He rubbed the edge of his eye with a finger. 'I was here when it ended, just out of bed and hobbling about the place. I'd made it through, when millions of others hadn't. Twenty-three people killed from this village alone; eleven had worked here. I knew them all, and countless others besides. But I was grateful because I thought

68

that was it, war over and done with for good—as far as we were concerned at any rate. Roger was two years old then, Michael just born, and it meant so much to know they would never have to do what I had done, what *all* my family had done for hundreds of years. Future generations were going to be spared. And now, out come the gas masks again, only this time we're all expected to fear the worst.'

'It seems so impossible though,' said Joss. He felt uneasy now; he wasn't sure he wanted to hear this.

'Impossible? Why impossible? Last time, they used to fire the canisters over but there was always the risk that it might blow back in their direction. No such problems now. *Now* they've got aeroplanes, and they can drop the stuff any damn place they like. Do you know what we're talking about here? Take Lewisite—smells like geraniums and one whiff and you're a gonner. Or mustard—virtually no odour at all, but blinds and eats your flesh away. Phosgene—fills your lungs with water, so you drown. Can cause gangrene too. I've seen it Joss. Seen it all before.'

He drained his glass. Joss watched him, unable to say anything.

'I'm sorry,' he said, 'making you listen to the bitter ramblings of a tired drunkard. But I thought I should at least have the decency to explain my recent behaviour.'

Joss began to speak, but David lifted a hand. 'Don't worry. I don't expect you to say anything. You can't possibly understand. I couldn't when I was your age. But if it does come to war, don't become a soldier. Don't make the same mistake Roger has made. Think how many people were

69

killed on the ground last time—and twenty years on the weaponry available is even more destructive. Joss, promise me this: if it comes to war, take to the skies. Fly where no one can reach you.'

Joss nodded.

'I've often been thinking of late,' David continued, 'what would have happened if fewer men had been killed in the last war. Chamberlain and his mob—they're old men. Tired men. What if there'd been a bit more young blood about? Probably wouldn't have got us into the mess we're in now.'

David poured the last of the wine, then slumped back in his chair. 'Do you know how I met Celia?'

'No. No I don't.'

'I was at school with her brother, Alex. Best friend in fact. We used to spend our holidays at each other's houses, a bit like you and Guy. Celia was a year younger than Alex, and I always thought she was wonderful. Probably in love with her even then. Then war broke out and of course, Alex and I joined up immediately, excited just like everyone else. Hell of a lot of flag-waving then. Everyone wanted it. I didn't get to see Celia again because Alex and I were sent off to France. Then one day, we were standing in a trench—it wasn't even the front line, but a communications trench a little way back—and there was this whistle and the next thing I knew, Alex had disappeared. Well, that's not entirely true. He hadn't completely disappeared because bits of him were hanging off my jacket and running down my face.'

Joss looked up, but David was staring ahead. A single tear ran down his cheek.

They were silent for a few minutes. Joss stared at

70

him, dumbstruck. David *looked* like a defeated man: strands of hair stuck to his forehead with sweat, his eyes rheumy and dull, cheeks blotchy.

At last, he pulled his handkerchief from his top pocket, his heavy breathing juddery. 'So,' he said, 'I was sent on leave after that. And I went to visit Alex's parents, and there was Celia. It was a German shell that killed Alex, but the point is, in all that time I don't think I ever really hated the Germans. Just the fools who led them. And I don't hate them now. Just that lunatic Hitler and all his loathsome cronies.' He was slurring his words now, but then he looked intently at Joss. 'You know Joss, we all think a great deal of you. It's probably wrong of me to say this, but in many ways I regard you as one of our own. Course it's wrong of me, bloody wrong of me, because, obviously I can't replace your father. But I want you to *know*. Know that you're always welcome here. *Always.'*

Joss swallowed, stunned.

'I'll always think like that, Joss. And so will Celia, I know. Whatever happens.'

Whatever happens.

Joss's mind raced, his heart dead in his chest. So, David knew about him. He and Celia both knew.

'Please,' said David, pushing himself out of his chair, 'forgive me.'

*   *   *

Joss flung open the door and strode over to Guy's bed.

'Wake up!' he said, 'Guy, bloody well wake up.'

Guy turned over, looked up with half-open eyes. 'What? Joss? What are you doing here?'

71

'What did you tell him?'

Guy, his hair on end, rubbed his eyes. 'What are you talking about? Joss, what is this?'

'Your dad. He knows. He just told me. Christ, Guy, I can't believe it. You promised, *swore* never to tell a single person. And I trusted you. My past, Guy, is *my* secret, and I trusted you with it.' He was pacing up and down the room, his hands clasped to his head. 'Well? *Well?* When did you fucking well tell him? And now your mother knows too. And probably Stella and Roger. Probably the whole bloody world. What does that make me look like? All this time I've been telling a lie and they've known *all along.* Jesus, Guy, how *could you*?'

'It's only Mum and Dad.' He was awake now, staring at Joss. 'Please, Joss. Just sit down for a minute.'

'Just tell me.'

'I had to,' said Guy.

'Why? Why did you have to?'

'Because what would have happened if they'd found out later? They might have turned you away. I couldn't risk that. After everything that happened to them before, I had to know.'

'But they wouldn't have found out would they?'

'Your stepfather did.'

Joss sat down on the end of the bed. He was silent for a moment.

'I had to, Joss.'

'When?'

'Before you first came here. Please don't hold it against me.'

'Christ, I don't know. I just—I don't know what to think now. I thought only you knew, Guy. You and no one else.'

72

Guy put a hand on his shoulder. 'It's nothing Joss. Means nothing. You've nothing to be ashamed about.'

Joss looked away. 'But I feel ashamed. I hate what I am, and I hate people knowing.' They were both silent a moment. He could feel Guy's warm hand still on his shoulder. 'I'm sorry,' he said eventually, 'I think all this war talk must be making me twitchy.'

'It's making us all twitchy.'

'But to find out now that they've known all this time—it's, it's a shock, I suppose.'

'I'm sorry. Forgive me.'

Joss breathed out deeply again. 'It's all right.' He turned and smiled ruefully, his anger spent. 'I don't think I could ever be cross with you for long. But please, Guy, no one else. Not a soul, and when we're at Cambridge, I don't want you ever to mention it again, not even to me. It's best forgotten about.'

'All right, Joss. I promise.'

Joss stood up and left.

He walked out onto the landing, but instead of turning to his room, walked back towards the main staircase. Switching on the light, he crept halfway down, and stood in front of David's portrait. Painted in 1916, the year after Alex's death. So young still. Joss tried to picture him, bloodied and shocked, standing there in the trench. A German shell. Joss ran a finger over the paint, smooth, delicate, but already beginning to crack, little lines etched across the canvas.

Cambridge—October, 1938

Dr Sleeman slowly stirred his tea, tapped the teaspoon three times on the edge of the rim, then carefully brought the cup to his lips. Thin lips, Joss noticed, a dull watery purple, edged each side by a few gingery bristles missed by the morning's swipe of the razor. It was a bright day, and warm; outside, the mid-afternoon sun shone down uninterrupted by any passing cloud and through the leaded window. A long shaft cut across the room, filled with tiny particles of dust, languidly dancing in the sunlight. On one side of this bright divide, sitting in an armchair by his desk, was Dr Sleeman. On the other sat Joss, and a fellow undergraduate, named Haskell, who, sitting back on his chair, appeared as at ease as Joss was stiffly uncomfortable; and this, their first time in Dr Sleeman's lair. Joss watched Haskell's foot jiggling and the disinterested way in which he drank his tea. And long hair too, so that every so often he would sweep it back past his ears. His skin glowed with good health, its colour far darker than the more pallid complexion Joss shared with most Englishmen in mid-October. A slightly protruding chin heightened the jaw-line, and although his hair was dark, he had fiercely pale eyes and arching eyebrows that gave him an air of perpetual amusement.

'In many ways, then,' said Sleeman, setting down his cup once more, 'the Normans were the political masters of their world. From Norman acumen and political organization stemmed the basis of kingship and national unity that remains with us to

74

this day.'

He paused and eyed his charges. 'Don't you agree Mr Lambert?' he said, fixing on Joss.

'Yes,' said Joss, 'well, that is, except that England was unified before the Conqueror—wasn't it?'

'Well said,' said Haskell.

Dr Sleeman gave Haskell a cursory glance, then turned to Joss and said, 'It depends on what you consider the word "unified" to mean. Inasmuch as there was one king, I would have to agree with you. But politically and militarily, I would say you were some way off the mark. And do you think there was any other way to unify a nation in the eleventh century than by a combination of political and military authority? You must remember that William of Normandy did what no king before had ever achieved: total authority over a country that had been rudderless for the previous six hundred years.'

Joss drank his tea, hoping by using his mouth for another purpose he might be excused further response. The ruse seemed to work, for Haskell cut in.

'But you cannot suppose Harold—the Anglo-Saxon King of England—was not capable of ruling a unified country. William was just a lucky opportunist, and unlikely to have won had the Saxons not been fighting off another invasion in the north. I think your military superiority theory is somewhat flawed.'

Joss looked at Haskell with a mixture of awe and horror, then at Dr Sleeman. But rather than berating him for insolence, the supervisor's mouth broke into an amused smile.

'The fatal "what-if", Mr Haskell. What if, what

if—unfortunately it's a phrase that cannot be applied to any study of history.'

'Of course not—I'm merely disputing your own assumptions.'

Back and forth they argued—Haskell defending Anglo-Saxon art, law, systems of government, and kingship, while Dr Sleeman patiently countered by citing the conquerors' military and organizational acumen. Joss listened, mesmerized, conscious he had become an invisible third party.

Eventually, Haskell sat back in his chair and prodding the air accusingly said, 'William subdued the English by slaughtering them. He was nothing more than a butcher, destroying the Anglo-Saxon ruling class. With the English nobility destroyed there was no one to lead the thegns and peasants; Norman subjugation would have been easy. And by imposing the feudal system, they enslaved free-born Englishmen. Like any dictatorships, the Normans were rotten at the core.' Joss stared at him.

Dr Sleeman smiled. 'Careful, Haskell. It's too easy to let romantic fervour get the better of you. You should not be under any delusion that the average English peasant was any more contented or "free" under the Saxons than he was under the Normans. Nor are we discussing the Theory of Modern State. William was neither Hitler, Mussolini or Franco.'

Haskell drummed his fingers onto the arm of his chair. 'It's not romantic fervour, sir, it's just a belief that the Normans have been grossly overrated and should be revealed for what they really were: fascistic, small-minded thugs who took existing systems of government and order and claimed them for their own.'

Sleeman chuckled. 'The Norman Yoke. That old chestnut. Nothing more than a myth, passed down from generation to generation, championed by the Levellers, regurgitated by Stubbs and then read and swallowed hook, line and sinker by impressionable young men like yourself. I'm going to enjoy this, young man. It'll be an interesting challenge converting you.' He stood up and trailed a finger along a shelf of books. 'Maitland,' he said, pulling a copy from the shelf and handing it to him. 'See what you make of that. You can read it too, Mr Lambert.' Sleeman moved towards the door. 'Well, gentlemen, I think that will do for today. I trust you're settling into college life well enough?'

'Yes, thank you,' said Joss.

'Till next week, then,' said Haskell, who without pausing to thank their new tutor, pushed past Joss and out of the room.

Joss caught up with him at the bottom of the steps.

'Patronizing bastard,' said Haskell. 'What the hell does he know? "You've set me an interesting challenge, Haskell",' he mimed. He stopped and turned to Joss. 'And he's right, it will be a challenge. I'm going to convert *him*. That'll wipe the smile off his face.' He brushed his hands through his hair, and felt his pockets.

'Christ, where are my cigarettes? You don't have one do you?'

'Sorry no—I don't smoke.'

'Must have left them in my rooms. Damn.'

'I thought you stood up to him very well,' said Joss, then added, 'I wouldn't have dared.'

'Why on earth not? Don't you think you should

stand up for what you believe?'

'Yes, but—'

'Believe me, you want to watch it with people like Sleeman. His sort like to forget this is a university and that we're actually supposed to develop our own minds. They get used to students swallowing everything they say. Anyway, I've always loathed the Normans.' He stopped abruptly and looking at Joss said, 'You're not a Norman are you? I hope not, because if that's the case, I'm afraid we'll have to be sworn enemies.'

'No, I'm definitely Saxon,' said Joss.

Haskell grinned. 'Good. I thought as much. I'm Tommy, by the way. Tommy Haskell.'

'Joss Lambert.' They shook hands, then continued walking round the Old Court, Tommy's hands thrust deep into his pockets.

'No, I'm afraid we have something of an ignoramus in our tutor, and he must be converted.' He stopped again. 'Where are your digs? Are you in college?'

Joss nodded. 'The other side of the river. In the new Fisher building.'

'Well I'm just here in Essex. Why don't you come and see where I am? Have a drink.'

Joss followed him up a narrow wooden staircase until they reached a landing and a door with T. Haskell inserted by the side. 'Come on in,' said Tommy, pushing open the unlocked door and taking off his gown. Joss was immediately struck by its neatness and by the level to which Tommy had already stamped his own mark. A silk bedspread, patterned with peacocks in deep mauves, blues and gold, covered the standard grey and brown blankets; on the dark wood chest of drawers stood

78

a narrow bronze vase full of white lilies. Their scent filled the room. An elaborately patterned rug lay before the sofa in front of the fireplace. Above the mantelpiece hung a highly impressionistic oil painting of a coastal scene: bright blue sea, white buildings, green-leafed palm trees, and on the opposite wall a framed bill-poster promoting *Die Zauberflöte* in Vienna from 1932.

'What a room,' said Joss, staying by the door. 'Mine looks very tame by comparison.'

'Amazing what you can do by putting a few bits and pieces here and there,' said Tommy, crawling underneath his desk. Joss wondered what he was doing until Tommy backed out again, clutching a bottle of wine. 'Here we go,' he said, putting the bottle on his desk and collecting a couple of glasses from a sideboard next to the fireplace. 'It's all pretty eclectic I know, but they all mean something to me. It's comforting.' He strained to pull out the cork, then handed Joss a glass. 'For God's sake, do sit, Joss,' he said, then went over to the Art Deco stand by the door. 'Here, take a look at this: at first a very ordinary walking stick, but then'—a flash of steel emerged from the wood—'we have a deadly weapon with which to send potential enemies—Dr Sleeman or some other hoodlum—packing.'

Joss laughed. 'Where on earth did you get that?'

Tommy swished the blade back and forth. 'Makes a good noise doesn't it? In Luxor, in a market there. I was there just a month ago. My folks live in Cairo.' He put the sword back in its scabbard and sat down next to Joss. 'Dad's in the diplomatic service, so we've lived all over really.' He brushed the dust off his knees, and said, 'I'm either going to have to move my stash of booze, or buy more trousers.'

Then he began to talk. He looked directly at Joss as he spoke, eyes intense and hands generously used to emphasize a point. It seemed he had spent half his life in English boarding schools and the other half in a succession of exotic locations. Paris as a child, then Vienna, a long stint in Washington and finally Egypt. Paris, he told Joss, was a great place to be a child. Did he know it? Joss shook his head.

'Ah well,' he said, 'then let me tell you, the French love children.' There were always things going on and Tommy and his family lived in a very grand house right next to the Place des Vosges. One of his favourite things was to walk with his mother to the Tuileries to watch the Punch and Judy there. Even at that age, he recognized there was a degree of glamour about the French. Paris, he said, was 'so *chic.*' Vienna was beautiful too, and because it was comparatively close to the mountains it felt a very clean city. 'Not like London, I can tell you.' The bill-poster hanging on the wall was a memento from those days—his first ever opera. He'd always longed to go to the opera because his parents were always going—part of the job he supposed—but then when you're a child you always want to be treated like a grown-up, *don't you*? And it was 'amazing, incredible'; he would never forget it. Just thinking about the Queen of the Night's arias made the hairs on the back of his neck stand up, even now. Washington was good—a sort of homecoming for his mother who was American. 'But just in case you're wondering, Joss, my mother's great, great grandfather came to Massachusetts from Dorset, and my father's family are from Somerset, so I'm definitely Anglo-Saxon through and through.'

Joss smiled.

'But America is so very different from Europe,' Tommy continued. Although he himself was half-American, he initially felt very little affinity with them as a nation or a people. 'Unbelievably insular and—well, I don't want to seem too harsh—but rather brash and ignorant too.' But the standard of living over there was *miles* better than anything Europe could offer. Everything was bigger too—bigger cars, bigger houses, bigger country. But then again, the United States were barely involved in the last war, so even with the Crash, never suffered in the same way that Europe did. At least, that was how it appeared to him, although having said that, he went to Colorado once and the people there—especially the native Americans—were among the poorest he'd ever seen. After a short while, he began to rather take to the Americans. He appreciated their 'optimism' and their unfailing friendliness. 'Taught me not to be so bloody stuffy and snooty.' And the girls he said, grinning, *loved* English accents. 'I may be half-American, but to those girls I played the fully-fledged English gent bit for all it's worth, I can tell you.'

In the end, he was rather sorry his father was moved to Egypt, although the prospect of going to Africa and seeing all the ancient Egyptian ruins was pretty good compensation, especially for someone interested in history and archaeology like him. But they did miss not having a refrigerator. 'Amazing how quickly you get used to new things, and then you wonder how you could ever have lived without them before. And especially in Egypt when

81

temperatures regularly reach a hundred plus in the shade. 'Believe me,' said Tommy. 'June, July and August—avoid Egypt like the plague. It's too hot for anyone and the chances of getting some terrible lurgy are ridiculously high. I should know—I spent much of last summer lying on my back chucking my guts up.'

Tommy emptied the bottle of wine into their glasses. Joss hadn't eaten anything since breakfast some four hours before and the wine was already going to his head. He swilled his glass. Drinking in the middle of the day and meeting people like Tommy; he'd hoped Cambridge would be like this, although it seemed incredible that someone his own age could have seen and done so much.

Pulling out another cigarette, Tommy said between his teeth, 'Well come on—what about you? I've been ranting quite long enough, but it's not fair to let me tell you my life story without hearing yours.'

'Oh, it's very tame by comparison,' said Joss. 'I've mostly lived in London, although I was born in Africa, so that's one up on you, isn't it?'

Tommy laughed. 'Whereabouts?'

'Kenya. My mother lost her parents as a child and so moved out to what was then British East Africa to live with her grandparents. They had a farm just south of Nairobi.'

'And your father?'

'He died before I was two. I don't remember anything about him.'

'So your mother brought you back to England.'

'Exactly. To London. Been there ever since, pretty much.'

'Mother remarried?'

'Yes.'

'Sorry, I'm prying aren't I? I'm so nosy. Terrible trait.' He left the sentence hanging.

Joss smiled apologetically and paused to drink from his glass. *Yes, let's talk about something else.* 'But I'm not an out-and-out Londoner, you know. One of my oldest friends lives in Wiltshire. His family have semi-adopted me, so I spend quite a bit of time down there. Much more fun being there in the summer than in London.'

'I'm sure. Brothers or sisters?'

'An older brother and Guy's twin, Stella.'

'I meant you.' He smiled quizzically.

'Oh. No—just me and my mother,' he said, then added, 'Actually Guy's here too.'

'At Queens'?'

'Yes, but mathematics. Don't hold it against him, though.'

Tommy laughed. 'I promise not to—anyway, I know one of those too.' Then he yawned, stretched, and said, 'So, what are we going to do?'

'What do you mean?'

'Here at Cambridge. We can't just be slaves to our textbooks.' He ran his hand through his hair again. 'I thought I might take part in a play of some kind. Row maybe—I've had enough of rugger. Rowing might be fun. And fly—I definitely want to fly. Join the University Air Squadron and get to buzz around the skies for free. What could be better?'

'All right,' said Joss. 'I'm not sure about the acting, but rowing and flying, definitely.'

'Get your chum Guy to join in the fun too,' said Tommy. He stood up and began peering intently at his face in a mirror by the door. 'I'm worried my nostril hair's growing,' he said. 'God, I dread getting old. My worst fear is that my hair will fall out. I can't think of anything worse than being bald.'

Joss laughed. 'Is your maternal grandfather bald?'

'No. No, he's pretty much got the lot still.'

'You'll be all right then.'

'Is that how you know? What a relief.'

*   *   *

Presently they wandered over to the Old Hall for dinner. Rows of gowned students lined the tables, standing chatting until the President arrived and they were called to grace. Joss spotted Guy and, with Tommy, made his way towards him. His friend was talking to a tall student with unkempt hair and a tweed jacket with sleeves that were far too long. His tie was loose, revealing the top button of his shirt, and his gown creased.

'Hello Noel,' said Tommy.

'Oh, you know each other then?' said Guy.

'We were at school together,' said Tommy, holding out his hand. 'Tommy Haskell.'

'So were we,' said Guy, nodding at Joss. 'Guy Liddell.'

'I know,' said Tommy. 'Joss has been telling me.'

'And let me guess,' said Noel, looking at Joss, 'you've had a crash course in the exotic, glamorous world of Tommy Haskell, *bon viveur* and man of the world.'

'Noel's bitter that he's never stepped out of Yorkshire—until now of course,' said Tommy. 'I mean look at you, Noel, you even dress like a country bumpkin.'

84

'Clothes should be entirely functional,' said Noel. 'I'm neither interested in fashion nor the vanity that drives it.'

'Nor am I particularly,' said Tommy, 'but good clothes make me feel better. I know for example, that if *I* wore that pullover of yours, I would end up as bitter and depressed as you are.'

'I can only feel sorry for you then, Tommy,' replied Noel. 'If you need something as materialistic as clothes to determine your mood, you must be a more pitiful individual than I'd ever appreciated.'

Tommy turned to Guy and Joss. 'Typical Noel comment that—brilliant mind, but no *joie de vivre.*'

The sparring between the two stopped as the diners were called to grace. A sudden hush descended on the room. After a brief pause, one of the scholars began, 'Benedic, Domine, nos et dona tua.' Just words, albeit Latin words; they meant nothing. Even if he was religious—which he'd long ago decided he wasn't—Joss knew he'd still find a lot of the prescribed prayers uninspiring; archaic collections of words, repeated over and over, so that habit and tradition were the only comfort they now offered. He wondered if even the Dean believed. How could a God who was so merciful and loved them all so much, still let them face another European war after all the death and destruction of the previous one?

Joss frowned to himself, annoyed that he'd allowed himself to admit such thoughts. David was wrong. There wasn't going to be another war. The Czechs had been sold out to save their bacon, and he and Guy had not been sent off to fight, but were at Cambridge after all, making new friends instead and talking about flying and rowing. Even the Vice-Chancellor, in his matriculation speech, had talked with optimism of the year ahead. Cambridge, he said, was beginning the new academic year with the worries and uncertainties of the previous weeks firmly behind them. Life *must* return to normal.

The hall was dimly lit. Large candelabras, now filled with electric light bulbs, hung over them. Darkened portraits watched them, as they had done to countless generations of young men before them. Much like school in many ways, Joss thought; and the same smell of boiled vegetables and floor polish. Tommy was swaying slightly, smirk on his face; Noel, staring straight ahead, brow furrowed with distaste. The scholar finished. *Amen*, said Joss, an automaton. Then benches and chairs scraped on the floor.

'So what do you think?' said Tommy, some minutes later, having outlined his plans.

'I'll try the rowing, but I'm not going up in any plane,' said Noel.

'Why on earth not?' asked Tommy.

'Wouldn't trust myself. I don't want to get killed just yet.'

Tommy sighed.

'Aren't you interested to know what the world looks like from up there, though?' asked Guy.

'Not enough.'

'And what if there's a war?' said Tommy. *There it is again, inescapable.* 'I suppose you'd rather be fighting on the ground, struggling around in the mud, cold and miserable. Or maybe at sea, the icy brine chilling you to the core, and where any moment you could be sent to a watery grave.'

'You could still be sent to a watery grave,' said

Guy, 'if you were shot down into the sea.'

'I don't intend to fight at all,' said Noel. 'I'm not going to get myself killed just because a bunch of idiotic politicians ballsed everything up.'

'Would you be a conchie then?' asked Guy.

'Noel's an advocate of Moral Rearmament,' said Tommy.

Noel smiled. 'I said I'm not going to get myself killed—I wouldn't *refuse* to fight, I'd just avoid it. Wars need mathematicians at home. You'll do the same Guy if you have any sense. Surely you don't want to fight?'

'Of course not, but—'

Guy was cut off by Tommy, who said, 'But Noel, wouldn't you feel a bit emasculated?'

'Why would I feel that?'

'Well, sitting in some office somewhere while everyone else is risking their lives. "What did you do in the War, Daddy?" Will you be able to answer your son and not feel just a little bit of shame and remorse?'

'I've never known anyone who values self-glorification more than you, Tommy. But it's not much use if you end up a fire-ball on some hillside.'

'Oh, I don't know. I've enjoyed my life. Of course I want to live to a ripe old age, but I think there's something to be said for dying in a blaze of glory. Especially if it's in a Hurricane or a Spitfire—what could be more exciting than zooming about in one of those? Better even than sex.' He paused and looked at Joss and Guy. 'Wouldn't you agree?'

They nodded. 'I'm sure,' said Guy.

'What do you think, Joss?' asked Noel.

'About what?'

'What would you do if there's a war?'

'Oh, I don't know. I find it hard to imagine. I still don't want to think it's possible.' He looked at the others, then said, 'Anyway, when are college rowing trials?'

'This weekend, I think,' said Tommy. 'Are we all agreed to try for a four?'

'Count me in,' said Joss.

'Me too,' said Guy.

Noel raised his knife.

'Good,' said Tommy.

'And what about getting into the air squadron?' said Guy.

'Oh, it's straightforward enough. Apply, then interview with the squadron commander and you're in. Luckily my parents know him—he's quite an old bloke, a fighter pilot in the war. He'll see us right, don't you worry.'

'Another warning about Tommy,' said Noel, 'he claims to know everyone from the Pope to King Tonga of Outer Mongolia.'

'This resentment is, of course, a by-product of Noel's sheltered background,' said Tommy. 'Don't listen to a word he says or you'll end up as miserable as he is.'

*   *   *

Much later that evening, Joss returned to his rooms in the Fisher Building. The beige carpet, only two years old, was already worn by the door and near his bed was a large stain of spilled wine. No exotic patterns covered his bed, nor was there a single picture on the wall. His desk contained a few books, his cupboard a couple of suits and jackets. When he'd first arrived, ten days before, this room had seemed a manifestation of his new-found independence and adulthood. Now, he realized, it represented his own short-comings. Tommy had shown him how one's character could be stamped upon everything one did. Even Guy had come armed with wine and whisky, photographs of Stella and the other Liddells, and a vast array of clothes. At the time Joss had mocked him, accusing him of being ludicrously over-packed. 'We're only going up for a couple of months,' he'd told him, 'not a round-the-world cruise.'

Guy had given him a withering look. 'I need these things, Joss. I'm not going to slum it, you know.'

What did this room say about him? he wondered. There was little in his sparse collection of belongings to give him away. He kicked off his shoes, and lay stretched out on his bed, his hands behind his head, staring at a yellowish water stain on the ceiling above him. He barely knew who he was himself.

Cairo—September, 1942

At last—a letter from his mother. She'd received two telegrams—one to say he was missing, another a day later to say he'd been picked up. *'For a moment I thought the worst,'* she wrote, *'but thank God you're all right. Surely they should send you home now? Tell them you've done your bit. Come and recuperate in the flat—I'll be a most attentive nurse.'*

No you won't, thought Joss. Maybe, for a day or two, then the novelty would wear off and her pressing social engagements would once again win the day. He smiled to himself: his mother could say such things in the knowledge that it would never happen.

The anger he felt towards her had long gone. At school she had always been a most infrequent letter writer, but since he left England her hastily scrawled notes had continued to arrive in a steady flow. Now she had even outdone Stella. His mother, the most unreliable person he'd ever known, was proving to be the one constant in his life after all. A life for which there was no reason any more.

Stella's letter. The most terrible words he'd ever read. *'I can barely remember the sound of your voice, except that I loved it.'* He sighed. *Stella,* he thought, *why couldn't you have waited?*

Joss looked up as a nurse entered the ward and breathlessly told them that Rommel had been forced to retreat. Montgomery had held firm. Now the Germans wouldn't be storming Cairo after all. She paused, beamed at them, and said, 'Isn't that the most marvellous news?'

The response was hardly euphoric. One muffled cheer that soon developed into a coughing fit, a grunt from another and silence from the other four. Alex Carter, in the bed next to Joss, was asleep; or at any rate his one eye was closed.

'Well,' said the nurse, 'I thought you'd all want to know.' She looked at Joss, and seeing he at least was awake and listening said, 'It was at Alam Halfa. Rommel attacked on the ridge there, but couldn't break the line. He had to withdraw. Your lot bombed them to shreds apparently.'

'Thank you,' he said, 'that is a great relief.'

Alam Halfa. He'd flown over it several times in the days before his crash. From the sky it looked much like any of those narrow ridges in the western desert: arid, bleak and uninhabitable—and uninhabited, save, of course, the two armies massed either side. An unnatural habitat for man.

He could imagine the celebrations that would go on that night. The bars and clubs would be teeming, the streets of Cairo full of drunken soldiers. *Good old Monty! Hooray for the Eighth Army!* Morale suddenly sky-high after the depths of despair in the preceding months.

He supposed he was glad. Pleased to hear the RAF had done well. He thought about the squadron and pictured Prior and Calloway insisting that they all have a few drinks that night. The men huddled in their greatcoats in the canvas mess. Prior always stashed away some of the precious beer and whisky supplies for special occasions; the CO had never been a great drinker himself, so perhaps that made it easier to be self-disciplined. Even so, Prior was a good man like that. Assuming he was still there, of course.

Later that night he heard the revellers on the streets outside, just as he'd predicted. Shouting, then breaking glass near at hand, noises that rose above the constant murmur of the city. There were animalistic yells from the group of revellers. But he'd been just the same on numerous occasions. That first year at Cambridge—sometimes it seemed as though they'd barely been sober.

Breaking glass.

That night after the Novice Cup. Emboldened by their drunkenness, they had wandered into Trinity, and Guy had tried to land a bottle in the fountain

91

but missed. The sudden noise, in that cold, still night, rang amplified around the courtyard, so that there was a moment of clarity when they looked at each other then turned to run for their lives to escape the Proctors. Joss remembered the clouds of hot breath on the air, the railings along King's Parade rushing past him, and the clatter of feet on the pavement. Quite hilarious at the time, but in retrospect, nothing more than the kind of high jinks which young men the world over get up to after too much drink.

The orange glow of the city at night seeped through the ward windows. Outside, Joss heard more shouting—Scots, by the sound of it. Another yell, English this time, then footsteps running away, disappearing into the night.

Cambridge—November, 1938

As the term continued, so the anxiety and panic that had gripped the country began to recede. At Girton, the air-raid shelters were left unfinished, and plans to make the college a war hospital for London children scrapped. Joss noticed that talk of war came up less in conversation; and he, for one, had other concerns, which, although having no bearing on the international situation, seemed to him no less important. Prime amongst these was their preparation for the Novice Cup at the end of November, a regatta for those new to rowing. As agreed, the four of them—Joss, Tommy, Guy and Noel—had gone to the college trials insisting they would stick together as a crew, or not at all. It was not an auspicious start. They had been laughing about something Noel had said, not concentrating properly, and since none of them had ever rowed before, they nearly capsized just trying to seat themselves in the narrow hull.

Roland Williams, the college captain, had squatted on the edge of the landing stage and steadied their riggers, then rubbed his forehead with exasperation. 'Most novices at least manage to get into the boat before tipping over,' he told them. 'I'm not sure this is going to work.'

'With your help it will,' said Tommy. 'Coach us and we can aim for the Novice Cup. We'll train hard, do as we're told—promise.'

'Is that so?'

'Might even win it for you,' said Noel. 'You'll never know if you don't give us a chance.'

'Think of the glory we would bring to the college,' added Tommy.

'And the glory we would bring you,' suggested Noel.

The captain stood up and rubbed his chin, clearly unsure whether these cock-sure freshers were serious or not. He was tall, broad shouldered, and wearing a cream university blazer trimmed with pale blue silk.

'Try us for a couple of weeks,' suggested Guy.

'Yes, just two weeks and if we're still no good then we'll leave you alone,' added Tommy.

Taking off his cap and smoothing down his already sleek, dark hair, Roland agreed to try them for a fortnight, on the strict understanding that if they could not balance the boat by then, the deal was off. Then, having found them a cox—a diminutive first-year called Tony Mullins—he told them to meet him at the boathouse at six o'clock the following morning.

When Tommy had first suggested rowing, Joss had imagined languid afternoons lapping down quiet backwaters of the Cam. Exercise, certainly, but relaxation too; messing about on the river had sounded appealing. Conversely, dark mornings of icy cold or driving rain had not been a part of his vision of the sport. But as soon as Roland had laid down the gauntlet, it became a point of honour to complete the challenge. The others, he knew, felt the same way, enjoying a kind of perverse pleasure in the discomfort of their early-morning starts. Meeting by the porter's lodge, heavy with scarves and pullovers, they would stomp up and down in the cold early morning air, blowing on hands, and then when they had all assembled, run together to the boathouse. Soon this routine was brought forward even earlier so that by the time Roland arrived on his bicycle, they were not only already there, but had taken the boat off its rack and out onto the landing stage too. The devil-may-care attitude—the arrogance—they had affected on the day of the trials vanished as soon as they put on their rowing shorts.

After two weeks, Roland told them they were hopeless, but that he would see them through to the Novice Cup. They hadn't a hope of winning, but he was feeling generous and was getting used to shouting at them from the riverbank.

Some days they made great progress, so that on their walk back to college they would all talk at once, prattling excitedly about how they had felt the lurch of the boat against their backs and that on a particular stretch they had begun to show some real pace. On others, they would regress; one, or all, would feel tired or hung over, their balance would be terrible, blades would plunge too deep, and Roland would bellow at them like a parade ground sergeant-major.

Joss liked the frosty mornings best, even though his teeth would be chattering and his knees white with cold. He liked the way the last stars faded away and the lines of pink and yellow gradually emerged on the horizon. He liked the smell of autumn, the pure, chilled air that refreshed his lungs. And he liked the mist that hung over the river—rowing past spectral figures lowering their boat into the water or watching other coaches on the riverbank emerging as if from nowhere on their bicycles. His favourite moment was when they were rowing well, over a long stretch. As one, blades would dip the water, a dull boom as they pulled; their seats would squeak and creak along the runners; Roland silently cycling alongside them. Occasionally, they disturbed a coot or swan, but otherwise they were surrounded by calm silence, their own entity shrouded by the river mist. Despite his exertions, Joss would be enveloped by a sense of profound calm.

'I think we should ask Roland if we can go out a couple more times a week,' said Joss one morning. They were walking back along the river path, damp with autumn and trodden leaves. The frost was already thawing and everything dripped. They had just had a good hour and even Roland had grudgingly admitted they were making progress. The good outings were beginning to outweigh the bad. 'We want to win the cup don't we?'

'Three's enough, surely,' said Noel.

95

'I'm with Joss,' said Guy.

'Under normal circumstances, early mornings are anathema to me,' said Tommy, 'but maybe we should, you know.'

'I don't mind,' said Tony.

'We've just got to persuade Roland, then,' said Noel. 'I can't believe I'm actually enjoying competitive sport.'

Roland agreed—just until the Cup—although they would have to do a couple of early evening sessions because he had his own commitments with the university squad. No one minded missing the odd lecture; as Tommy was quick to point out, it was only until the Cup.

*   *   *

One weekend Stella came to see her brother. Guy had been vague about their plans beforehand. 'Oh, I expect I'll show her a few of the sights, that sort of thing,' he'd said when Joss had asked. There had been no invitation to join them. On the Saturday morning, however, Guy did knock on his door and walk on in, before Joss had a chance to reply.

'Stella—hello!' he said jumping up from his seat and frantically trying to tidy his room up a bit: there was rowing kit strewn across the floor, dirty mugs and a pile of books and papers across his desk.

'Sorry Joss—but I'm afraid Stella absolutely insisted on seeing your room too. You see,' he said turning to her, 'it's much the same as mine really, only less tidy and more Spartan, if that's at all possible.'

'We're just about to go on a tour of the town,'

said Stella, 'would you like to come too?'

Joss swallowed and looked at Guy. 'Well—' he said, but Guy cut him off.

'I think Joss has probably got better things to do than traipse around Cambridge with us.'

Stella shrugged. 'Oh well,' she said, her eyes sweeping the room.

Damn! Joss cursed to himself—of course he *wanted* to spend time with her, but in that split-second moment when he had to make his decision he had felt certain that Guy did not want him to join them.

'Perhaps later then?' he said, the chance slipping ever further away.

Stella smiled. 'Yes, maybe,' she said.

As soon as they had gone Joss closed his eyes and lightly banged his head against the wall. 'Damn!' he said out loud. 'Damn, damn, damn.' He was still feeling wretched and cursing the missed opportunity when, a short while later, Tommy came in.

'What are you doing?' said Tommy, wandering over to Joss's desk and helping himself to an apple from Joss's newly-acquired fruit bowl.

Joss lifted his book. 'Maitland,' he said, 'but I've been rereading this page about half a dozen times.'

'Come on then, let's go to Grantchester and have lunch. You don't really want to be working do you?'

'Not especially.'

'Well, grab a coat and let's go.'

They headed out of the college and began the walk across the water-meadows.

Their attempts to convert Dr Sleeman had not been going well.

'We'll probably discover that Sleeman's forbears

were Normans,' said Tommy. His scarf was wrapped round his neck so it covered half his face. His hands, as usual, were deep in his pockets. 'His family tree probably goes back to before the conquest, when his people were shield bearers in William's army. I think even in this day and age, one empirically feels drawn towards one's roots, even if those roots are nearly a thousand years old. Are we Anglo-Saxonists because we really, truly believe their laws, systems of government and art were more sophisticated than they have been given credit for, or is it because we feel an affiliation to a people from which we ourselves descend?'

'Both,' said Joss. 'I'm certain of the first part of what you said, but my interest derives from wanting to believe the latter.'

'Wanting to believe, Joss?'

'Yes.' *But just not in the manner you think,* he thought to himself.

They climbed a stile, Grantchester's church now clearly visible across the fields. 'You know Joss, you and I are rather alike in some ways. At least in interests. We both have an obsessive streak.'

'Do we?'

'Don't look so offended. What I mean is that when I get an interest in something, I get *really* interested. Have to know everything there is about it and have to be better than everyone else. And although I never lose that interest, I do move on to something new.'

'I don't think I'm especially like that,' said Joss.

'Well what about this fascination with the Anglo-Saxons then? You and I hardly talk about anything else at the moment, yet before you came here I bet you'd hardly given them a thought. Now you're banging on about Harold and Hastings and going on digs.'

Joss frowned.

'Don't get me wrong—I'm all for it. It's great to have found a fellow-enthusiast—I certainly don't get any encouragement from Noel. And then what about the rowing? Your idea to increase the training.'

'I just want to win that cup.'

'Exactly, and now you're driving us all towards it with your quiet determination. Honestly, Joss, I'm with you all the way. But think about it: we're investing all this time and energy and yet we haven't the first idea whether we've got the slightest chance.'

'But it's fun though. You're enjoying it, aren't you? Getting satisfaction when we're all working well together? And all this exercise first thing in the morning. Makes me feel alive.'

They walked on in silence for a few moments, then Joss said, 'Do you think we'd have become obsessive about flying?'

'Definitely. I already am, only I have no means of channelling my obsession. I should never have gone to Marshall's—just made matters worse.'

For the current term at any rate, the University Air Squadron was full; all three had had their applications turned down. To Tommy's consternation and to Noel's delight, the Haskell family connections with the commanding officer had counted for nothing. But they had still gone to the opening of Marshall's new airfield near Cambridge, having heard that some Spitfires were doing a public display for the first time. Three of the RAF's newest fighter roared past, cowing the

99

crowd below. The planes were so fast, they had become nothing more than insects on the horizon in just a few moments. Then they were back, their engines purring with a rich, guttural throb, twisting and turning with breathtaking agility. Tommy had talked of little else for days afterwards.

'Well, maybe you're right,' said Joss at length. 'About being obsessive, I mean. Although I wouldn't call it obsession; rather just a healthy interest in things.'

Tommy laughed. 'All right—a healthy interest then. What others have there been? Your childhood must be littered with them.'

Joss laughed. 'Let me think. When I was much younger I was very keen on all those Rider Haggard books—tales of daring and adventure and big-game hunters. And Baden-Powell—I loved his books about Southern Africa. All I ever wanted to do when I grew up was to go to Africa and become the biggest of big-game hunters. Guy and I both read absolutely everything we could about it. Highlight of the week was getting *Chums*.'

'I know the thing: *Valour in the Veldt;* brave British colonials showing the natives how it's done.

'Exactly.'

'But you don't want to do that now?'

'No. No I don't. As you said, one moves on.' Joss paused, tugged at his ear. He was aware that Tommy sensed there was more. Part of him wanted to tell Tommy everything. Part of him didn't. Indecision—and an awkward gap in the conversation. A matter of seconds only, but inwardly Joss cringed at his sudden paralysis.

'So what came after African Adventurers?' said Tommy, making the decision for him. *Relief.*

'After that, well, there's Alvesdon Farm, I suppose.'

'Which is what?'

'Where Guy's family live. It's the most beautiful place, Tommy. A Queen Anne farmhouse at the foot of a ridge of chalk downs. His family have lived there for hundreds of years, farming the land.'

'A good Anglo-Saxon name, Alvesdon,' suggested Tommy.

'Yes, isn't it? For all I know, his family were farming there even then. Guy's not at all interested in its history, but I think it's fascinating. Because they've always lived there they have centuries of family belongings. All the old books, letters, ageing pewter—you name it. And relics too: a sword used in the Battle of Waterloo. A Civil War set of armour. It's like a museum to one family, only the place feels so alive.'

'How amazing.'

'It is. Although they were farmers, the second sons always seemed to become priests or join the army.'

'And brought back mementoes of their experiences.'

'Exactly, or at least, the soldier sons did. And it's all documented. There are letters from these people writing about the things they've seen, and then you feel their possessions in your hand, hold them where they would have held them. The character who was at Waterloo came back and took over the farm—Arthur Liddell—Guy's great-great grandfather. He was an officer in the Queen's Own Royal Wiltshires. Followed Wellington for much of the Peninsular War. He was wounded at Salamanca by a glancing sword-blow from a French hussar, but

101

survived. And a great letter-writer. I suppose there was plenty of time for that sort of thing, but reading them now, the interesting thing to me is how much he was like any young man. He had good moods and bad moods, wrote enthusiastically about things that excited him and grumbled if he was ill or they'd spent too long in the field. He mourned lost friends and hated the Spanish almost as much as the French. They're all there: neatly folded, with surprisingly legible handwriting. You can really imagine him sitting in his tent writing them. Some even have ink blobs and food stains. And then you see one of his tunics and he becomes even more real. A few moth holes, but as scarlet as the day he first wore it. Fortunately Guy's father is a proud guardian of all this stuff and so it's carefully looked after. I think he rather likes it that I'm so interested in it all. But Tommy, you must see some of these things. The big events of the last four hundred years and one or other of Guy's family was there every time. It's extraordinary.' He stopped and grinned at Tommy. 'So maybe I'm a bit obsessive about that.'

'I thought it was a healthy interest.'

'Touché.'

'I don't think I've ever heard you talk so much in one go. The Liddells are obviously quite a family. And I wouldn't mind betting you're quietly in love with Guy's sister too.'

Joss reddened.

Tommy slapped him on the back. 'That's shut you up again. I suspected as much when you first told me about them that day we met. Don't worry, your secret's safe with me. Anyway, I don't blame you—I saw her with Guy this morning.

She's lovely.'

Joss looked away.

'Sorry,' grinned Tommy, 'that was mean of me—none of my business. Please forget I ever mentioned it. But I was right. You *are* like me: you get hooked by a subject and want to know everything. I'm like that every time the folks move somewhere new. Just have to know all about the place—its history, its culture, the little side-streets that only the home-grown know about.'

They reached the edge of the village. Grantchester was a quiet community of farmers, tenant labourers, land-workers, and dons, but made famous by students of the nearby university. Byron had swum in a pool there; Rupert Brooke had written a poem about it, and most weekends its normally quiet lanes and public houses thronged with students, so that it became less a village and more an undergraduate excursion centre. Then during much of the week, and certainly throughout the university vacations, it returned—without fuss—to being an English village much like any other in Cambridgeshire. But on that Saturday, a clear, bright mid-November day, six weeks into term, Grantchester was pullulating with young men and women.

A loud murmur hung heavy across the pub, disturbed every so often by a sharp laugh or exclamation. The air was thick with tobacco smoke, which, with the winter sun pouring through the windows, swirled with a blue-grey phosphorescence. The grate crackled and then spat, sending sparks up the blackened brick chimney. Joss noticed the clock, similar to the one in the Blue Lion in Marleycombe, and wondered whether on quiet evenings, when the place was less busy, the pendulum would tick with the same audible constancy.

Tommy raised his glass once they had sat down, and peered at the dark fluid. 'Perfect day for it,' he said. 'Nowhere in the world has pubs like England does. You'd never find this kind of place in America or Austria, or even France for that matter. Bars, yes. Pubs, no, and believe me, there's a big difference.' He felt his pockets. 'Damn it. Where the hell are they?' Then the frown disappeared and he produced a rumpled packet of cigarettes.

'But you never lose your lighter.'

'I never would,' said Tommy flicking open the lid of his American Zippo on the table. 'I value it far too much, and I think subconsciously, one knows how to look after the things one values in a way you wouldn't with a tuppenny pack of cigs. But I tell you, Joss, the British may have been the best inventors in the last century, but America makes the best of *everything* now. And that includes cigarette lighters.' He snapped the lid shut and laid it flat underneath his palm on the table. Then taking a draught of his beer, he stretched and said, 'Anyway, don't think I've forgotten about the flying, because I absolutely haven't.'

'A dormant obsession, then,' suggested Joss.

'Exactly. But when this war comes, they're going to need a whole stack-full of pilots. Then we'll get our chance.'

Joss didn't say anything.

'There will be one, Joss, you must know that.'

'Will there? I don't see why. Anyway, let's talk about something less depressing.' He glanced around, hoping he looked bored.

Tommy eyed him for a moment, then said, 'Fine,

if you like. But it's not going to go away just because you don't want to talk about it. Hitler took Czechoslovakia and no one lifted a finger, even though in doing so he broke a whole load of international treaties and alliances. He must think invading countries is the easiest thing in the world, so he's certainly going to want to do it again. Hungary maybe, or Poland. My old man thinks his main aim is Russia.'

'Russia? That's ridiculous. I mean, no offence to your father, but why would Hitler want Russia?'

'He wants an empire. Probably wants the world. God knows, but he's fully rearmed, has successfully absorbed Austria and Czechoslovakia into the Third Reich and I see no reason why he'll stop there.'

'He'll stop because he doesn't want to go to war with Britain and France.'

Tommy took another long drink of beer, then said, 'There'll be a war Joss. Maybe not next year, maybe not even the year after. But it will happen, and it'll be people like you and me who'll have to fight it. It's much better to accept it. I have and I feel fine about it. I'm enjoying myself here much more now that I know I've got to make the most of life while I can. I'm not so careful. *Carpe diem*, and all that.'

Joss glanced down into his pint and gently swirled the liquid, watching the grey particles at the bottom of the glass rising lazily, jostled by the sudden swell.

'Cheer up. Look, if war's declared and we join the RAF, we'll probably still be training by the time it's all over again. They're not going to fling us straight into the thick of it, you know. In the meantime, we'll be getting paid for flying around in those amazing planes. So you see, there's really very little to get depressed about.'

Joss looked at him across the table: the hand sweeping back his fringe, those piercing blue eyes, and the slightest of smirks that said, *nothing worries me.*

'All right,' said Joss, 'I'll try not to worry.' If only it were that simple, he thought.

The shafts of sunlight slid across the room and disappeared. Tommy craned his neck and looked out of the window and up at the sky. A looming front of low, grey cloud had arrived, shutting out the sun like a giant rug. In only a few minutes, what had been a cool, bright day had become, dark, damp and wintry.

'Looks ominous,' said Tommy.

'I think we might get wet,' said Joss.

'And then we might catch pneumonia and die, in which case, your worries about future wars will have been a waste of time.'

'Or I might get run over by a bus tomorrow.'

'You might. And if you were, you wouldn't be the first to suffer such a fate.'

But he wasn't, nor did they catch pneumonia, even though by the time they reached Cambridge, both were wet through.

Cambridge—December, 1938

By three o'clock, they had won four races. During the first, Noel's rigger had broken just after they'd started, and so the rest of them had been forced to complete the heat without him. It should have been

106

an easy win, but had ended up being far closer than any of them cared for. During the second there had been no such hitches, but then on their way to start the third, it had begun to rain. There had been a false start on the race before them, so they had ended up waiting for over half an hour, becoming increasingly wet and cold. 'Keep moving,' Roland had shouted at them from the riverbank; that was all very well, but there wasn't much room for manoeuvre, nor did they want to exert themselves just before the crucial semi-final. While they rubbed their legs and blew on their hands, the crew from Jesus had leisurely entered the water from their landing stage near the starting point.

'Bastards,' Noel had muttered, as the opposition's cox tipped his cap towards them. Roland had warned them that the Jesus crew were good. 'Pull so much as one false stroke, and you'll lose it.' He'd eyed them all in turn. 'So concentrate like you've never concentrated before.'

Eventually the race had got underway, although both crews started badly; a stroke of luck. But from then on, they pulled together, Tony shouting and goading them to a half-a-length victory. Afterwards, they all agreed that Tony had coxed the race of his life.

'. . . And lower,' said Tony. They leant over the edge of the landing stage and with a gentle smack their boat, the *Lady Elizabeth,* had settled on the water. Roland held down the riggers as they lowered themselves onto their seat, much as he had done on that first outing. What a long time ago that seemed. Now the boat barely rocked as they called their readiness: Guy at bow, then Tommy and Joss—the two tallest—in the middle at two and three, and finally Noel at stroke.

The next time I'm on dry land, it will all be over, thought Joss. In just over twenty minutes' time, theirs would be victory or defeat. Joss rested the blade on his legs and looked at his hands. They were beginning to hurt: the calluses that had gradually built up during the preceding weeks had proved no protection against a whole day on the river, and a large blister throbbed angrily on the fleshy part of his hand.

'All right then,' said Roland. 'This is it. You've worked damned hard and deserve to be here, but all that matters now is the race ahead. Row your best and you can do it.' He stooped and shook their hands in turn. 'Good luck.'

Slowly they paddled their way to the start. The rain had all but stopped, leaving a dampness that hung in the air. Above them, the sky was a watery and constant grey, dulling the light. The trees along the river had darkened almost to silhouettes. Joss glanced at the people lining the bank in their long coats and scarves. Shouts of encouragement were accompanied by small clouds of warm breath.

The Trinity crew were there already, staring not at them, but straight ahead, their eyes fixed in concentration. At Tony's command, Joss and Guy paddled forward, Tommy and Noel backwards, so that the boat turned, and then they were drawing towards the starting punt, an official squatting down to grab the prow of their boat as they glided towards him. His cream blazer glowed luminously in the fading light.

The official held the prow firm in his hand. *No turning back now.* Joss wanted to retch. His stomach had knotted and his throat tightened.

He'd been nervous before, but nothing compared to how he felt now. He wanted so badly to win, yet it seemed impossible to think they would.

'Crews forward,' shouted the referee. Joss jolted to attention. He slid forward on his runner, arms wrapped either side of his legs.

Silence—an eternity, poised in this crouched position.

'Ready,' said the referee at last. Joss tensed, as did the others.

'Set.' Blades turned in the water, snappy like drill. Deep breath. Hold it . . .

'Row!'

Yelling from both coxes, the squeak of seats rolling frantically up and down their runners and the furious pounding of eight blades hitting the water. They had come through the start well, but so had the Trinity crew. From the corner of his eye, Joss saw the prow of the Trinity boat inch forward then back, then forward again as the crew heaved their blades through the water.

Directly in front, Noel was gasping, the muscles across his back stretched taut.

'And give it ten—come on, pull!' Tony yelling his orders, veins pulsing on his neck.

Halfway, and the two crews were still neck and neck. The blister on Joss's hand had burst—with every stroke pain shot up his arm as the raw skin chafed against the wood of his blade. His legs were beginning to throb, and he felt himself begin to tire—he wasn't sure how much longer he could keep going at such a pace—but then Noel groaned, and his blade only skimmed the surface, spraying Joss with water, the boat wobbled, and for the first time the Trinity crew took the lead.

'Come on!' shouted Tony, 'They're gaining on us. Don't lose this now. Go for twenty!'

Twenty! Joss cursed inwardly, but as he came up the slide, he reached forward with his arms that bit further.

Three-quarters of the way through the race—pain for just one more minute. Anyone could put up with that.

Still their blades hit the water together, and the boat surged forward then decelerated as they drew up the slide, then thrust forward again. The Trinity boat was now dangerously close to them, almost clashing.

'Move away Trinity!' shouted the referee from the launch trailing them. 'Move away.'

'Don't look at them,' shouted Tony. 'Come on, keep going! Come on! One, two, three, four!'

'Move away Trinity,' came the mega-phoned voice again.

Fleetingly Joss glanced at their rivals. They looked panicked. The warning from the referee had upset their rhythm, and in pulling away they had lost precious inches of lead. It was the chance they needed. He knew the others sensed it too. Tony's voice was now hoarse, but he barely needed to speak—all four knew what had to be done. Joss forgot the pain; excitement overrode all other sensations.

They crossed the line a quarter of a length ahead. The sense of elation was so overwhelming, Joss thought he might even cry. He leant back in his seat laughing. Tommy shook his shoulders. 'We've done it, Joss. We've bloody well gone and done it!'

Joss gasped, still short of breath, but turned and grinned at him. His legs and arms were flushed

110

pink, and his face burned. He leaned over and scooped some water, icy cold, over his head. It felt delicious.

*   *   *

Much later, they stumbled back from having been presented with the small, yet solid silver cup, to Roland's digs near Magdalen. They were drunk.

'I know it sounds silly, but going over that finishing line was the greatest moment of my life,' said Joss.

'Mine too,' said Guy.

'I hate to admit it, but I agree with you,' said Noel. 'Never thought I'd feel that about a sport.'

They turned onto St John's Street.

'I know in the big scheme of things the Novice Cup probably isn't incredibly important, but it's very important to me,' Joss continued, his words slurred.

'Hear, hear,' agreed Tommy.

'Look Trinity,' said Tony. 'Let's go in.'

They stole past the porter's lodge. 'Shh,' said Guy.

The front quadrangle was quiet. A couple of figures crossed the far gateway, but otherwise the place was still and silent. Suddenly Guy grabbed the bottle from Joss's hand and hurled it in the air.

'One in the fountain for them,' he said as the bottle cartwheeled through the night sky. It fell short, the glass smashing into a thousand splinters, reverberating round the four sides of the courtyard, and shattering the silence that hung heavy over the college.

For an instant, they all looked at each other, the

111

violence of the noise bringing them to momentary clarity and sobriety.

'Run!' said Tommy, and together they turned and fled, clattering past the porter's lodge and down Trinity Street and King's Parade. They did not stop until they reached Queens'. There, leaning on the old wooden bridge, they gazed into the water, the same river that had earlier borne them to victory. For a moment, they were silent, catching their breath; then they began to laugh. The more they laughed, the more they couldn't stop. Five young men, quite hysterical, doubled-up at this moment of personal, yet shared triumph.

London—Christmas, 1938

With his toe, Joss slowly turned off the hot tap, then sank down into the narrow bath. Outside, it was still dark, but despite the early hour, he could hear activity—cars, horses hooves, dull, but distinct. They *had* to be awake at that hour, but he didn't. *He* should still be asleep, but having woken and unsuccessfully tried to read a book, he had run a bath instead.

Less than a day this time. He cursed himself. After all these years, he should be used to it.

Yesterday, when he'd arrived back from Cambridge, his mother had seemed as pleased to see him as she ever had, clasping him tightly to her, and kissing him repeatedly on the cheek. She had insisted they sit down right away and that he begin telling her 'absolutely everything' about his time in Cambridge. And so he had happily told her about

112

Tommy and Noel and the rowing and Dr Sleeman, and about his rooms and funny incidents which he knew might shock some mothers, but not Diana.

'I want to meet these new friends of yours,' she'd told him, 'they sound heavenly.' They had gone out for lunch—to a small restaurant near Victoria run by an Italian friend of hers—and as they'd walked down Belgrave Road, she'd looped her arm through his and told him what a treat it was to have her son all to herself for a day.

Joss had talked almost without pausing. Whenever he'd asked her about what she'd been doing, Diana would soon steer the conversation back towards him. She was so proud of her clever son, she told him; all her friends now knew about his scholarship. And he had become so handsome too—in fact, she couldn't believe she was having lunch with such a clever, handsome, grown-up son. She felt very lucky indeed.

Afterwards, they walked in St James's Park, just as they had on so many occasions when he'd been a boy. The bandstand was empty, nor were the lawns littered with deckchairs as they were in summer, but Joss liked the way the frost gave the place a magical air. Dog-owners, wrapped up against the winter cold, impatiently hurried past. By the water, the park's ducks and geese squatted with puffed-up chests.

'Gosh, it is cold,' Diana said, and then gripped his arm even more tightly.

And as always, Joss was won over by his mother once more, the trials of the previous summer—the fights about money, the bickering, the brooding resentment—all put to one side. If only she could always be like this, he thought.

For that day, he believed himself to be quite the most important person in the world to her, and he forgave her everything: for not writing to him once whilst he'd been at Cambridge, for never visiting him, for her apparent total lack of interest during the previous three months. For making him feel as though he mattered very little to her, despite being her only son.

And as she could when she chose, she made him laugh, made him love her once more. Perhaps they would spend the fortnight without arguing even once. He enjoyed her company more than he had in ages. Really, he thought, it should be very easy for them to get on this well all the time.

Then came the disappointment; deep down, he'd expected it, but perhaps not so soon. They arrived back at the flat with Joss thinking of all the things the two of them might do over the next couple of weeks, but as Diana was taking off her coat, she said, 'What are you going to do with yourself tonight then, darling?'

'I rather hoped to have dinner with you,' Joss told her.

'Oh, you are sweet, but I've got to go out I'm afraid. You don't mind do you? But I have had a lovely time, darling. You've been quite a gent putting up with your mother all day.'

'I can't believe you're leaving me here on my first night back,' said Joss.

Diana paused. 'Now darling, don't be difficult. It's just a few people you don't know. You'd be bored stiff. Why don't you go out with some of your own friends, or something?'

Joss nodded, although his mother knew perfectly well he wouldn't be going anywhere. Guy was in

114

Wiltshire, and would almost certainly be sitting down to a family dinner; Tommy was in Yorkshire, spending Christmas with his aunt and uncle. Noel, too, had gone home, to Nottingham. Other friends from university were dotted about the country, or away. Anyway, he was short of money. Guy had invited him down to Alvesdon, of course, but this time Joss had resisted; he'd been there most of the Easter holidays, much of the summer too. And while he knew the Liddells treated him like an extension of the family, he didn't want to start taking them for granted. Or rather, he didn't want *them* thinking he was taking them for granted. But it didn't stop him wishing he was there now.

'So am I going to see you at all? Or does your busy schedule preclude spending any time with your son?'

'Now darling you know perfectly well I have a life to lead too. I can't just stop everything because you waltz back from university. Anyway, we've spent the whole of today together, haven't we?'

'And what about Christmas? Or do you have other arrangements?'

'Oh, Joss, honestly. There's really no need to take that tone. We're going to have lunch with the Redmans.'

'I thought you hated Margaret Redman.'

'Not at all. I don't know where you picked up that idea.'

Joss let it pass. 'I'm allowed to come to that one am I? You're not worried I'll be bored then?'

'Oh, do stop going on, Joss. Why do you have to spoil everything?'

'Me spoil everything? That's rich.'

They were both silent for a moment; he sitting on

115

an armchair in their sitting room, disappointment seeping through him, and angry with himself for having shown that disappointment so blatantly; while she sat at her writing desk shuffling through some papers.

So, nothing has changed at all. Already they were back where they had left off in the summer.

Eventually Diana looked at him and said, 'Oh don't sulk, Joss. It's terribly unbecoming in a grown man. I can't have you trying to make me feel guilty for going out without my nineteen-year-old son.'

'Well I am sorry,' he said, standing up, 'I'd certainly hate you to ruin your evening over me.' Then he left, retreating to his bedroom. It was a scenario that had been played out with unwavering regularity for as long as he could remember.

Lying in the bath, the following morning, he wondered why he let it bother him so much. Partly, he knew, it was because she was the only family he had; as such, he expected there to be a stronger bond between them. But there was more to it than that.

He gazed at his pinking skin, then at the wall, running with condensation. Underneath the taps, green calcium deposits, matching the colour of the walls, stained the sides of the enamel bath like solidified lava.

The day before, when he had forgiven her everything, he saw her defects as a mother in a different light. Major pitfalls became eccentric foibles. And he began to make excuses: perhaps he was too quick to criticize; and, *well, it couldn't have been easy for her, after all.*

Pah! What a gullible fool he was. After all this time, he really should have known better. And how clear everything was now: she'd believed a mere day of her undivided attention would make up for the previous few months' negligence. But he wasn't one of her lovers or suitors to be cowed by a few hours of flattery; he was her son. He chewed at his nails, grown soft from the warm water. *What does she really think of me?* Fond of him, perhaps. Little more than that. Really, he was a hindrance, a nuisance who got in the way of every plan she ever made.

Little scenes from the day before kept entering his head over and over. He thought about how, in the park, he had walked with his back that little bit straighter; and then how he had noticed people noticing her—a woman who looked younger than her forty years, and who, despite her limited resources, always managed to maintain a sense of style and sophistication. He had liked it then, his good-looking, elegant mother on his arm as they strolled through St James's Park, just as he had enjoyed playing the gallant chaperone, opening the door for her in the restaurant, or standing behind her chair as she took her seat. He cringed. He wished he was back at Cambridge or at Alvesdon, surrounded by people who valued his company and who would never fob him off with false flattery and empty words.

*   *   *

He barely saw her over the next few days. He didn't believe she was deliberately avoiding him; rather, she had other people to see, with lunch and dinner dates almost every evening. Sometimes she would be back in the afternoon and they would converse

117

briefly in the sitting room, before she disappeared to her room to get herself ready for the next excursion. She had always seemed to rush from one thing to the other, even when she'd been married to George. Now she was surpassing herself.

Christmas came and went. They spent the day with the Redmans at their house in Kensington. With her beaky nose and wide eyes, Margaret Redman reminded Joss of a startled bird. And she never stopped talking; about the latest fashions, or restaurants, or clubs, but mostly about other people, people in her world of 'smart' society: did Diana know about X and Y? What a scandal that was! Or had Diana seen such and such? No? Oh well, you simply *must* darling, she's to die for. Joss loathed her, and spent most of the lunch reinforcing this opinion. He began creating little fantasies, imagining her suddenly sprouting wings and flapping round and round the room with increasing hysteria. He would have almost felt sorry for John Redman, had he not treated Joss with the same polite indifference as his wife.

Joss had been seated next to the children, Timothy and Peter, aged ten and twelve. Having lunch with the grown-ups was a special Christmas treat for the children, and they were both as overexcited as their mother. The only other guests were Sir Anthony and Lady Cunningham. A Member of Parliament, he was in London, rather than their house in Yorkshire, because he'd recently become a junior minister and needed to spend time near the Commons. Margaret Redman fawned over them, desperate to impress, laughing raucously whenever he made a wry aside and agreeing with any shared observation. The

Cunninghams, though, were the only two there who showed some small interest in Joss, although as soon as lunch properly got underway, conversations around the table became less general and more isolated; Joss listened to Peter and Timothy talking to him about motor cars, of which he knew very little, and then football, about which he was slightly more knowledgeable. Diana was immersed in conversation with Sir Anthony. For two people who professed to not knowing each other, they looked comfortably familiar with each other. *Poor Lady Cunningham*, thought Joss, wishing he was sitting next to her instead.

* * *

Salvation was at hand, however. He might not have gone to Alvesdon, but perhaps Guy could come up to London? And so he had written, beseeching his friend to come and relieve him from his current state of purgatory.

A letter from Guy arrived three days after Christmas.

Alvesdon Farm, Christmas Eve, 1938

Joss,

All right, then, I'll drag myself up to that stinking cesspit that is our capital. I think I can recognize a distress signal when I see one. But won't Diana mind? Or don't we care about that? I'll come up on New Year's Eve, but expect lavish entertainments to be laid on, especially for seeing in the New Year. Stella's coming up too, to stay with Charlotte—and no doubt to drape herself over Philip—so I will travel with her. I hope I can

119

trust you to survive until then.
Guy.

Well, that was something, he thought to himself, although he felt a pang of irritation at the thought of Stella with Philip. At least Guy disliked Philip too, although he seemed to take against any man who showed an interest in Stella. Sitting on the sofa, alone in the still, scented atmosphere of the flat, he thought about that. *Of course:* Guy was every bit as jealous as he was. Not in the same way, obviously; more because Guy liked to think of himself as the most important man in Stella's life. Philip made him feel threatened. Well, at least they wouldn't have to see it first-hand. As ever, Stella would disappear into a different world—a world more familiar to his mother than either he or Guy.

The same day a telegram arrived. It was from Tommy, saying he was coming down south early and could he please camp down at Joss's flat?

'*Yes*,' Joss replied immediately, '*come right away.*'

Diana was not impressed.

'I do think you might have asked me first,' said Diana later that afternoon. 'I'm not running a boarding house, you know.'

'You'd never notice even if you were—you're never here.'

'It's still my flat, Joss, and I don't want it overrun.'

'For God's sake, it's only for a few days. Anyway, I thought I lived here too. Or am I also just a boarder?'

Diana sighed. 'Joss, *please*. No of course you're not. You're welcome here anytime you like, and it's lovely having you. I just thought you might have asked me first before inviting half the world, that's all.'

'It's only Guy and Tommy.'

'And where are they going to sleep? One could have the spare room, but what about the other?'

'In my room—on the floor. Does it matter?'

'No,' Diana sighed, 'I suppose not. Especially if they stop you moping about the place feeling sorry for yourself.'

*   *   *

Late the following morning, Diana stood in front of the long mirror in the hallway, putting on her lipstick, flicking something from the corner of her eye and then lowering a hat carefully onto her head.

Leaning against the door leading into the drawing room, Joss watched her. 'Where are you off to?'

'Hm? Oh, lunch.'

'Who with?'

'No one you'd know.' She turned and smiled, then took the few steps towards him and kissed him on the cheek. 'Be good darling, and have fun with that friend of yours.'

'Tommy.'

'Yes—Tommy. When's he getting here?'

'Later today.' Or at least, Joss hoped so. He hadn't had a response to his reply. He wondered whether Tommy had changed his mind.

Diana left, the front door slamming behind her. Joss walked over to the mirror and wiped the lipstick from his cheek.

Half an hour later he was stretched out on the long sofa, his shoes kicked off, reading *The Woodlanders* and wishing he lived in a cottage in some Wessex wood, when there was a loud knock on the door. It startled him; he'd been close to sleep. Laying the book face down, he stood up and wandered into the hallway, just as the knocking started again. 'Just coming,' shouted Joss.

Standing on the step was Tommy, the collar of his coat turned up, his hat low over his brow. By his side stood a small brown leather suitcase.

'Tommy! You're here!'

'Sure am.'

Joss ushered him in. 'I would have met you off the train you know.'

'Thought I'd save you the bother.' He took off his coat and hat then walked into the drawing room and dropped himself on the sofa. 'Boy, am I glad to be here. Joss, remind me never to stay with my aunt and uncle again.'

'That bad?'

Tommy ran his hands through his hair. 'That bad.'

'Well, it can't have been worse than being here.'

'Joss, all I'm going to say is this: I don't think I felt any hot water the whole time I was there. My uncle banged on endlessly about 'that Hitler chap having a point' and how Britain was going to the dogs; he hates the Frogs and the Eyeties. The Yanks are even worse, and frankly, he doesn't know how his brother-in-law does it, having to live and deal with these ghastly people on a day-to-day basis. On top of that, there was nothing but mud for miles, the house was freezing, and my cousins, whilst sweet, were far too earnest and cowed by the overbearing presence of my uncle to be of any sustainable interest.' He leant back and stretched. 'Ah! The relief of being back in civilization!'

Joss laughed. 'What about Egyptians? Did he disapprove of them too?'

'Did I leave them out? My God, they were the worst! "Filthy little Arabs" he called them, the ignorant bastard. It was gruesome. I can't work out if he really, genuinely disapproves of what my father does, or whether he's simply jealous.'

'At least he's not a blood relative.'

'Well, yes, there is that to be thankful for. I don't think I could cope with the shame of being related to that dinosaur. Why my aunt married him, I have no idea.' He looked rueful. 'I don't know Joss, what a miserable pair we are. And to think Christmas is supposed to be fun.'

'There's always next year.'

'Very true. Maybe we should go abroad—make a pledge now, that Christmas 1939 will be spent with friends only. I know someone who could lend us the perfect place in Brittany, although, to be honest, anywhere without relatives would be fine with me.' He shifted to the edge of the sofa and picked up a photograph of Diana from a small table to the side. It was a studio shot, taken at George's insistence some years before. She was wearing a pale satin dress, a demure glance over her bare shoulders. 'Who's this? Is it your mother?'

Joss nodded.

'She's stunning. Doesn't look a bit like you, though. Look at that dark hair.'

'What are you implying?'

'Nothing—that you must take after your father, I suppose. Any pictures of him?'

'No,' he said, then was silent for a moment. 'My mother's still very good looking. Striking, I suppose.'

Tommy eyed him curiously and nodded. 'Where is she anyway?'

'Out. Lunch with some friend or other. I'm sure you'll see her later.'

'I hope so. You're so peculiar about your family.'

'I'm not—it's just there's nothing to tell. Let me show you your room,' said Joss, picking up Tommy's suitcase, 'then let's go out.'

'All right, Joss—I know better than to pry.'

'And Guy's coming tomorrow too.'

'Oh good. We're going to have fun. Nice flat, by the way,' he said standing up, and looking round the room.

'Yes. I suppose it is.'

But hardly home. Diana had bought it eighteen months before, after her separation from George. Part of a Pimlico mansion block, it had three small bedrooms, a drawing room, dining room and a kitchen, which, although modern and fitted with ample storage space and rotating cupboards, was rarely, if ever, used. She used to cook once upon a time, so she said, but Joss couldn't remember ever seeing her do so. Certainly she couldn't afford a cook, or any full-time servants for that matter; there was a housekeeper, Mrs Goodson, who came in every morning for an hour, and who could, sometimes, on occasion, be coerced into providing basic meals. It was certainly a comedown after the comfort of George's Chelsea home, with its five floors, and maid, housekeeper *and* cook. They had moved in there immediately after the marriage. Joss had been just three at the time. He had a vague memory of the reception party, held in the large downstairs drawing room with its high ceiling, long windows and ornate cornicing: he had been a page-boy, complete with cream breeches and silk ruff. The ruff had chafed his neck and he had spent the time trying to get it undone. The first time he managed to untie it, someone put it back on for him; this happened again a second time; the third, George had lost his temper and bent down, impatiently tying it again so that it hurt even more.

A wedding party full of strangers: stiff, old men and women, impossibly ancient and frightening. He distinctly remembered wandering between their legs, searching for his mother. Spying her, he clambered through the throng, only to find she had moved by the time he got there.

It had always been George's home though. As a bachelor, he had lived there on his own for many years, and even once he had a wife and stepson, there were few changes about the place. After all, Diana and Joss brought virtually no possessions with them. But when she first bought the flat she would often say, 'It may be smaller, but it's all mine.' It was painted in plain pale colours rather than the heavy wallpaper that George had favoured. The walls were left largely bare, save for a few prints and paintings; no more dark, austere landscapes. If George's house had resembled a gentleman's club, then the flat was the epitome of understated feminine *chic*. Even the smell was different: in Chelsea, the faint whiff of stale cigar smoke pervaded every nook and cranny, with the exception of the kitchen and basement, where vegetable steam and animal fat overrode everything else. There were none of these odours in the

Pimlico flat. Just the gentle aroma of lilies (which Diana always had in the drawing room) and scent.

So, as George's house had always been very much his, the flat was very much Diana's. Nevertheless, the novelty of it had long since worn off. Joss suspected his mother missed living in the comfort of George's house more than she would care to admit.

* * *

Tommy and Joss went out. It was another fine, cold winter's day, without any sign of smog, and so they decided to walk rather than take the Underground. With the collars of their coats turned up and their hats lowered, they set off. As they ambled along the winding pathways of St James's Park, Joss noticed that the grand painted terraces of the Mall and the white stone of Horse Guards seemed to accentuate the cold, standing out icily through the dark, leafless trees. Under the Admiralty arches and on to Trafalgar Square, where even on the coldest and wettest days the pigeons still milled. Then up Charing Cross Road, with its theatres and endless bookshops. A chance to talk—that was something one could always do with Tommy. Joss told him about Christmas and the Redmans. Margaret Redman's accent and her excitability were lavishly exaggerated in his retelling, so that she became even more of a caricature.

Tommy laughed. 'I hate people like that, though. Snobs and social climbers. As bad as my uncle in their way. Why does your mother want to be friends with her?'

'God knows.'

'So what have you been doing in between?'

'Not a great deal. Walks, reading. I've been to the British Museum once already. The thing is Tommy, I'm fairly short, as usual. If I'm going to spend money I'd rather do it when friends are around. And London's so expensive. I always nearly choke when I realize how much cheaper a pint of beer is in Marleycombe.'

Near the Seven Dials, Tommy showed Joss a 'great little tea-shop' he knew. It was run by Italians, and the coffee, he assured Joss, was the best anyone could get in London.

'Buongiorno, Tommy,' said one of the waiters as they entered. He was a squat, middle-aged man, with greying dark hair and a black bow-tie, and carrying a tray of dirty plates and cups.

'*Ciao, Fredo. Come sta? Cosa stai combinando?*' said Tommy. For a minute or two they talked in Italian.

'I've ordered us some coffee and meatballs,' said Tommy, turning to Joss. 'A jolly little place, this.' He lit a cigarette. 'I'm so happy to be back in London.'

It was good to have Tommy here, thought Joss. He never allowed life to become too serious; he envied his friend that.

From the café, they went to the British Museum. Looking at the Anglo-Saxon displays was, Joss reflected, much more fun with Tommy than it had been on his own. Tomorrow Guy would join them too. He felt lighter, as though a heavy fog had lifted.

*　　　*　　　*

'I can't believe you're expecting me to sleep on the floor.' Guy was standing in the bedroom, his suitcase at his feet. 'After all the times you've been to stay with us, had your own room—not to say *large* room—all to yourself, you drag me all the way up here, and this is the treatment I get.' He turned to Tommy. 'Honestly, you should have seen his letter: "*Please Guy, come and stay, I'm so bored Guy, save me from this torture, Guy.*" So of course, realizing my good friend was in need of help, and being the kind-hearted generous person I am, I rushed up without pause for thought.'

'Guy, I absolutely insist you have my bed,' said Joss.

'No, no, I wouldn't want to deprive you of your comforts, Joss. The hard floor will be perfectly adequate for me.'

'Well, I've got plans,' said Tommy, 'and they don't involve going to bed either early or sober, so this argument is academic.'

'Sounds worrying,' said Guy.

'No, no, this will be fun. Trust me. After all, it is New Year's Eve.'

'Well, I'm hungry,' said Guy, 'so please tell me the first part of the plan involves dinner.'

Tommy put an arm around Guy's shoulder. 'It does, Guy. Doesn't pay to drink on an empty stomach, after all.'

*   *   *

They took the Underground to Piccadilly Circus. Tommy steered them towards the Lyons on Coventry Street. The place was heaving, the windows all heavy with steam and condensation.

They were briskly ushered to a table on the first floor.

'Seems everyone's got the same idea as us,' said Joss, glancing around the room. On the next table, a young man with glasses wearing evening clothes was talking loudly, his hands waving to illustrate every point. His companion smiled or nodded occasionally, but Joss saw she was bored, and disinterestedly twiddling the foot of her fur that was still draped around her shoulder. Then another man came to join them and her face lit up, leaving the other hanging mid-sentence.

'Oh dear,' muttered Tommy, having seen the same thing, 'I think he'd be better to push off and leave them to it.' He looked at Guy and Joss. 'Happy?'

'Perfectly,' said Guy, 'after all, it is just fuel we're after, isn't it?'

They ate their meal then headed back to Piccadilly. They were going to go to a party, Tommy had explained to them earlier, of an old school friend of his called Ronald Wilkes. He hadn't seen him since leaving school, but he thought it had potential as Ronald had always been good fun. 'And anyway, I'm intrigued to see what his place is like. Albany's a pretty exclusive block of flats, you know.'

Cars, buses and carriages filled the streets, bringing with them the constant hum of traffic, while even on a clear night like tonight, the air smelled heavy with soot and burning fuel. On the pavements, men and women hurried by. Around Eros, people milled, hawkers shouted. Joss caught a fleeting whiff of chestnuts and sweet pipe smoke. Light bathed everyone and everything with an unreal glow: from the streetlights, from the London Pavilion, from the huge façade of advertising, glaring reds and whites and yellows. A man wearing evening clothes but no overcoat hurried past, his shirt-front glowing a luminous blue from the garish lights. Up above, the night was perfectly clear, but the stars had all but vanished.

They turned up a short roadway, beneath high ornate grey buildings, the light suddenly darkening, then past the porter standing at the foot of the steps, and into the building. The hubbub from the party had spilled out onto the landing two floors up.

'Well, we're in the right place,' said Tommy.

'Just like Cambridge, this place,' said Guy, as they headed up the narrow staircase. 'Look, they even have the same kind of nameplates outside the doors.'

'Cambridge transported to London,' agreed Tommy, 'but no Proctors.'

A small group of people were smoking and drinking on the landing. One man slouched against the doorway. He looked them up and down then, with a grimace, straightened himself so they could pass. On into the hallway, already crammed with people. The three of them paused a moment, until Tommy waved to a thick-set man with wavy hair and flushed cheeks at the end of the corridor.

'That's Ronald,' said Tommy. 'He's put on weight.'

Ronald side-stepped his way towards them, one arm raised so as not to knock his drink, cigarette between his teeth.

'Tommy—very jolly to see you,' he said. 'Hello there,' he said to Joss and Guy. 'Come on in—let's

130

get you a drink. I'm afraid everyone's been very punctual tonight for some reason.'

'So I see. The place is bursting, Ronald. Were you always this popular?'

'I don't think so—although to be honest, I haven't a clue who most of them are.'

Joss and Guy followed them towards the kitchen, Tommy occasionally holding up their progress by pausing to shake hands or kiss a cheek. He dutifully introduced people to Guy and Joss: this was Christina whom he hadn't seen since they'd been in Le Touquet together the summer before last; or Peter, whom he'd met at a weekend bash of somebody or other. Smiling faces, a shake of a clammy hand, and Joss would nod and smile in turn. *How d'you do? Oh really? Well, good to meet you.* How did Tommy do it, Joss wondered.

Ronald found three glasses then filled each with vermouth, pouring in one continuous flow so that the liquid spilled onto the counter. 'Should get you started,' he said, then someone bumped into him, and he turned, his attention drawn away.

'All right?' asked Tommy. He sipped his drink and looked around. 'A few familiar faces here.' Then he spotted someone else he knew, and his face relaxed into a broad grin. 'A-ha. And a particularly lovely one too. Excuse me a moment.' Joss and Guy followed his eye. In the corner stood a girl with very blonde hair, long slender neck and wide eyes.

'Who's *that*?' asked Guy.

'Don't know—but she's very beautiful.'

'Typical bloody Tommy.'

They weaved through the throng and clouds of cigarette smoke into the next room. Joss began talking to a short thin-haired man. He had also been at school with Tommy. 'Always seemed to go off somewhere exciting in the holidays,' he said. 'We'd all go back to our people, but Tommy would turn up the next term with tales of Countesses in Austria or lucky escapes from an Alpine mountainside.' Joss laughed.

'Known him long?' asked the man.

'Not really—we're at Cambridge together.'

'Hm. Decided to give that one a miss, myself. Couldn't really see the point.'

'It's fun,' said Joss.

'But delays a career by three or four years.'

'Good. The longer the better.'

'I'll remind you of that in four years' time,' said the man. Then he looked down past Joss and said, 'The music's stopped.'

'I wasn't even aware it was on.'

'No, well, it is a bit noisy in here.' He stretched past to the squat black gramophone and began to wind it up.

'Make sure you play something good,' said a familiar voice behind Joss. He swung round, startled. 'Stella,' he said, feeling his heart quicken. 'What are you doing here?'

'You sound as though I've just caught you red-handed at something,' she said. Her hair was down, but immaculately curled on her shoulders. She looked even more beautiful than he remembered.

'No, no, I just wasn't expecting to see you here. Guy never mentioned it.'

'Well, nor did Guy to me.'

'Actually, I suppose he didn't really know. Neither of us did until today. Ronald's Tommy's friend. It was Tommy's idea to come.'

'There you are then. Who's Ronald?'

'The person who's holding the party.'

'Oh.' She shrugged.

He quickly looked down at his glass. It was empty. No wonder he was beginning to feel a bit light-headed.

'Can I get you a drink?'

'Come on let's both go and get one.'

Joss followed, inching his way back out of the room and down the corridor. He couldn't see Tommy or Guy.

'I've come with Philip and Charlotte,' said Stella, reading his thoughts. 'But she's latched onto some man and he's gone and deserted me, the rat. Talking to some bore about Hitler. I think if I hear one more thing about that man I'm going to go mad. As you can imagine, it was a great relief to spot you.'

'Have you seen Guy then?'

'Only in the distance.' She found another bottle of Martini and filled their glasses, then put a cigarette between her lips.

Joss picked up a matchbox and struck one but it went out. 'Sorry,' he said, 'try again.' This time it remained lit.

'Honestly, Joss, I can't believe you don't smoke. How can you be so strong willed?'

Joss felt himself redden, but when he looked at her again, she was smiling.

'I'm teasing you.'

'I tried once. Didn't like it though.'

'Hm,' said Stella, looking round. 'So who is this Ronald? Funny place he lives in.'

'We think it's a bit like the rooms at Cambridge.'

Stella thought for a moment. 'Yes, you're right. I

133

knew there was something familiar about it.' She glanced around the room, then turned back to Joss. 'I enjoyed my trip to Cambridge. I'm very envious of you all.'

'Come up again next term,' said Joss.

'I might well do, although I do think next time you might be a bit more sociable. I'd like to see you too, you know.' She eyed him keenly, and Joss smiled awkwardly, then said, 'I got the impression Guy wanted you all to himself.'

'Hm—it's funny. I suppose he can be a bit possessive. But when I'm next up—' She never finished what she was going to say. Philip Mornay had sidled up behind her, and, seeing Joss, conspiratorially put a finger to his lip—*Don't give the game away*—then folded his arms around her waist, and she started, then turning, relaxed. 'Oh, it's you. You gave me a fright.'

'Sorry darling—got a bit stuck with that chap.'

'So I saw, but don't pretend you weren't happy talking about the Nazis.' She looked at Joss. 'War, war, Hitler, war. It's his favourite conversation.'

Philip chuckled. 'Don't be sulky. It's serious stuff. Joss will back me up on this one.'

Joss kept quiet.

'Perhaps not the right subject for parties though,' added Philip. He smiled and kissed Stella on the back of her head. He'd grown a thin moustache since Joss had last seen him. He was wearing evening clothes; his starched shirt-front and white waistcoat appeared unnaturally bright in the dim light.

'Philip,' said Stella, 'I'm ready for some supper. Can we go on now, do you think?'

'Of course we can, darling; after all, this isn't my

134

crowd. Where shall we go?'

'Oh, I don't know. You choose. Might be fun to have a dance though, especially to see in the New Year. No chance of it here—I can barely hear myself think let alone the poor gramophone.'

Philip patted his pockets then said, 'Well, good to see you again Joss.'

'You too.'

'Bye, bye Joss, and Happy New Year,' said Stella, and this time she kissed him in such a way that he felt her lips lightly brush his cheek. 'Now, I must quickly find that brother of mine.'

*   *   *

It was a while later, when the party had begun to thin, that Tommy suggested they move on.

'I'm already feeling a bit drunk,' said Joss, 'I'm not sure I'm going to be able to stay awake much longer.'

'Oh, come on Joss! Don't be a killjoy. You've got to see in the New Year, and anyway, I've got to show you this little club before we call it a day. Guy's on for it, aren't you Guy?'

'Definitely,' said Guy. 'Raring to go.' He began dancing up and down the hallway. So Guy was drunk too. It was harder to tell with Tommy.

Outside, Joss tripped on the edge of some paving and fell forward, the hard ground stinging his hands.

'Oh dear, Joss,' said Tommy, helping him back on his feet. 'Look, tell you what, fall asleep in the club if you want, but try and stay awake until then, all right?'

They wandered on, Joss uncertain of where they

were going, although the glare and vibrancy of Shaftesbury Avenue soon gave way to much darker, narrower streets. Other passers-by flitted, indistinct, into the shadows.

Music floated out from somewhere along the street, faint at first, and then louder as they turned and went through a doorway and down some steps. A man in black tie stood by a counter and after a brief discussion with Tommy waved them through. Although they had come from the Albany party, the air in the street had, for once, been clear and fresh, so that Joss took several moments to adjust to the new haze of cigarette smoke. At the far end, on a slightly raised rostrum, a small band was playing. The man at the piano wore a white dinner jacket, and sang dreamily as his fingers fluttered over the keys. A few people were dancing on the linoleum dance floor by the stage, lazily twirling round and round.

A waitress led them to one of the tables by the wall. Joss sat down, taking it all in. The band was pounding out old—and some new—numbers: a small five-piece, just about right for the size of the place. Old gas lamps in frosted glass flickered from the windowless walls, giving the place a tight, dim atmosphere. Faded photographs of George V and Queen Mary hung on the wall. Joss wondered when the new king and queen might make the grade. The place was busy without heaving. Opposite them, a party of young men in evening dress were making a scene with one of the waitresses, until a couple of girls arrived and sat down with them instead.

Tommy ordered champagne, and it arrived shortly after, in an ice bucket with no ice.

136

'The champagne's always warm,' said Tommy, 'and in any other circumstances completely undrinkable, but somehow I rather like it like that here. A bit like communion wine—I always think that's delicious when I'm kneeling there in church, but if I had a glass of the stuff at dinner it would probably be revolting.'

He raised his glass, drank, then sighed deeply. A moment later, he stood up and said, 'Won't be a moment,' then disappeared to the far side of the room.

'Where's he gone?' said Guy.

Joss shrugged.

'What a night!' said Guy. 'Rather insalubrious, isn't it? I suppose that's all part of it. Or maybe it only seems so because we're drunk.'

'Probably,' said Joss. 'But how does Tommy know about these places? I've lived in London most of my life, but I wouldn't know how to find this again.'

It was true: this new world of restaurants and bars and parties and nightclubs was unfamiliar, part of an adult existence upon which the curtains were only slowly being drawn back. Guy sipped his champagne, anxiously looking around the room as he did so. *We're fish out of water,* thought Joss.

Tommy returned with three girls. 'Gentlemen, some introductions. Joan, Emily and Dorothy. They're after some dancing.' The three girls smiled coyly, and together, a little too abruptly, Guy and Joss pushed back their chairs and stood up. There was a moment of awkwardness as each wondered who should dance with who, but then Tommy led Dorothy away and the others followed, Guy and Joss trailing behind. On the dance floor, Joan turned to Joss and took his hand. The pianist

137

struck up again, waggling his head from side to side as he began the jaunty intro. With a nod, the others came in too. *When Somebody Thinks You're Wonderful,* he sang.

'I like this song,' said Joan, 'don't you?'

'Very much,' said Joss. He hoped he was being gentle with her, but all this swinging around was making him giddy. He tried to focus on her face instead. Not bad-looking, really: a high forehead, with dark hair parted in the centre and then curled neatly behind her ears; large, almost child-like eyes with long lashes and a small, neat mouth; lips painted dark, dark red. Seemed good on her feet too. But he wished he could have been dancing with Stella instead.

'Don't look so serious,' she said suddenly. 'What's to be serious about?'

'Sorry,' said Joss, 'nothing, I wasn't meaning to.'

She laughed. 'You're funny.'

Was he? Joss couldn't quite see why, but he smiled back.

'Do you like dancing, then?' he asked her.

'Oh, yes.'

'Well, you're very good at it.'

'Why, thank you.' The song came to an end. 'Another one?'

He bowed to her. 'I'd be honoured,' and took her hand once more. It had suddenly dawned on him that it was actually quite straightforward playing the gentleman, and that there was no reason to be shy or bashful in any way. He smiled at her again, this time from the side of his mouth. It was something he'd noticed Philip Mornay did rather well. He glanced round at the other dancers. On the far side of the floor, Guy span round, laughing.

The band stopped then began playing *Auld Lang Syne.* It caught everyone off-guard—*midnight already?*—but after checking watches, the singing began.

'Happy New Year,' said Joan, leaning up and giving him a kiss.

They carried on dancing, but then he began to feel hot, and with it, his giddiness increased. He was struggling to focus. His face was flushing, he was sure, and he needed to sit down, just pause for a moment. Try and stop his head spinning. After a great flourish, the song came to an end. A light ripple of applause.

'Would you like to sit down, now?' asked Joan, peering closely at him.

'Yes please,' said Joss. His attempt at debonair panache had evaporated.

'Come on then. You are sweet, you know.' She took his hand and led him from the dance floor, not to their table, but up some steps to the side and then through a curtain and into a dark hallway.

'Come on, you,' she said tugging at his arm as Joss paused at the foot of a set of wooden stairs. Silently, he followed her, wondering vaguely where they were going, but lacking the will to find out.

She paused on a landing and opened a door into a small room with a bed and couch. A single dim light hung from the centre of the ceiling. The bed was piled with a number of maroon velvet cushions.

'Everything in this place is so dark,' mumbled Joss. He was squinting, trying to absorb his surroundings. He could barely see into the corners of the room. It was as though there were no walls, just darkness.

'That's because it's a club, silly,' said Joan. 'Come

here, you.' Pushing him onto the bed, she sat beside and began to run her hands through his hair.

'That's really nice,' said Joss, 'thank you.'

She continued, silently, her fingers stretching over his scalp, then began loosening his tie. Joss began to drift; he was too tired—too drunk—to resist.

Then suddenly, he was awake again.

Panic. Her hand was on his crotch, unbuttoning his fly. He briefly craned his neck down to see, then lay back, amongst the cushions, paralysed, his mind in turmoil. Joan began singing softly, and then her hands delved into his underwear and grabbed him. He looked again, appalled by what he saw.

'Relax,' she said and smiled at him. Joss let his head drop again. His entire body tingled. He thought of Stella once more; he felt as though he were betraying her.

'That will do for the moment,' she said, leaving him exposed and vulnerable. 'Let's get out of these clothes.' She turned, motioning him to undo the buttons that ran down the back of her dress.

'Oh, sorry,' he said, 'of course.' His hands were clumsy, shaking slightly. Despite her mastery of the situation, she still seemed delicate, even vulnerable. As the buttons came undone, one by one, the dress slowly folded away to reveal soft white skin. He ran his hand down the tiny humps of vertebrae. She raised her hands, carefully pushed the dress off her shoulders, and turned to face him once more. She wore silk underwear, although it was old and worn. The tiny hairs on her arm rose as her body became covered in goosebumps. While she tugged at his tie and started undoing the studs on his shirt, he continued to half sit, half lie on the bed, incapable of doing anything. *Perhaps I'm bewitched,* was all he could think. Her hands spread across his chest.

'Now you help me,' she said, and lifted up her arms. He reached for the bottom of her camisole and lifted it gingerly. 'That's it,' she said. He watched her, barely daring to breathe, as she removed her knickers. Her body was so young, soft and curvaceous. He'd often fantasized about being in this situation, but now the moment had arrived he was at a loss as to know what to do. Staring in wonder, he felt her take a hand and place it over one of her breasts. Like her hands, it was cool; and softer, more giving than he'd imagined.

Squatting before him, she helped him remove the last of his clothes, tossing them onto a heap on the floor. Naked and defenceless, Joss watched with a mixture of horror and mounting excitement as Joan began fumbling with something. 'Don't worry,' she said, 'it's only a French letter.' Joss closed his eyes for a moment. Hardly very romantic, but then— well. 'Best to be safe,' she said, by way of explanation. Joss nodded. His mind was buzzing too much to offer a response. But Joan had experienced hands and in a moment had straddled her thighs either side of him. To his amazement she grabbed him again, and guided him inside her. So this was what it was all about: he was lying back on this strange bed actually doing *it,* and despite the seedy circumstances, despite barely knowing Joan, it was better than he'd ever imagined. He wondered if it would be like this with Stella. Guiltily, he ran his hands over Joan's skin; it was warmer now, and as he kissed her arms and shoulders and breasts, he breathed in deeply her faint smell of lavender and

141

sweat, and thought he would never forget it. Then she was rocking back and forth more quickly, her hair falling over her face, arms stretched out and clasping at his chest.

*   *   *

The light was still on when he awoke. Joan had gone. Conspicuous in his nakedness, he grabbed his clothes and began to dress quickly. The noise of his legs sliding down his trousers and the snap of his braces were the only sounds to jar the oppressive, sudden silence. He had an overpowering desire to leave the room as quickly as possible. Looking at his watch, he was relieved—and surprised—to discover he'd not been away that long. Even so, he wanted to find Tommy and Guy again as soon as possible, then get away from there.

Just as he was leaving, he noticed his wallet on the couch. He knew what he'd discover. Picking it up, he opened it out. The money had gone.

'There you are,' said Tommy. He was still at the table with Dorothy. Guy was there too.

'What happened to you?' asked Guy.

'I think we can all guess,' said Tommy, 'but Joss, please spare us the details.'

Joss rubbed his head. Dorothy was smiling—or laughing at him; he couldn't tell. He glanced around, suspecting everyone in the room knew him for what he was.

'Joan had to go home,' said Dorothy, 'but she said to thank you very much.'

Joss nodded then looked at Tommy. *Please, let's go, now.* A stabbing headache began.

Guy said, 'Well now you've reappeared, shall we

142

get going?' *So, Guy to the rescue—as always.* Tommy nodded and pushed back his chair.

Back out onto the street, they were met with a sharp blast of cold air after the warm fug of the club.

'What a night, Tommy, what a night,' said Guy.

'It was good fun.'

'And Joss—what happened to you?'

'Yes, come on, Joss, spill the beans.'

Joss walked on silently.

'She took your money,' said Tommy. 'Well, nothing to worry about, it happened to me too, the first time.'

'Joss—did you, you know, *do it* then?'

'Joss is too embarrassed,' said Tommy, 'and now he can't talk. Well, there's nothing to be ashamed about. Relax! So you lost a quid or two, but it was worth it wasn't it?' He nudged Joss. 'Pretty damn good wasn't it?'

Joss began to smile. He couldn't help himself.

'There!' said Tommy, 'What did I tell you? Joss got his end away with Joan!'

'You lucky sod!' said Guy, 'all I got was Emily sitting on my lap for half an hour. And she was quite heavy after a while.'

Joss turned to them, grinning. 'My lips are sealed. What happened is between me and Joan.'

Tommy laughed. 'Quite right, Joss, quite right.'

*   *   *

Despite the late hour at which they arrived back at the flat, Joss was awake early the following morning. The floor was hard and he couldn't get comfortable. And he couldn't stop thinking about the previous night.

'Joss,' Guy whispered. 'Are you awake?'

'Yes.'

Guy shifted and leant over the edge of the bed.

'What was it like? Last night with that girl?'

'Very embarrassing to begin with, but then rather amazing.'

'I think Emily wanted me to do it too, but I wouldn't follow her.'

'Why not?'

'I'm not sure. I didn't think she was very pretty. Maybe I should have been more drunk.'

'Well, I must admit, I do wish it hadn't been so— well, *seedy*. Tommy was right—she *did* take my money.'

'At least you've done it, though.'

They were quiet for a moment, then Guy said, 'Do you remember last Christmas? At Alvesdon? Still at school, Cambridge not even on the horizon. I don't remember any mention of war then. God, the sheltered life we led. Everything's changed so fast.'

'But we're having fun aren't we? You're enjoying Cambridge?'

'Yes, of course. I just—oh, I don't know. Roger wasn't able to make it back this year. The first time ever we haven't had the whole family together at Christmas. It seemed empty there without him. I know he's older now and in the army and all that, but everything *is* different now.'

Yes, thought Joss, *he's right*. But for the most part, he was glad for it. Perhaps, if he'd been Guy, brought up at that wonderful place, surrounded by the other Liddells, he'd feel differently. But he hadn't. Cambridge, Tommy, even Joan: with their help, his childhood was rapidly receding.

'Joss?'

'Yes?'

'Happy New Year.'

Cairo—September, 1942

He was flying a Spitfire again, and coming into cloud. The land below was faint, hazy, then there was a moment of pure clarity, before losing the glare of sunlight once more. Now the cloud was so thick he could see nothing. Just a whiteness, and although he could see the propeller whirring in front of him, could feel the constant vibration of the airframe, and hear the numbing background throb of the engine, it seemed impossible to think he was flying at over 300 miles an hour. He might not have been moving at all. He could see nothing, and nothing could see him, and he was calm content.

Sudden screams through his headset, cries piercing into his brain. *'Help me, help me! Oh, God no! Mother, please God! Mother! Help me!* The cloud had disappeared and there in front of him was a burning plane, so close he could see the terror of the pilot's eyes—wide, almost bulging out of their sockets. Hands on fire—were they his hands? The flames were right under his nose. Then the plane fell from view, a great plume of black smoke following behind and he was alone again, flying over English fields, silence, save the thrum of the engine. Not *his* flames then. He put his hand on his heart—*thank God, calm once*

145

more, but then when he looked ahead again, there was blood streaming over the canopy, and his Spitfire was beginning to dive. He pulled on the stick, but nothing happened; pushed the rudder one way then the other, but his controls were useless. The arms on the altimeter were spinning backwards, and he was powerless to do anything but watch the ground rush towards him. At less than a hundred feet, he put his hands up to shield his eyes. So this was it, his final moment, and he was engulfed by sheer, uncontrollable, terror.

Joss opened his eyes. His hair was sodden. Sweat ran down the side of his face; he had another crushing headache. These dreams—they were getting to him. Always the blood on the Perspex followed by the dive, the crash that never quite happened. But the screaming pilot—this was a new development. Christ, he'd heard enough men cry their last; felt their pain, terror, and panic drilled into his headset.

What did it mean? The screaming pilot: that was the easy bit. Obvious: his guilt, his very own Jacob Marley. But why was the out-of-control dive so terrifying? What was he scared of? Was it the pain? Because if he crashed like that he'd never feel a thing. Or was it the fear of dying? Only a few weeks before he'd have welcomed it. Sometimes he believed he still would. It made no sense.

In the desert, he used to long for sleep. The one time when he was unconscious and able to forget what was happening to him. But now—well, now, he dreaded it. Lying in his bed in this accursed place, he would try and keep himself awake as long as he could. Try and think of other things.

That night with Joan. She must have seen his

146

type many times before. Perhaps that was her speciality: bedding young virgins. Joss thought of the guilt he'd felt at betraying Stella. He'd never betrayed her again. He'd stayed true. Perhaps if he ever got out of here, he would find another Joan in Cairo. Perhaps that was what he needed: to go and fuck some girl.

He didn't mean it, though; and nor would he. Not yet. He couldn't writhe around with someone else knowing he would be thinking only of her.

But back then it had been different. Yes, he'd felt guilty all right, and ashamed, especially when he'd realized his money was gone. But there had been relief too: relief that one of the world's great adult mysteries had been revealed. What a prude he'd been. *You did it with a tart!* Guy had said, and Tommy had said, no, not really a *tart*, it was just that Joan could be a little light-fingered.

'And what about you, Tommy?' Guy had asked, *'Are they still light-fingered with you?'* And Tommy had laughed and said, no, they did it with him for free.

Joss smiled, remembering. Remembering the Zippo lighter and the Americanisms that crept into the way Tommy talked.

A nurse with a trolley pushed through the doors. Suppertime for those who could eat it. There was more variety to the food than they'd ever had in the desert, but even so, bully beef was bully beef, however you cooked it up. Where would the Allies be without it, he wondered.

'Here you are, Joss,' said the nurse, handing him a bowl of corned beef hash.

He picked at it with a fork. The quality had been better since the army had been halted at Alamein.

147

Improved stocks were coming in. In the desert they had become bully beef experts. The best came from the Argentine; Canadian or British tended to be less good: not so much meat and more fat and other *stuff.* Anything with Arabic on the tin was bottom of the heap. Beef—fat chance! Goat or dog, more like. They were able to tell the success of the desert war by the kind of bully beef they were given: quality meant victory—or stability—in the field. Arabic on the tin suggested the line was over-extended or things were going badly wrong.

He put a forkful in his mouth. This seemed to be all right, although of course, he hadn't seen the tin. Tasted not too bad, either. A bit salty, but definitely a meaty texture to it. Hardly a cause for celebration, however.

Cambridge—February, 1939

Winter passed. Joss had gone back to Cambridge early, relieved to be away from his mother and from the increasingly oppressive atmosphere in her flat. It had been cold and lonely, those first couple of weeks in January, but then his friends had returned, bringing with them the camaraderie and jollity of the previous term. His mood had soon lightened.

Although none of them actually said as much, there was an understanding that their rowing career may have peaked with the Novice Cup; with no major cup to aim for, and without that necessary incentive, their enthusiasm had wavered. Nor was Roland as committed. He was busy with the university squad training for the Boat Race. They

148

still spent time on the river, but five times a week was reduced once more to three; three became two; and six-thirty in the morning became eight o'clock.

But if this diminished enthusiasm had created something of a void, it was soon filled. At the end of the first week of February, Joss found a note in his pigeon-hole asking him to attend an interview with Squadron Leader G.B.G. Fraser at Marshall's airfield. There was no explanation for this sudden request, just a date and time. But after his initial elation he began to fear what Tommy and Guy might say if they had not been granted interviews too, especially as their pigeon-holes appeared to be empty; he spent the rest of the afternoon in a state of nervous excitement, desperate to share the news, but not daring to.

His concern was unfounded. At dinner Guy and Tommy could talk of little else.

'We've got to get through the interview, though,' said Joss. 'We're not there quite yet.'

'Oh, rubbish, we're in all right,' said Tommy. 'It's just about giving the right impression. All we've got to do is look smart, and sound as though we'd do anything to fly and we'll sail through.'

Two days later, having had his hair cut especially, Joss cycled over to Marshall's for his meeting with Squadron Leader Fraser. He was the first of the three to be interviewed. Arriving with more than enough time to spare, he hovered uncertainly by the two University Air Squadron huts. The airfield was quiet. He supposed most of the planes were in the large hangar, although beyond that he saw a Tiger Moth and a Miles Master parked up on the grass, and a flutter of renewed excitement swept

149

over him. Gingerly he knocked on the door of the first hut and entered. A man in oily overalls sat on an old armchair reading a paper.

'Yes?' he said, not looking up.

'I'm here to see Squadron Leader Fraser,' said Joss. 'I'm a bit early.'

'Have a seat. I'm sure he'll be here soon.'

Out of some sense of misplaced decorum, Joss perched himself on a fold-away wooden chair rather than one of the other armchairs. The hut smelled of dust and dry wood. Large cobwebs stretched from the narrow rafters. Then from outside came a sudden roar and the windows shook. Joss craned his neck and watched a plane glide into land, the wings wavering slightly in the final approaches.

'Better get going,' said the man in the overalls, standing up and dropping his paper back on the chair. Joss nodded.

Quarter of an hour later the silence was broken as the door burst open and in walked a tall man with a grey moustache and a narrow, pointed nose. He looked at Joss and said, 'Come on in.' Joss followed him into an adjacent office, straightening his tie and smoothing down his hair as he did so.

'I'm Squadron Leader Fraser,' said the man, closing the door behind Joss and then retreating behind his desk. He looked at a piece of paper, squinted, then said, 'You are Lambert, I take it? Mr J?'

'Yes, sir. How do you do, sir?'

'Very well, thank you, Mr Lambert.' He pointed to a rickety chair in front of the desk, and Joss sat, back straight, his hands clutching his knees. Fraser was, Joss guessed, in his mid-forties, although it was hard to tell. His hair and moustache were almost entirely grey, but his face surprisingly unlined. He took a cigarette from a blackened silver box on the desk, and struck a match. His hand trembled by his mouth, the tiny flame flickering as he tried to connect it with the end of the cigarette. Eventually a red glow appeared and he drew deeply, then exhaled a large, lazy cloud of smoke. The cobwebs reigned in this room too—from the single light that hung from the centre of the roof, in the corners, and on the black identification charts that hung on the wall, left over from the last war.

'So you want to fly, do you?'

'Yes, sir. Very much.'

'Well, flying is not just about being in the air, you know. Plenty of classroom stuff too. You prepared to study?'

'Yes, sir.'

Fraser leant back in his seat, stretched and yawned. 'You're probably wondering why you've been called in for an interview now. What's this—the third week of term?'

'Yes, sir.'

'Well, it's simple. At this squadron we have a high turnover. Less than fifty per cent who start ever pass their proficiency certificate. Cocksure young students come here in the mistaken belief that flying is somehow a frivolous pastime. Some think they know it all before they've even started. Others decide they do quite enough studying as it is and ignore the theory. A few think it's going to be for them, then find they chuck their guts up the moment they set foot in a plane, or that they're scared of heights. I don't want any of these people

151

here, Mr Lambert, and so they're given the chop. Simple as that. And those who don't take it seriously are a danger to themselves and others. I want you to enjoy it, Mr Lambert, but I want you to work hard too. Work hard and remember the UAS does not operate as a social club. Clear?'

'Of course, sir.'

'Good.' A sudden gust of wind shook the hut and whistled against the window frame. Fraser looked out—it had begun to rain. 'Weather is a constant problem I'm afraid. Always holds things up this term, so it means we usually have to double the amount of flying in the summer. Longer days, of course, but even so. And the bloody university won't let us fly in the mornings, so it's only afternoons, I'm afraid. Look out for timetables on your college notice board, but with luck you'll get nine flights this term, starting next week.'

'Thank you, sir. Thank you very much.'

'Planes: mostly you'll be on Moths, although we've got a couple of Masters too. And a Link Trainer. Know about these?'

'No, sir.'

'Funny little box thing, like a miniature plane, for synthetic flying. You sit in the cockpit and it actually responds to your movements. Gives you an idea as to what it feels like flying a plane. Through the headset the instructor tells you what to do and lets you know when you've crashed and killed yourself. Ingenious really.' He stubbed out his cigarette. 'Roll on summer, eh?' he said, looking out of the window again. 'You play tennis? I love tennis.'

'Yes, sir. That is, I enjoy it, sir.'

'Oh well, you're definitely in then.' He smiled.

Was he joking? Joss couldn't tell. 'See you next week, then, Mr Lambert.'

*   *   *

Tommy and Guy's interview had been just as informal. The three of them were walking towards Taylors to be kitted out with their UAS uniform, as instructed.

'Did he call you mister?' asked Joss.

'Yes,' said Guy, 'Mr Liddell and then "The Mathematician". He seemed very taken with the fact I was studying mathematics. Said it would be very useful and then told me that flying was as much about theory as it was practice.'

'Said that to me too,' said Tommy. 'Then we talked about my parents.'

'Funny bloke,' said Guy.

'I thought he seemed bored,' said Joss.

'He was quite an ace in the war,' said Tommy. 'Apparently he shot down twelve planes over the Western Front. Probably a bit of a comedown having to teach a bunch of students.'

At the tailors they tried on their new dark blue blazers and grey flannels.

'I hope I don't get kicked out now,' said Joss. The uniform cost him £11.13.6d, an outlay he could ill afford.

'Think of it as an investment,' said Tommy. 'Anyway, if we're flying there won't be so much time to spend money on other things.'

*   *   *

Tuesday 12th February 1939—*at last.* The previous

153

day's rain had passed; in its place came soft, bulbous clouds and patches of clear blue. This time, more planes were lined up on the grass. One engine was already roaring as they reached the flight HQ, the propeller a faint blur, mechanics watching intently. The three of them wandered over to the first plane, a Tiger Moth. Joss held out a hand and ran it softly over the wing—smooth, taut, not like linen at all. *I am a part of this now,* he thought. And that distinct smell: oil, petrol, dope and metal; he knew he would never forget it.

There were three other new students. The six of them milled about in the flight HQ. Their apprehension was palpable.

'Fraser's an ace, you know,' said one of them to Joss.

'So I heard,' said Joss.

'Apparently shot down sixteen Huns in the last war.'

The door of Fraser's office opened and he walked in with three other men, two of whom wore flying suits and the third overalls. A cursory welcome, and an introduction to the other instructors: Sergeants Carter and McLean; Flying Officer Paterson. 'Lambert, Liddell and Stevenson?' he said, looking up. 'You three follow Sergeant McLean and get your flying kit on. The remaining three stay here for a moment.'

Joss glanced at Tommy, who winked.

'This is it!' whispered Guy as they walked across to the neighbouring hut. Overalls, flying suits and flying paraphernalia hung from rows of hooks lined along the wall of the changing room.

'Get rid of your jackets, and find yourselves a set of overalls each. Then put on this.' He held up a

154

padded suit. 'This is a Sidcot suit, and believe me, you're going to need it.' Pausing by a large wicker basket he said, 'And here are goggles, flying helmets and gauntlets. Boots if you want them. And over here,' he was now standing by a row of shelves, 'is possibly your most important piece of kit: the parachute. Just grab one each and you'll be shown how to put it on by your instructor.'

Then they were stumbling across the grass, unaccustomed to the heaviness of so much clothing. Joss put on his flying helmet. Tight and hugging, it smelled of leather.

'Lambert, you wait here,' said McLean as they reached the first Moth. A glance from Guy and a discreet pat on the shoulder. Joss felt a jingle of nerves once more.

He was peering into the rear cockpit when a voice made him start.

'All set then, Mr Lambert?'

Joss turned. 'Yes, sir.'

'Good,' said Squadron Leader Fraser. 'You've got me today, so aren't you the lucky one?' He looked intently under the wing and then said, 'All right Lambert, let's have a good look round.' Joss listened intently as Fraser explained the basic theories of flight, and what each part of the plane played.

'Get in and I'll talk you through the controls,' said Fraser. Carefully Joss lowered himself onto the seat. 'In many ways it's obvious,' said Fraser. 'Hard right on the rudder and the plane will yaw to the starboard and vice versa. Just like a go-cart.' The joystick was equally straightforward—push forward, the plane went down, pull back, the plane went up. Joss began to think flying might not be as difficult as he'd feared.

Back out of the cockpit and a lesson in how to use a parachute. 'It's easy,' said Fraser, 'count to three then pull on the ring. Bend your knees as you land.' Then back into the cockpit once more, but this time Joss was properly strapped in. 'There,' said Fraser, 'we don't want you falling out.' The straps dug into his shoulders. It was as though he'd been glued to the seat. Nimbly, Fraser hopped into the seat in front. A rigger had appeared and with both hands turned the large wooden propeller. Nothing, then another turn and with a burst of smoke the engine spluttered into life and the machine began to shake. Fraser tied the strap of his flying helmet then gave the thumbs up sign. The engine roared louder, and the grass either side of them flattened in the slipstream. Then they were moving, bumping along the rough field, the double set of wings flexing with the uneven movement. At the end of the field, they turned and Fraser opened the throttle further. Forward they surged. The Moth appeared to be shaking so much, Joss thought something must be wrong and that the whole plane would disintegrate at any moment.

Suddenly, the shaking stopped, and the end of the airfield disappeared beneath them. Realizing he'd been holding his breath, Joss began gulping lungfuls of air. He peered over the side as much as the harness would allow, watching in amazement as the ground receded. In moments they were rising over neat squares of brown and green, over woods and villages, the soft undulations of the Cambridgeshire countryside spread beneath them like an enormous rug.

'All right?' came a voice through the

communication tube.

'Yes, sir. It's wonderful, sir.'

The wind battered his face and his eyes began to stream so Joss lowered his goggles. Gently, the plane turned, revealing a whole new panorama. He wanted to shout for joy. Oh, yes, this was wonderful all right! They flew through some light cloud—*so this is how high it is,* he thought; from the ground it was impossible to tell such things. Joss glanced across at the wings, with their wooden struts and wires. Bumping along the runway he had feared they would snap at any moment, but now, as they effortlessly scythed through the air he realized the machine was performing as designed.

'All right, now you try.' Joss was jolted from his reverie. 'Come on,' said Fraser, 'wake up and take the stick, feet on the rudder.' Clutching both hands on the control column, Joss felt the plane lurch.

'Gently!' yelled Fraser. 'Treat her like your girlfriend.'

Gripping tighter, Joss tried to stop the jolting, but if anything the plane bucketed even worse.

'For Christ's sake,' said Fraser, 'softer! You should be able to do this with one finger.' Joss loosened his grip and to his amazement, the machine did not drop from the sky. For a few moments he was actually flying straight and level.

*   *   *

Once they had landed, Joss pulled off his flying helmet and followed Fraser back towards the flight HQ. Despite the weight of his kit, he felt lighter, as though slightly drunk. He'd never known anything could be quite so exhilarating. What was rowing?

157

Or cricket? Nothing in comparison. Up there, the sky was so peaceful, so beautiful, and yet swirling and gliding through the air—with danger a sliver away—provided new, unequalled thrills. He wanted to jump back in and head to the skies once more. Already he resented the week he would have to wait until his next flight.

Tommy was just as effusive about this new addiction, but the same could not be said of Guy. On the journey back to college he remained quiet while Tommy and Joss could barely get the words out quick enough. Apologizing, he complained of a headache. Over the next few days, it became clear to Joss that something must have happened to Guy that day. His friend did not call on him once—which was unheard of—and whenever Joss went over to his rooms, Guy claimed he was too busy to do anything other than work. Then one lunchtime, he snapped. Their next date at Marshall's had been posted and Joss had started to talk about it when Guy said, 'Look, Joss, I'm not sure Noel wants to hear all this.'

'Don't mind me,' said Noel, wiping soup from his chin.

'Yes, well I'm sick of it,' said Guy. 'All we ever talk about is flying. We used to have such interesting conversations.'

Later, he apologized. A quiet knock on Joss's door, then a sheepish face appeared. 'Am I forgiven?'

'I'm not sure.'

Guy sighed and lay down on Joss's bed, his hands behind his head. 'I'm sorry,' he said. 'I didn't mean to take it out on you.'

'Guy, what is it? What happened last week? I've

barely seen you since. I've missed you.'

'I've missed you too—I'm sorry. But it's so embarrassing,' he said. 'I can barely tell you now.' He sighed. 'I discovered I'm scared of heights. There, I've said it.' He sat up, hugging his knees. 'It was awful, Joss. As soon as we'd taken off, I realized I was never going to be able to do it. I was scared rigid, and for most of the trip kept my eyes tight shut. On landing I couldn't get out of the plane quick enough.' He paused and looked away. 'I feel so humiliated. But I can't go back. It was torture.'

'I'm so sorry,' said Joss. 'But, Guy, it doesn't matter, really it doesn't. Lots of people drop out. Fraser said so. No loss of face in that.'

'But we've always done things together.'

'It's only an afternoon a week, if that. It's not like the rowing. That really *did* overtake our lives.'

Guy nodded, unconvinced.

Joss stood up and looked out of the window. He'd forgotten to draw the curtains. Outside it was dark, although distant lights illuminated other windows. Other students, studying, talking, drinking —doing what undergraduates do. But already he felt apart from them. He had lied to Guy. Flying had already taken over his life.

Cambridge—March, 1939

It was towards the end of the Lent term that Joss was sitting in Guy's room, trying to write a review of a film they had been to see the previous evening. Early evening, and still light outside;

159

winter at last receding. A rap on the door, and without waiting for a reply, in walked Noel and Tommy.

'Hallo. We're after some tea, Guy,' said Tommy. He made straight for one of Guy's armchairs, then immediately stood up again and wandered over to the desk where Joss was writing.

'What are you doing?'

'A review. The Errol Flynn film last night.'

Tommy snatched the piece of paper Joss was writing on from beneath his nose.

'*The action is as fast-paced and relentless as the flash of Flynn's rapier.*' Tommy laughed. 'Yes, but I know the real reason you liked that one so much— Saxon Robin making fools of the evil Normans.'

'But he's also noble and fair—"*It's injustice I hate, not Normans.*" '

'I hate injustice *and* Normans,' said Tommy. 'I'm not so generous.'

'And I hate people banging on pointlessly about people who've been dead for a thousand years,' said Noel.

'You're such a philistine, Noel. It's your tragedy that you can't see that,' said Tommy.

'Rubbish. I just don't see the point in constantly harping back to the past. It's over, and can never be altered. We should be looking ahead.'

'I'll tell you the point: because the past is inextricably linked to our future. How can we plan for the future if we don't understand our past?'

'So, by that reasoning you are implying that if we understand why Bismarck unified Germany and why the victorious Allies made such a hash of everything in 1919, then we can understand why Hitler is threatening world peace now?'

'Exactly.'

'And what good does it do us? We might understand Hitler's motives—power, greed, insanity, whatever—and we might even understand why all the Germans have fallen for him—jingoism, pride, better conditions and so on—but does that make us any better equipped to deal with the situation? I don't see how it does. There's only one thing that will stop him, and that's the threat of losing all these gains he's made, and that means us having more guns and arms and planes and supplies than he does. To achieve that, Tommy, we must look forward, not back.'

'And for that we'll need mathematicians, I suppose,' said Guy.

'Of course. Mathematicians and accountants—people good with figures. Number crunching—that's the bottom line.'

Tommy was silent for a moment, distractedly picking at the loose stuffing on the arm of his chair.

'Well, despite all you say, I don't see how an entire nation could fall for Nazism. Anyone with an ounce of intelligence can see Hitler's rotten at the core.'

'But you've never been part of a defeated nation, or so poor you've begun to starve. Hitler's turned all that around.'

'We've had the Crash. Even worse in America—I don't see the Americans turning to fascism.' He paused for a moment, then brightening, said, 'You know what? Perhaps we should go there—to Germany, I mean. Have a look. See if we don't get sucked into the allure of Nazism.'

'When?' said Noel.

'We've got holidays coming up. Let's go then, all

of us.'

Guy, who had briefly disappeared to fetch the boiling water, returned with the teapot.

'You'd come wouldn't you Guy?' said Tommy.

'Come where?'

'To Germany, in the holidays.'

'Germany? But it's full of Nazis.'

'That's precisely why we should go—so we can see for ourselves what the fuss is about.' He stood up and began pacing the room. 'I know: we can go skiing—skiing is wonderful, you'd all love it—and I've a friend who has a chalet in the Bavarian Alps that I'm sure she'll let us use.'

'Of course you do,' said Guy.

'So we can ski for a few days then have a look around Munich—the heart of Nazi Germany. In fact, there's the most wonderful violinist in Munich who my folks got to know when we were in Vienna. We could look her up—I'm sure she'd show us around. Just think how much fun it'll be.'

He looked round expectantly. 'Well?'

'All right,' said Noel. 'In theory, you may count me in.'

Guy looked at Joss. 'I'd have to think about it, Tommy.'

'Come on—it'll be fun. What about you Joss?'

'Oh, I don't think so. I'm a bit broke, you see.'

'We can take my car,' said Noel. 'It'll be much cheaper that way.'

'And we certainly won't have to pay for the chalet,' said Tommy. 'I'm certain of it.'

Joss picked at a finger. *Why did Tommy have to suggest this?* 'I'm not sure,' he said. 'But you all go. You don't need me to come.'

'But I *want* you to,' said Tommy. 'You and Guy

both.'

Joss said nothing.

'Well, tell you what,' said Tommy, 'no need to decide now. I'm going to have to send a couple of wires and it will take a few days to sort out.'

'All right,' he said, 'I'll think about it.'

*   *   *

Later, once Tommy and Noel had gone, Guy said, 'I'm sorry, that must have been a bit awkward for you.' He eyed Joss, then added, 'Look, I know I vowed never to mention it again, but perhaps we should go. *You* should go, Joss? I can lend you some money, you know.'

Joss bit at his lip. 'Thanks. But it isn't really that, as you well know.' He sighed. 'Oh, I don't know. Maybe you're right. But thanks Guy—for being so loyal. I don't know where I'd be without you sometimes.'

'Tell Tommy.'

Joss looked up.

'Maybe.' *Maybe. Maybe not.*

Much later he was about to go to bed, when something made him change his mind. He'd slept little the previous night and the prospect of a repeat performance depressed him. Having put his shoes back on, he left his room, taking two steps at a time down the staircase and out into the night. It was raining. He cursed, and started to run. On the wooden bridge he nearly tripped, but made it to Essex before he was too wet. Up the stone staircase and a light knock on Tommy's door.

Tommy opened it a few moments later. He was wearing an open-necked shirt and sleeveless

163

pullover, his hair in disarray, cigarette between his lips.

'Joss.' He looked surprised. 'Come in.'

'Sorry to come round so late.'

'It's all right. Just doing some work. D'you want a glass of something?' He stretched under his desk, pulled out a bottle of Scotch, and without waiting for a reply, poured two measures. 'Here.'

'Thanks,' said Joss, taking a sip, and sitting himself down on the sofa.

Tommy looked at him expectantly. Joss barely knew where to start.

'Joss, are you all right?'

'Yes, sorry, I'm fine.' He fingered his glass, swivelling it round and round. The room was lit only by a couple of lamps and a flickering church candle on the mantelpiece. A moth fluttered around the lamp by the desk. Tommy peered at him, his face half in shadow, so that his normal humorous expression appeared hardened, set somehow. 'You're acting most oddly. What is it?'

'Nothing. Well, that's not entirely true. There is something.' He took a deep breath and then a sip of his drink.

'Come on Joss—the anticipation is killing me.'

Joss apologized again. 'I just don't want you to think differently of me that's all.'

'Very unlikely.'

Joss looked into his drink again, then said, 'You know how you say I'm mysterious about my family?' Clouds of smoke from Tommy's cigarette snaked across the line of light then diffused and disappeared.

'Ye-es.'

'Well, there is a reason for it, but if I tell you, you

164

must swear—promise on your life—that you won't say a word to anyone else in the entire world.'

'Scout's honour,' said Tommy holding up three fingers.

'Tommy—I mean it.'

'Yes, yes, I promise on my mother's life, stick a needle in my eye, *et cetera*.'

'All right then. You see, I have to tell you this for you to understand.' He ran his hand through his hair. 'It's difficult to know where to begin.'

'At the beginning?'

Joss smiled briefly. 'Yes, of course.' He swallowed again, then said, 'The thing is, Tommy, when I was fourteen I found out I wasn't really who I thought I was.'

*   *   *

His father had died when he was barely one year old. That was what he had been told. A tropical fever—Diana never specified which one. Kenya was a hard place at the best of times, but for her, having already lost a husband and not willing to risk her son, the only alternative was a return to England. She sold the farm and with all her belongings in a couple of trunks, took a ship from Mombasa. To begin with life in London was hard. Her own parents had died when she was young although there was an aunt in Hampstead who took pity on them and welcomed them into her home. There were few opportunities for young widows with small children, but with her aunt's help, Diana was able to earn a living as a governess, tutoring three young girls at a nearby house. Whilst there, she met George Smythe, the brother of the father of the girls and within a year they were engaged and then soon after married. Joss and his mother left the aunt and moved into George's house.

Joss could remember nothing about his time living with the aunt. She, too, had died, not long after his mother's wedding. His mother's wedding was almost his first memory. And George—well, perhaps it was a child's jealousy. Sometimes it was hard to tell whether he had, even at that young age, distrusted and disliked him, or whether it was his older self imposing different memories. Certainly he had always been a source of frustration and irritation to his stepfather: always there, getting in the way, the living reminder of his wife's former life, and former lover.

George: already in his early forties when he married Diana; the prosperous bachelor, with the house to match. With its leather and cigar smoke, its heavy dark furniture and gilt Victorian landscapes and sporting prints, it was an uncompromisingly male environment. Even Rose, the housekeeper, and Susan, the cook, seemed to be cut from the same block: two spinsters, devoted to George and wary of the newcomers. But for all its comparative luxury, George's house was cold and overbearing. Apart from his mother, only Phoebe, the maid, showed any kind of interest in Joss, but she had her duties to do. Once, Joss heard George chastise her severely for spending too much time 'with that child'.

Of course, his mother looked after him some of the time, although he was aware at an early age of George discouraging her. There were servants to look after children—there were when he'd been a child and so there would be now. At some point—Joss couldn't quite remember when—George took on a nanny. What was her name? Just Nanny. Then he remembered: it was Rebecca, because he'd once seen it on a letter left on a desk that began 'My Darling Rebecca'. He'd felt so ashamed of himself he'd immediately turned and not read any further. It had shocked him though, because he couldn't imagine anyone being passionately in love with Nanny. Even at that age, he could tell she was not the sort of person people fell in love with. Unlike his mother, Nanny was not in any way beautiful, but rather plain with a large mole on her chin that had hairs growing from it; and nor did she share his mother's sense of fun and humour. But she fulfilled her assigned role assiduously: took him to the park, knitted whilst Joss played, read to him, and kept him out of the way of George and Diana as much as she could. But sometimes Diana would take him out for the afternoon herself. Those were times to be looked forward too. Most days she would come and see him before he went to bed and read him a story. It was his favourite time of day and he would be plunged into gloom if, for some reason, she did not appear. Had she been aware how much he yearned to be with her? He wasn't sure; but if George had been his real father, or a loving stepfather, his long hours with Nanny would have been no different from any other middle-class young boy.

Not long after his seventh birthday he was sent to boarding school. When his mother told him what was about to happen, he believed his life was as good as over. The thought of leaving her distressed him greatly and for several days he was inconsolable. He remembered the first trip down there, sitting quietly on the back seat of George's Alvis wearing his new uniform. The school lay nestled amongst Dorset parkland, a ramshackle mansion with a number of tall brick chimneys. He hated it at first. But despite being so quiet, he soon proved himself good at games and reasonably bright and so was left alone, an oddball but ignored by the school bullies.

Although he missed his mother, he was only too glad to be away from George and his house, and soon became one of the few pupils who dreaded the holidays. Nor was there any Alvis to meet him at the end of term. After that first trip, he was expected to take a train with a few of the other boys back to London.

Perhaps, then, it was unsurprising that Joss began to create a fantasy world in which large, greying men with big moustaches would be the villains, and young, fair-haired, handsome crack shots were the heroes. Joss had only one picture of his father. In it, he was standing on what looked like a small outcrop, a shotgun slung over his shoulder. He was smiling, almost squinting in the bright sun. Hatless, strands of fair hair had flicked down over his forehead. His other hand rested on his hip. 'Where was it taken?' he'd asked his mother several times; but she couldn't remember. It didn't really matter: the circumstances were obvious. It was clearly some kind of safari. His father had probably just shot a lion, maybe two.

The photograph was kept safe and close to him at all times. The only time he ever became really animated was when he spoke about his father and life in Africa: about shooting big game, or the war against Germany and the raids into Tanganyika. He told his friends about the MC his father had won in the war, for leading a surprise attack on a German hill-station. And not a day passed when Joss didn't wish his father was alive, and that they were still living on the farm in Kenya.

As soon as he was old enough, he began reading Rider Haggard and books about scouting in the veldt. Anything—books or magazines—that involved adventure in the bush and big-game shoots was lapped up. *King Solomon's Mines* was his favourite book of all time, read over and over again. George might be a clever man and good with money; his stockbrokering business might have done well while many others had crashed; but Joss regarded such a life with contempt when compared with the possibilities for heroic adventure in East Africa. London, with its teeming streets and pollution, was overcrowded and oppressive. East Africa was wild and open and fresh.

When Joss was older, he vowed he would return, and become a big-game hunter like his father.

*   *   *

At thirteen, Joss left his prep school and was sent to a small public school in Somerset. George himself had been at Harrow, but since the sole purpose of sending Joss to boarding school was to keep him out of the way, a lesser establishment was deemed perfectly sufficient, although Joss had heard him begrudge the cost to Diana on numerous occasions. Most of the four hundred pupils came either from military and colonial backgrounds, or were the sons of local farmers, as was the case with Guy Liddell. And most followed their fathers, heading, at eighteen, straight to one of the military academies or back to the farm.

In that respect, Joss was something of an oddity, although his African roots ensured he had something in common with a few of his contemporaries. Even so, it was with Guy Liddell that he became friends in that first term. Although Guy was a farmer's son, and had never been abroad, he shared with Joss an appreciation of Rider Haggard and other African adventure stories; and like Joss, Guy also intended to head for Kenya when he was older, where he too was going to run a farm and go hunting. His older brother, he explained, would inherit their farm in Wiltshire, so it was up to him to go out into the world and make his own mark. The two of them spent much of that first term reading about, and discussing, their future plans. Guy couldn't decide whether to have cattle or plant tea. Both agreed coffee would be disastrous. Or perhaps they should both forget their plans to farm and make a living hunting instead. They could be the new Allan Quartermains.

Joss had made friends at his prep school, though he had never had a particular best friend. But on returning back to London for the Christmas holiday he found himself missing Guy's company. His bedroom at the top of the house seemed more isolated and lonely now that he was back on his own once more. Guy's house sounded wonderful: wide, open, with plenty of places to amuse oneself. His friend had painted a picture of an idyllic childhood making dens and camps, building dams across the stream, bicycling for miles along the roads and tracks that linked the villages along the valley. Throughout his life, Guy had been surrounded by people: a twin sister and an older brother, a mother and father whom he adored, other boys in the village. He had told Joss of all this. Not bragging, but rather, snippets of his upbringing that emerged gradually, as though the most normal thing in the world.

Joss had been back in London a few days when the argument began. He'd noticed a tension in the air since he'd been back; George had been unusually terse, even by his standards, so when he began to hear raised voices from below, it didn't surprise him.

It was evening, after dinner, and he was in his room. His mother and George had had arguments before; never in front of him, although in that house, sound easily travelled up the floors. A reedy violin had drifted through the house from the gramophone in the drawing room, a background noise that he noticed only once it had abruptly stopped. Muffled voices followed, indistinct at first, but then louder. Joss moved to his door, not opening it any wider, but just leaning against the frame, straining to listen.

'How dare you! How *dare* you!' His mother. Then George answering back and Diana trying to speak over him. Joss tiptoed out, skirting the edge of the landing to avoid the creaky floorboard, and gently slid on his backside, a stair at a time, until he almost reached the next landing. He peered over the edge at the floor below. From his position he could just see the bottom of the doorway into the drawing room. George was pacing up and down and occasionally the lower half of his legs and his feet crept into view.

'You had no right to go in there, George, no right whatsoever,' his mother was saying. There was a tremble in her voice: panic, or fear; maybe both, Joss wasn't sure.

'Well, it's a bloody good job I did, isn't it? I mean, *Christ,* Diana, don't you think you should have told me this some time ago? Didn't it cross your tiny little mind that I should know this?'

What? What should he know?

'No George, you had no right whatsoever. Going into *my* drawers, opening *my* box, my *locked* box! My God, you've got a nerve! It's so—so underhand, the very thought of you pathetically scrabbling about trying to find the key.' She laughed, but there was no humour, just contempt. 'I suppose you've been trying to work it out for years. For God's sake, George, what kind of a man are you?'

Then a smack and for a brief moment, silence. Joss bit his lip, his hand clenching round the bannister.

'You bastard!'

'I've never lied to you, Diana. Never pretended something that wasn't. If you'd told me the truth right away, I'd never have had to find all this out for myself.' There was a pause and then George added, 'And to think that all this time I've been paying his bloody school fees.'

Joss stiffened. Until then it hadn't crossed his mind that this could be about him.

'You leave him out of this,' Diana hissed, 'and for God's sake keep your voice down.'

Then George began laughing.

'Shut up, George! For God's sake, shut up!'

'Oh, but it is funny. His father, the brave

Englishman, war hero, big game hunter—'

'Don't George, don't you dare.' Real panic now.

George stepped out into the hallway, and looked up, as though he'd known Joss was there. For a moment, the briefest of moments, they stared at each other. George, utterly expressionless.

'No, George, don't—please, George.'

He looked down again, towards Diana and said, 'Not only German, but a deserter as well.'

Time froze. Everything stopped the moment he heard George say those words. He was no longer conscious of anything around him. Instead, like a wave, a coldness swept over him, draining him, sucking out his lifeblood. Then he ran, down the stairs, past the doorway to the drawing room, along the hall, out through the front door and down the steps onto the street. Something made him turn left: his legs were moving, signals were telling his body to run, but he was not conscious of what or how; he just had to get away, from George, his mother, from the house. Get away and never return. It was dark outside, and although there was not a thick smog, the air was hazy, the streetlights providing only small circles of filtered light. Joss kept on running, past these intermittent beacons, past other people in the street, past cars, and a taxi that had to brake suddenly to avoid him and which blared its horn, until at last, his energy spent, he stopped. Slowly, more rational thought returned. He wanted to believe George was lying, but knew he wasn't. Diana's reaction told him that. And the look on his face before he said those words: he would never forget it. But how could it be? He wanted to know, wanted to hear the truth from his mother, but at the same time, the thought of seeing

George again was unbearable.

He stayed out all night, unable to think of another way of ensuring he avoided his stepfather. Gradually, the numbers of passers-by began to dwindle and the sound of engines rumbling along the roads receded until a strange quiet descended over the city. Joss walked and walked—it was too cold to lie down. No wonder he felt different from everyone else at school. He *was* different, barely English at all, but German. *German!* It was unthinkable. This simply couldn't be. Not him. He stopped and picked up a discarded beer bottle then smashed it on the ground. He wanted to smash in windows, kick down doors, reap destruction on everything that crossed his path. Stumbling on, like a drunk man, he spotted a bench, and, suddenly exhausted, sat down. Burying his head in his hands, his throat tightened and then he could hold back no longer. He began to sob uncontrollably. His father had been his guardian, watching over him, his source of solace; but now, suddenly, he was there no more, gone forever. As though his father had died for a second time.

His mind remained clear about one thing: he must avoid George. Images of the man standing in the hallway, puffy cheeks and jowls, greying moustache, those dark eyes boring into him, flickered across his mind over and over again, like a tune that wouldn't go away. *German and a deserter too,* delivered with such vindictive relish. He never wanted to see George again as long as he lived.

He left the bench behind and stumbled on. If only it wasn't so cold. He wrapped his arms around his sides and hunched his shoulders. In his panic to leave the house, he'd not paused to take a coat. All he had was his pullover and thick trousers. His teeth began to chatter. A frost was forming. A man in a thick overcoat, collar up, hat low over his face, hurried past.

He rubbed his sides. Where was he? He'd walked into a square, tall houses, six floors high, red brick, towering over him, and surrounding him and the garden square in the middle. He heard two cats fighting nearby, their screeches shrill and clear. So cold. He spotted a large maroon car parked in the street—something familiar about it. He should keep walking, but he was tired, very tired, and so sat himself on the footplate of the car, his shirt collar turned up against his cheek, his knees tucked under his chin, close to his chest. He would pause for a moment, and think about what to do. As long as he didn't have to see George.

*   *   *

When he awoke, he was in his bed, and he was no longer cold, but hot, the sheets clinging to legs, his body clammy with sweat. His head throbbed if he moved it, and he found it hard to focus. His mother leant over him.

'Joss? How are you feeling?'

'All right I think.' For a brief moment he had forgotten what had happened. Then, with clarity, he remembered, and his chest seemed to lurch, an oppressive weight dropped on him once more. 'I'm tired though.' He didn't want to speak to her. He wanted to be left alone.

'I've been so worried,' she said. 'The milkman found you. Recognized you and brought you home. We even had the police out looking for you. Joss,

175

I'm so sorry.'

Joss looked at her, then turned over on his side.

'You must sleep, darling. Rest, that's what the doctor said.' She kissed his head. Joss closed his eyes.

He barely spoke for three days, then one morning, he awoke feeling much better, the fever gone.

'Is it true?' he asked his mother when she came in to see him.

She sat on his bed, and stroked his head, but he moved her hand away. She looked hurt, but nodded. 'Yes, Joss. I'm so sorry.'

'Why did you lie to me? Why did you let me believe all those things about him?'

Diana sighed. 'Joss, I'm going to tell you a story. A story about a young girl. A young girl who lost her mother—and really her father too—when she was about your age, and who was sent to live with her grandparents in Africa.'

'You.'

'Yes. My mother, your grandmother, died when I was twelve, and my father was left to bring me up on his own. I suppose I was a difficult child for my father, always getting into trouble. But I missed my mother. My father didn't know what to do with me, so sent me out to my grandparents who had a small farm south of Nairobi, in British East Africa as it was then. Perhaps it was just as well, because not long after the war began and my father went off to fight.'

She was, she told Joss, miserable. Her mother had died and her father abandoned her. Africa was a long, long way away, and hot and dry and with too many flies. Her grandparents seemed

176

impossibly old and although they looked after her as best they could, they were Victorians and too strict with such a headstrong young girl. They would go to Nairobi once a month for provisions, but apart from that she was stuck on the farm with no one to talk to apart from her grandparents and the African boys who worked for them. Even that was frowned upon and she found herself in trouble on more than one occasion for talking to one particular boy. Eventually she stopped because they flogged the boy so that he could barely walk for a month. She longed to return to England and to her father. Once the war was over, things would be different and she could go back to him, but then came the news of his death—killed in action in November 1917. The telegram didn't specify where or in what circumstances.

Then one day a stranger arrived, a Dutchman, called Martin Lambert. He was only a couple of years older than her and immediately she fell in love with him. 'It was such a relief, you see,' she told Joss, 'to have a white man of a similar age appear on the farm.' And he was good-looking too, with very blond hair and a wolfish smile. Her grandparents took him on and he lived in a little shack a short way from the house. Whenever she could she would sneak away and visit him. To begin with, he tried to discourage her, worrying that her grandparents would be angry, but then he fell in love with her too, and they began talking of absconding together.

They agreed they would slip away the next time they went to Nairobi. Diana counted the days. She felt very little for her grandparents and now that she was eighteen, the regimen of her life at the

177

farm seemed even more oppressive. She just wanted to be free with her handsome Dutchman. But as the day grew closer, the Dutchman grew quiet and wistful. She knew something was troubling him, but she couldn't draw it from him. Then the night before they were due to go to Nairobi he sat her down and told her the truth: that he was German, not Dutch, and that he had deserted from the German Army. He'd been on the Western Front. He was a gunner but had been wounded and then once he'd recovered, been sent to Tanganyika. But he'd had it with the war. Terrible things had happened in France. He'd joined with four friends from home and all had been killed. He wasn't scared, he assured her, just sick of fighting. Sick of killing people and watching those about him be killed. He didn't have anything against the British—it wasn't their fault. It was the fault of the politicians. When he arrived in Africa he soon realized how easy it would be to just walk away from it all. And that's what he did. One night he left the camp and started walking. He had a rifle and plenty of ammunition and having stolen some clothes from a farmhouse, eventually made his way to Diana. He'd felt he couldn't allow her to elope with him until he'd told her the truth. He loved her too much to spend the rest of his life living a lie.

'What did you say?' asked Joss.

'I told him I didn't care and that I still loved him.'

'And did you?'

'Oh yes. It wasn't just because he was my means of escape. He was lovely, Joss. Haunted, but lovely and I adored him. The truth is, I still do.'

Diana and Martin slipped away as planned. He had a small amount of money saved and so they

178

married then began looking around for work on another farm as far away from Nairobi as possible. The war was over by this stage and soon they met John McKinley, a Scotsman who had just arrived in Africa and who had bought a large cattle ranch in the north. She wrote to her grandparents, apologizing for running off with Martin, but telling them she was well. Months later came a reply, terse and perfunctory, disowning her. But what did she care? She had a new life now, with Martin on McKinley's farm, and she was blissfully happy. It was there that Joss was born. And it was there that Martin caught blackwater fever and died.

'It was the war, you see. It had weakened him. Every so often he would go off into another world and I knew he was thinking about France. It was terribly sad. You hear about all those who died in battle, but you don't read about those that died afterwards, as a result. When Martin caught blackwater fever he had very little resistance left.'

With her husband of two years' dead, Diana began to panic. She could never go back to her grandparents, and nor did she want to stay on the farm without Martin, with its constant reminders of their life together. There she would simply wither away. Nor was it any place for a young widow to bring up a son. Africa held nothing for her any more. She would go back to England instead. After all, she was twenty, quite old enough to look after herself and there she could start again, be whoever she wanted to be. She was clever, good-looking and suddenly the world seemed full of possibilities.

'And when we arrived in England?'

'I took us to London and to my aunt in Hampstead. She was my mother's sister and knew nothing about what had happened in Africa. Her husband was killed in the Boer War before they'd had any children. She adored you.'

'So you lied to her too. Why did you when my father never did?'

Diana sighed. 'Because. Because things were very different then. The war was still so recent. There was a lot of anti-German feeling around. It was hard enough being a widow with a small child. There seemed to be no point in making our situation harder.'

'But why didn't you tell me?'

'I meant to. But then you started to believe he was someone else. I couldn't have told you the truth. Not for a long while, at any rate. '

'But why let me believe all those things about him?'

'Because it was simpler. And because in many ways he was all those things you wanted him to be: brave, honest, decent, loving. And funny. He was funny.' She smiled, remembering.

'But not English. I'm not English. I'm half-German. Even Lambert is German, not English at all.'

Diana ran a hand through his hair, but he turned away.

'George should never have said those things,' she said, 'but it doesn't matter. There's nothing to be ashamed of. People don't mind about such things so much any more.'

'George hates me.'

'No, no he doesn't. He just—' Joss looked at her. 'He's been good to us, Joss. Given us a home, you a good education. If I hadn't married George, God knows where we'd be now. It's a harsh world when you're poor.'

Joss said nothing, just drew the sheets close to him and turned away from her. 'Get some rest,' she said, then silently, she left the room.

He waited a few minutes, then pushed back the sheets and forced himself out of bed. He was weak still, and felt giddy. Steadying himself, he reached onto the top of his chest of drawers and found the old photograph of his father. Taking it from the frame, he held it for a few moments in his hands. The same face, the same strands of fair hair falling over his brow. But a different person. Slowly, deliberately, he began to tear the paper, into two, then four pieces, then more and more, until all that remained of his father were dozens of tiny fragments. Waste paper. He gathered the bits together and, opening the window, flung them out into winter sky.

*　　　*　　　*

Tommy poured another drop of whisky into his tumbler.

'So you really are Anglo-Saxon, through and through.'

Joss laughed. 'Yes, I suppose I am.'

'And you've never told anyone?'

'No—apart from Guy. As you can imagine I was delighted to be away from London and back at school, but even so, Guy was quick to realize something was up. I suppose I no longer wanted to talk about Africa or compare notes about Rider Haggard. I desperately wanted to tell him—tell someone—but I was so too terrified that he'd hate me for it and tell everyone else.'

181

'But you did.'

'Yes. Because if I didn't tell someone, I thought I'd burst, and then one day, we were walking in the school grounds and it just all came out. And I needn't have worried, because of course he was brilliant about it all and swore my secret was safe with him and that during the next holidays I wasn't to go back to that fiend George, but to come with him to Alvesdon Farm. Which is exactly what I did. David and Celia virtually adopted me. To be honest, I don't know where I'd be without Guy and the Liddells.'

Tommy sat forward on his chair and rubbed his hands together. 'Joss,' he said eventually, 'I can entirely understand why you were so upset at the time, but why such a big secret now?'

'I suppose because I *am* ashamed,' Joss told him. 'Even then the Nazis were already in power, but now look at them. Hitler ranting and raving, marching into Austria, then Czechoslovakia. Persecuting the Jews. I don't want anyone thinking I'm somehow a part of all that.'

'But that's ridiculous. No one would think that.'

'They would. If people here knew I was half-German I would have to spend my whole time explaining myself, telling them I have nothing to do with Germany, Nazis or their warmongering. People would think I'm somehow a sympathizer. They would—it's human nature. I've lived a lie for so long now, it's easier to keep it that way. And I don't sound German in any way, so no one suspects.'

'Pretty much what your mother has done, then.'

Joss looked down at his glass. 'Yes, I suppose so.'

'And what about your father? You can't still

182

hate him.'

'I don't think I ever hated him—not really. I just felt betrayed. But you know Tommy, the hero I created was make-believe, so it's hard now to feel much for someone I never met. I do sometimes wish I hadn't torn his picture up, though. But I was so angry and upset then. I blamed him for my humiliation.' He ran his hands through his hair and sighed. 'Oh, I don't know what I feel really. I just wish I was English and had a normal English family. My father was from a country I neither know or understand.'

'You must have family over there still?'

'Probably. Diana didn't know too much about my father's relations. His father had died when he was young, but there were two older brothers. One was killed in the war, and the other he fell out with over something—I don't know what. But he also had a sister, whom he apparently adored and missed very much. They never even considered going back, though. He told my mother that Germany was finished, and that as far as he was concerned he became an orphan the moment he walked out of the army.'

'Two orphans together. It's incredibly romantic, Joss. And you've never wanted to find out more? I don't know how you can let it lie. I'd be over there in a flash. I'd just have to know.'

Joss shrugged. 'I try not to think about it. Germany may have seemed finished in 1921, but who knows? Had he lived, he may well have returned. Things might not have worked out in Africa, and then when you look at Germany now ... He deserted because he was fed up with fighting, not because he hated his homeland. So you see, if he hadn't died, I might be living in Germany now, speaking German, waving swastikas, a fully-fledged Nazi. I could have been one of them, Tommy.'

'You must know where he came from, though?'

Joss nodded. 'Yes, I know that much. Munich.'

'Ah.'

'Exactly. So you'll understand why I'm hardly going to come with you.'

'Don't be ridiculous! Don't you see? That's precisely why you've got to come. So you can see how completely different you are. You're as English as the next man, Joss. It's not who your family are that counts, it's where you feel you belong. Where you feel most at home.'

'What about you? Where do you feel you belong?'

'Well, I'm different. I'm very at home wherever I am and I fancy myself as something of a man of the world. But deep down I feel English too. After all, this is where I was educated, and even at the embassies we have always been surrounded by other Brits.'

'So you don't consider yourself American in any way?'

'No. No, I don't. I *like* America, and I'm very fond of my American family, but really, we're chalk and cheese. And after twenty-five years of marriage to my father, my mother isn't very American either. Only the faintest accent now, although she was a New Englander in the first place.' Tommy leant forward on his knees and looked intently at Joss. 'Please come, Joss. It'll be fun, and I promise, will put any doubts you have to rest.'

It had stopped raining by the time Joss wandered

184

back to the Fisher Building, but the bridge and the path still glistened in the faint light from the porter's lodge. Joss paused on the bridge and looked into the river, now running more swiftly after the rain. Little else moved. All around him was still and deathly quiet. *What to do?* He was grown-up now, a young man of nineteen. Tommy had a point, after all. Perhaps it was time to go there and confront his fears. The knots in his stomach tightened. It had been his decision to tell Tommy, but now that he'd done so, he knew his secret was slipping away from him. Guy, the Liddells, and now Tommy. It was becoming harder to bury his head in the sand. Harder to pretend he was something he wasn't. Harder to sustain the lie, a lie which, as Tommy had quite rightly pointed out, was the same for which he had cursed Diana.

Germany—March, 1939

In March the Germans marched into the rest of Czechoslovakia unopposed. Beneš, the Czech president, resigned. For a moment, even Tommy had wondered whether they should forgo their trip, but then neither the British or French governments batted an eye, and so they decided to head to Germany as planned. Leaving together straight after the end of term, they crammed themselves into Noel's small Wolseley, their luggage strapped to the back with an excessive number of belts and lengths of cord. They had three days and two nights in which to reach Munich; time, Tommy declared, in which to see some other sights on the way.

185

'The great thing about motoring,' said Tommy, 'is you can set your own timetable, and stop and see things you could only glance at if you were passing by in a train. I really must get a car one of these days.'

Guy wanted to visit the Somme battlefield, where his father had served during the last war. David had never spoken much about his wartime experiences, and nor had Guy asked, but, he told Joss, he had felt he should write to his father to ask for his blessing for the trip to Germany, 'bearing in mind what he went through and with Uncle Alex being killed and so on.' David had written a long letter back. 'It was incredible really,' said Guy, 'all about the importance of forgiveness and understanding that most people in any war are innocents caught up in something they neither want nor care very much about.'

Yes, Joss had thought, *David was a remarkable man.* He understood why Guy wanted to see the fields of the Somme; he wanted to as well, not just because David had been there, but because his father had too. Already the trip was stirring confusing emotions within him.

A blanket of flat grey hung heavily over them as they wandered amongst the network of old trenches and bomb craters, now green with grass and shrubs where once had been raw earth. Parts had been levelled out and were being farmed again, young wheat shoots springing into life above the bones and debris of battle.

At the monstrous monument at Thiepval, they paused, silent, open-mouthed, staring at the names of the tens of thousands of missing men never recovered from the lush farmland that lay round about. Joss craned his head back, looking up at the massive monument, jutting high, still and silent on that outcrop. Then in silence they drove to a cemetery where Guy's uncle Alex lay, in a grave identical to the other 832 in the neat rows around him. Bleached white stone and manicured lawns. Alex had been twenty-four, but most of those lying there were younger: nineteen, twenty, twenty-one. In the far corner of the cemetery, a woman was kneeling, tending some flowers. She never glanced up at them once. Joss wondered whether she'd seen them at all.

Their mood, and the grey sky, lifted as they approached Paris. Tommy was determined to see his old house again and so they rented a room together in a tired pension near the Place des Vosges, and spent the evening and the following morning ambling lazily around the heart of the city, pausing at cafés along the way. A puppet show was still being performed in the Tuileries, children gathered round the front of the striped tent, the mothers and nannies sitting on benches discreetly to the side. The sun shone, bathing Paris in a wash of clear, spring light.

Then they continued on their way again, through towns and villages, land that had been fought upon, and over, time and time again for hundreds of years, until at last they reached Strasbourg and the Rhine, and the black, red and white border control box with its grey uniformed soldiers. They reached Munich late in the afternoon.

Tommy had arranged for them to stay with Freya and Erich von Thadden; she was an eminent violinist and he a businessman whom his parents—and Tommy—had known well during their days in

Vienna. The plan was to spend a night there, then leave the car in Munich and take the train into the mountains to Garmisch-Partenkirchen for some skiing. The von Thaddens lived on Fürstenstrasse, near the Hofgarten and Odeon Theatre, but despite detailed instructions, they still managed to get themselves hopelessly lost. Munich teemed with people, cars and trams, although what struck them the most were the number of Nazi banners that lined each and every street. The flagpoles were almost horizontal, so that the swastikas hung fully spread. The city appeared to be awash with vivid scarlet.

'Christ, they're everywhere,' said Noel, 'just about every house has one.'

'Quite pretty really if it wasn't so sinister,' said Tommy. 'Very different from the last time I was here.'

'Still, this *is* the birthplace of Nazism.'

'Even so, I don't think there were this many Union Jacks in London even on Coronation Day,' said Joss. 'Are they forced to put them up or is it just a sign of spontaneous fervour?'

No one knew, and they continued, past landmarks occasionally recognized from their guidebooks until they somehow found themselves on Ludwigstrasse and close to their destination.

Fürstenstrasse was a quieter residential street, and although a few swastikas fluttered in the afternoon breeze, the street was not the sea of red that the public parts of the city had been. There was not even a flagpole from the von Thadden house. With a high pointed red slate roof and ornate dormer, it had long narrow windows and a façade painted pale yellow. On the second and third floors, the central windows jutted outwards, creating room-height alcoves.

Freya was not there to meet them; instead the task was left to her maid and Erna, her daughter.

'Hello, Tommy,' she said, wrapping her arms around his neck in an enthusiastic embrace. 'How lovely to see you.' She spoke in English, but with a heavy accent.

'I hardly recognized you,' said Tommy, while the others stood behind, awkwardly clutching their cases and bags. After she had solemnly shaken their hands, she said, 'I'm so sorry mother's not here to meet you. I told her you were bound to turn up as soon as she left, but she had to go to a rehearsal.' She wore a neat blue sleeveless frock over a white shirt, her dark hair still long and held in place by a band across the top of her head: a sixteen-year-old girl, on the cusp of becoming a young woman; her hair and clothes had yet to catch up with her face, which was pale and oval, and rather striking.

She led them up the staircase, with its marble steps and curving bannisters. A collection of prints lined the wall. 'But she will be back soon. You will probably want to have a wash after your journey, anyway. But we're holding a dinner in your honour tonight, you know. Papa will be back and Willie's bringing a friend from the university. The Count's coming too.'

'The Count?' asked Tommy.

'Count Max von Tietz.'

'Von Tietz . . .' Tommy looked thoughtful. 'No, I don't think I've met him before.'

'He's known our family for years. Max is very charming and owns the most beautiful place in the

189

mountains. Near Berchtesgarden. You would love it, although Garmisch is lovely too. That is where you are all going isn't it?'

'Yes,' Tommy nodded, 'skiing. This lot haven't done it before and I told them it was a must.'

'Oh, it is. It is wonderful.' She smiled, then added, 'Anyway Max seems to spend much of his time in Munich these days, which is lovely for us, and means he can come to your dinner tonight.'

Not so very different, thought Joss, as he was shown his room. Just like any other teenager trying to be more grown-up than they really are. Even so, he was already looking forward to leaving the following day. The dinner Freya had planned—it sounded too formal and he worried he might say the wrong thing. And tomorrow morning—before they took the train; he would find the address Diana had given him. All the way out he had been telling himself not to, but now he was here, he knew it was unavoidable; something he *had* to do, something that deep down he had known all along he would have to confront from the moment he had agreed to the trip. He had begun biting his nails again. He wanted to relax but couldn't, and wished Tommy had taken them straight up to the mountains.

He thought of his mother's startled expression when he'd told her he was going to Munich.

'Are you really sure you want to, darling?' she'd asked.

'No, not at all. But I think I should.' He didn't try to explain.

'You're not going to find Martin's family are you?'

'No, of course not, but I want to know where he

190

lived. I just want to see.'

He hadn't seen her look so flustered or upset in a long time. 'Well, I've still got some of his letters from his sister,' she said. 'They were very close, and I think she was still living with his parents. If you're really sure, I expect I could probably dig something up.' Then she looked at him, her eyes pained, and said, 'You are an enigma to me sometimes. I thought you wanted nothing ever to do with him and yet now, suddenly, after all these years—' Diana left the sentence unfinished.

She found one of the letters: a weather-beaten scrawl that had crossed continents, the paper so thin it seemed a miracle it had survived at all. *My aunt,* Joss thought, feeling the fragile tissue between his fingers. *Pflugstrasse.*

Pflugstrasse was in the Lehel district, he'd discovered since. He'd found it in Baedeker—close to the river, a few steps away from the Isar Gate. As soon as they'd reached Munich, he'd started wondering whether they might pass by it. They did not, but as more obvious landmarks appeared, it dawned on him that these were sights his father would have been only too familiar with. The big triumphal gate, the strange clock-tower. He wasn't sure how he should be feeling. Many of the buildings were magnificent and there was freshness that was absent in London, but whether this was an objective opinion or due to some deep-rooted subconscious affinity, he could not tell. Certainly there was nothing physically familiar; even the von Thaddens' house was markedly different to any London town house. And the Nazi banners. Perhaps they were merely an expression of patriotism, but to Joss, their omnipresence was oppressive.

Tommy had warned them to pack their evening clothes, but standing in the drawing room later that evening, his collar digging into his neck as he was introduced first to Herr Erich von Thadden, then Count von Tietz, Joss wondered whether he would have been more at ease in a straitjacket. The room, although high-ceilinged, was warm, and a trickle of sweat ran down his back, causing his shirt to cling to his skin. His brows, too, were becoming moist. He wiped a hand across them and into his hair as discreetly as he could. Herr von Thadden was asking him, in impeccable English, whether he had been to Germany before; grey eyes fixed on his. Joss tried to hold his gaze. He was older than Freya, possibly sixty, Joss guessed, with short grey hair at the sides and a gleaming bald pate. But he looked lean and fit, and although Joss was the taller, he still seemed to be looking up, rather than down at his host.

'No, never,' Joss told him. *But my family live just round the corner.* 'It looks like an impressive city, though.'

'Ah, yes, well, we have several princes and their very able architects to thank for that.'

'And slightly cleaner than London, I think,' added the Count, who had asked to be called Max. 'None of your pea-soupers here.' He chuckled, his eyes following the movement of Joss's hand as he wiped his brow again. Max was much younger, perhaps thirty-five, with fair hair like Joss and a humorous face. Under his bow-tie hung a blue ribbon and a star. In many ways he was rather like Philip Mornay; they shared the same urbanity and self-assurance. Put me in any situation, Max's

192

expression seemed to be saying, and I will still make decent conversation. Joss smiled briefly. 'Yes, well, being so close to the mountains here you must—'

Max cut in. 'Actually, I remember once being in London and you literally could not see your hand in front of your face. It was'—he turned to Herr von Thadden, searching for the word, then said something in German, before adding—'almost pitch black, and yet it was still only early evening. I am sorry, I am still learning English.'

'You seem perfectly fluent to me. So does Erna.'

Max bowed. 'Thank you. Most educated Germans speak English to a lesser or greater degree. It is useful for us.'

'I insisted our children speak English,' said Herr von Thadden, 'and French too for that matter. How is your German?'

'Sondern schlect.' *Rather bad.* He could have avoided learning German at school, but some part of him had urged him to do so. He still understood more than he would ever care to admit.

Max laughed and patted him on the back. 'In that case I think it a good idea if we all try and stick with English tonight, don't you agree Erich?'

The dining room was dominated by a large portrait of Freya playing her violin at one end, and tapestries of an extended stag hunt along both of the sidewalls. Tommy was seated next to Freya, with Max on her left. Joss was next to him, opposite Erna. Noel and Guy were placed either side of Herr von Thadden, with Willie and his friend Rudolf in between. Silverware covered the table: wine coasters, enormous candleholders, salt and pepper cellars, four rows of knives and forks, and wineglasses for each course. Although electric lighting ran throughout the house, in the dining room there were two large crystal chandeliers holding over thirty candles each. These above, and the candles on the table below, burned steadily, filling the room with centrally focused light, their heat adding to Joss's discomfort.

Before they began the consommé, Herr von Thadden stood up and formally welcomed their 'English friends'. Tommy raised his glass in acknowledgement.

'It is lovely to have you all here,' said Freya, turning to Joss then Tommy. 'I have always loved young Englishmen. So polite. And when we were in Vienna we were *such* friends with Edward and Barbara. Do you remember those days, Tommy? You were such a charming young man, but, I think a trouble to your parents too.' She clasped her hands together and gave a silent laugh. Slight, with a small narrow face and highly defined cheekbones, Freya had dark hair like Erna's, but cut shorter. Her hands were pale and slender; she reminded Joss of a porcelain doll—delicate, and finely sculptured.

'And I always thought I'd been the model son,' said Tommy.

'Mothers always worry about their sons. It is their life's role, is it not, Freya?' said Max.

'True, very true. I certainly worry about Willie enough, now more than ever.' Both Max and Tommy let the comment pass, but Joss noticed Willie look at his mother and catch her eye; he thought she look sad, and he was reminded of Celia that time last autumn when Roger had left to go back to the army.

194

Joss glanced at Guy and Noel, then back at Tommy. They looked to be doing better than him, talking easily, enjoying the von Thaddens' more than generous hospitality. If only he wasn't overheating; but the more he thought about it the worse he felt, like an itch once scratched. He wondered when the conversation would eventually turn to the situation in Germany. After all, they couldn't all make small talk for ever. Noel had earlier vowed to walk out of the house if the von Thaddens turned out to be ardent fascists. Tommy had pestered him until he promised, under pain of death, not to do any such thing. The von Thaddens, Tommy assured them all, were no Nazis, but then reminded them that one of the reasons for going had been to find out more about the situation in Germany. Joss smiled to himself; Tommy needn't have worried: Noel, in deep discussion with Herr von Thadden, was far too cowed to make any such remonstrance.

It was Max who eventually brought the subject up. 'I hear you are going skiing this week,' he said to Joss. 'It is a funny thing you English and skiing. No mountains high enough to ski from in England and yet you still managed to turn it into a popular pastime over here in the Alps. "The English have claimed these mountains as their own," my father used to say. Still, with things as they are, I think you will find rather fewer of your compatriots passing you on the slopes than you might have done a few years ago.' Joss looked at him to see whether there was any sign of resentment, but detected nothing but good humour. 'And if you are going to Garmisch, you must see the Olympic Stadium. It's magnificent, built for the games three years ago. If

I remember rightly, both Britain and Germany did rather badly.'

'It's always been just a pastime for us, you see,' said Tommy. 'Skiing was never meant to be treated as a competitive sport.'

'Well, that is where we differ then, Tommy, because Germans are competitive about everything.'

'One of the reasons Hitler is so popular,' said Herr von Thadden. 'Brought some pride back. Versailles was a terrible, terrible thing for us Germans. Nearly the ruin of the country. Dark, dark days.' He placed his spoon back in its bowl, looking up at some ill-defined point on the wall, unaware all eyes at the table had turned to him. Joss shifted in his seat uncomfortably.

'But you survived the Depression, father,' said Willie.

His father nodded. 'But think how we have prospered since '33. The economy is stable, there are jobs for everyone, *demand* for everything. Rearmament has brought prosperity and crucially, it has brought pride. When Germans see these parades the Nazis are so fond of having, they see gleaming machinery and row upon row of neatly uniformed men. They see banners and eagles, things upon which they can focus. It gives them pride. Military might gives pride. We were vanquished, but now we have risen again, even stronger than we were before. Hitler and the Nazis have brought about all of this. It is understandable how they can be forgiven a few imperfections.'

There was silence around the table. Joss saw Noel rub his chin thoughtfully; even Tommy looked momentarily at a loss. Erna, opposite him, looked at her father then her mother, then at Max.

'But no one wants war again, father,' said Willie.

Herr von Thadden glanced up suddenly at his son. Joss expected a rebuke, but instead he said, 'If there is war, it will not be like the last time, but a silent war instead. Germany is using its new-found military might to take back the lands we lost in 1919. And so far we have not had to fire a shot. Do you think Britain wants war? Or France? Of course not. Chamberlain isn't going to risk losing another generation of young men over a bit of land in Eastern Europe that has changed hands countless times before. I think even the British government realizes that Versailles was unsustainable. Military might and a preening of wings prevents war. Germany's rearmament programme is a deterrent.'

'But what about Czechoslovakia, sir?' asked Noel.

'Czechoslovakia? I think most Czechs are only too glad to come under German rule. If they had not, do you not think there would have been fighting? But not a shot was fired, not a shot. I do not see that German occupation of Czechoslovakia is any different from the British occupation of most of their dominions. The British have something to offer most of these countries: law, order, peace, commerce, and most feel they are a better place for it. Just because we are talking about Slavs rather than Negroes makes no difference.'

'What about you, Max? What do you think?' asked Freya, laying her hand on his.

'I expect Erich is right. I do not know much about politics, and even less about war.'

'But you have your commission.'

'Yes, but only in the reserve. I turn up for

197

exercises every summer, do my bit, then come back here. I do know a few high-ranking Nazis, though, and although some of them are a bit—well, *ardent,* I suppose is the word—most are fairly ordinary fellows, really. Bureaucrats in military uniforms, most of them. There are a lot more rules now, though.'

'Like being forced to join the Hitler Youth,' muttered Willie.

'I didn't realize it was compulsory,' said Tommy.

'It is,' said Willie. 'Hitler Youth for the boys, BdM for the girls.'

'Well, it is not going to be to everyone's taste, is it?' said Freya. She smiled at her son.

'Learning a bit of discipline did not do you any harm, Willie,' said Herr von Thadden.

'Well, I love the BdM,' said Erna, brightening. 'We sing and hike in the mountains and dance and make things. And in the summer we go into villages and help in the kindergartens. It is fun.'

'Volk und Vaterland,' said Willie. Rudolf smirked.

'What is wrong with that? I like being patriotic and I rather like Hitler, although I do feel sorry for the Jews.'

And suddenly there it was, the one subject everyone else had been deliberately avoiding, out in the open because of a teenager's ingenuousness. Unaware of the significance of her comment, she continued, 'Anna, a really good friend at school, was not allowed to join the BdM because she was Jewish. It seemed so unfair as everyone else in my class was joining. She was really upset about it. Then her parents decided to leave Munich and move to Switzerland instead.'

198

'One does feel sorry for the Jews, of course,' said Herr von Thadden, 'but they have found themselves in this situation time and time again through history. They have always been, and I suspect always will be, an itinerant race. They arrive at some new quarter and because they are so naturally good with money, make themselves rich. But as newcomers, this causes resentment. Then when things go badly wrong, people look for a scapegoat. This is what has happened in Germany. The Jews are being blamed for the misery of the Twenties. I am glad to say, though, that all the Jews I know have left the country. Like Erna's friend, they have gone to Switzerland or America. It is hard for them, of course, but they will be all right. They have been moved on before and come through it.'

'But Erich, Kristallnacht was terrible,' said Freya. She looked at Tommy, 'Really frightening. I thought the world had gone mad. You should have seen Munich the following morning—glass and debris everywhere, as though a hurricane had ripped through the city. But one does feel sorry for some of the Jews, you know. Maria Lundt—she was a young violinist I played with, and with real promise too—she just disappeared. At least, she never turned up to a performance we were giving. I know it was only a small recital, but it was unlike her. That was just a couple of weeks ago. I have been feeling ever so worried about her. I went round to her house, but there was no sign. No one could tell me anything. I do hope she is all right.'

'I am sure she is, Freya,' said Max. 'Probably playing her heart out in London or New York by now.'

Freya smiled briefly. 'You are probably right.'

Joss glanced again at Noel then Tommy and Guy. None of them had said a word. Any moment, Noel would speak out, say something that would insult their hosts, and then there would be trouble. Joss wished he could excuse himself, slip outside into cooler air, away from the heat and tension that now suffused the room. Even Tommy, he could see, was taken aback. There was no disguising it, and from the glance between Freya and her husband, it was clear their hosts understood that too. For a moment there was a pause, so that the only noise was a spoon being laid down on china and the chink of a wineglass knocked against a knife. Noel dabbed his mouth with his napkin and cleared his throat, but at that moment the maid entered to clear away the bowls and he was distracted. Herr von Thadden turned to them and spoke. 'You must understand that despite this, what you saw as you drove through Bavaria today is a thriving Germany. And for that we have to be thankful. No government is perfect. One always wishes they might do this, or not that. But in most respects Hitler has brought about a change for the better.'

'One wishes there might not be Gestapo watching every move,' said Willie. All eyes turned to him.

'Willie—that's enough.' Herr von Thadden glared at his son. 'I do not want to hear any more of such talk.'

Willie reddened, glaring silently back at his father. Tommy looked furtively at Joss, then Max said, 'So what are you all reading at university? I've been to Oxford once, but I believe Cambridge is, if anything, more beautiful. Is that so?' It was an obvious ruse, but the collective sense of relief was palpable. The conversation drifted back to more general subjects. Rudolf and Willie were both at the university in Munich, although Rudolf was from Hamburg, in the north. They were reading architecture.

'So when we come back from skiing, which buildings should we add to our sightseeing list?' asked Guy. 'I know I'd like to see a bit more of Munich.' He looked at the others, who nodded agreement.

'You should show them around, Willie,' suggested Freya.

'All right. Yes, let us do that.'

'And make sure you stop at a few beer halls too,' said Max. 'You cannot visit Munich and not drink some Bavarian beer.'

'I don't think any of us need much persuading on that score,' said Tommy.

'On Saturday, then?' said Willie.

So it was settled. Even once Erna had been sent up to bed and Freya had retired, further talk of politics was kept to one side. Did Tommy remember such and such from Vienna days, Herr von Thadden asked. Yes? Well, they were in Munich only the other week. Someone else had sadly died. A terrible shame—only in his forties and with three teenage children.

Mutual acquaintances were then put aside once Max revealed himself to be something of a motor-racing driver. It turned out he'd even taken part at Le Mans in 1932. A number of amusing anecdotes followed involving dares, wagers and spinning off the road into a shed full of chickens. An expensive hobby, he confessed with a rueful smile, that would one day be the ruin of him. In more ways than one,

201

Herr von Thadden had suggested, the speeds they did. Everyone laughed. Yes, Max, admitted, it could be dangerous, but the exhilaration of going so fast and pushing oneself and the machine, were what made it so addictive. And if he did have to die, that was the way he wanted to go. Tommy nodded—*a man after my own heart.*

Despite the lightening of the mood over dinner, it was not until he was safely in his room and scrabbling to undo his tie and collar that Joss was able to unwind from the tight coil that had constrained him all evening. He flung his jacket on the bed and opened the window, cold air soothing his face. He was conscious he'd said little at dinner. Mostly he had listened, unable to assemble his thoughts into any kind of coherent order. He wondered how different he would have been if he had been brought up in Germany instead. The von Thaddens were well-off, educated and successful, but was their view representative of other Germans? Had *he* been brought up a German, would he have responded to the treatment of the Jews in the same way as they had? It was clear why Herr von Thadden preferred to play such matters down; even by driving through Munich, it was obvious the city was thriving. Buildings gleamed, advertisements glared along every street. Cars, taxis and trams jostled along the roads.

He stripped and washed, then slid into bed. Opening his book, he tried to read but was unable to concentrate, and his eyes glazed over the words. *Tomorrow,* he thought. Their train was at ten; plenty of time beforehand, as long as he rose at a reasonable hour. He'd told no one of his quest, nor that he even knew where his father's family had lived. When Tommy had asked him about it, he had adopted his usual ploy, shrugging his shoulders and changing the subject. He could not bury his head in the sand now, and the same unanswerable question kept turning over and over again in his mind: how much of himself was his own, and how much was conditioned purely by where he lived and with whom he spent his time? He feared what the truth might be.

He was awake at seven, and downstairs shortly after. The von Thaddens were all at breakfast, but there was no sign of the other three. That was something. 'If you'll forgive me,' he said to Freya, 'I'd like to take a brief walk for half an hour.'

'But of course,' she told him. 'Have some breakfast when you get back.'

Clutching his Baedeker, he stepped out into the heart of Munich. Above him, the scarlet flags and banners flapped in the early morning breeze, and the ropes pinged against the flagpoles. Trams trundled past, their bells ringing. People hurried to work, just as they did in any city. He repeatedly glanced at his map—then hurried on, through Odeonsplatz and past the Hofgarten and Residenz, until he crossed the wide mall of Maximilianstrasse and found himself among a tight network of winding roads and dense buildings.

Pflugstrasse, when he finally reached it, was a short road of poorer, shabbier buildings than most he had just walked past. It was quieter, too, away from the hubbub of the main part of the city. Joss felt his heartbeat quicken as he turned in. The narrow street, with its cracked plasterwork thick with soot and dust, gave it a dark, almost oppressive appearance. A few swastikas hung from

203

windows, but there was none of the regimentation here that was so evident elsewhere. With something approaching dread, Joss walked past each building, until he came to number twelve. He paused, looked up, then approached the door—a large, heavy door, of dusty brown, not painted in years. It was divided into apartments, a line of doorbells and names to the side of the main door. Freising, Meinz, Hildebrand—and Lambert. Joss took a step back, and put his hand against the wall to steady himself. It *had* to be them; surely it was too much of a coincidence to be otherwise. With a jarring clatter that startled him, the door suddenly opened and two boys, not much younger than himself, stepped out. Brothers—they looked so similar they might almost have been twins were it not for the obvious difference in age. They both glanced at him then hurriedly walked past and off towards the Isar Gate. A moment later, a middle-aged woman appeared, calling after them and holding a bag aloft. 'Martin!' she shouted. 'Martin!' The older of the two boys slapped his head—*of course! how could I have been so careless?*—and ran back and snatched the satchel from her hand.

'Danke, Mutter,' he said, grinning sheepishly. Joss watched him run back down the street, then realized the woman was staring at him strangely. He looked at her—greying blonde hair, rounded face—and saw the bewilderment in her pale blue eyes as she searched his.

'Grüß Gott,' she said.

'Frau Lambert?' Joss asked.

'Nein. Mein Mutter—' she pointed to the apartment above. Then more slowly, said, *'Wer geht es Ihnen, mein Herr?'* *Who are you?*

'Ich heiße ...' he began, then faltering, said, *'niemand.' Nobody.* He turned away, his mind reeling. *'Auf weidersehen, gnädige Frau,'* he said, walking away from her.

'Halten!' she called after him, but Joss did not look back. Instead he quickened his step and hurried back the way he'd come.

Cairo—September 7th, 1942

It had been a mistake, going to Pflugstrasse like that. He'd known that the moment he'd seen his aunt standing there in the doorway. Before, his father's family had been an unknown—a possibility, but nothing definite—and so long as they'd remained that way, they might just as well have not existed at all. But from that point on, they had become real—real people who lived and existed and who then became harder to put out of mind. And worse: his aunt had two sons, boys whom he might one day fight against. He really wished he'd never known that.

For a long time, he'd kept his discovery a secret; he did not want these people to exist in Guy or Tommy's mind too. He had also been sparing with the truth to his mother: yes, he'd admitted seeing the house, but there has been no mention of any meeting. He could remember little of the walk back to the von Thaddens' that morning—he'd felt too shocked to think coherently. Looking back on it now, he realized he must have seemed even more reticent than usual, but none of the others had passed comment; they'd probably all been too excited about their trip to the mountains.

Now that *had* been fun, Joss thought to himself, although it was less the skiing he remembered than the mountains themselves. In Garmisch-Partenkirchen there had still been swastikas and portraits of Hitler, but the mountain slopes themselves were their own. The pervasive, suffocating, presence of Nazism had been left behind along with Joss's new-found family. The Alps had seemed so vast—peak after peak, jagged and proud. Nothing would ever conquer them: no artificial boundary, separating one people from another and from differing rules of government. He'd never appreciated the futility of such a contrivance before. Those untamed mountains had belonged to one another, and always would.

He still thought about his German family. He often wondered what had happened to those two boys he'd seen that morning. They were, after all, his cousins. Both, he was sure, would be old enough to fight. Perhaps they'd already fought; already died. But one day, after the war . . . He also wondered what had become of the von Thaddens; where the war had taken them. To his mind, they had been essentially decent people, pushed into uncomfortable choices by circumstances beyond their control. He remembered something Willie had said to them on their return from Garmisch. As planned, he'd shown them round Munich, and they'd been standing in Königsplatz, surrounded by Nazi flags and banners, when Tommy had asked him what he intended to do when war came. Willie had sighed. 'Probably I will accept my call to arms along with everyone else,' he'd told them. 'There is no alternative if one wants to survive.' Should

Willie be blamed for toeing the line, as Noel had insisted? Joss could not be so judgemental, then or now.

Then, just a month ago, he had seen Max, at the small field dressing station he'd been taken to after his crash. What a place that had been: a steaming collection of canvas five miles behind the front line, the stench of blood and death heavy on the air. Just a couple of overworked doctors, their overalls stained and splattered, barking instructions above the groans of the dying and wounded; even during the lulls, the fighting continued. At some point during his journey in the truck, Joss had passed out once more, waking later amongst this hubbub of activity. How much later, he had no idea. It had not, however, been the noise that had awoken him, but rather a tickling sensation all over his face and neck. He opened his eyes and it momentarily stopped. Dark blots circled in front of him and then a whirr in his ear: flies, welcoming him back from the dead. Lifting his head he saw he was lying on a stretcher, only a few inches from the ground. He felt very little pain, rather, just light-headed, as though he were somehow removed from what was happening to him. His arms and shoulder had been heavily strapped, and around his wrist hung a ticket, exactly like a luggage label—even down to the small ring of reinforced card to prevent the string tearing into it. Various options were printed on it, and 'Combat wound' circled. 'Gunshot upper arm, burns to arms and legs' had been scrawled in the appropriate section. Joss looked at it with curiosity, surprised that a piece of card could have such a dehumanizing effect.

'If you can read it, it means you're going to be all

207

right,' said a voice next to him. Joss turned his head and saw a captain lying on a stretcher alongside him. Beads of sweat ran lines through the dust clinging to his brow. His mouth twitched and he gasped; he had some kind of wound on his thigh. Joss was still looking at the captain when he was aware of a sudden shadow falling across him. Looking up, he saw two stretcher bearers manoeuvring another casualty next to him. The underside of the canvas sagged with the weight of the body. Blood had soaked most of it dark red—almost brown—and was now dripping through at a steady rate onto the dusty soil beneath, like a tap not properly turned off.

'And down,' said one of the bearers, and together they roughly dropped the stretcher onto the ground. The wounded man's head lolled towards Joss and his arm slipped limply from his side. He was wearing an Afrika Korps tunic, a double row of ribbon across his chest. Both sides were obliged to treat wounded prisoners, but even Joss could see this one was beyond hope. The stretcher bearers had better things to do. Then the man opened his eyes and stared, and Joss knew he'd seen him before. Older, more lined and weather-beaten, but there was no mistaking him.

'Max,' he said. 'Good heavens—Max.'

The man stared back, frowning a little; then his face softened, his eyes began to blink and he smiled. 'I know you,' he mumbled in English. 'I know you, I'm sure.'

'Yes, yes, you do—I'm Joss Lambert. We had dinner together. With the von Thaddens in Munich before the war. You drove motor-racing cars.'

'Yes, I remember now,' said Max, almost

208

inaudibly. 'Our skiing friends from England.' He blinked again, and Joss saw tears roll over his nose and down his cheek. 'I can't feel my legs,' he said. His groin was a dark and glistening mess.

'They're still there,' said Joss.

'Ah. Well, that's something then.' His eyes flickered and then he began to convulse, his neck and chest lurching, as though he had something stuck in his throat. Panic shot across his face, and then he was calm once more. He closed his eyes and groaned.

'It's good to see a friendly face,' said Max eventually.

'I wish—' Joss began. 'If only it could have been in happier circumstances.'

Max smiled faintly. 'What a stupid place to die.' Another tear ran down his cheek. Two flies landed, following the path of the salty fluid. 'I don't want to die now—not here. Make sure they bury me properly, won't you? I've seen what happens to people who don't get buried. Terrible, terrible.' His teeth began chattering and he clenched his arms about him. He suddenly looked quite different: an age older, cheeks sallow, pale despite long months under a relentless sun. Words kept coming, mutterings, a jumble of words in German then sometimes French and English.

'Max, Max,' said Joss, but the Count was somewhere else. Joss pushed himself onto his elbows and called for help. A medic came over.

'Yes, sir, what is it?' he said, running a hand across his brow then irritably whisking flies away from his face.

'My friend here needs urgent attention.'

The medic squatted and put a hand to Max's

neck. 'Dead,' he said. 'One less Kraut to worry about.'

'He was no Nazi,' said Joss, 'so watch what you say.'

The medic lit a cigarette, then said, 'He's still a fucking Kraut though, isn't he? So what's the difference?'

Joss dropped back on the stretcher, exhausted. Max was right. This was a terrible place to die. A place unfit for human habitation. He'd barely known him, and yet he felt more sad now than when many of his colleagues had died. The medic wandered a few yards away and called over two stretcher bearers who had been pausing for a smoke by their truck. Throwing away their cigarettes irritably, they slouched towards the medic.

'Move this one out of the way, will you?' said the medic.

'It's a German,' said one of them.

Joss pushed himself up further on his elbows and said, 'Make sure he gets a decent burial won't you?' Then catching their surprise, added, 'I knew this man before the war.'

'Course we will, sir,' said the shorter one. 'Doesn't do anyone no favours not burying them, you know.'

Joss nodded, and watched them take Max away. Some fifty yards from the station, they halted by a pile of stone and sand, then tipped the stretcher on its side. Max rolled off and disappeared, another piece of war refuse safely out of the way.

That had been over a month ago, and despite his best efforts, Joss was still alive—alive and making a good recovery. The hole in his arm had closed and was healing and were it not for the skin grafts to his legs, he would already have been up and out of the hospital. He'd read every book that had been brought round. Another Jeffery Farnol, a couple of Dickens' and *Vanity Fair*; the bigger the better. The day before one of the English ladies who brought round the mobile library had scolded him for bending the spines of some paperbacks he'd been loaned. 'You should take good care of them,' she'd told him, 'so other people can enjoy them after you. It's no good if all the pages fall out. These books are precious commodities for the likes of you, so treat them properly. There is a war on, you know.'

Oh, piss off, Joss had wanted to say. *I haven't risked my neck to be told off about some tuppenny paperback novel.* But instead, he'd said, 'Sorry, won't do it again.'

'No, I should think not,' said the lady, moving on.

As soon as she had left, he opened the Agatha Christie and folded it back on itself. Funny, but before the war, he wouldn't have dreamed of treating a book in such a way. He had always taken such good care of his books.

Before the war.

David had often used that phrase, a clear and very defined means of dividing the two parts of his life, as though the years leading up to 1914 had been a golden age, a rural utopia. And yet in many ways, life at Alvesdon Farm must have continued afterwards in much the same way as it had for decades before. The same lower fields were still ploughed for wheat and oats, and for grazing the dairy herd; the downs, as before, kept for the sheep, or just left wild, their slopes rich with flowers and wildlife. The daily routine of porridge on Mondays, and kippers on Friday and Sunday was, Joss knew, a Liddell tradition that had continued unchanged for generations. Dinner was always at 8.30 in the evening. The grandfather clock in the hall had been losing five minutes in every twenty-four hours in 1914, just as it probably still was now. There had been change over the years, of course, but change was gradual. It wasn't something that could happen overnight.

Joss knew differently now. It was not that everything around David had changed, but rather his view of that world. *He* had become different. The war had shaped and altered him irrevocably, so that he would always mourn the unscarred innocent he had been before. Joss understood because this new war had changed him in turn. In the same way that a snake sheds its skin, he had discarded his former self. The nineteen-year-old he had been in 1939 had long since died, replaced by someone he barely recognized.

He'd read the opening paragraph of *Murder in Mesopotamia* five times but not absorbed a single word, and so with a sigh, put the book down. Above him the fan still limped round, its relentless creaking a source of far greater irritation than relief from the heat. One of these days he would grab a stick and smash it from the ceiling, then stamp on it, crushing it into tiny fragments.

Alvesdon Farm—April, 1939

On their return from Germany, Guy invited Joss to

spend the rest of the Easter vacation with him at the farm; in fact, Guy said, 'You'll come to Wiltshire afterwards, won't you?' It was a statement rather than a question and Joss agreed immediately, satisfied that honour had been maintained by staying away at Christmas. And with the trip to Germany behind him, a weight had been lifted from his shoulders. Ahead lay two weeks of blissful seclusion: walks on the downs, beer at the Blue Lion, perhaps another giant jigsaw, long talks over dinner; lots of rest. As Guy and he stepped off the train at Salisbury, Joss smiled to himself. *Hooray,* he thought, *back where I belong.* And he *did* belong there, in a way, because that was where he was happiest. When everything else around him seemed invariably uncertain, Alvesdon Farm and the Liddells never wavered.

But he was wrong. It had happened four days before. David had crossed the yard and begun climbing the steps to his office when he had suddenly collapsed, tumbling backwards and cracking open his head. Sam Hicks had found him shivering at the foot of the steps. Doctor Chawley had been sent for and David taken upstairs to bed. Four stitches had sorted out the gash in his head, but the high temperature and wheezing were another matter. Had he been feeling ill before, the doctor wanted to know. Celia had shrugged and mentioned a cold that hadn't properly cleared up; but otherwise he had seemed all right. Apparently that had settled it: David had contracted pneumonia. What he needed was complete rest. He was to drink plenty of water to get the temperature down and to be very carefully monitored.

Celia had kept up an almost constant vigil by his

213

bedside, patting his brow with a cold flannel when he began to sweat and bringing hot water bottles as the shivers started. When he wasn't sleeping, she read to him, and arranged for the wireless from the office to be brought to his bedside. By the time Guy and Joss arrived, Celia looked exhausted and in need of a day in bed herself.

'Why didn't you tell me sooner?' Guy said to Celia as soon as they reached Alvesdon. Joss had never seen such a look of panic on his face before.

'There was no need, and I didn't want to worry you. He needs rest, that's all.'

'Well, I must see him immediately,' said Guy, heading for the stairs.

'Shh,' said Celia. 'Go gently. He's asleep.'

Guy and Joss tiptoed into his room. David was lying there, head propped up by several pillows. His face looked gaunt, the skin yellow. His hair was far greyer than Joss had remembered. Celia had filled the room with the last of the season's daffodils, but the bright colours and soft fragrance could not lighten the depressing scene before them.

'My God,' whispered Guy, 'he looks terrible.'

'He'll be fine,' said Celia, placing an arm round Guy's shoulders. David's chest rose and fell gently with a reedy wheeze.

'But Dad's never been ill,' said Guy. 'I can't believe how different he looks.' At that moment, Joss saw Celia turn, put her hand to her mouth, then look back at her son. 'Rest—lots of rest, that's all he needs. Come on, let's leave him to sleep.'

'Is he eating anything?' asked Guy once they were back on the landing. 'He's lost so much weight.'

'A little—soup, mostly. He's been off his wine a

bit lately, so he'd lost some weight anyway, you know.'

Later, Guy and Joss took the dogs up the track to the downs behind the farm. There was a cold wind, but the sky was clear. The hedgerows were just beginning to fatten. An abundance of blackthorn flower shimmered boldly white against the greenery. Two buzzards circled above them, their strange catcall shrill and mournful. After winter, the valley was now bursting back into life.

'I'm sure everything will be fine, but it's just such a shock to see him like that,' said Guy.

'I know,' said Joss.

'Dad's always been so fit and strong. Such a pillar. No matter what went wrong, Dad was always there. Someone we knew we could always rely on.'

'He still is. A couple of weeks in bed won't change that.'

'I know. I suppose I've realized he's not infallible, that's all. Instead of looking young for his age, he's suddenly become an old fifty-two. That's what has upset me more than anything. Very selfish of me, I'm sure, but I don't know what I'd do if anything happened to Mum or Dad.' He stopped and looked at Joss. 'Sorry, I'm being insensitive.'

'No, no you're not. I feel a bit the same, to be honest.'

Guy stooped, picked up a small flint, then flung it far away down the steep slope of the hill. 'Too much change, all of a sudden. That's the problem.' Then he looked at Joss and said, 'God, I hope there isn't a war.'

*　　　*　　　*

215

David did recover. Slowly, over the next two weeks, his strength grew. He began to sit up in bed for longer periods. Guy and Joss helped Celia, taking it in turns to read to him from the armchair next to his bed. Several letters arrived from Roger—he was in Scotland somewhere, training. One evening he even rang, and David was helped out of bed so that he could speak to him. 'Says he's going to have pneumonia soon it's so cold up there,' chuckled David after he'd handed back the receiver to Celia.

At the weekends, Stella came down. With Guy, the two of them half-read, half-acted out Shakespeare plays to David in the bedroom. It cheered him up greatly. One afternoon, Joss was roped in too. He did not have the flair of Guy and Stella, but David applauded his performance all the same.

'That was quite the most wooden Prospero I've ever heard,' Guy said once their performance was over.

'Don't be so mean to poor Joss,' said Stella, then turning to him, touched his arm and said, 'I thought you did it perfectly well.'

Joss laughed. 'Thank you Stella, although I think it's fair to say I won't be signing up for drama school.'

'I think you'd all have given Henry Irving a run for his money,' said David, and laughed wheezily. 'I could get used to this, you know.'

For some reason Joss could not quite put his finger on, he found it easier to talk to Stella now. Perhaps it was because at mealtimes there were just the four of them round the dining-room table; perhaps it was because both Guy and Stella were less jocular, less glib—for while the prospect of war may have been of grave concern, their father's

216

illness was more palpable. Or perhaps, Joss wondered, it was just that he was now more self-assured than he had been before. Her presence set his heart beating just as much as it ever had, but he felt less tongue-tied than he had of old.

In a strange way, it had been one of his happiest times at Alvesdon Farm. Life had not been quite so carefree but David's illness had brought about a quiet closeness and intimacy that had made Joss feel more included and more a part of the Liddells than ever before. He was almost sorry to be heading back to Cambridge.

When it was finally time to pack up their cases for the start of the new term, David even managed to come downstairs to see Guy and Joss off. Resting one hand on Celia, his brown checked dressing gown wrapped tightly around him, he waved to them from the open doorway.

Sitting in the back of the car, watching the figure disappear from view, Joss was struck by a powerful sense of foreboding, something that was pecking away at him, ill-defined in the background, but *there*. He glanced across at Guy, who was picking his lips and staring distractedly out of the window, and knew that his friend felt the same way too.

Alvesdon Farm—August, 1939

His shoes were covered in dust: chalky grey dust from the track. It had been raining when he'd arrived three days before, but already the water had filtered through the chalk and the subsequent days of sunshine had baked the surface hard and dry once more. They were baking him too, and as Stella climbed the gate, he paused, waiting for her, taking the opportunity to wipe his brow, hitch up his trousers and turn his shirtsleeves another roll. He could feel his knapsack sticking to his back.

The picnic had been her idea. There was the harvest on, and they'd all been helping—even Stella—but then that morning she'd said, 'Let's have a picnic—it's such a lovely day,' and Guy had said, 'You two go if you want but I don't think I can really.'

'All right,' said Stella, 'Joss, you'll come for a picnic won't you?'

Joss had looked briefly at Guy, but Guy had said, 'I don't mind, honestly. Go.'

'Yes, all right,' Joss had told her, his mind joyous with excitement, 'why not—if you're sure I can be spared Guy?'

'Of course—it's not forced labour here, you know.'

And so that had been that, and now he was alone with Stella, walking up the opposite side of the valley.

They continued climbing, the track now passing through a hillside wood. A rabbit scurried across the lane fifteen yards in front of them, disappearing into the undergrowth. Then the woods cleared and Joss saw they were approaching the top of the hill.

'That's the old Oxdrove,' said Stella, pointing to another track running across their own just up ahead. She walked on, then stopped, and placing both hands on her hips, turned back towards him and said breathlessly, 'There—how about that?'

Joss followed her gaze and for a moment said nothing as his eyes swept over the view before him.

There below was Marleycombe with its square-towered church and houses peeping through the trees. Beyond lay Alvesdon Farm, and the long ridge of chalk that ran parallel to where they stood now, and which enclosed the villages along the way so neatly. Blue-green woods nestled at the base of its curves, the sun casting dark shadows that accentuated the spurs as they gently rolled down to meet the golden fields dotted with stacks of corn. Beyond lay the hazy blue ridges of Salisbury Plain.

'Look,' she said, pointing westwards, 'there's the cathedral. You can see the spire, ten miles away.' Joss eyed the narrow silvery sliver shining in the distance, then turned again to look at the view stretching away to the south. 'My God, you can see for miles and miles,' he said.

'That's the Isle of Wight,' said Stella, shielding her eyes from the glare of the sun. 'You can't always see that far, but it's very clear today. It often is after rain.' Joss continued to gaze: at Cranbourne Chase, and beyond to the Purbeck Hills. Barely a sound could be heard. The world seemed to be still, as though captured in a particular moment of time.

'Why haven't I been here before?' said Joss.

Stella shrugged. 'It's not our land and the wrong side of the valley.' She started walking again. 'Come on, I want to show you something.' She led him a short way along the Oxdrove. The track dropped slightly and curved, and then to his surprise, Joss saw there was a house. 'It used to be a pub once upon a time,' said Stella. 'When this was a major thoroughfare, it was a coaching inn.'

As they drew nearer, Joss realized it was derelict—grass and weeds sprouted around the chimneys and tiles were missing from the roof. The stone windows were empty whilst most of the surrounding outbuildings had long since collapsed.

'What a place to live,' said Joss.

'Remote, though.'

'Yes, but—' He was going to say romantic, then stopped himself. Positioned just below the southern side of the ridge, he realized why he had never seen it before. The hill dropped away from the house, a line of beech trees leading the way. Joss followed Stella as they walked around. He rubbed a finger along the plum brickwork—rough but warm in the afternoon sun. A wood pigeon flapped above, disturbed from an upstairs window. The sudden noise startled them.

'That gave me a fright,' said Stella, putting a hand to her chest. Then she added, 'One day I've half a mind to restore this place and live here.'

'What would you do?'

'Do?' she said, as though surprised by the question. 'I don't know. Just be happy, I suppose.' She smiled at him fleetingly and said, 'Anyway, I just wanted to show it to you. Let's go back up the track and have the picnic.'

They clambered over a gate and into an empty grass field where they could see either side of the ridge.

'Here,' said Stella. 'About here.'

Joss stopped and took the canvas knapsack off his back, hoping Stella wouldn't see the line of sweat on his shirt where the pack had rubbed against him.

'There used to be a gibbet here, you know,' said Stella, as Joss unrolled the rug. 'In the olden days. Because it's such a good view. Everyone coming along the ridge road would see it, and so would

220

everyone in the valley below. A warning to highwaymen and other thieves.' She smiled. 'Now, of course, it's just a wonderful place to picnic.'

They sat down on the rug, Joss leaning back on his elbow, Stella sitting up, staring at the view before them. He followed her gaze but would have rather looked at her instead, her dark hair, the faint hint of freckles on her nose and the way her dress was drawn tight across her breasts. He wondered if she knew how much he thought about her. Surely not, but then when she suggested the picnic, perhaps she had noticed that his feigned casual acceptance was just that, a poorly-disguised act?

'Hmm,' she said, closing her eyes for a moment and lifting her face to the sun, 'it's good to be away from London.'

'Hear, hear. If I had it my way, I'd live here all the time.'

Stella opened her eyes again. 'You almost do.'

Joss felt himself flush.

'I'm only teasing, Joss. No need to look so hurt.'

Joss looked down awkwardly. 'I'm always torn,' he said, 'between wanting to come down and not overstaying my welcome.'

'Well you shouldn't. Everyone loves having you down. To be honest, I'm so used to it, I barely notice you now.' She laughed, and stretched back. 'Poor Guy—he's really missing out.'

'I know—I feel a bit guilty.'

'Well you really shouldn't. You've helped him quite enough already—you're entitled to a bit of time off. Anyway, it's good for him—he's so lazy. It's about time he did something useful. Even so, I must admit, it is a bit strange to see him suddenly trying to act responsibly.'

They were silent for a moment, Joss searching for the right thing to say. It was ridiculous, really. He knew Stella so well in many ways and yet they had never shared a single confidence together; however much he had wished it might be otherwise, she had always been diluted by other people—the Liddells, Philip Mornay, guests at a party.

'Tell me what you've been doing the past few weeks,' she said. 'Any more tutoring?'

'No, not this year. I've been flying quite a bit.'

'Lucky you. I bet it's wonderful.'

Joss sat up once more. 'Oh it is—the most exhilarating thing I've ever done. Up in the sky, darting in and out of the clouds, turning and diving—the thrill of travelling and moving about so fast, faster than you could ever go on the ground. And England looks so beautiful from up there— you'd never know how beautiful. And in a way, it's so peaceful too. You feel so free. As soon as I land, all I want to do is get in the air again.' He took a quick sip of his beer.

Stella looked up at the sky, and then said, 'I think I'd like to see what the ground looks like from up there.'

'I could take you up one day.'

'Could you? Really? I'm worried I'd be too frightened. Is it very dangerous?'

Joss shrugged. 'I don't think so. Not if you're careful.'

'Which you are?'

'Yes—well, you get more careful all the time. With practice. I suppose it's a bit like driving a car. Seems very odd to start with, then you suddenly get the knack.'

'But a bit hairy until you do. I think that's what would put me off.'

He thought about his first solo, during the University Air Squadron summer camp a month before, and decided to tell her about it: how he'd longed for the moment, but then, when it had arrived, how he'd sat in the cockpit, his mind a whirr and a sickening feeling of dread building up in his stomach. Flying, he explained, was all about being relaxed—smooth, gentle handling—yet his fingers had been struggling to even tighten the strap on his helmet. Then had come the moment of truth. He'd paused for a moment at the end of the airfield, taken a deep breath, then gunned the throttle and the plane had rattled and shaken across the grass runway. But although his speed had been good, he'd pulled back too far on the control column, so that no sooner had he taken off than the plane almost stalled. The frail biplane had seemed to pause, then drop, and Joss had felt his stomach heave into his chest. Somehow, the plane had recovered and Joss had exhaled, realizing that for some reason he'd been holding his breath since taking to the air. Then he'd relaxed, the momentary panic over. Turning the plane gently, he'd banked and begun a circuit around the airfield. He remembered looking down below and seeing the camouflaged bell-tents—their homes for the two-week camp—and the other planes lined up along the edge of the field. And then he'd shouted out loud—a whoop of joy—for he was flying, just he and the plane, soloing for the first time.

After a couple of circuits, it had been time to come in and land. Once again, his hand had tightened round the control column, then he'd

223

chided himself. *Relax, relax, remember.* Slowly pulling back the throttle, he'd watched his altitude drop. The airfield was approaching all too quickly, looming large ahead of him. He'd landed countless times before, but now, with no instructor in front— no safety net—he'd felt his limbs tense. Twenty feet above the ground, the plane had wobbled from side to side, the ground rushing towards him at a horrifying speed. He'd actually closed his eyes the moment the wheels touched the ground, half expecting the plane to flip over and crash in a pile of burning wreckage, but instead, he was gently knocked forward at the moment of impact, before the plane gently bounced into the air once more. A few bounds later and both wheels were on the ground, the tail dragging along the ground behind, and he was taxiing the aircraft back across the field. His first solo, and he'd survived.

'Could have killed yourself on that take-off of yours,' Rodgers, his instructor, had said as Joss had climbed out of the cockpit. 'How many times have I got to tell you, sir? Treat her like a lady, not a truck.'

Stella laughed, then said, 'Well, I can see that must have been very exciting.'

'Yes—it's a big hurdle. What everyone aims for from the moment they start, really. We flew a fair amount at Cambridge, but I learnt more in the two weeks of camp than I did in the two previous terms. We lived and breathed flying from the moment we arrived to the moment we left. And we were lucky—the weather was perfect. Not a drop of rain the whole time.'

'You know, Guy's green with envy about all your flying,' she said.

'I know. Although he pretends he isn't.'

'That's just Guy. Secretly, he wishes he'd been at camp with you and Tommy too, although, actually, I think it's less to do with the actual flying and more that you and Tommy are so wrapped up in something of which he can't be a part.'

'But I still see more of Guy at Cambridge than anyone else.' Joss plucked at some grass. 'You're right, though. I'm sure I'd feel the same way if I were him. And I suppose it has taken over a bit, to be honest. I'd promised him it'd only be one afternoon a week, but it's much more than that.'

'I can't say I blame you. You two can't be inseparable forever anyway. He's got to get used to that. I don't see him for weeks at a time, but I don't love him any less, and I'm sure you won't either.'

Joss looked away, then said. 'Actually, Tommy and I have also joined the RAF.'

'What do you mean?' She looked shocked. 'Guy never told us about this.'

'Well, it was only a few weeks ago. After the end of camp. We were having a drink in Cambridge and I told Tommy I couldn't bear the thought of not flying again until term started, and he said we didn't have to. We'd both soloed on the camp and passed our Advanced Air Proficiency and so were eligible to join the Volunteer Reserve. So I said I thought we should both do it straight away, and so we did. That afternoon we walked over to the recruiting office, were sent off for a medical and then joined 629 (City of Cambridge) Auxiliary Squadron.' He looked at Stella, then added, 'We've flown a lot, although they've not got enough planes at the moment so we've a couple weeks off. Actually, with everything that's happening at the

225

moment, I'm rather expecting to be mobilized at any moment.'

Stella looked aghast. 'Oh, God, it really is happening, isn't it? I can't believe it. First Roger, now you and Tommy. Even Philip's talking about joining his father's old regiment. Charlotte's brother says he's going into the Navy. Next Guy will be off. What's happening, Joss? Has the whole world gone mad?'

'It's a storm in a teacup,' he said. 'You'll see. It'll blow over, with everything back to normal by Christmas.' He paused then added, 'Actually, it was your Dad who told me I should fly. He told me I should take to the skies where no one can get me.'

She bit her lip and looked away, then said, 'Dad's dying.'

What? Joss's mind raced. *What can she mean?*

Her face was still turned from him. 'There I've said it. No one else will. We've all been so busy carrying on as normal, pretending nothing's wrong, assuming the pneumonia took a bit more out of him than it might have done. Mum knows, but by not thinking about it, hopes it'll go away. Even Guy won't talk about it. I've always been able to talk to Guy about everything, but he just refuses. But it won't go away. It can't. He's got cancer, Joss, and he's dying.'

She turned back and Joss stared at her; stared at the tears teetering on the edge of her eyelids, the trembling mouth she was fighting to control. She put a hand to her face.

'My God,' said Joss at length, his mind numb, 'you're right aren't you? Oh, God. Stella, I'm so sorry.' He felt his voice catch, but even so, the enormity of what she had just said had yet to

226

sink in.

'And to think they're still intending to carry on with the party,' she said, the tears now flowing. 'It's madness. Dad's dying, war's around the corner, Roger's on standby and the marquee men are coming on Wednesday to put up a tent so that we can laugh and sing and pretend everything's *exactly* the same as it's always been. But I just can't carry on pretending. I just can't.' She buried her face in her hands, then composing herself said, 'I'm sorry, Joss. I should pull myself together.' She took the handkerchief he offered and wiped her eyes, then sighed heavily. 'Thank you. It's just this refusal to talk about it has been making me go mad.'

Joss looked at her. A terrible hollowness had begun creeping through his body. A life without David—it couldn't be true, but of course, it was. Joss thought, *I have known hurt, sadness, disappointment, even hate, but never grief.* Not until now.

*   *   *

Joss always slept well at Alvesdon, but that night sleep evaded him. There was too much to think about. Eventually, after lying on one side of the bed then the other, he got up and went over to the window. It was already open, but he pulled back the curtains and pushed up the sash to its full extent and then sat there gazing out. The night was still and a three-quarter moon bathed the house in soft light. It had been a hot, sticky day and was still warm. The air was now fresher, though. He could smell the dew settling on the lawn below.

He'd known Stella had been right about David

227

the moment she'd said it, but then at dinner it suddenly seemed even more obvious. He'd looked yellowish and sallow. Normally David had been a healthy eater, never leaving anything on his plate. It had been a family joke that he would lick it clean given half a chance. Joss remembered when he'd first come to stay watching David's jaw mechanically grinding and chewing each mouthful. That evening, his plate had hardly been touched. It had been torture to watch. He'd said little, even when Stella suggested they should call off the party.

'But we can't possibly,' Celia had exclaimed.

'Why not?' said Stella. 'We'll be at war any moment, and Roger's not going to be here. It's supposed to be a celebration, but I can't see there's much to celebrate. I'm sorry, Mum, but surely you can see I've got a point.'

'Bit late to say this now, isn't it?' said Guy. 'Especially after all the work that's gone into it already.'

'But Guy, you've already got more than enough to do sorting out the harvest. And anyway, it's not as if Dad's up to partying.'

There was silence around the table. Joss noticed Celia give several glances towards David, appealing to him for help. 'But what about the invitations?'

'Mum, most of the people from London won't be able to come. Philip's already told me he's not sure he's going to be able to make it and suggesting we leave him out of the cricket. The people who *can* make it will mostly be local. It'll be easy enough to let them know. They'll understand.'

'And what about all the food?'

228

'But we've barely started.'

Celia sighed, and clasped her hands together. 'We've had the party every year since 1919. It's a tradition. And it's my favourite day of the year. My absolute favourite.'

'But, Mum, how much would you enjoy it this year? Really, honestly?' She looked at her imploringly. 'Mum, please.'

'David?' said Celia.

'Let it go, Celia,' he said. Then he smiled at her, and Joss noticed his watery eyes were shining. At that moment Joss thought he might cry himself.

Celia put down her napkin, but after a few moments, got up and left the room. Stella sighed and ran her hand through her hair. 'Wonderful,' she said.

'Guy, go and see your mother,' said David. Nodding silently, Guy scraped back his chair and left the room.

Later, when everyone else had gone to bed, he and Guy had sat swilling whisky around their glasses. Joss had only been there a few days, but this late-night time in the drawing room had already become something of a routine. It was the only chance the two of them had really had to talk. With David hardly leaving the house, and with two of the farm workers already gone to join the army, Guy had been needed to help with the harvest. Joss too: for the first two days of his visit he'd spent most of the time standing on top of a long wooden cart, feeding sheaves of corn into hayricks. He'd enjoyed it, being outside all day. And the sweet smell of fresh-cut wheat and dust was a pleasant change from high-octane fuel or the coal-dust of the city. But it had been back-breaking too. Breaks were necessarily short—a brief pause for bread, cheese and a few glugs of beer; the chatter mostly about the job in hand.

As he and Guy had sat in the dim light of the drawing room, Guy had lit a cigarette and said, 'Thanks for all your help this week. Didn't mean to drag you into toiling on the farm as well as with the party.'

'I enjoyed it,' said Joss, truthfully.

Guy nodded then said, 'Amazing when one actually does some work, how much one appreciates moments like this.' Shaking out the match, he flicked it into the fireplace. He was sitting in the leather wing-backed armchair normally considered to be David's. 'I've really enjoyed this quiet time the last few nights. A drink and a smoke. Bit of a chat.'

Joss was sitting opposite on the long sofa, and swilled his glass once more. 'Yes,' he said, 'I know what you mean. Funny to think how much time we used to have. What *did* we do all day? Nothing— just lounged about and drank beer down the Blue Lion.'

Guy chuckled silently, then stared pensively at the fireplace. At length he said, 'I suppose Stella's right—about the party, I mean.'

'Probably.'

'I don't think anyone really feels in the party mood. In fact, it's all a bit depressing, isn't it? Or are you still vainly clinging to your belief in world peace?'

'I don't think we should get hysterical just yet.'

'We're finished at Cambridge, though, aren't we?'

'Are we?'

'Well, you are. You'll be too busy playing the

230

pilot. I still can't believe you've joined up. I always thought you'd be the last of us.'

'I haven't really. Only the Volunteer Reserve. It's the greatest flying club in the world, remember? Anyway, how else am I going to fly for free? And besides, I've got months of training ahead of me before they throw me to the lions.'

'In the last war you were lucky to get ten hours. They were all slaughtered.'

'Things have changed. More like a year now.' They were silent again for a moment, then Joss said, 'Do you really think you won't go back? To Cambridge, I mean.'

Guy stubbed out his cigarette, swallowed the rest of his drink then muttered something.

'What?' said Joss.

Guy sighed, then stood up, took Joss's glass and went over to the sideboard. 'It's Dad, Joss,' he said, pouring two more whiskies. 'I don't think he's getting better. Mum hasn't said anything, and I don't think Stella yet suspects the worst, but Dad's got cancer. I'm sure of it. I tried to collar Dr Chawley, and although he wouldn't say exactly, he didn't deny it either.'

Joss felt himself freeze. 'Guy,' he said. 'I—' But Guy cut him off.

'I know, it's unbelievable. I still can't really accept it's true. But you must see, that without Dad, and without Roger, I *have* to stay here and run the farm. I've been talking to one or two of the other farmers round here and there are already war committees being set up to reorganize the way we farm. Make us more productive.' He was pacing about now, an unlit cigarette between his lips. 'They reckon we're going to have to plough up just

231

about everything. Too much wasted land, too much livestock and not enough wheat and barley. There's going to be a hell of a lot to do, Joss.' He fingered his glass, watching the amber liquid as it swilled round and round. 'I'm sorry,' he said, not looking at Joss, 'I know this must be a terrible shock, but I had to tell someone. I've so wanted to talk to Stella about it, but I don't think I'd be able to hold it together.'

Joss knew he had only a few moments in which to decide whether to tell Guy about Stella, but while his unhappy mind raced, Guy said, 'You're shocked—I know how fond you are of him.' Then he stood up quickly and said, 'Perhaps we can talk about it in the morning. Give you a chance for it to sink in. Come on, let's turn the lights out and try and get some sleep.'

*   *   *

And so Joss had not mentioned his conversation with Stella. Now, sitting by the window, with the moon bathing him with creamy light, he thought about how crazy everything had become. David must know, so must Celia. Now Guy and Stella knew too, but not one of them was prepared to admit it to the other. And he'd been gutless enough not to tell Guy that everyone knew. He felt weighed down with sadness, for what was happening now, and for what was about to come. The spell had broken at last, as, deep down, he'd always feared it would.

*   *   *

The following day, the Liddells cancelled the party; even Celia had looked relieved, although nothing more was said about the seriousness of David's condition. Joss, too, played along with the pretence, not mentioning his conversation with Stella to Guy. Stella even remarked to her father that he was looking much better. 'Soon be more myself,' he said and kissed her lightly on the forehead.

Then two days later came the news that the Nazis had signed a treaty with the Russians. 'That's it then,' said David as they sat around the wireless in the drawing room. 'There's no stopping it now.' Then he shuffled out of the room and went back to bed, where he remained all the following day. At ten the next morning, a telegram arrived for Joss. He was in the fields and had to be fetched in.

'I'm sorry Joss, but I thought it might be urgent,' said Celia once he reached the house. She was standing in the hallway, by the round table, kneeding her hands together, the telegram sitting on the silver platter.

Come back to London quick. Mobilization papers arrived. Diana.

Joss turned to Celia, then noticed Stella standing in the doorway to the drawing room. 'I've got go,' he said. 'I've been called up.'

Celia put her hands to her mouth and said, 'Oh no, not you too.' He saw Stella bite her lip—she looked worried. They were still standing anxiously in the hall as he climbed the stairs to pack.

Before he left, he went to say goodbye to David, who had noticeably worsened since the news of the Nazi-Soviet pact. There was not the slightest sign of his former vitality.

'I joined the air force, as you suggested,' said Joss. 'When I can, I'll come and fly down here. Buzz over the farm and wave to you all.'

'That would be good,' said David. 'I'd like to see that. Bet the place looks even more beautiful from up there.'

So this is it, the last time we'll speak, thought Joss. He was struck by the awful finality of the conversation. He wanted to say more, to thank him for treating him like a son, for welcoming him into his wonderful, beautiful, home; for all their many chats in the office, and for the time they'd spent looking over the family books and records; for supporting him whenever he needed it. For being the one man he respected and loved above all others. Instead, he said, 'Make sure you get better soon, won't you?'

'I'll do that.' He smiled, then said, 'I'll be thinking of you.'

Joss nodded then left the room, without a backward glance. Close to tears, he didn't trust himself to speak any more.

As he walked downstairs, Stella came out to him from the drawing room.

'I can't believe you're going,' she said.

'I have to.' Her eyes were searching his. She looked weighed down by the strain of the past few days. 'Please be careful, Joss,' she said as he reached the bottom of the stairs, then she put her arms around his neck, and held him tightly for a few moments. 'Take very great care.'

'I'll try my best,' he said, smiling.

Celia appeared with the dogs, and a moment later Guy strode in, insisting on driving Joss to the station despite the harvest.

Final goodbyes, then the two of them were walking across the gravel and getting into the car. It had been just a little over half an hour since Joss had opened the telegram. Perhaps it was better this way, but he still felt an icy knot in his stomach. He and Guy spoke little on the journey, but at Salisbury Guy said, 'Christ, I can't believe it's come to this. Write, won't you? Write as much as you can.'

'And you.'

'Course. Goes without saying.' He flicked his cigarette into a gap between the carriages of the waiting train, then said, 'This is the end of it all, isn't it? Childhood and everything?'

Joss nodded, then clasped Guy tightly. 'Try not to work too hard.'

Guy pulled away and smiled, sadly. 'Good luck, Joss. Christ, I hate saying goodbye.'

The whistle blew and Joss picked up his case and stepped onto the train. Moments later, it began inching its way out of the station. He leant out of the window and waved at Guy, standing forlornly on the platform, until he could see him no more.

England—September, 1939

He reached his mother's flat in Pimlico only to discover he wasn't expected in Cambridge until Saturday the 2nd. This meant a whole week kicking his heels in London.

'Why on earth didn't you tell me this?' he demanded. 'I could have stayed in Wiltshire another week.'

235

'Darling, there's about to be a war. You can't possibly be cross with me for wanting to see you,' Diana said. 'Who knows when we'll next have the chance?' Her lover, Anthony Cunningham, had told her that the government was preparing for hundreds of thousands of casualties in London alone. 'I might be one of them,' she added.

He let the matter drop. There was no point telling her about David; after all, it was a part of his life in which she had no part; as far as he could remember, she'd only ever met the Liddells once, during his and Guy's last sports' day at school.

At least this enabled him to see more of Diana than usual, even if only because so many of her friends had already moved out to the country. Anthony Cunningham had also been less than attentive of late. Diana had feared he was going to leave her. 'It *is* a time of national crisis,' Joss had pointed out, 'and he *is* a minister. It's hardly surprising he's busy.'

Although Joss and his mother never discussed her romantic involvements, Joss had become aware that Anthony—or *Sir* Anthony, as he referred to him—had begun to play a large part in his mother's life some time soon after Christmas. It was noticeable that since his arrival, she had appeared less concerned about money and had stopped worrying Joss about his fees at Cambridge. Whether Sir Anthony was now contributing to his education, Joss neither knew nor wanted to know. His feelings towards him on a personal level, however, were mixed. Sir Anthony would never leave his wife—that was perfectly clear—and Joss disliked his mother's status as a mistress. On the other hand, this state of affairs seemed to provide her with both a sense of security and happiness, for which he could not bring himself to begrudge her. And anyway, it was hard to imagine anyone could be worse than George. Joss had been in his last year at school before Diana had finally left her husband. She had then immediately travelled all the way down to Somerset to tell her son the news.

'What took you so long?' Joss had asked her. By that time he was seventeen and barely even talking to his stepfather on the rare occasions he was neither at school nor Alvesdon Farm. He hadn't seen or spoken to him since.

'I didn't want you to have to drop out of school,' she'd replied.

That was nearly two years ago. For now, he was determined to make the most of this time with her. Time before who knew what might happen. And so they went for walks, drank tea at half-empty teahouses, and watched the capital prepare for war. Above the blue September skies, the grey barrage balloons floated once more. *Like giant grey goldfish*—Stella had said. Whitehall had become barricaded with mountains of sandbags, while most people had lined their windows with criss-crosses of tape; at least they were doing *something* against the effects of bombing.

One day, Joss helped Diana make her own blackout boards.

'Anthony says London could well be destroyed,' Diana said as they fitted the boards in place, 'but I just can't believe it.'

'I can't either,' he replied, 'but couldn't you move out for a bit—just until we know what's going to happen?'

'Where would I go?'

'I don't know. There must be someone. What about Anthony—can't he find somewhere for you? Or what if I rent you a small place?'

Diana shook her head. 'You are sweet, but I'll be fine here. You're going to need what money you get. If the bombers come, I'll head straight for the air-raid shelter.'

'Promise?'

'Promise.'

Later she said, 'I'm so glad you're here, darling. I'd have been bored to tears without you.'

Joss had kissed her affectionately. 'Well, aren't you lucky then?'

On his last night, she took him out to dinner. She was on sparkling form: attentive, funny and Joss enjoyed every minute. She spoiled him too—champagne, more wine than either of them should have drunk, and sumptuous amounts of food. They had even taken a taxi back to the flat. Having an attentive mother was, he reflected, one definite upside of being on the brink of war. But once they were back in her sitting room, she suddenly looked grave.

'Darling, there's something I want to say to you,' she began, as Joss poured them both a nightcap.

'What is it?' he said.

'Come and sit down, and I'll tell you.' She patted the sofa.

'Must be serious.'

'I suppose it is, in a way.' She eyed him, then said, 'It's about your father—now, don't be cross.' Joss said nothing. 'I think before you head off to war, you should have something of his. I *want* you to have something of his.'

Joss sipped his Scotch. 'What?'

238

She stood up and went over to her writing desk. 'I'm afraid there are no more photographs . . .'

'Diana, please, don't start that again . . .'

'But there are a couple of other things I think you should have.' She gave him a small cardboard box. 'Open it,' she said.

Joss took a deep breath, looked at his mother suspiciously, then lifted the lid. Inside, resting on cotton wool, was a silver cup, with the words, 'Martin Lambert, 1/9/1895'.

'His birthday,' said Joss.

'Yes,' said Diana. 'It's his christening cup. He would have been forty-four today.' He looked at it, the silver clean, fresh and untarnished.

'And there's something else,' she said, handing him the box once more. Joss looked inside, and saw there was a medal—a black metal cross.

'It's his Iron Cross,' she said. 'He won it in France for carrying four wounded men to safety.'

'You never said he'd won a medal for bravery.'

'You never gave me the chance.'

He clenched his fingers over the cold metal, and was silent for a moment.

'Thank you,' he said quietly.

'Well,' said Diana, 'I hope you'll treasure them. I've been wanting to give you something of his ever since you went on that trip to Munich, but there just never seemed to be the right opportunity. You know, Joss, he may have been German, and on the "wrong" side, but he was a wonderful person. You must never, ever feel ashamed of him. I'm sure this may be hard to believe, but even now, there's not a day when I don't think about him.' Diana looked at him and smiled.

'Thank you,' said Joss. 'Thank you for these and

239

for a perfect evening.' He could feel tears at the corner of his eyes.

'My pleasure.' Then she kissed him and stood up. 'Good night, Joss,' she said.

*   *   *

At long last, he was on his way to Cambridge, as ordered. Answering the call to arms, as his father had all those years before. Joss leaned back in his seat, as the train hurried onwards, and closed his eyes; a moment of calm after the chaos of King's Cross. The platforms had been heaving with people, mostly women and children trying to flee the capital. Joss had struggled to make his way through the throng and reach the right train. On the seat opposite him, a boy and a girl, presumably brother and sister, were talking excitedly about living in the country, and for a moment he listened to their chatter. They'd obviously never left London before, but even so, their ignorance surprised him. 'Enid, what are *those*?' said the boy at one point. Joss half opened an eye and followed the boy's gaze. For a second he couldn't understand what he was referring to. Then the girl said casually, 'Oh, they're just farm animals.' *They mean the cows,* he suddenly realized.

*   *   *

Cambridge. The train clattered across the tracks then jolted to a halt. Doors snapped open and the remainder of the passengers stumbled out onto the platform. Joss paused for a moment, and straightened his uniform. *A student no more,* he

240

thought. Then he realized he was hungry. He looked at his watch—1.30 p.m. *No wonder.*

'Joss! Joss!'

He turned—*ah, Peter Benson, and smiling as ever*; his mood immediately lightened. Peter was one of Joss's 'new flying friends', as Guy called them. They'd met at the University Air Squadron, although having finished his second year, and with more flying hours than Joss and Tommy, Peter had joined the RAF Volunteer Reserve earlier in the summer. Joss couldn't imagine why anyone would dislike Peter. He'd never seen him in a bad mood, or treat life as anything other than a non-stop source of amusement. Flying, girls, drink, parties, golf and rugger in that order. Joss envied him.

'Good to see you,' Peter grinned, shaking Joss's hand vigorously. Joss was several inches taller, but Peter's round face and stocky frame gave him the impression of being even shorter. He always blamed this for his limited success with girls. 'It can't be my lack of charm,' he once told Joss.

'D'you know where we're supposed to go?' Peter asked as they headed out of the station.

'Jesus College, I think,' said Joss.

'Good job I bumped into you then. I was all set to head off to Marshall's.'

They paused first at a pub—a half-pint of beer and an omelette—then made their way towards Jesus. Turning down the walled path of The Chimney, they reached the red-brick gate tower and walked into First Court.

Large numbers of young men milled about on the lawn. Some were in uniform, others in summer jackets and flannels; some carried neat holdalls and suitcases, others with vast trunks and mountains of luggage. 'We're not even at war yet but the whole country's in chaos. Chaos in London, chaos on the trains, chaos at Jesus College,' said Peter.

As they approached one group, Peter said, 'What's going on?'

One man shrugged. Another said, 'God knows. We're told to turn up, but no one's here.'

Then Joss suddenly spotted Tommy on the far side of the Court, leaning against a doorway, smoking and reading a newspaper. 'Come on, Peter, let's go and see him.'

Tommy grinned and waved as they approached, then folded away his paper. 'Well, I think we're just about ready for war, don't you?'

'Mayhem, utter mayhem,' said Peter. 'Let's just hope Hitler doesn't switch his attention from the Poles and make a lightning strike on Cambridge.'

Two warrant officers eventually arrived. Looking at the mountains of luggage with disdain, they began reading off lists of names. All but two had made it. Then they split the recruits into two groups: those already in the Volunteer Reserve and those who were not. The two groups were to form themselves into orderly queues and then, one by one, they would be told where they were to be billeted.

'No flying today, then?' said Peter as he reached the warrant officer at the head of their line.

The man eyed him suspiciously, uncertain whether Peter was being serious or just plain cocky. *These long-haired boys,* he seemed to be thinking, *who the hell do they think they are?*

'No, sir. Just watch the college notice board and wait for further instructions.'

'Just like the first day of term,' said Peter, once they'd been allocated their billets. All three had been put in St John's College.

'*Just* like the first day of term,' agreed Tommy. 'Except we're being paid to be here rather than us paying them.'

'At least we're not being put up in Queens',' said Peter.

'Coming from a Peterhouse man, I find that very rich indeed,' said Tommy.

They passed through the Tudor gateway of St John's. The porter, looking slightly baffled by his new role, was standing outside the lodge.

'All a bit strange this, isn't it?' said Peter, as the porter handed them their keys.

'Yes, sir, it is. Don't normally expect to see the young men back this early in September, least of all in uniform.' Peter chuckled. The porter continued, 'They say we'll be at war by Monday morning. Who'd ever have believed it after the last one?'

'You out there were you?' asked Joss.

'Yes, sir. A nasty business. Reckon you've been very sensible taking to the skies. I wouldn't wish the trenches on anyone.'

Joss nodded. 'You're not the first person to tell me that.'

*   *   *

Later, they went to The Eagle. Joss had checked the notice board every half-hour and in between had written a letter to Guy, but by seven o'clock it was clear nothing else was going to happen that day.

'Let's get drunk,' suggested Tommy as they

243

crossed over King's Parade.

'But what if we're flying tomorrow?' said Joss.

'I'll bet you five shillings we won't be flying tomorrow. Or the next day. Or the next day after that.'

'What do you mean?'

'Well, you saw how disorganized they were today. It's going to take a while to sort everything out.'

Joss's heart sank. He wasn't sure what he'd been expecting, but it wasn't this. Why weren't they all better prepared? Mobilization was no surprise. As far as he was concerned, he'd been just about the only one refusing to accept that war was coming. No one had really believed Chamberlain the previous year, yet now it seemed very little had been done since then.

'Relax, Joss,' said Tommy. 'We're going to have all the flying we want and more. Make the most of this while you can.'

The pub was busy, mostly with other young men.

'I wonder if we'll ever get back to the squadron,' said Joss, as they stood at the bar, buying their drinks.

'They've been sent up north,' added Tommy. 'Hurricanes.'

'Well that's something,' said Joss. 'At least they're on fighters.'

'I don't think we can assume we'll get sent back,' said Tommy. 'The way everyone's talking, it's going to be the bombers that do all the work. Slow, heavy cumbersome, bombers.'

Peter groaned. 'No, they can't make us do that!'

'I do *not* want to be flying bombers,' said Joss.

Tommy shrugged and lit another cigarette. 'Look, I agree. I want to fly fighters too. But none of us have a clue what's going to happen, so there's no point worrying for the sake of it.'

'But it's the not-knowing that's the worst of it, don't you think?' said Peter. 'I don't mean us, and what we end up flying, but *everything*. Everyone in the village—my parents included—seems to think there'll be some great air attack before we're even at war. Mass annihilation forestalling any kind of formal hostilities. Seems rather unlikely to me, but who's to say? You're right: the bottom line is that we don't know anything. What Hitler plans to do, or if we're ready to fight; whether it'll all be over in a matter of weeks, or whether this is going to go on forever. My parents seem very depressed about it all, but I'm not really sure what I feel. Just happy to be flying, I suppose.'

Peter talked more about home. His family were from Kent, and, he admitted, he was quite glad to have got away for a bit. The past week his house had seen a non-stop line of people trooping in and out—someone coming about the ARP services, someone else about the evacuees. Another checking the blackout curtains fitted properly, another just to listen to the wireless. The radio had never been off air, he told them. 'I don't think the newsreader can have gone to sleep all week. Did you hear him? So bloody depressing! Then playing those awful songs—if I hear *Land of Hope and Glory* one more time I'll go mad.'

Tommy's parents had been posted home. Now working in Whitehall, his father was commuting into town every day from their newly-rented house near Guildford.

'Glad to have them back?' asked Joss.

'Of course, although there's a part of me that

245

thinks they might have been safer in Egypt.'

'I thought your father thinks Hitler's after Russia?'

'You *what*?' said Peter. 'Russia? Surely not. I thought he's just signed a pact with them?'

'Only temporarily,' said Tommy, 'until he's sorted out Europe. *Then* he'll go for Russia. But Dad thinks we *will* see German bombers coming over.'

Peter looked at Tommy—*if you say so; what do I know?*—then stood up to buy more drinks.

Tommy sighed. 'The porter's right, you know—Chamberlain can't hold off much longer now.'

*   *   *

They left at closing time, tight—but not drunk. After a hot, cloudless day, the air was now warm and close.

'Feels like a storm brewing,' said Peter, then added, 'actually and metaphorically.'

Later Joss lay in bed unable to sleep, listening to the peals of thunder and the rain beating down against his window. Peter had been absolutely right.

Cairo—September, 1942

Three years ago. Three whole years and three weeks. *It's the not-knowing that's the worst of it,* Peter had said, but Joss was glad he hadn't known what was coming; that he'd end up festering in some hospital in Cairo, sick at heart and in mind.

That morning—the day they went to war. A Sunday. Everyone crowding around the radio in

246

the JCR listening to Chamberlain's tired and reedy voice saying that they were now at war with Germany. There had still been no orders posted on the notice board and he had suddenly wanted to speak to Guy and to see how David was and how they were coping. He'd rung from the telephone in the porter's lodge, although there were so many calls being made he couldn't get through for a while. Then eventually the line had begun to ring. It was Guy who'd answered. He'd sounded strained.

'Guy—it's me, Joss! I just wanted to see how you are.'

'Joss, my God. Joss, it's happened.'

'I know, it's terrible. But even *I* realized it was inevitable. No bombers yet, though.'

'What? What do you mean?' Guy had sounded confused. Then suddenly he'd said, *'No, I don't mean the war. It's Dad, Joss. He's died. In the night.'*

*   *   *

He still mourned for David, even now. The day he died, it seemed as though the old order had crumbled forever. Sitting on a wicker chair in the hospital gardens he thought about that. The war had heralded the dawn of a new age—a modern age of progression, of accelerated mechanization. Age-old barriers and traditions had broken down, the fabric of society altered irreversibly. In his mind's eye, he wished Alvesdon Farm could remain for ever as it had been before the war, yet this new world—as Tommy had so ably demonstrated—had promised endless possibilities too. The new order had enabled him to fly, enabled him and Stella to

247

fall in love, given him chances that would not have been possible a few years before. Did he regret it now? Before he'd received Stella's letter, he would have said no, despite all that had happened. Now he wasn't so sure. He wondered what David would have made of it all. Would he have blessed the relationship of his daughter and his son's best friend? David had been fond of Joss, had loved him even, but was Joss—penniless and with few prospects—the kind of person he would want his daughter to marry? Possibly not.

It was still stifling, even in the shade, although it had been hot, too, that September of 1939; beyond the garden walls, the never-ceasing rumble of the city continued its daily pulse. A soldier with a heavily plastered leg was practising with his crutches, accompanied by whoops of encouragement from one of the VADs. *These memories,* he thought. During the past couple of days, he'd tried to recall every time he'd been to Alvesdon Farm, and the main things that had happened—principally as a way of passing a couple of hours. He reckoned he'd accounted for every visit. But memory was strange, for while he could remember almost every day of his month with the Liddells during the summer of 1936, there was much about the time following the outbreak of war that was already hazy.

How long had they all remained in Cambridge? He tried to think. A couple of weeks, or was it longer? At some point they'd been drafted into one of the Initial Training Wings and divided into little squads of a dozen or so. It had been something of a shock to begin with: early morning parades, being yelled at by Warrant Officer Woodman—a soldier with twenty years' experience in the Indian Army—

for their general slovenly appearance and for having kept their hair too long. Practising drill around the Second Court. Joss remembered Tommy had been most indignant, refusing to cut his hair and blustering at the pointlessness of drill as a part of flying training. 'It's like being back at the bloody school OTC,' he said, 'and I hated it then.' But not all the training staff had been as fierce as Warrant Officer Woodman. One time, they'd been sent on a route march, but on reaching Grantchester, had stopped at the Red Lion, drunk a hasty pint, then ambled back.

The massed raids of bombers had not appeared. Britain did not send any troops into Poland, and nor did France. Instead, they stayed where they were, patrolling the Maginot Line and carrying on in much the same way as they had before September 3rd. The only shots fired were at sea, and although Roger Liddell had to remain with his unit in France, Joss had no difficulty in securing 24 hours' leave to attend David's funeral in Marleycombe.

What of that day?

A packed village church. Celia, with Guy and Stella either side, standing beneath the yew tree in the south-west corner of the churchyard, the coffin slowly lowered into the gaping hole in the ground. So brave and dignified.

How many funerals had he been to since? Countless. He couldn't remember half of them. Certainly couldn't remember much about most of those being buried.

Then back to the house for the wake. A low murmur in the drawing room. Sandwiches and sherry. And the four evacuees skulking miserably

249

on the stairs.

'Why has Celia been made to take them on?' he'd asked Guy.

'She offered. Apparently, she'd agreed to take some on last year, and didn't want to back down now. Said it would give her something to do and take her mind off things. It's been a nightmare, though.' They'd come from South London, somewhere, and had arrived at the farm full of nits and with only the clothes they were standing in. The two younger ones, an eight-year-old boy and girl, both regularly wet their beds. Their table manners—or rather, lack of them—had shocked even Celia, while the little boy was scared rigid of the dogs and horses. 'Stella has stayed down all week and has been helping mum,' Guy continued, 'but they couldn't have arrived at a worse time. It hasn't made life easy for us, or for them, for that matter.'

An aunt then collared Guy, and Joss stood there listening for a few minutes, clutching his sherry, until another relation appeared and blocked him from the conversation altogether. The densely packed room was becoming hot, and not feeling much like talking anyway, Joss quietly slipped outside, where the air was cool and fresh. Rather than walk round to the garden where he could be seen from the drawing room, he turned into the yard. Sitting on the steps leading up to David's old office he was surprised to see Stella. She looked miserable, smoking a cigarette, her head on her knees.

'Stella,' said Joss. 'Are you all right?'

She lifted her head. 'I couldn't bear another person telling me how sorry they are. Too much

250

sympathy becomes a bit overwhelming after a while, so I thought I'd escape for a few minutes.'

'Sorry—I'll leave you to it.'

'No, no, don't. Stay and chat for a moment.' Then she said, 'You look very smart in your uniform.'

Joss smiled bashfully. 'Still feels a bit strange, to be honest.' He came over and sat on the bottom step. 'How are you coping?'

'Oh, all right, I suppose. I know it sounds dreadful, but I can't wait to get back to London. It's been awful this week—mum's being very brave, but the evacuees are a nightmare. It's not their fault, though, poor lambs, just shocking timing.' She tucked a strand of hair behind her ear. 'At least we haven't been bombed yet.'

'No.'

They were silent for a moment, then Stella said, 'I still can't believe Dad's gone. That I'll never see him ever again. It doesn't seem possible somehow.'

'I know.'

'I thought the funeral was awful. I desperately wanted to cry, but I knew that wouldn't help mum, and so I spent the entire time clenching my fists and willing myself not to.'

Joss picked up a pebble and threw it across the yard. 'I don't mind if you want to cry now,' he said. 'I won't tell, I promise.'

Stella smiled at him, and said, 'Thank you Joss. You're a sweet person, you know.' Then she looked away, and buried her face in her hands. 'Oh God,' she sobbed, 'now I *am* crying. Sorry Joss, it's just so bloody—'

'Here,' said Joss, passing her his handkerchief. She took it and he said, 'Would you like me to leave you alone now?'

251

'No,' she said, looking up. Her face was wet with tears, and she said, 'Actually, would you mind terribly just holding me a moment?'

'No, no, of course not,' he said, standing up awkwardly, and taking her arms in his. He felt her warm head against his, and her hands clenched against his back; he closed his eyes and breathed in her scent, and wished he could hold her like this forever. Her body shook gently, and then with two heavy sighs, she let go of him and sat back once more. 'Thank you,' she said softly. She dabbed her eyes, then held out the handkerchief.

'Keep it,' said Joss. 'For the time being anyway.'

'Thanks.' She sighed again, then said, 'I suppose I had better get back. Do I look terrible?'

'Not at all.'

'Liar.' She smiled, dabbed her eyes once more, then said, 'Philip should be here looking after me really, but thank you, Joss.'

'Any time,' he said kindly, then, feeling emboldened, offered an arm. As he felt her hand clutch onto him, he said, 'I suppose he couldn't make it down?'

'No, the sod. He's involved with some kind of war-work—not sure what exactly—and has become terribly self-important. Said he was very sorry but he couldn't get away.'

They reached the front door and Joss said, 'Are you sure you'll be all right now?'

'Yes, I'll be fine.' She paused, then said, 'I'm sorry about that. I hope I didn't embarrass you, but I do feel much better now.'

Joss looked at her reddened eyes and the slight smudge of mascara. *I'd look after you forever if you like,* he'd wanted to say to her, but instead said,

'Good,' then followed her back into the hall.

Shortly after, one of the guests at the wake had given him a lift back to the station, and he'd caught the next train back to London, and then on to Cambridge. It had been the last time he'd seen any of the Liddells or Alvesdon Farm for many months.

*   *   *

The square-bashing had eventually come to an end, but his training had only just begun. Joss, along with Tommy and Peter, had been promoted from 'Sergeant Under Training' and then commissioned to 'Acting Pilot Officer'. At the same time, they were posted to their flying training school at Kinloss, high in the north-east of Scotland. For the best part of seven months, they had lived a cocooned existence, cut off from the war and the rest of the world. Joss saw almost nobody other than those involved with the course. His only real contact with the outside world had been a handful of letters from Guy, three from Celia and one from his mother. At Christmas they had been given 48 hours' leave, but they were so far north, only the Scots among them had bothered leaving the station. The rest had celebrated in the mess and on a drinking spree to Nairn. It had been easy to forget there was a war at all. At the time, Tommy, especially, had bemoaned the isolation, but really, Joss thought, it had been a good thing. Being in the middle of nowhere had kept them all together; had enabled them to immerse themselves in flying and the task of becoming fully trained pilots.

He couldn't remember ever really thinking about killing other people, or what would happen if he were to be shot at, or that many of them would, in a year's time, be dead. They'd been young men then, in love with flying, their goal only to get through each stage of the course.

*   *   *

Joss whisked away a fly from his face, and rubbed his itching arms in turn. How callow they'd all been then, he thought.

Scotland—January, 1940

A cold, but fine morning, and thankfully, little wind. Joss had known nothing like the icy winds that battered their airfield. At night, long after the embers in his tiny stove had gone out, the flurries from across the North Sea would whistle through the wooden Nissen hut, and no matter how many layers he wore, or how much he pulled the blankets tightly around him, he was still cold. A few weeks ago, it had rained solidly for a week, bringing most flying to a halt. His room had flooded, so that one morning he'd woken up and put his feet straight into a puddle of freezing-cold rainwater. Their batmen had been doing their best, making sure their little iron stoves were regularly stoked. Both Joss and Peter were looked after by Mr McLeish, a small, thin Scot from nearby Lindhorn. They guessed he must have been well into his fifties, but the only concession he ever made to the cold was to button up his jacket and wrap a scarf round his neck. He'd explained that a lifetime living by the

254

sea, and facing the north-east winds, hardened both the skin and the soul.

Today, however, conditions were perfect for flying. Joss walked over to the flight hut, looking for Heyward, his flight instructor, but could see no sign of him. He stamped his feet up and down, blew into his hands and watched other trainee pilots carrying out their pre-flight checks, then, one by one, taking off. Tommy and Peter, both in 'B' Flight with him, roared past. After ten minutes, Joss began to feel irritated. Where *was* Heyward? After twenty, he was decidedly annoyed. Ideal conditions, and his Wings Test fast approaching. He was wasting valuable practice time.

He walked up and down, flung his helmet up into the air then caught it again, hoping he was making himself conspicuous. Eventually the Flight Commander appeared, apologizing for keeping him hanging about. Heyward, he told Joss vaguely, was held up, but in the meantime, could he please take 4126 over to Lossiemouth? They were expecting him and someone would then drive him back.

'Oh, one other thing, Lambert,' he said, almost as an after-thought. 'Make sure you're back in good time. You'll be taking your Wings Test this afternoon—about 1400 hours, all right?'

'Right, sir,' said Joss. Calm-as-you-like, *piece of bloody cake, sir*. His brain was screaming as he strode over towards 4126, a Harvard he'd flown numerous times during the past few months. Half-past nine now: that meant three-and-a-half hours to think about the test, to make himself so tense he'd never be able to fly properly. In four hours' time he would probably be kicked off the course, his flying career over.

Joss had arrived at Kinloss four months before
itching to get back in a plane and confident that he
could handle an aircraft as well as the next man.
His very first flight with Heyward had soon crushed
such confidence. 'You're aerobatics are appalling,'
Heyward had told him. 'Your slow roll was a
disgrace. You let your nose drop away and you lost
far too much height. Haven't you ever heard of
using the rudder? You're heavy-handed, too, and, if
you're going to avoid getting the chop, you're going
to have to start listening to what I say.' He hadn't
stopped there. 'Bet you thought flying was easy,
didn't you?' Joss had nodded miserably. 'It's typical
of you VR boys. Think the RAF's just one big lark,
here so you can have a good time and learn how to
fly for free. You're all the same—think you're
God's gift and complacent to boot.'

Later that day he'd gone to his first lecture and
had been given twenty-three separate textbooks.
'You will need to know all of these backwards,'
they'd been told. 'There are absolutely no
opportunities for cutting corners.' Over a quick
drink in the mess that night, he'd discovered
Tommy and Peter had been given similar warnings
about complacency; that had made him feel
marginally better until he discovered neither had
been chastised for their poor flying ability. They'd
also been told that typically, around forty per cent
failed to complete the course. Joss had come to
Kinloss believing his progression would be
straightforward, his wings casually handed over
after a few months. By the end of that first day,

he'd realized he'd be lucky if he made it to Christmas.

He'd worked hard since then, promising never to take any part of the RAF for granted again. After all, how many great men had yearned to do what he was doing? And just how lucky was he—an ordinary nineteen-year-old with barely a few pounds to his name—to be flying and paid to do so. He must never squander this opportunity. Never.

Under the patient tuition of Flight Sergeant Heyward, he had begun to progress well. Manoeuvres that had once seemed impossible were gradually mastered, bad habits ironed out and his belief in himself had grown once more. They'd progressed from aerobatics to navigation, and although he'd struggled with the classroom mathematics, he'd discovered he was particularly good at finding his way about in the air. Not so Tommy, for whom navigation was proving his stumbling block. He'd got lost a number of times, landed at wrong airfields and shouted back at his instructor. Having proved himself a naturally gifted pilot, ahead of the rest of the field, he had suddenly found himself hauled in front of the Station Commander and threatened with the sack. A number of trainees had already gone: there in the mess one day, but mysteriously absent the next, a blatant reminder against complacency.

Joss and Peter spent many extra hours over several weekends goading him through the basic principles of navigation and meteorology, so that Joss was almost as triumphant as his friend when Tommy successfully completed a triangular navigation test.

That had been three weeks ago. The following

day, he and Heyward had had a particularly good flight. In the classroom that afternoon he'd grasped all that was said to him; suddenly everything about engineering that had previously seemed so incomprehensible had clicked into place. For once, he'd taken a night off from studying and had a few drinks in the mess. With around a month until his Wings Examination, he'd felt certain all would be well for the first time since his arrival at Kinloss.

Then there'd been night flying. The prospect had not especially alarmed him, and his first flight with Heyward had been straightforward enough. 'There's nothing so terribly difficult about it,' his instructor had told him, 'just one golden rule: as soon as we leave the ground, whatever you do, don't look outside the cockpit. You must rely entirely on the instruments and trust in what they tell you.'

His first solo had been a few nights later, the night the course had its first fatality. It had been another freezing night, but after successfully completing two circuits, Joss was preparing to land, dropping to around three hundred feet and turning for his approach towards the airfield, when his cockpit was suddenly filled with a bright orange glow. Instinctively he looked up ahead and saw a huge column of flame spurt into the sky. His stomach lurched, his hands tensed and the plane dropped a wing. He quickly righted himself, but he was no longer looking at the instrument panel—but rather at the line of the flare-path and the mass of flames at the far end of the flare-path. For a moment he was unable to focus, numbed into a sense of detachment from where he was and what he was doing. The Harvard was rapidly dropping, the line of flares and the fire ahead of him approaching too quickly.

A green light flashing caught his eye and suddenly he breathed again. *Come on, take a hold of yourself.* His hand gripped the control column—too tightly, he knew, but all he had to do was land. *Concentrate, think,* he told himself, pulling back the throttle and glancing at the altimeter and artificial horizon. Swaying a bit, but steady enough. Seventy-five feet, sixty, fifty. *Oh Christ, the undercarriage!* The flares were now right in front of him. Forty feet, and the wheels whined back down into position, a click as they reached their full extent. Just seconds later, the Harvard jolted as it touched the ground—*Jesus, that was close*—the flares speeding under his wings once again and the flaming wreckage at the end of the airfield rushing towards him. Cutting the throttle, he bumped across the rough field. But he was in one piece, safe.

Joss pulled back the canopy and heaved himself out and onto the wing, then jumped onto the ground. For a moment he stayed there on his knees, breathing in deeply, the air sharp and cold. The lantern in the nearby flight tent and the flames still burning at the end of the runway cast the parked Harvard in a curious glow, making it look ugly, menacing and lethal. But now silent, apart from the engine ticking as it cooled.

'You all right, sir?'

Joss glanced round. Heyward was standing behind him. He hastily got up, but felt light-headed and put a hand out onto the wing to steady himself.

'Fine, thank you, Flight,' he said, forcing a smile. 'Really, quite fine.' Then he said, 'What the hell

259

happened?'

'Parker, sir. I'm afraid he crashed as he came into land. A minute or two before you came in.'

'Christ.'

Heyward put a hand on his shoulder. 'We'll talk about the flight tomorrow. For now, go and have a drink, then get some sleep.'

Tommy had bought him two Scotches. Most of the trainees were in the mess, but it was a subdued crowd that night, stunned into silence by the news of Parker's death. Joss had barely known him; he'd been one of the older ones—a surveyor before the war. It was like that—groups had quickly formed; but the isolation and sense of shared purpose bound them all together.

'Better now?' said Tommy.

Joss nodded. 'Thought I was going to crash too,' he said. 'For a moment, I lost control up there. Recovered in the nick of time, then realized the wheels weren't down. I thought I'd had it, Tommy, I really did.'

'Well, you're fine now, that's the main thing.'

'He was married, you know,' said Joss. 'Two children.'

'Accidents happen.'

'I know. But it doesn't make it any less shocking when it does. I mean, that could have been us, Tommy.'

Tommy drew on his cigarette, then leant his head back and exhaled a series of perfectly formed smoke rings. 'But it wasn't Joss. We'll be all right, don't you worry.'

*   *   *

The following day they'd been called together by the station commander, who'd given them a lecture about cockpit drill. It was, he told them, entirely due to the pilot's carelessness that Acting Pilot Officer Parker had been killed. Had he done his cockpit checks properly he'd have realized his artificial horizon wasn't working. As a result, two small children were without their father and a wife without a husband, not to mention the wrecked Harvard.

Joss couldn't stop thinking about the column of flame and the panic that had nearly caused him to crash too. Nothing wrong with *his* cockpit checks, just a failure of nerve when the going got tough. Heyward insisted they fly again immediately, but Joss found it hard to concentrate. The control column was stiff in his hand, his aerobatics appalling, and they bounced four times as he landed. The following day was little better. As Joss turned in to land, the Harvard lurching from side to side, Heyward said nothing. Nor did he say anything as they hit the ground and once more bounced several times along the runway. Joss knew he'd flown badly, that he was letting himself down, but that made him worse. Miserably, he taxied over towards the flight tent and came to a halt.

'Don't unplug any of your leads yet,' said Heyward. He paused for a moment then said, 'Incredible though it is, that was even worse than yesterday. I told you when you arrived here that you were a bloody awful pilot. Well, you're even worse now. In fact, you ought to be kicked off the course right away.'

'I don't know what's the matter with me,' said Joss. 'I just can't do it any more.'

261

'I do,' said Heyward. 'I know exactly what's the matter with you. You had a shock the other night and you're feeling so bloody sorry for yourself that your fragile confidence has been shattered. But having a delicate disposition is no fucking good in the middle of a fucking war. Believe me, sir, if you ever make it out of here, you're going to see a lot worse than Parker blowing himself up. So bloody well get a hold of yourself. Try and grow up and behave like a man and not a bloody schoolboy.' He was silent again. Joss was glad he didn't have to look him in the eye. 'Now, I'm going to give you just one chance for you to show me what you're made of. I want you to take off, head out over the coast then practise flick-rolls, barrel rolls, Immelmans and a couple of stalls, and I want them to be perfect. Then I want you to fly back and perform the best landing of your life. I'm not going to say a word until we get back. All right? And sir?'

'Yes, Flight?'

'Don't you dare let me down.'

For a moment, Joss sat in the cockpit, stung with anger and humiliation. How dare Heyward talk to him like that. What did he know? He hadn't been there, hadn't seen the ground looming towards him. He hadn't felt the total lack of control, or the paralysing terror of those moments. The engine spurted into life once more. *I'll show you*, thought Joss.

Forty minutes later they glided onto the runway. Throughout the flight, Joss's anger had been increasingly replaced by triumphant elation as the Harvard turned and rolled about the sky with seemingly effortless ease. What a cunning old sod he was! thought Joss. Of course, Heyward had been right. *Of course he had.*

'Right,' said Heyward as they walked back to the flight tent, 'I think we can start really working up towards your wings examination now you've remembered how to fly.'

*   *   *

That had been a week ago, and now, having safely delivered the Harvard to Lossiemouth and been driven back, his examination was almost upon him. At half-past one, wearing his Sidcot suit and gauntlets, his parachute slung over his shoulder, he was back by the flight tent, waiting to be told which plane he would be flying. Heyward appeared. 'Take 4925, sir,' he said. 'Go and do your checks then wait for your examiner. And good luck, sir. Remember: make sure you stay relaxed.'

Calm down, calm down. He paced round the Harvard, waggling the ailerons and elevators, checking the rudder. Then he clambered into the cockpit and with one of the riggers, checked all the instruments. Out again, another check around the outside. Still working. Back into the cockpit. Three times in and out before the examiner—the Chief Flying Instructor—arrived, walking briskly towards him and looking at his watch.

'All right then, Lambert, let's get on with it.'

Joss tried to take his time strapping himself in. *Relax, remember.* He flexed his fingers, took a deep breath. Never before had a particular moment in time been so critical. In under an hour his future would be decided. He could even be packing his bags and leaving Kinloss in a few hours' time. *Mustn't think like that.* Heyward had told him he was as ready as he'd ever be. He must draw comfort from that. If Heyward believed he could do it, then surely he could. One chug, then another, the propeller jerking. Then a whirr in front of him and the whole plane trembled and rattled.

'All set Lambert?'

'Yes, thank you sir.'

'Good. Taxi, then take off and climb due north to nine thousand feet.'

As soon as he was airborne, a strange calmness settled over him. It was odd how one minute he could be hurtling down the runway, yet the next that sense of speed had evaporated. Up over Lindhorn, where Mr McLeish lived, and out over the grey-green North Sea.

He knew what to expect. Spins, stalls, then some aerobatics. A week before he'd thought he was finished, but now, as he climbed through the cloudless winter sky, he knew he was in total control. He had tamed the Harvard, so that it did whatever he wanted of it.

Back over land, the highlands stretching away beneath them. Joss checked his altimeter: 9,000— time to level off. Instructions from the examiner: a spin to the left until he was told to recover. Joss pulled the stick as far back as it would go into his stomach, and pushed his foot down hard on the left-hand rudder. The Harvard shuddered then the port wing dropped and they were spiralling out of the sky, the mountains below spinning and twisting, and growing all too quickly.

'Recover.' Flat, dispassionate, despite corkscrewing down through thousands of feet of sky in a matter of seconds.

Joss pressed down fully on the opposite rudder,

and pushed the stick as far forward as it would go, and—*thank God*—the spinning stopped. Throttle open, stick eased back once more, and the Harvard was flying straight and level again. He grinned to himself. How many times over the past months had Heyward to come to his rescue? Well, he'd wished Heyward could have seen that one. *Bloody near perfect!*

They climbed again, up to 6,000 feet. Aerobatics next. 'Relax, don't grip the stick too tight,' Heyward had told him over and over again, and for so long Joss had had to really concentrate not to clench his fingers around the control column. But now— suddenly he understood, and it gave him a sense of empowerment, as though the Harvard were a trained animal, and he its master. A perfect barrel roll, the height exactly the same as when he began the manoeuvre. 'And another one,' his examiner told him. Joss watched the altimeter, pushed down a bit more on the rudder. *Piece of cake.* Loops, steep turns, stalls. Then an imaginary forced landing on a lone bank of cloud, the engine cut, the Harvard drifting silently through the January sky.

'Thank you, Lambert. Back to Kinloss please.' A fleeting moment of panic as they flew through more cloud—*where had that come from?*—and, for a few moments, Joss lost his bearings. Then there was the coast and Inverness. Easy. A short stretch up the coast and they would back. Joss signalled the airfield and was given the all-clear to land. Throttle back, undercarriage down—*watch the height and speed*—and only the slightest of jerks as they landed on all three wheels. Joss taxied off the runway, the engine now quietly idling, and punched his thigh. Surely he'd done it. Must have been good enough. He'd done everything asked of him, hadn't he? Joss looked at the examiner in the mirror, hoping for a sign, but the instructor was casually undoing his harness and helmet straps, and making no effort to engage in telling eye contact.

'Thank you, Lambert. That's enough for today.' They both stepped out and back onto the grass. A quick note on a clipboard from the examiner, then he strode off as purposefully as he'd arrived. Joss suddenly felt exhausted, his legs weak as he stumbled back to the flight tent.

*   *   *

Heyward later congratulated him. 'The CFI was pleased, sir. Thought you seemed very competent.'

'Does that mean I passed?' Joss asked.

'The flying part, certainly. Well done, sir.'

'No, thank *you* Flight, thank you very much.' He shook his hand vigorously. 'It was your doing not mine.' *Thank God,* thought Joss. After all that time, he'd done it.

A day later both Tommy and Peter passed theirs, too. But elation soon evaporated. One hurdle had been jumped only for them to face another. The written examinations were, as their instructors repeatedly told them, every bit as important as the practical test. Three more nights of staying up late and cramming over their books, then they were sitting in the examination hall, Joss staring at the sheet of white paper face down on the desk in front of him, the examiner looking up at the clock at the end of the room. The minute hand clicked into position.

'All right, gentlemen. You may begin.'

Results were posted at the end of the week on a notice board outside the mess. Joss, Tommy and Peter were trying to jostle their way forward to see, but there were a number of other trainees in front of them crowding around the results list. One man looked ashen. Others grinned and shook hands. A sudden gap at the front and Peter squeezed in.

'We're in!' he shouted, turning to Tommy and Joss. 'We're bloody well in!' Joss pushed in alongside him. And there it was: APO J Lambert, on the list of those now entitled to wear the flying badge on their tunics.

'Well, I don't know about you,' grinned Peter, 'but I'm going to go and get those wings sewn on right away.' They almost ran back to their rooms— round the main buildings, and across a short pathway to the rows of curved Nissen huts. Joss swung open the door, and there, hanging on his wardrobe, was his blue tunic, the pilots' wings already sewn on above the breast pocket. *Mr McLeish.* But how had he known? Joss ran his finger across the bumpy needlework. Could there be anything more coveted in the entire world?

Cairo—October, 1942

For all those weeks he'd lain festering in the hospital, he had heard the city, smelled the city, but seen little of it. A constant rumble of noise—the noise of millions of Arabs, Australians, Africans,

Americans, British, New Zealanders, Canadians, Indians, donkeys, mules, cats, dogs, pigs, goats, monkeys, chickens and rats all flung together into the seething melting pot of Cairo.

A never-ending background murmur, but the shock of stepping beyond the hospital confines had been quite overwhelming, similar to the bewilderment that had struck him the first time he'd arrived in the city eighteen months before. He was going to a convalescent home—to stay with Mr and Mrs Harberry, an English couple who owned a large villa in one of the more respectable suburbs. Mrs Harberry had sent a car—a sleek, shining American Chrysler of deep maroon and chrome— which had been waiting for him as he'd hobbled out of the main entrance. A dapper Egyptian had dashed out of the driver's seat and rushed to open the rear door.

'Please, sir,' he said, holding out an arm.

'Thank you,' said Joss, handing him one walking stick then the other, and swinging himself onto the back seat.

A quick glance in the mirror from the driver and then they pulled off, along the driveway through the hospital grounds and up to the main gate with its swing barrier. A nod from the guard, the barrier lifted and then—whoosh—like opening a door on to a loud and drunken party, there was Cairo. In the road in front, cars jostled with animals and people, horns blared. Two, then five children clawed at the open window of the car. 'Baksheesh, baksheesh.' Plaintive brown eyes staring at him, grubby little hands cupped open.

'I don't have anything to give you,' said Joss. He patted his pockets. 'I don't have anything.' The driver turned round and spurted a tirade of Arabic, then lurched into the road. Joss looked behind him, but the children had already scurried off, looking for their next target.

It was true. He had nothing. Ill-fitting khaki-drill shirt and trousers—rather than shorts—to protect his legs, his shoes, underpants and socks and two letters from Stella that had been in his breast pocket when he crashed. Not even a handkerchief, and he never liked to be without one of those. He wondered what had happened to his trunk. When someone died, one or other of them would go through everything, then it would be sent on to GHQ in Cairo and there, presumably, eventually returned to his family. But what happened when someone was wounded? He couldn't really remember.

Ahead was the back-end of a cart piled high with some kind of green plant. The driver was pressing his hand almost continually down on the horn, then leaning out of his window and yelling at the cart-driver. Huge billboards towered over them by the side of the road. Lana Turner and Hedy Lamarr roughly painted in garish colours stared down at him—all ruby lips and white teeth. Below, street vendors shouted, whilst a couple of men stood by high-piled crates of cooped-up chickens. Next to them, stacks of watermelon, oranges and lemons. A sudden waft of cooking, sweetly savoury. Two soldiers were being accosted, but they were walking onwards, refusing to look the Egyptians in the eye. An old woman, dressed in black sitting in a doorway. More shouting: an argument on the pavement, three Egyptians all gesticulating wildly. A tram hurtling past, bell clanging. *'We guarantee our watches are sand, water and shock proof—ideal for the desert,'* he read on a sign above one shop. Past a large terrace crammed with officers and safragi carrying trays of drinks.

'Shepheard's Hotel,' said the driver, as though Joss were a tourist.

Then onwards, the traffic on the road slowly thinning, past the Abdin Barracks and the Egyptian Parliament and away from the hub of the city towards Maadi, until they reached a quieter residential suburb, with wide tree-lined streets, partially hiding the large European villas and houses.

The car slowed and they turned into a drive lined with bougainvillaea and towering palm trees. At the top of a gentle rise lay the house, a large modern villa, creamy white but with bright blue shutters either side of its windows. A pillared veranda spread out onto the garden. There were some people sitting there. Both the villa and gardens were almost entirely hidden from their neighbours by more trees—varying kinds of eucalyptus and a banyan that also offered large patches of gentle shade.

The car drew up by a widened semi-circle at the front of the house. A safragi dressed in a long white djellaba and red fez scurried down the steps and opened the door.

'Welcome to *Villa Jacaranda,* sir,' he said, as Joss passed him his two sticks.

'Thank you.' He carefully swivelled his legs out onto the drive and pulled himself up. Taking his sticks he rested a moment then began walking to the steps. At that moment a lady wearing a red silk dress with large daisies printed on it breezed onto the porch.

'Now you must be Flight Lieutenant Lambert,' she said. Her bright lipstick and smile reminded Joss of the billboard painting of Lana Turner. Her hair was even curled in a similar fashion. 'It's *so* lovely to have you. Walter and I just *adore* having so many dashing young men about the place.'

She came down the steps to greet him. 'I'm Mrs Harberry, but everyone calls me Binny—I know, silly name—and so must you. Here, let me help,' she said, taking his hand. 'And what should we call you?'

'Joss. Everyone just calls me Joss.'

'Joss,' she repeated. 'I knew a Joss once. Scottish chap. Or was he Irish? Doesn't really matter. But he became a sailor. Anyway, Joss, I hope you'll be happy here. There's quite a few of you staying, actually—six at last count and now you, so that makes seven—although you're the only pilot. And I hear a fighter pilot too.' Joss nodded, uncertain how to respond. 'It must be terribly exciting flying those planes of yours,' she continued, 'I once went up in a Tiger Moth over the Pyramids before the war. Quite the most marvellous thing I've ever done.'

They went through the open front door into a spacious hallway. At one end stood a large stone fireplace, although it looked as though it had never been used. 'It can get really rather icy in winter,' she said, following his gaze, 'not that you'd think it now.' On the walls hung hunting prints—scarlet tunics, England in winter—and a large antelope head. The furniture looked as though it had nearly all come from England: an oak sideboard, hatstand and a round table rather like the one in the hallway

271

at Alvesdon Farm.

'Now, you're down here, sharing with Dobbo. Well, his real name's Walter, but my husband's called Walter too and we can't have more than one—it would be too confusing. But since we were here first, my Walter takes precedence, and so we call him Dobbo, short for Dobson. He's lost a leg, poor fellow, so like you, we try to keep him away from stairs. There is a downstairs loo—lap of luxury, but when we moved here I absolutely *insisted*—but I'm afraid you'll have to hobble upstairs if you want a bath.' She opened the door onto a large square room with whitewashed walls, two beds and a walnut tallboy with brass handles. 'Da-dah!' she said, ushering him in.

Joss smiled. 'Thank you,' he said, 'this is wonderful.'

'Used to be our son's room, but he doesn't need it for the moment.'

'Is he back in England?' asked Joss.

'Yes—boarding school in Shrewsbury and then with his aunt and uncle. Haven't seen him for just over three years. He's sixteen now.' She looked wistful for a moment, then said, 'Which is why we love having you young chaps here. Keeps us entertained. And look,' she said, leaning by the one unused bed, 'what we have here.' Joss hobbled over to help her, as she began pulling out his old leather trunk from underneath. 'It arrived just yesterday.'

Ah, at last! Funny how in the car he had felt curiously unconcerned about it, but now that it was sitting there on the floor in front of him, he wanted to open it immediately, to reread old letters, to see those few belongings that *were* his and his alone.

'Dobbo's out on the veranda, I think,' she said,

'with two of the others. The other three are all doing part-time work now at GHQ.' She looked around the room thoughtfully, then said, 'I'll leave you now to settle in. Come and join the others whenever you're ready.'

*　　　*　　　*

As soon as he heard Binny's footsteps disappearing down the hallway, he went over to the door and quietly closed it, then immediately returned to his trunk. There was a blast of mustiness as he pushed back the lid, then lifted out three bundles of letters: those from Stella, a bunch from Guy and then a bundle of miscellaneous others—from Tommy, Diana, Celia, other friends from the air force— each tied neatly by a bootlace. He picked up his letters from Stella, put them to his nose, and breathed in for a moment, before looking at them once more. There was her unmistakable high-looped handwriting on each of the envelopes; but the ink was already fading, and with it, the fragile thread that linked her to him The thought of her, of the way she looked, sitting at her table in her room in Alvesdon Farm, was harder to picture now. Carefully, he placed them back in the trunk.

A glance at his watch. *Mustn't be too long.* But these moments alone were precious. Binny seemed to understand. He picked up the bundle from Guy. The writing more irregular—slanting to the left in one letter, to the right in the other, his scrawl distinguishable simply because it was so unlike any other. Joss flicked through the envelopes. *February 15ᵗʰ 1940.* He pulled out the pale blue paper and began to read. First of all a reproof. *'Thanks for my*

273

overwhelming flood of letters. Not one for over a month! What fickle friends you and Tommy have become. Is flying really so wonderful that you haven't the time to drop me a line?' Well, partly, that had been true. Another of those obsessions Tommy had once talked about, but there had been more to it than that. The workload had not lightened once they'd won their wings. The second part of the course had been just as intense: formation flying, gunnery, more navigation, more lessons. And up at Kinloss they'd been so isolated, that if he didn't write about flying—and he had been mindful to try not to—there had been little else to say. A week off after the wings, but it had hardly been worth trekking down south. Instead he and Tommy had gone walking in Skye.

'You'll be pleased to hear you're not the only ones doing your bit,' Guy had written. *'Regular notices from the government assure me the land is Britain's battlefield now. We're down to just nine men now, including me. Do you realize there used to be at least twenty-four in Dad's day? I'm having to work like a Trojan. Up at the crack of dawn every day—me! can you believe it?—toiling to keep you fed. It'd be quite funny if I didn't feel so damned exhausted.'* Joss smiled to himself; Guy had never once made it to any of his nine o'clock lectures during their time at Cambridge. He said getting up early simply didn't agree with him. *'At least Sam Hicks has stayed—I don't know where I'd be without him. There's so much to learn—I'd never appreciated farming was so complicated. You'll laugh, but the men all call me 'The Boss'—if only I felt I deserved it.* Then a passage about Stella. She was being impossible. *'She's already bored by the war. Bored of her*

274

secretarial job, bored of nothing happening, and, as she puts it, bored of seeing Philip and all the other chaps prancing about in uniform pretending to be soldiers. I keep telling her she should pack in London and come down and give me a hand with the farm. I'm almost serious, too.'

By that time, Guy had been effectively running the farm for six months, and from his letters, it had been clear he'd been having a hard time. Local farmers had been galvanized into committees to make farming more efficient. Wiltshire alone, Guy had told him, had been ordered to farm an extra 40,000 acres of land every year if they were to have enough food for everyone. Most of the land that ran along the Herepath at the top of the downs had been turned over to crops. The sheep that had grazed there for centuries were put onto only the steepest land. Many were culled. Cereals had become the prime concern. Cereals and milk, and so the dairy herd had remained. Whatever the weather, Guy had to be up to milk the cows. Then there were the never-ending tasks of re-fencing, ploughing, and harrowing. Two of the evacuees had gone back to London, but two had remained, so Guy made them help too, after school and during the holidays and at weekends.

'I feel exhausted,' he had written in this particular letter. *'I see Mum briefly at mealtimes, but I hardly have the energy to speak. It's very odd living here all the time, just Mum, me and, of course, Francis and Ruby. But then I'm not really living here—not like we used to—because I seem to spend all my time on the farm. Were those carefree days really less than a year ago? I'm mourning their passing, and I don't care if that sounds melodramatic. What I would do to*

rewind the clock and have those times again. Wouldn't you love to spend a night by the hearth of the Blue Lion? Actually, you're probably having too much fun flying over Scotland to miss our long-lost youth. Pity us real war-workers!'

Joss folded the letter, carefully slipped it back into the envelope and tied it up again with all the others. He did mourn for those days. He mourned them very much.

*   *   *

On the veranda, Joss met the 'stay-at-homes' as Binny called the house-bound convalescents. The three of them were sitting in wicker chairs, drinking coffee and reading newspapers, which they lowered with half-smiles as Joss emerged through the French doors. Trying their best to look interested, but the months of pain, boredom and increasing disenchantment were difficult to disguise. Joss raised a hand—a half-smile back, a nod. *It's all right, I understand.*

Binny, who had been sitting with them, immediately stood up and cheerily introduced him. Another burns victim—Brian—a twenty-year-old lieutenant who'd managed to escape from his burning tank when it had 'brewed up'; his new room-mate, Dobbo, a curly-haired captain of twenty-four; and Mark, a young lieutenant who'd had his right arm badly 'mucked about' by a tank mine. It was pretty useless now, he told Joss, but he'd been lucky not to have had it amputated. A bit of cursory chat, then back to the newspapers.

Later, Binny insisted she show Joss the garden. 'I'm very proud of my garden,' she told him. 'We

276

have a dazzling array of plants, you know, far more exotic than anything one might have back home. I say "home", but in fact, we've been living here for nearly ten years. Still, England is home, isn't it? Even the man who's lived in Africa nearly all his life thinks that.'

'Yes, I suppose it is.'

'And where's home for you, Joss?'

He didn't answer straight away, then he said, 'Wiltshire—near Salisbury.'

'Oh lucky you,' said Binny. 'Lovely part of the world.'

'Yes,' said Joss. 'What about you?'

'London, I suppose—that's where Walter and I lived when we were first married, although my parents still live near Alton in Hampshire.' She looped an arm through his, occasionally pausing to smell a flower or inspect a leaf. Zinnias, more bougainvillaea, poinsettias, oleander, jasmine—all proudly pointed out by Binny. A light, fragrant smell, reminding Joss of the *pot pourri* Tommy often kept in his room at Cambridge, suffused the dry autumnal heat. Although they were still within the suburbs of Cairo, the grounds were quite large: lawns of dry grass, edged by borders overflowing with plants and shrubs, and a variety of palms and other trees that shielded them from their neighbours.

'It's Mark that I'm most worried about,' she told him. 'Don't ever let on, but it was a friend of his who'd actually stepped on the mine. His foot landed on Mark's head. Ghastly for him.'

'Awful.'

'Makes me shudder just thinking about it. No wonder he's in a bad way.'

'I suppose I've been lucky being a pilot,' said Joss. 'We don't get to see too many bodies.'

'No,' said Binny, 'I suppose it's more about shooting down a machine than the men who are in it.'

'I've always tried to think of it that way.' Not too many bodies, thought Joss, but enough. Each one had sickened him: the Germans in the Junkers that crashed above Alvesdon Farm; the pilot in that spectral Spitfire; the man whose parachute had caught on the plane as he'd baled out of that Dornier; not many, but enough. Then there'd been the Italian in that Macchi he'd shot down a few months before. *That Italian.* His goggles had been off his face, and Joss had seen him—seen the expression on his face. Not surprise exactly, nor fear—but bafflement. 'Never shoot until you can see the whites of his eyes' had been Mac's line; well, Joss had seen them clear as day. A beam attack at about fifty yards— unbelievably close. He'd pressed his thumb down on the tit and bang! Suddenly there'd been no more eye contact, as he'd shot half the Italian's face away. He hadn't meant to—he'd *meant* to just get him in the engine, force him to bale out. 'Get anything?' Robinson, the Intelligence Officer had asked. 'A Macchi 202,' Joss had told him, after he'd safely made it back to the landing ground. The machine, not the man.

'He needs all of us to help him, I think,' said Binny. She looked at him, seeing his confusion. 'Mark?'

Mark—yes, of course.

'He's so young. Of course, you're all young, but he especially so.'

'I'll certainly try,' said Joss, and then, having safely imparted the main purpose of their stroll, Binny began talking about inconsequential things once more—Cairo, plants, the merits of their cook.

*   *   *

Joss met the rest of the household later. Although October, the British still stopped work at lunchtime, then returned to their offices some time in the middle of the afternoon. Walter, Binny explained, rarely came home during this siesta, instead preferring to head off to the Gezira Club for a swim and some tennis. 'He likes to keep fit,' she said. The other convalescents, Binny told him, were not expected back at GHQ in the afternoon. 'They usually pitch up in time for tea on the lawn,' she said, and so it proved. There were three of them: Colin, a captain with the sappers, who'd lost an eye; Rick, another youthful-looking lieutenant; and Tony, who, with a moustache already flecked with grey, appeared noticeably older than the rest of them.

The chatter became more animated now the others were back. Sir Miles Lampson had been at GHQ and had spoken to Rick; the ambassador had told him they were soon going to rid Egypt of Rommel and his army. Tony agreed that the mood at GHQ was certainly much improved: more and more reinforcements were being sent to the front. There was news that two more of Rommel's tankers had been sunk *en route* to Tobruk. Colin told them about another large shipment of American Sherman tanks that had safely reached Alex, although, he added, this was not to be repeated. 'Keep it to yourselves, all right?'

Tony then asked if anyone was up for a game of Scrabble. Colin and Binny put up their hands.

'Anyone else?' said Tony. 'Joss, what about you? Make the fourth?'

'All right,' said Joss, and the four of them moved back to the veranda.

Walter Harberry appeared not longer after. On first meeting, he appeared every bit as affable and hearty as his wife. Firm handshake—drink?—*tell me all about it.* Then a bit about himself. A lot of his friends were now in uniform, but he'd stayed with the bank. 'They need us money-men even more than ever,' he told Joss, 'Of course, you chaps are taking the brunt, but the thing about this war is: everybody's doing their bit. Even pen-pushing bankers like me. Been out here long?' he said, suddenly changing the subject.

'On and off, yes. Early last year, then a stint instructing in Khartoum, then back again in April.'

'Back home again in that time?' *There it was again—'home'.*

'No.'

Walter rubbed his chin. He had a large beaked nose, which dominated an otherwise good-looking face. His still-dark hair was brilliantined neatly to his head. 'You're not by any chance related to Johnny and Edwina Lambert are you? Got a place down on the south coast. Lymington, I think it is.'

Joss shook his head. 'No, I'm from a very small family.' *A small family in England, at any rate.*

'Oh well. Just thought I'd mention it. Funny how often one does discover these strange coincidences, though.'

'Yes I know. When I was first wounded, I ended

280

up lying on a stretcher next to someone I hadn't seen since we'd been at the same dinner party a year before the war.'

Walter laughed. 'Really? Well I'm blowed. Just goes to show doesn't it?'

*   *   *

Tea on the lawn, Scrabble, drinks, dinner. A seamless flow of English hospitality.

'You must ask Tony how he got his "wound",' Rick said to Joss at dinner. Smirks from the others.

'Now, now, Rick,' said Binny.

'It's all right, Binny,' said Tony. He smiled wearily. 'It's the cause of much amusement to this lot, Joss, but I did in my knee jumping off the back of a fifteen-hundredweight truck. Kneecap halfway round my leg. Agony, though, I can assure you.'

'He's such an old man,' said Rick, 'his joints aren't up to it any more.'

Joss smiled. 'I know someone who did much the same thing jumping down from his plane. He'd already survived a bullet through the shoulder and reckoned the knee was the far more painful of the two. And he was only twenty.'

'Hear that, Rick?' said Tony.

'I still think you should leave the fighting to us younger chaps,' said Rick.

Tony looked at Joss. 'You'd have thought I was fifty not thirty-two.' He took the ribbing well. 'All I can say is that it's a good job the big-wigs at the War Office don't agree with you,' he said. 'Otherwise I'd be stuck in England with the Home Guard rather than eating this delicious dinner with our delightful hosts.'

281

It *was* delicious, *and* a proper dinner, even if only a couple of courses. Perhaps in peacetime Joss would have found the chicken a bit stringy, but it had been the first time he'd sat down to a hot meal with a proper knife and fork, *and* wine since his last leave in Cairo back in May.

'What have we got for pudding?' asked Walter Harberry as two safragi came to clear the plates.

'Spotted dick and custard,' said one.

Walter nodded approvingly, then turned the conversation back to the British build-up at the front. Colin repeated his news about the Shermans.

'Good,' said Walter. 'I'm fed up of hearing the bloody gyppos taunting us about the Germans. I know we're not out of the woods yet, but after Alam Halfa, well—'

Colin cut in. 'Rommel's clearly over-extended himself. I'd say we've got him pretty much where we want him, to be honest.'

'I do so hope you're right,' said Binny. 'I don't think I could bear to go through another flap like the last one.'

*   *   *

After dinner, Joss still felt wide awake. He'd become used to sleeping little at night and was glad when Walter suggested a nightcap in the main drawing room. One whisky became three and when he returned to his room, Dobbo was already in bed and fast asleep. His room-mate had said little, and Joss wondered whether he had always been quiet, or whether he'd become so since losing his foot. Moving around as quietly as he could, Joss undressed and washed, then eased himself into his

282

new bed. He'd thought the whisky had made him drowsy, but now that he was lying there, sleep still felt a long way off. It was at times like this that he wished he could write to Stella—or Guy for that matter. *'Well, I'm out of the accursed hospital at last,'* he began in his mind, *'and living in a luxurious villa abounding with safragi and sociable, affable hosts. Although I'm surrounded by the ever-present sound of insects and the smell of heat and dust, this is about the most English environment I've been in since leaving home, and it makes me long for Alvesdon Farm more than ever.'*

He sighed and turned over. His wounds would probably buy him a ticket to England, but what would he find when he got there?

*   *   *

At some point he must have drifted off to sleep for he was dreaming when he first heard the noise. He was looking at a brick-paved stableyard and someone was sweeping it with a large broom, but very slowly. Then the stableyard changed to sand and he was in Egypt, watching the safragi who'd brought in the spotted dick; and then he was definitely awake, but for a moment was disorientated and couldn't think where he was. He turned over saw that Dobbo was sitting up in his bed, reading by the light of an electric torch. It had been the turning of the page he'd heard in his sleep.

'Sorry,' he said, 'did I wake you?'

Joss rubbed his eyes. 'Don't worry.'

'I can't stop waking up in the middle of the night, I'm afraid, and then I can never get back to sleep again. Tend to lie here brooding. But I've discovered reading something boring helps, and the Harberrys have lots of boring books.' He looked at the spine. ' "The Life of Benjamin Disraeli",' he said. 'Fascinating to some, I suppose.'

'But not to you.'

'No.' He dropped the book onto his lap and stared at the end of his bed. The half-light of the torch cast an outsize shadow of his head and shoulders on the wall beside him. 'Keep thinking I've still got my leg. Itches like hell, but there's nothing there. What kind of a trick is that?'

Joss shrugged.

'I used to be really good at sport,' said Dobbo. 'Bloody useless in the classroom, but good with a ball. Even captained the school at rugger and soccer.'

'What happened?'

'Trod on a mine. Hardly a unique case. Just wish it had been an anti-tank one and done the job properly instead of leaving me a one-legged freak.' He rubbed his cheek, then said, 'Sorry. I don't mean to bang on about it.'

'It's all right.'

Dobbo sighed, leant back, and banged the back of his head gently against the wall. 'This war's been going on too long. What's the chance of sticking it out for three years and not picking a wound or worse? Not much, I suppose.'

'You joined before the war?' asked Joss.

'Straight out of school and off to OCTU,' said Dobbo. 'You?'

'Volunteer Reserves. Got called up two days before war broke out.'

'Battle of Britain?'

Joss nodded.

284

'Could have done with your lot at Dunkirk.' A familiar jibe, and one ignored.

'You were out in France?'

'Yes—survived that. Picked up, and home briefly. Then packed off to Egypt and back and forth across North bloody Africa. Foot left somewhere in the desert, a variety of hospitals then the lovely Villa Jacaranda and our oh-so-charming hosts.' He looked up and apologized again. 'I'm sorry. I've become rather bitter.'

'Don't be. To tell the truth, so have I.' They were silent for a moment, Joss wondering whether he should elaborate. He guessed Dobbo was thinking much the same. Instead he said, 'I lost a good friend in France.'

'Who was he with?'

'Queen's Own Royal Wilts.'

'Really?' Dobbo brightened. 'We were with some of them just before Dunkirk. What was his name?'

Joss sat up in bed, quite awake now. 'Liddell. Roger Liddell.'

'Well I'm damned. Yes, I certainly remember Roger. Don't think I'll ever forget him. We joined at the same time. Went through OCTU together. After our training I didn't see him again until those last few days in France.' He gave out a laugh. 'Old Walter was right about strange coincidences. So how come you knew him?'

'Known him half my life, but tell me, do you know what happened to him. Could he still be alive?'

Dobbo paused a moment, then looked at him curiously, as though he were suddenly unsure whether he should say any more. Then he said, 'You know, Roger Liddell was probably the bravest man I ever knew.'

England—May, 1940

Dunkirk. Joss had barely heard of the place until a few days ago, but suddenly it had become one of the best known spots in the world, the British Army's last hope.

They drove in silence, across the Thames at Southwark then on through Peckham, New Cross and Blackheath and out onto the Dover road, Tommy at the wheel, Joss next to him and Stella in the back, biting her nails and staring out of the window as London gave way to the Kent countryside.

'When do you think we'll get there, Tommy?' said Stella suddenly.

'Perhaps another hour. Depends on what else is on the road,' he told her.

Stella clicked her tongue impatiently then said, 'Have you got a cigarette, please?'

Tommy patted the pockets on his tunic, then stretched over to Joss's side and pulled open the glove compartment. 'Have a look in there will you, Joss? Should be some somewhere.'

Joss found a crumpled packet and passed them over. Tommy shook out two and put them both in his mouth, then pulled out his Zippo and with half an eye on the road, and half on the end of the two cigarettes, lit them and passed one back to Stella.

Smoke filled the car and Joss opened his window and watched the everyday life going on outside. The distinctive Kentish oasthouses peeked through the lush countryside, bursting with greenery and the first flush of summer. A little overcast, but warm enough. There was nothing in this peaceful scenery that betrayed the enormity of events unfolding sixty miles away on the French beaches. There were, however, a few hints that times were changing: farmers were cutting their hay, but although there were still a few fields where lines of workers swished the long grass with their scythes, there were now noticeably more tractors carrying out the lion's share of the work. Mechanized farming was the future, Guy had told him, a future accelerated by a government anxious to make as much from the land as was possible in this time of crisis. Alvesdon Farm had recently gained two brand-new tractors—bright blue Fordsons, of which Guy was very proud. *'These machines go just about anywhere—even up the side of Prescombe!'* he'd written, and promised to take Joss for a ride next time he was down.

A week before Joss and the others were due to leave Kinloss, the Germans launched their attacks in the Low Countries. For months on end the war had stalled but suddenly the Germans were trampling all before them. The news had shocked those at the small RAF station, none more so than Joss, because he knew that Roger was over in France with his regiment. He could hardly imagine what the Liddells were going through. After trying unsuccessfully for two nights to place a telephone call through to Alvesdon Farm, he eventually got through on the third time of trying. Guy had sounded strained. Had they heard anything, Joss had asked. Nothing, Guy had told him, nothing other than what was reported in the paper and on the wireless; they were all trying to keep busy. He was worried about his mother the most. 'She's

287

finding it hard to sleep. She's being brave, as you'd imagine, but she did say this was worse than last time when Dad and Uncle Alex were away.'

'Poor Celia. And are you all right?'

'Just about. It's sickening to think of Rog caught up in all this. But please come down as soon as you can—I'm longing to see you. It's been such a long time.'

Nearly nine months. After Kinloss, Joss was due some leave. He would, he told Guy, come down then.

The end of the course had brought disappointment, however. Neither Joss, Tommy or Peter had been posted back to their old Auxiliary squadron, but instead had been earmarked for Army Co-Operation. Of the twenty-nine who finished Flying Training School, twelve had been sent to bomber squadrons, four to fighters and the rest to Old Sarum to complete an Operational Training Unit on Lysanders. There had been a collective groan among the students as the announcement was made. Everyone not already training on bombers had fighters as their goal and they had assumed that this was where they would end up. Flying Lysanders—slow and ungainly—in whatever capacity was seen as a regressive step, not a move forward. Tommy was not only disappointed, but furious. 'What the hell do they want Army Co-Operation for?'

Peter had shrugged. 'I suppose someone's got to do it.'

'Rubbish. It's insane. We'll be lucky if we've got an army left in a few weeks' time. If the Germans can sweep through the Netherlands and France this easily, they're going to have a crack at Britain too aren't they? What good will Lysanders be then? The only thing that will save us are fighters and fighter pilots.'

'Well, maybe they'll change their minds then,' suggested Joss.

'They'd better,' said Tommy. 'Because at the moment their reasoning is totally incomprehensible.'

The one consolation for Joss was Old Sarum's proximity to Salisbury and Alvesdon Farm. Instead of spending evenings either studying or in the mess, he and Tommy could slip off and spend the night in the Blue Lion with Guy. Perhaps he could even spend his weekends at the farm.

They were given ten days before the course began. His training had been intense and the time had whistled by, but even so, he'd missed the Liddells and Alvesdon Farm very much. He'd thought about them often—especially Stella. The time away had done nothing to quell his feelings for her. As they left Kinloss and began the long drive south, it suddenly seemed as though he'd been away for an age and that life had altered far beyond the normal levels of progress. He'd felt impatient to be back.

But first he had to see his mother. Tommy dropped him off and he stood outside her door adjusting his cap to a jaunty angle and making sure the top button of his tunic was undone before ringing the bell. Although she had promised to be in, he was still relieved when she finally opened the door.

'Darling, you're back! And look at you—so handsome!' She embraced him and Joss smelled her familiar scent. She looked as well as ever. A few lines around the eyes, but nothing to suggest a

289

woman of over forty.

He held her for a moment at arm's reach. 'You look well. New haircut?'

She patted the back of her head with her hand. 'Yes, well, I've decided to go a bit shorter. D'you like it?'

'I think you look stunning.'

She laughed, then took his hand and led him inside. 'Come on—let's sit down. I want you to tell me *all* about it.'

'Look,' he said, pointing to his chest, 'my wings.'

'Darling, you are clever, and I'm very proud. Does that mean you've been promoted then?'

His heart sank. 'No. It means that I'm a proper qualified pilot. I wrote and told you, remember?'

'Of course I do. Sorry darling, but my brain's a bit all over the place today. Must be the excitement of seeing my son again. Shall we have some tea? Would you like some tea and a bit of cake?' Before he'd answered, she stood up and disappeared into the kitchen. Joss followed her.

'Not looking too good in France is it?' he said.

'No, but at least something's happening at last. Can't tell you how dull it's been here in London. Everyone's so strict, you know, with the blackout and everything and we've scarcely heard an aeroplane in months. So much for Anthony's talk of mass-bombing.'

'You sound like Stella.'

'Stella?'

'Guy's twin sister. You remember Guy?'

Diana raised her eyes. '*Yes.* I know who Guy is. There's no need to be sarcastic. So she's bored of the war too is she?'

Joss chuckled. 'Well, according to Guy she is.'

290

'Don't blame her. All the men are rushing about being frightfully self-important but with little to actually do. At least, not until a couple of weeks ago. Now I barely seem to see Anthony, although the good news is that he's taking us both out to dinner tonight.'

Joss looked crestfallen. 'Really? Does he have to?'

'I thought you'd be pleased. A decent meal after all that time stuck away up in Scotland.'

'I want to see *you*.'

She kissed him lightly on the cheek. 'But we've got each other to ourselves now. It'll be fun to go out later. Anyway, I want to show you off. And you must wear your uniform so he can see your wings.'

Not wanting to argue so soon after his arrival, he acquiesced. 'All right, then,' he smiled. 'You win. But I do want to talk to you about something else.'

'Sounds serious,' she said.

'I suppose it is.' On the drive down from Scotland, he had decided he would try and persuade Diana to leave London. Tommy was convinced London would be attacked before long and even Joss found his reasoning convincing. 'Things are not looking good,' he told her. 'Those bombers Anthony talked about might still come and I don't want you here when that happens.'

'Oh Joss, please don't start on that.'

'Maybe you should just listen to me a moment.'

'And maybe you should stop telling me what to do.'

'It's only because I don't want anything awful to happen to you.'

She softened. 'I know, and it's very sweet, but I'll be perfectly all right. I know how to look after myself.'

Joss dropped the matter, but brought it up again later on at dinner. Anthony had taken them to the Criterion. The place was packed, throbbing with uniforms and silk dresses.

'I've been trying to persuade her for ages, Joss,' said Anthony. 'Like talking to a brick wall.'

'And do you think we should be worried?'

Anthony looked around furtively, then leaning in closely, said, 'Of course no one's certain, but the Germans can't just sweep into Britain like they have everywhere else because there's the Channel in the way and we still have the RAF. Hitler's got plenty of bombers, though. We know that much. So it seems very likely they'll be over here before too long, and the capital's an obvious target. Winston's giving us plenty of fighting talk, but we need a miracle in the next few days if the army's going to be saved. It probably would be safer for you if you left town, Diana.'

Joss looked at his mother. 'Please consider it at least.'

'Oh all right—I'll *consider* it,' she said, then dabbing her mouth with her napkin added, 'Now can we talk about something else?'

Anthony gave Joss a look as though to say, *We've tried haven't we?* but really, Joss didn't think *he'd* tried very hard at all. Diana was his mistress— someone to entertain him when he was in London, and with a wife already in the country, he had the best of both worlds. *Of course* —suddenly it was all so blindingly clear: Anthony had no intention of forcing Diana to leave; and his mother never would because she feared he would leave her the moment she did, and then she would have nothing. Joss glanced across at Anthony. That man was making a fool of his mother; using her for his own amusement. He wished he had the nerve to stand up and punch him in the face. It was nothing less than he deserved.

His sense of disappointment and frustration had not left him the following morning and so he was delighted, when, during breakfast, he received a call from Guy.

'Guy! At last! Any news of Roger? Is it still all right if I come down tomorrow? I was thinking of catching an early train.'

Guy sighed. 'Um, well, I'm not sure.'

'What d'you mean? What's happened?'

'Listen, Joss—it's Roger. He's missing in France. We've just had the telegram.'

'Oh Christ, no.'

'I've already spoken to Stella and she's determined to go down to Dover and see if she can find out some news. And, well, to be honest, I'm not going to try and stop her. Anyway, Mum was wondering—we were both wondering—whether you'd go with her. It's going to be madness down there and I think it would be better if there were someone with her. Philip can't go and everyone else has work or something on. Do you think you could go? I wouldn't ask, only—'

'Of course I'll go with her. I'll do anything I can.'

'Thanks, Joss. We won't forget this.' His voice was beginning to break, so Joss took down Stella's address then called off. For a few moments he sat motionless in the hallway. Diana was singing gently in the bathroom, but otherwise the flat was still. He felt his throat tighten and a chill run down his back. *Why Roger?* It wasn't fair. And then he thought of

293

Guy and Celia opening the telegram in the doorway at Alvesdon.

* * *

Joss had phoned Tommy who immediately offered to take them down in his car. He would, he said, like to help, and anyway, wanted to see the British troops returning. Furthermore, he knew Dover well having made countless trips across the Channel from there. If Joss went to Stella's flat, he'd be with them in an hour. By eleven all three of them were in the car and crossing back over the Thames.

So far, Stella had not cried. On the bus to Kensington, Joss had worried about how he should react to her tears, then chided himself for being selfish. But then when he saw her, he realized there was anger in her eyes rather than grief. She'd said little, and even now, sat in the back of the car smoking her cigarette in silence. Joss glanced round at her, and gave her what he hoped was a reassuring smile, but she barely acknowledged him; instead she continued to stare out of the window, her eyes focused on some far off and indeterminate point.

They reached Dover early in the afternoon.

'My God, look at this,' said Tommy. The streets were heaving with khaki-clad men. Mostly British, but French too. Hollow-eyed, dirty, some with only half a uniform, but most—the British at any rate— were smiling despite their fatigue. Just glad to be home. Many of the doors along the streets were open, with women lining up to hand the troops mugs of tea and pieces of fruit and other food. Tommy inched his way forward then suggested they park and continue on foot. Joss watched, open-mouthed. For the past couple of days, this had been little more than a newspaper story. Now it was for real, the end-piece of a heroic retreat. He watched two particular men stumble past. Their faces were covered with oily grime and several days' growth of beard. One could barely keep awake—his friend gripped onto his arm while they staggered forward.

Stella unwound the window and leant out. 'Where are the Royal Wiltshires?' she asked over and over. Most barely looked up. One shrugged, another said, 'Dunno, miss.' Another asked for a cigarette.

Tommy parked the car in a quieter back street. No sooner had they stopped than Stella was out of the car and striding away from them.

'Stella, wait!' said Joss as he and Tommy ran to catch up.

'Stop a moment,' said Tommy. 'Please.'

'There isn't a moment to lose,' she said, 'I've got to find my brother.'

Joss grabbed her arm, so that she swung around to face him. 'Stella,' he said, 'there's thousands of troops all over the place and if you go charging off we won't get anywhere. We've got to think about this logically. The ships are going to be coming into the harbour so that's where we must go first. There's bound to be some officials or someone there who'll help us. Otherwise this is going to be like looking for a needle in a haystack.'

She blinked, as though startled by his sudden authority, then looked at his hand still gripping her arm. Following her gaze, he quickly let go.

'All right,' she said, her voice quiet. 'Let's go to

the harbour.'

They walked through streets crowded with soldiers. Most looked too tired to even notice them, but one barged into Joss and said, 'Where the hell were you then?' Joss was so startled he couldn't think of anything to say.

'What did he mean?' asked Stella.

'I've no idea,' said Joss.

Another group of soldiers saw Joss and Tommy's uniforms and looked at them with contempt. 'You've got a nerve being here in that kit,' muttered one.

'Beginning to wish I'd been in my civvies,' said Tommy, 'although what this is about I've no idea. It's not our fault we do our fighting in the air and not on the ground.'

'Perhaps we look too clean and well-rested,' suggested Joss.

As the harbour suddenly revealed itself, Stella whispered, 'Oh my God,' and put a hand to her mouth. Rows of ships were lined up along the harbour, stacked side by side, in places three deep. The quays extended out into the sea, lined with cranes silhouetted like giant gallows against the dull overcast sky. Troops were disembarking from an old cross-Channel ferry, now painted grey, as more ships inched past the breakwater. Further out to sea, the rest of the convoy approached the harbour. Elsewhere, smaller boats were queuing up to moor at the marina. No matter how large or small the vessel, every one was swarming with troops.

'It's like 1588 all over again,' said Tommy. 'Look at all these boats. There's even little pleasure cruisers out there.' More boats were slipping out of harbour, presumably heading back to the beaches

296

of Dunkirk.

Stella, followed by Tommy and Joss, almost ran towards the main harbour where there was a stack of three ships ready to disembark. A crowd of people had already gathered at one end of the quay to cheer the returning troops. Stella, with Tommy and Joss close behind, squeezed her way to the front.

'Sorry, miss,' said a soldier, conspicuous in his peaked cap and clean uniform. 'Can't go any further just at the minute.'

'But I'm looking for my brother,' she pleaded.

'Look, I'm sorry miss, but not now, all right? We've got thousands of troops just about to disembark and we need the quayside kept clear,' he told her, then seeing her crestfallen expression added, 'Try the station. We're sending most of them there.'

The three of them remained where they were, watching the spectacle unfolding before them from a distance. Lining the quay nearest to them was a rusting destroyer, and the wounded were being lifted off first, carried up the gangway by stretcher-bearers, leaving the standing crammed anxiously on deck. On the quayside, underneath the corrugated roofing that extended out from the port's depots and warehouses, were a number of VAD nurses standing by olive-green ambulances and lorries ready to take the badly wounded to hospital. Red-capped military police and a number of soldiers also stood by waiting to usher the returning army. Everyone waiting there appeared to have a specific job to do. Joss watched these scenes open-mouthed, and thought about how strange it was that amidst the chaos there was still that peculiarly

British sense of order.

Two medical orderlies stepped onto the quayside carrying a wounded man who was groaning loudly. Suddenly he tried to sit up and even from a distance of over a hundred yards, they heard his plaintive calls for his mother.

Now it was the turn of the walking wounded to disembark. Joss looked round and saw the men were already stomping up the gangway. Some clean-shaven, others with several days' growth of beard; some with torn and bloodied uniforms, others with little uniform at all. But although they looked tired and dirty, he was surprised by how many still had their tin hats and rifles. The soldiers and military police waiting for them began yelling instructions as the thousands began to stream onto British ground once more. Rifles were laid down against one of the warehouse walls, then the men were led forward. Those without shoes or basic items of clothing—one man was wearing pyjamas under his greatcoat—were also pulled out and taken to one side where piles of folded clothes and army boots were ready and waiting.

Then without warning, Stella suddenly made a dash past the guards and ran towards the edge of the quay where the soldiers were disembarking.

'Stella!' shouted Joss.

'Don't worry,' said Tommy, 'they'll bring her back.' They could see an angry red-cap call to another waiting soldier and order him to take hold of her. Taking her arm he pulled her out of the way of the men swarming onto the quay, and led her back. There was some laughter from the crowd.

'Get your hands off me!' said Stella, wriggling free from the soldier's grip.

'Come on Stella,' said Joss, 'this isn't the way.'

'I've got to find out about Roger,' she repeated.

'Not here,' said Joss. 'Come on.' She looked at him, her eyes wild, then seemed to relent.

'All right,' she said, pushing a strand of hair off her eyes.

As the first boat emptied, so the men from the next clambered aboard and in turn stumbled up the gangway like an enormous swarm of ants. Now the quayside had already become thick and dark with khaki. The front of the line was inching forward along the harbour's edge as more poured into the column from the stacked ships.

'What about a cup of tea?' shouted one of the men to the soldiers leading the way.

'Just as soon as we get you to the station,' replied one of the officers. 'Plenty for everyone there.' But there were already a number of civilians—older men, women and children—gathering ahead of the column, armed with boxes of fruit and sandwiches.

'Come on,' said Tommy, 'that's where we need to go.'

'Where is the station?' asked Stella, 'we don't know where it is.'

'I do,' said Tommy, 'follow me.' They turned, leaving the spectacle behind. Gulls cried overhead, and then they walked away from the harbour and down a street that was now empty. A distant booming, dull, but quite distinct. Joss said, 'Thunder?'

'No—I reckon that's the German guns.' They stopped to listen.

'Do you think they'll ever get over here?' said Stella. The colour had gone from her face, and she wrapped her arms about her, even though it was not at all cold.

'History doesn't support it.' Tommy looked at her kindly.

'Are you all right, Stella?' asked Joss.

She nodded, then turned and continued walking down the street, while above, a lone Union flag flapped noisily from a sudden gust of wind blowing off the sea.

*　　*　　*

The sight that greeted them at the station was no less astonishing. While several thousand weary troops were disembarking at the harbour, a further several thousand were boarding the extra trains hurriedly laid on at Dover station. As at the quayside, it was left to those troops not sent to France to ensure the onward journey of the BEF from the port bottleneck continued as quickly as possible.

Stella once again hurried forward, side-stepping through the throng, with Joss and Tommy following behind until, for the time being at any rate, they could move no further. A large number of troops had just been shunted onto one of the platforms where empty carriages were waiting. But first they needed feeding and so fresh troops had begun the process of handing out pies, sandwiches, bananas and oranges already stacked up ready on trestle tables set up along the platform. Others were pouring large milk-pails of tea into enamel mugs and tankards and any other drinking vessel they had been able to lay their hands on.

'It's not even this busy in August,' said Tommy. But it didn't take long for the crush to subside as

300

those armed with food and drink stepped back onto the train. Eventually the platform began to clear until most of the troops were on board.

'Now's our chance,' said Stella, pointing to the FANYs and ATS girls that were now walking up and down with trays of cigarettes and more buckets of tea, answering the outstretched arms calling to them from the doors and windows of each carriage. She strode over to one of the trestle tables and grabbed a tray of sandwiches. 'Come on,' she said to Tommy and Joss, 'give me a hand,' then began trawling the length of the train asking the same question over and over: 'Is anyone here from the Royal Wiltshires? Royals Wilts, anyone?'

*   *   *

By ten o'clock that night, the light was finally fading. They'd had a fruitless day. They'd wandered up and down the carriages along each of the platforms asking over and over, but nothing. Then the train would pull out and another come in. More men would surge on, but again, nothing.

But while the never-ending stream continued, Stella was loath to stop. 'And at least we're helping,' she said, clutching another tray of sandwiches. 'At least we're doing *something*.' Tommy wanted to know how long they were expected to keep searching. 'Until I get some news,' Stella told him. 'But I don't expect you to keep at it. I'll be all right on my own.'

Tommy ran his hands through his hair. 'No, we'll work in shifts. We said we'd help and we will. That OK with you Joss?' Of course it was, Joss told him.

'But I need a drink,' said Tommy, 'just a quick

301

one.' When they'd been at the harbour, they'd noticed a number of smaller boats were also arriving, and their passengers, not subjected to the same level of efficiency as those on the larger vessels, were filling up the pubs and teahouses of Dover. Surely, Tommy suggested, they were worth a quick scour?

Back they went to the seafront, and into the first pub they came to, crowded with soldiers. Tommy and Joss squeezed in and made their way across the room. The place was thick with cigarette smoke and the smell of beer and damp clothes. Tommy nudged his way to the bar through a handful of Scots who were standing there and on their way to getting drunk. 'The fucking RAF are here lads!' said one of them and they all lifted their drinks and cheered.

'Can I get any of you a drink?' said Tommy.

'Supposed to make up for the fact you've been sitting on your arses over here is it?'

'What is all this?' said Tommy. 'I haven't even completed my training yet, so how am I supposed to have flown over France?'

'We're looking for a friend who's gone missing over there,' said Joss.

One of the soldiers prodded Tommy in the chest. 'Listen sonny, we've just spent six days getting bombed and strafed to bits on those fucking beaches and none of us ever saw a single fucking plane from the RAF. Saw plenty of Messerschmitts and plenty of Stukas but not a single Spitfire or Hurricane. We didn't get one bit of help from your bloody lot.'

Joss looked at him. He had congealed blood across his battle-blouse and a blackened cut across his chin. His hands were covered in dirt, his nails black.

'Well, they were there. I know they were. Shooting down enemy aircraft and getting killed themselves trying to help you lot,' said Tommy. 'They were probably too high for you to see, or hidden by cloud.'

'Were they fuck,' said another of the Scots. 'Do you know how many men we lost over there? Most of our entire company. Over a hundred and sixty men.'

Joss stepped in between them. 'Look, did you ever see the Royal Wiltshires?'

The soldiers looked it him—*who the hell are you?*—then the first one said, 'We saw a lot of people. A lot of Froggies going in the wrong direction and a lot of Jerries coming at us.'

A few chuckles, then another said, 'Last I heard they were at St Floris.'

'Where's that?' said Joss.

'I suppose about thirty miles south-east of Dunkirk. But listen, I haven't a fucking clue. That was a while ago now, and things changed every hour, you know. It was fucking madness out there.'

Tommy interceded again. 'Listen, you've been more helpful to us than anyone else so far today so please let me get you all a drink.' He nodded to get the barman's attention, then added, 'And I'm sorry you feel let down but really, you've no need to, I promise you.'

'Aye, well it's going to be up to you lot now, that's for certain,' muttered the man with the bloodstained jacket.

*   *   *

303

7.30 a.m. the following day. A pale pink sky had given way to bright sunshine. Tommy and Joss wandered across the port. They'd given up waiting at the station and instead returned to the quayside. Joss reckoned he'd had two hours' sleep, Tommy only one. Stella had curled up on the back seat just after midnight and had been sleeping so soundly the other two hadn't wanted to wake her.

Ahead of them, the latest arrivals marched off towards the station. At last the numbers on the returning boats were beginning to thin, and the talk amongst those at the harbour's edge was that over 300,000 men had been picked up off the beaches. A miracle, they said. And another miracle: among those just landed had been some men from the Queen's Own Royal Wiltshire Regiment. They hadn't gone to Margate or Folkestone or any of the other ports along the Kentish coast, but had reached Dover. And they had told Joss and Tommy what had happened across the Channel in France.

Joss felt a leaden weight bearing down on him as they walked in silence towards the car, not from fatigue, but sadness. He wondered how they would tell Stella; how she would react. He'd always looked up to Roger—they all had. He'd been so decent, so good natured. Then he thought about how terrible it was that he'd already begun thinking of him in the past tense.

Stella was still asleep when they eventually returned to the car, but then she awoke while they were still wondering what they should do.

'What is it?' she said, suddenly sitting up, a look of alarm on her face.

'We found some Wiltshiremen,' said Joss. Her

eyes were darting back and forth, searching his face for clues before he spoke the words. 'They'd been at St Floris, but there they were separated from the rest of their company. They managed to slip away, but they said it was hopeless—they had been completely surrounded by Germans and were already down to their last ammunition. Roger had been their platoon commander, but he'd been wounded in the leg a few days before. They were supposed to slip away in two groups, with Roger in the second.'

'Roger was wounded?' She looked pained, then brightened. 'So he could have made it too?'

Joss shook his head. 'He was already wounded in the leg. There was no transport left and they thought he was in a bad way. They said there was little chance he could have made that distance back to the coast. Stella, I'm sorry, but the best we can hope for is that he's been captured.'

She was silent for a moment, sitting there on the back seat with the door open, staring across the road and biting her lips; Joss wondered whether he should say anything more. But what could he say? It was no time for platitudes. Then she said, 'Could I have another cigarette please Tommy?'

Tommy felt in his pockets and passed her one, then stooped to light it for her. A single tear ran down her cheek. 'Poor Roger,' she said, then turned to Tommy and Joss. 'Well then. There's nothing more to be done. We can go back to London now.'

Joss felt exhausted. They all were. Perhaps his tiredness increased his sense of despair. David, now Roger—and the Nazis waiting to pounce on Britain.

Cairo—October, 1942

In Cairo, it was no longer quite so hot. The terrible summer heat had subsided and Joss could breathe more easily again; the room he shared with Dobbo was even pleasantly cool.

He sat at the writing desk Binny had proudly pointed out the day before. Before him lay a sheet of paper and a pen. It had been a long time since he'd written a letter and the pen felt curiously strange in his hand. *How to begin?* The nib poised, hovering above the paper. *MEHQ October 11, 1942. Dear Celia,* he began, *I hope you are well and in good spirits.* Then he stopped, frustrated by his inadequacy for the task.

He put the pen back down, and rested his chin on his hands. Talking with Dobbo last night had brought back a lot of memories. Seeing the returning troops from Dunkirk had been a shocking experience. How distant the war had seemed in Scotland, and how palpable it had become in Dover.

The experience had prompted something of an epiphany for Stella. 'I've got to change my life,' she told them. 'I've been selfish, shallow and not very nice. What have I been doing for the past nine months? Nothing. Typing a few letters during the day, gossiping with the other girls in the office and waiting until the evening when there'd be another party or another dinner. Except even that was becoming dull. The war was beginning to *bore* me. It was all anyone talked about, Philip included, and I resented it because I wanted them to be witty and

306

entertaining and to talk about me.'

'I think you're being a bit hard on yourself,' said Tommy. 'None of us knew this was going to happen.'

'No, I'm not. We all heard the guns. The Germans are laughing at us. I've got to do something useful and help make sure Roger wasn't fighting for nothing. My God, you two are doing your bit. You're prepared to risk your lives. Even poor Guy is working all hours trying to keep the country in food. He's given up university, taken on far more than he can handle and never once complained.'

'What will you do?' asked Joss.

'I don't know yet. Maybe the RAF. Become a WAAF. Something, anyway. I can't sit back any more.'

Stella. He thought of her sitting in the back of Tommy's Riley that first day of June. Her dark hair dishevelled in a way he'd never seen before; the look of defiance; the anger burning in those pale grey eyes. Stella without make-up, as though she had cleansed herself from a world of artificiality. Stella more achingly beautiful than he'd ever seen her before.

And he thought of her grief. Grief for her adored older brother, enhanced by the burden of the news she carried. 'What am I going to say to Mum and Guy?' she had said at one point during that drive back to London, and Joss had wished he could hold her and protect her, and that he might say just one thing that might make her feel better.

In London she'd asked him to accompany her back to Alvesdon Farm.

'I'm not sure that's a good idea,' he told her. 'You

307

should be together as a family at this time.'

But she was insistent. 'Joss, please. You were in Dover too. You spoke to the men from the Wiltshires,' and so he relented. She'd *needed* him. And he felt ashamed remembering about how thrilled he'd been, when really, he should have been thinking only of Roger and the Liddells.

They went straight on to Waterloo, found a train and an empty compartment.

'Thank you, Joss, for doing this for me, and for coming with me to Dover. You and Tommy have been very kind. I'm sure your leave must be very precious.'

'It's the very least I could do,' said Joss. 'I owe your mother and father a lot. You've all been like a second family to me.'

She looked exhausted. 'I wonder,' she said, 'whether it's better to have had a large loving family and then have the pain of losing a father and brother, or to have been like you, and not had them in the first place.'

'I miss David terribly,' he said, 'but at least I knew him. I can't say that about my own father, and I regret it. I regret it very much.'

Stella looked thoughtful for a moment, then said, 'Do you ever wonder what would have happened if he'd lived?'

Joss looked out of the window. *So Guy had told her after all.* And the strange thing was, he didn't mind. He turned back to her and said, 'You mean, would I have ended up in Germany? Yes, I do, all the time.'

'I'm sorry, Joss, I shouldn't have asked you that. It's really none of my business, and—'

'No, no, it's all right. Really. And you know, the

funny thing is that I've got more German family than I have English. Over here there's just my mother and me. In Munich I know I've certainly got a grandmother and an aunt and two cousins.'

Stella looked surprised.

'I found out last year, when we went to Munich. I saw them—my aunt and her two sons. Guy doesn't know. I've never told a soul before now.'

'Joss—I don't know what to say.'

'There's not much *to* say.'

'But doesn't it bother you, that we're now at war?'

Joss smiled ruefully. 'Yes, of course. I didn't really think about it too much when I was training, but now—well.' He tapped his fingers together. 'The chances are I'll be seeing action before too long, and so you can't help wondering about it. I keep thinking about my cousins. For all I know, the older one might even have joined the Luftwaffe.'

'But you don't know them. They're your family in blood only. You're English, and your home is here. I certainly don't think of you as being anything else.'

Joss smiled. 'You're right. I should try and put it out of my mind.'

Stella bit her lip and stared out of the window. 'Poor Roger,' she said. 'I can't put him out of my mind at all. Can't stop thinking about my lovely brother stuck out there.' She shivered. 'But do you know what I kept thinking as we drove back to London? I kept thinking, "thank God it's not Guy". Is that a terrible thing to have thought?'

'No,' said Joss gently. 'You're Guy's twin. Just make sure he stays where he is.'

They took a bus from the station. The valley and

the house, when they eventually reached it, looked as beautiful as ever, if not more so: the hedgerows were bursting with life and vitality, the trees dripping with thick, dark leaves. Only the house seemed dead and weary. Even Francis and Ruby, the two evacuee children seemed to know it was not appropriate to laugh. Celia had looked frail, greyer, her vibrancy snuffed out. Guy tired and irritable, shaken by the news of Roger and harassed by the responsibility of the farm. 'I've got to cut the damned hay, but I don't know when. It rains one minute, then it's hot the next, but if I cut it when it's wet, it'll be ruined, and scorched if I leave it too long in the sun. I haven't got enough people to do it anyway.' He'd looked desperate, at his wit's end. Joss had helped build the first rick, but Guy had ordered the first field of hay to be cut too soon and the following day the innermost part of the haystack had become so hot they'd had to dig a hole from the top to the bottom for fear it might catch alight. Five of them had taken it in turns with the knife, clambering down into the smoking hole and hacking away for a few minutes, then coming up again, pouring with sweat from the heat. They'd saved most of the rick, but wasted a fine morning's haymaking.

How difficult those few days were. Joss had felt a stranger then, as though he had no right to be there, and had regretted ever agreeing to come down with Stella. For allowing his heart to rule his head.

Celia and Stella spent much of the time fruitlessly trying to find out what had happened to Roger. But those in the know had more pressing calls on their time now. If he had been captured, there was certainly no news about it from the Red Cross or anyone else. 'Promise me one thing, Joss,' Celia had asked as he prepared to leave for his course at Old Sarum, 'if you ever hear anything about my Roger, be sure to let me know.'

* * *

Joss picked up the pen again. He'd promised, and now he knew.

Dear Celia,
I hope you are well and in good spirits. I am convalescing in Cairo at the moment and have at last discovered news about Roger—the worst news, I'm afraid. I am sharing a room with Walter Dobson, a captain in the Durham Light Infantry who was with Roger when he died. Apparently, Roger's Company had been involved in a fierce battle near St Floris. Many of them were killed, and Roger was wounded in the leg. He and a few other men from his platoon managed to safely retreat but they lost contact with the rest of the Company and ended up falling back with the Durhams to St Venant, where they dug in for a couple of days along the outskirts of the town. There was a canal in front of them, and the Germans were on the other side. They were very low on ammunition, but were repeatedly told that they had to hold the line at all costs. They knew the Germans were preparing to attack and equally knew their position was helpless, and that if they didn't make a break-out soon, they would all be killed or captured. Roger discussed the matter with Dobson. They had very little medical kit

other than field dressings and no vehicles with which to get him back to hospital. He knew his wound was becoming infected and that he had little chance of getting any help, and so he agreed with Dobson that he would cause a diversion with all the guns and ammunition they could muster, while they and the remaining Wiltshires made good their escape. He also asked Dobson not to tell his men what he was up to. That night, 27th May, they decided the men should try and escape without the Germans noticing. A sergeant in the Durhams led the first batch of soldiers away, including the men from the Wiltshires. Dobson was to lead the remainder. Roger lay behind a ditch with two Bren guns, their remaining supply of grenades, and a few rifles. The idea was that he should occasionally fire off a round, or give a spurt of the Bren gun to give the impression the line was far more heavily defended than it really was.

Dobson had been gone about twenty minutes when the German guns began opening fire. In no time the sky above Roger was lit up with flares, and Dobson, on a slight rise in the ground, could see it all. Roger was still firing away, but then several shells came over and landed right by him. After that Roger's guns were silent. His shots had given the Germans a chance to range their guns. He didn't have a chance.

All the men made it to Dunkirk and all, bar one, made it back to England. Dobson was later posted to North Africa and has seen much fighting. He says that Roger's action was the bravest thing he ever saw.

When he was back in England, Dobson said he

told this story to his new company commander and assumed the War Office had been notified. He said that in his opinion, Roger should have been given the VC.

I hope this at last puts your mind at rest. It was obvious Roger was going to be a brilliant soldier and his bravery does not surprise me one bit.

With love,

Joss

PS I think of Alvesdon Farm and the happy days before the war often. It is a constant source of comfort to me.

England—June, 1940

Tommy had been right about the need for more fighter pilots. Just four days before, they had still been at Old Sarum, flying Lysanders and wondering which Army Co-Operation squadron they might join. Then without warning, they were all called into the mess and were told that due to the loss of so many pilots over France, Fighter Command was now short of fighter pilots for the inevitable battle that lay ahead. Ten of the fourteen on the course were to join fighter squadrons with immediate effect. Joss, Tommy and Peter Benson were among those picked out. Shortly after this announcement they were ushered in to see Squadron Leader Jennings, the commanding officer at Old Sarum.

'You're all going back to your original squadron, 629, at Northolt,' he told them, then glanced out of the window as a Lysander sped past. He was a well-built man, late thirties to early forties, too old for combat now, but too young last time round, and so stuck forever as an instructor and desk-man. 'Apparently,' he continued once the Lysander had taken to the air, 'they've been up in North Yorkshire for much of the time since the war started.' Perusing the notes, he mumbled to himself as he skim-read his brief. 'Sent down to Northolt 11th May, in action over France throughout evacuation. A number of losses, including squadron leader.' He tapped his papers on his desk, stood up, and smiling, said, 'I envy you. Make the most of it.' The three of them stood there, until Jennings waved a hand of dismissal. 'Off you go then' he said, 'and good luck.'

*　　　*　　　*

They were given 24 hours' leave. While Peter headed back to Kent, Tommy suggested Joss spend the night with his parents near Guildford. 'Then we can drive up to Northolt tomorrow together.' Joss agreed. Having heard so much about them, he was intrigued to finally have the chance to meet Tommy's mother and father.

They were, of course, charming. He was tall, bald, but still handsome, while she was an older female version of Tommy: the same dark hair and eyes. When she spoke, it was with only the slightest hint of an American accent; it had evidently been softened from years spent playing hostess to countless diplomatic functions. She seemed modern, too, like Tommy: she wore black culottes and large round sunglasses, and as they went outside into the garden for drinks, brought out a portable gramophone on which she played the latest big band numbers. Inside the house, there were still a few packing boxes in the corridors, but the house reflected equally eclectic tastes as their son's, with paintings and artefacts from several continents and a lifetime spent abroad.

It was a sombre evening, however. Tommy's father had just received news of the French collapse. 'Petain's a misguided fool,' he told them. 'And the French equally foolish for believing an old general can save them again.'

'It doesn't sound as though the French were much help anyway,' said Tommy. 'Now that we're on our own we can do what we like and we certainly won't have to risk any more fighters the wrong side of the Channel.'

His father nodded. 'I suppose there's something in that.' Then he added, 'Events are moving too fast. To think the Gestapo will soon be running Paris.' The Haskells had friends there.

'What news from Isabelle and Jean?' asked Tommy.

Mr Haskell shook his head. 'None, I'm afraid. I assume they're still there.'

'I can't imagine they'll be the most co-operative of Nazi subjects.'

'If they want to survive they're going to have to be.'

Tommy's mother said, 'It's all so awful. When I go outside and see the garden with everything looking so gorgeous, it's quite impossible to believe the terrible events going on. I don't think I've ever known such a lovely spring evolve into such a sweet summer, yet the news brings us one calamity after another.'

' "The fields are fair beside them, the chestnut

towers in his bloom; But they—they feel the desire of the deep—fallen follow their doom." Tennyson,' said Tommy's father, 'rather apt, don't you think?'

Throughout the evening, the conversation never veered far from the rapid escalation of events. Tommy's father was certain Hitler would turn on Britain next. 'Winston's not going to sue for peace,' he told them.

'You don't think?' said Tommy.

His father shook his head. 'Good God, no. I don't believe he's ever had any intention of it, but certainly not now. Not after Dunkirk and with the country rallying behind him. And I agree with him. Someone's got to stand up to Hitler. He and his cronies are nothing but thugs and bullies.'

So there it was; not spoken about openly, but understood by all: a battle must surely come in which Joss and Tommy were likely to be first in the firing line. Joss watched Tommy's mother: so similar in looks and character, but tonight quiet, even demure, a woman torn apart by the thought that her son was about to go off to war, a fate that she was powerless to do anything about.

*   *   *

Mid-afternoon the following day. Tommy's mother insisted on a last cup of tea and a slice of cake. 'It's a wonderful English custom and you shouldn't be driving on an empty stomach.'

Tommy laughed. 'Mother that's very sweet of you, but I am twenty, you know, not eight years old.'

'A mother never stops caring about her son,' she said, brushing a fleck of dirt from his tunic. So they

316

had tea and cake, and then, at last, it was time for them to leave.

Speeding through the Surrey countryside, they did not speak for a while. Tommy, hands gripped tightly round the steering wheel, appeared to be deep in thought and Joss knew better than to disturb him. Then eventually he said, 'You know, mother tried to persuade me to go to America.' He laughed. 'I mean, bless her and everything for trying, but what did she think I'd say?'

'I suppose she felt she had to try.'

'Yes. I must say, I worry about them worrying about me far more than I worry about myself—if that makes any sense at all.' He turned to Joss and grinned.

'I think so.'

'Really, having no father and a dissolute mother puts you at an enormous advantage in these circumstances. No guilt to deal with.'

'Maybe not of that kind,' said Joss, and immediately knew he should have kept his thoughts to himself.

Tommy glanced at him. 'You can't still be worrying about your German-ness?'

'Can't I? How would you feel if we were at war with America and Hitler was President?'

'That's a ludicrous argument.'

'Why? Why is it? I have German blood, Tommy, and it's Germany who started all this. Germany who has caused countless deaths already. Of course I feel guilty, and so would you if you were me.'

Tommy was silent for a moment, then without warning, he pulled the car off the road and stopped. 'Listen to me, Joss. I don't know what lies in store for us, but pretty soon we're going to be fighting. We're going to have more than enough to think about without you worrying about your father's blood every time you get into a plane. You're an Englishman, Joss, through and through —defined by your upbringing and by those who have surrounded you. You should feel no confusion about this and not let any misplaced sense of guilt distract you from the job in hand. Otherwise—well, let's just agree you'll be making life even more difficult than it need be.'

Joss said nothing.

'Come on—I've no more English blood in me than you, and I've lived half my life abroad, but this is still the place I think of as home. And I'm proud that I'm about to do my bit defending it. It's an honour.'

'All right Tommy, you've made your point,' said Joss, 'but let's not talk about it any more.'

'Very well,' said Tommy, putting the car back into gear, 'lecture over.'

In fact, let's not talk about it again. He knew Tommy was not just trying to make him feel better, but believed every word he'd said. But Joss couldn't help the conflict in his mind, and one that was mounting as his direct involvement in the war drew ever closer.

It had been easy to put it to one side when he'd been training—the war had seemed a long way away then. But since Dunkirk everything had changed. Any moment, he would have to face up to his fear of being found out, and his fear of killing his father's countrymen. This anxiety gnawed away at him, impossible to bury, even though he believed, as Tommy believed, in the need to help preserve England and all that England meant to

318

him—the Liddells, Alvesdon Farm, his mother—from the menace that was sweeping across Europe. *If only*, he thought; if only George had not opened his mother's box; if only George had kept silent; *if only* he had shut the door to his room and stayed where he was. It was amazing how a life could be changed by just a handful of carefully chosen words.

*　　*　　*

They reached Northolt just after five. A lone Spitfire was landing as they pulled up outside the main building, but otherwise the place was quiet, with barely a soul about. For a moment they stood by the car, watching the Spitfire taxi to a stop.

'That'll be us soon,' said Tommy. ' I still can't believe we're finally going to get to fly one of those things. Think about that every time you start worrying again.'

A tall man in his thirties appeared. He wore horn-rimmed spectacles and had a trim moustache. 'Can I help?'

'I hope so,' said Tommy, 'we're looking for 629 Squadron.'

'Ah,' said the man, 'replacements. You're the third and fourth today.'

'Really?' said Tommy.

'Yes,' said the man. He had a gentle voice, rather at odds with an appearance that suggested brusqueness. 'A Pole and an American. One can barely say the word "Nazi" without spitting hatred, the other barely knows what a Nazi is.'

'So which is which?' said Tommy.

'Ha, ha,' chuckled the man, 'you'd never guess.'

He led them round a large building, then paused to light his pipe. 'My name's Reynolds, by the way,' he told them through cupped hands. 'Adjutant. You must be Lambert, Haskell or Benson?'

'Lambert and Haskell,' said Joss.

'Well, no doubt Benson will be here in due course.' He squinted up at the sky. 'Lovely afternoon isn't it? Can you hear the skylarks? Such a summery noise they make.'

They were given a room to share, then taken down to the mess. It was a large room with a variety of seats and armchairs, and a bar at one end. A number of pilots were there, two playing a game of snooker on the half-size table, others reading magazines or newspapers.

Reynolds clapped his hands and raised his arms. 'Gentlemen, two more pilots have joined us. Pilot Officers Lambert and Haskell.' One of the pilots stood up and, cigarette between his lips, extended a hand.

'How d'you do? Mike Drummond. I'm afraid we don't have a CO at present, but I'm one of the flight commanders. Very pleased to have you on board. What shall we do? A drink first or shall I introduce you to everyone?' Answering his own question, he said, 'Introductions, I think.' He had a wide, humorous face and dense ginger hair. He'd discarded his jacket and was wearing his pale blue shirt with the sleeves rolled up and his top button undone. The others were similarly dressed. One even wore a loose cravat rather than a tie. Joss felt conspicuously overdressed.

Sensing this, Drummond said, 'Oh, we're all a bit slack around here. I'm afraid it's the legacy of being an auxiliary squadron. Rather feel as though

320

we're above petty rules and things. The adj here is always trying to get us to smarten up our act, but until the new CO arrives we've decided we're going to make the most of our wayward habits.'

To the snooker table first: Johnnie Reeves and 'Pip' Winters. Pip, Drummond explained, was the other flight commander. 'He's been with the squadron since it was born, haven't you Pip?'

Pip nodded. 'July 1936,' he said, then squared up for another shot.

'While Reevesy's a comparative new boy—when did you arrive? '38?'

'Yup. Two years ago,' said Reeves. Neither seemed to want to talk much and so Drummond decided to forgo any attempts at conversation, pointing out the remaining men instead.

'Colin Bishop over there, Gordon Bowyer and Norman Malling next to him and the ugly bastard at the far end is Tony Simmonds.' Each lifted a hand in turn, then returned to whatever they were reading. 'We've all become a bit lethargic since Dunkirk,' said Drummond, directing them towards the bar. 'Not a lot going on, and I think we all feel we need a bit of a breather.'

'Hard work was it?' said Tommy.

Drummond whistled. 'You're telling me. At least three sorties a day and then we'd get there to find the sky swarming with German planes. We lost three on the first day, including the CO, although apparently he's all right and a POW.' There were now just seven of the original fourteen pre-war members left. The first to be killed had done so during a training exercise just after the outbreak of war. The other six had all been lost over Dunkirk: four killed, one definitely taken prisoner and another very probably. 'We saw him bale out OK, so I expect he's all right.' It was, he admitted a bit strange. They'd all flown together every weekend for so long before the war, and become close friends in the process. 'You could hardly not be,' he told them. 'After all, we were all much the same age, from the same part of the world and all loved aeroplanes.' Joss glanced at the fireplace. On the mantelpiece were various bits and pieces—an old cricket bat and ball, a faded photograph of a naked woman, and four upturned beer glasses. He was just about to ask whether they were significant, when the door opened and another pilot walked in, his Mae West still round his neck and wearing his flying boots.

'Our American back from his flight,' said Drummond.

'I tell you,' he said out loud, but to no one in particular, 'that aircraft is *amazing*.' He walked over to the bar, mopped his brow and flung down his gloves. 'Hi,' he said turning to Joss and Tommy, 'I'm Henry. Henry Karlitsky, of Polish descent but not to be confused with the other guy.'

'Was that you landing in the Spit a short while ago?' asked Joss.

'First time ever,' he nodded. 'It's fantastic. I don't know what you've been training on, but this thing is a thousand times more powerful and manoeuvrable than anything I've ever flown before. Gave me the biggest kick of my life, I can tell you.' He'd just got himself a beer, when suddenly the radio was turned on.

'Ssh,' said Drummond to the American, putting a finger to his mouth. Everyone in the room stopped what they were doing. Reeves and Winters put down their cues and went over to stand by the set. The others lowered their magazines. Through the muffled speaker came the sound of the bells of Big Ben chiming the hour then a crackly voice announced the Prime Minister. To begin with, Joss could barely make out what Churchill was saying. It was the first time he'd heard him speak and his words were so mumbling that he wondered whether the man was drunk. *'What General Weygand called the Battle of France is over,'* he told them. Consequently, the Battle of Britain, he warned them, must soon begin. Much rested on this battle: *'Upon it depends our own British life, and the long continuity of our institutions and our empire.'* They, as Britains, Churchill told them, had to withstand the fury and might of the enemy. If they did, then the world, not just Britain, would be saved. If they failed, he said, the whole world would be plunged into a new and protracted Dark Age. *'Let us, therefore, brace ourselves,'* he concluded, his rumble strangely rousing, *'that, if the British Empire and its Commonwealth last for a thousand years, men will say, "This was their finest hour".'*

The room remained silent after the radio was switched off. Then Pip Winters said, 'Well, that's that then. Time for a beer or five, I think.' The ice was broken. Colin Bishop returned to his magazine, but the others all followed Pip to the bar.

Tommy turned to Joss. 'Brilliantly melodramatic, didn't you think? A new Dark Age. And on the anniversary of Waterloo, too.'

'You might think it funny,' said Joss, 'but I thought it was pretty unnerving. It's us who are going to be taking on these hordes.'

323

'Feeling scared are you?' Tommy grinned.

Joss eyed him—*how can he still talk like this?* He said quietly, 'Yes, I am as a matter of fact.'

'But Joss, just think: we're on the brink of another Waterloo and we're going to be a part of it. Now that's something to be proud of.'

'Is that all this is for you? A chance for glory?'

'No—it's also a chance to fly fantastic aircraft.'

Joss shook his head. Suddenly he wasn't in the mood for Tommy's flippancy. The enormity of what confronted them had been mounting ever since their trip to Dover, but here, in the mess at Northolt, the sense of crisis seemed to be staring them all in the face. He could see it in the eyes of the pilots, men who had already tasted battle, and who had seen half their number shot down in just a few days. And these were experienced pilots, flying the RAF's most advanced fighter. How would they cope when the full force of Hitler's air armies were flung at them? A rudderless squadron with its heart ripped out. Churchill had just warned them, in the clearest possible terms, that they were facing a gargantuan struggle for survival. *'That's that, then,'* Pip Winters had said; not understated bravura, but defeatism. It hung like a shroud over every one of them. *We haven't a hope in hell,* they seemed to be saying, *so let's get drunk instead.* Joss wanted to grab every one of them and shout and scream and tell them to pull themselves together. He felt overwhelmed by the sense of disappointment, not because he'd expected so much more, but because in this room it seemed as though England were already dying. No matter what conflicts raged within, he knew he could not let that happen. Not like that.

A new day: the sun bright and warm, and the sky a luscious blue with barely a cloud in sight. Standing by a Spitfire, his first flight was just minutes away. The despair—the sense of *dread*—of the previous evening had evaporated. A light breeze drifted across the airfield, bringing with it the sweetened scent of grass still damp with dew. The same skylarks they'd heard on their arrival were singing high above him now. In the distance the sound of a mechanic working, a spanner tapping on metal, resounded across the quiet morning air.

For a moment, Joss stood looking at the aircraft. The wide curve of the wings, the nose pointing imperiously up towards the sky—barely a straight line anywhere. He ran a hand over the cold stressed metal of the wing, still wet with early morning condensation. There was, Joss reflected, an almost feline quality to its sleek lines and curves. What was it Drummond had called it? A 'real thoroughbred'. *Yes,* thought Joss, *I see what he means.* The sun was already well over the hedgerows at the far end of the field and as he walked around the engine cowling he was suddenly blinded by the gleam of brilliant light.

'All right sir?' said his fitter, who was standing on the wing root and polishing the canopy with a cloth.

'Yes, fine thank you. Perfect morning,' said Joss. He hoped he sounded nonchalant.

'Certainly is, sir,' said the rigger, who was busy fixing the cable from the starter trolley into the nose of the Spitfire. Joss looked back up at the fitter and noticed he was smiling. Was he laughing

325

at yet another inexperienced recruit or just being friendly?

'When you're ready, sir,' said the fitter.

Joss muttered 'Right,' then stepped up beside him. The paintwork by the footplate was chipped, revealing flecks of bare steel. A tiny half door hung open, allowing Joss to lower himself into the narrow cockpit. His fitter helped strap him in—Sutton harness clipped in tight, oxygen mask strapped across his face and fastened onto the leather flying helmet.

'OK sir?' asked the fitter.

Joss nodded, and then the door was shut close. He took a few deep breaths, the air around him suddenly close, then began going through his cockpit checks and trying to remember everything he'd been told. The cockpit was so narrow, his shoulders almost touched the sides. Throttle, undercarriage pump, magnetos, canopy release, temperature gauges, oil pressure. Look at it any longer and he'd never get off the ground. He waved a gloved hand at the two ground crew then pressed the starter button. A chug from the engine, then another, the propeller creaking, then suddenly flames spurted from the blackened exhaust stubs, the propeller whirred and the Merlin burst into life, a deep, guttural roar, noisier than any engine he'd heard before. Its pounding pistons vibrated his seat and shook the airframe. *Christ,* he thought, *this is the moment.* The moment he'd looked forward to—*yearned* for—ever since those Spitfires had roared over them at Marshall's. And yet he knew he had just one chance to get it right. There was no Heyward sitting behind him talking him through what he had to do. Drummond's casual briefing had not given him much confidence. 'You'll be fine,' he'd told Joss. 'Yours for an hour. Go and have some fun.' Then he'd turned back and said, 'Just watch you don't push the nose too far forward when you take off or else you'll go arse over tit. And another thing: bear in mind that this machine is much, much more powerful than anything you've ever flown before. Oh, and I almost forgot: wreck this aircraft and there'll be hell to pay. Serious hell to pay.' Then he'd winked and wandered off. Some briefing, thought Joss. Above his feet lay a tank full of high-octane fuel; beyond that, the giant Merlin engine, a thousand horse-power, capable of 350 miles per hour; ahead of that, the whirr of the variable pitch propeller, very different from the single-speed Harvard. Very different from anything he'd ever flown before. Nausea rose from his stomach. His mouth tasted sour.

Joss released the brakes and gently rolled forward. He couldn't see anything, then he remembered Drummond had warned him that forward vision was terrible and that during taxiing he should weave from side to side until ready to start his take-off. He'd also been warned that the controls were more sensitive than any other plane he'd have flown— well, he could tell that just from the way the rudder responded.

He swung the plane round at the far end of the airfield. A glance at the temperature gauges— already above a hundred degrees. Now facing into the wind, he counted to three. *Here goes.* Brakes released, throttle open, and then the Spitfire was hurtling across the grass, the surge of power intense. Joss glanced at the vast elliptical wings, straining as the Merlin growled deeper and the speed increased. Stick forward a shade, and the nose dropped, so that Joss could now see the perimeter rushing towards him. Fifty miles per hour, sixty, seventy, ease back on the stick and suddenly the two of them had left the ground and were surging through the air.

Hedgerows, houses, trees, flashed beneath him. In what seemed like a few moments, the airfield was nothing but a tiny patch of grass behind him. Beads of sweat ran down his forehead as the Spitfire continued to rapidly climb. Turning his head from side to side, he tried to work out where he was.

Shocked by the unaccustomed power, Joss felt completely out of control, as though the Spitfire was running away with him. *Think,* he told himself. Throttle back, coarsen the pitch—*much better.* Then he remembered the undercarriage. A manual pump. He looked down and realized he needed to swap hands, but as soon as he started pumping with his right hand, he found his left began aping the other and the Spitfire began bobbing through the air.

As soon as both wheels clicked into place within the wings, he levelled off. *Six thousand feet already! And so light on the controls!* Perhaps this machine wasn't quite so formidable after all, and for the moment, his fears evaporated. As Joss took the plane through a gentle turn, the horizon tilted. Arcing through the sky, he left behind the expanse of clear blue and flew into a mass of rolling white cumulus. Joss shouted out loud with joy—however many hundreds of thousands of people would wish to do what he was doing, cavorting and dancing around the sky in this wondrous machine?

Effortlessly, he climbed over a towering column of cloud, then laughing, rolled and dived and climbed once more. *This is perfect,* he thought. For this moment in time, he had become the master of all he surveyed: the sky, the clouds, were his; time had stopped. The war no longer existed. A glorious solitude, in which he had discovered harmony with both machine and nature. The morning sun gleamed across the top of the clouds capping them in a brilliant shining gold, and Joss understood why many believed heaven lay somewhere high in the sky. And at just the slightest command— the lightest pressure—the Spitfire twisted and pirouetted as it was bidden, a mighty beast indeed, but one already tamed. Never before had he experienced such sheer, unbridled joy.

*   *   *

Afterwards, Joss walked back towards the dispersal hut, his legs weak, conscious he'd just experienced the most exhilarating sixty minutes of his life. Landing had considerably quickened his pulse— the Spitfire's speed, the enormous nose masking his view, the ground flashing past beneath him— but it had eventually rumbled to a halt undamaged and with Joss still in one piece. A blast of heat from the engine had greeted him as he'd eased himself out of the cockpit and clambered onto the wing. The hot metal clicked furiously as it began to cool.

Away, towards the main building, he watched a car pull up and a man in uniform step out. The figure looked around, then was ushered inside.

At dispersal, a variety of deckchairs and a couple of tired-looking armchairs had been brought outside, and were now occupied by a few pilots. With their yellow Mae West life jackets around their necks and flying helmets either on their laps or by their feet, Joss supposed they were on duty despite the air of listlessness.

Pip Winters was one of them. 'How was it?' he asked. 'Your landing looked all right. A bit bumpy perhaps.' He was a small-framed man in his mid-twenties. Quiet, but observant. When he did speak, it was slowly, in a tone that might have been sardonic, or might just have been his way. Joss found himself wanting to be liked by Pip.

'A bit more powerful than what I've been used to,' said Joss. He wiped his hand through sweat-soaked hair.

Pip smiled. 'Just a bit. And designed specifically for shooting down Germans.'

Joss wondered whether the designers had ever meant it to be flown by a half-German. 'Who was that arriving?' he asked. 'Looked very official.'

'New CO,' said Pip. 'Don't know much about him, but apparently he's a career pilot. Cranwell, no doubt a bit of service overseas, instructing. The usual. Anyway, Mike's gone off to meet him with the adj.' He yawned, then added, 'Your two friends are somewhere up there.' He pointed to the sky, then returned to his paperback. Two of the others—Colin Bishop and Gordon Bowyer—were fast asleep, while Antonin Szafraniec, the Pole, sat apart from the rest, carving a stick with a penknife. To the side of the dispersal hut, Johnnie Reeves was practising his putting, tapping a golf ball into an old tin mug.

Joss stood in the doorway, desperate to talk to someone about his Spitfire flight, but sensing none of his new colleagues would be interested. His desire not to make a fool of himself outweighed his urge to share his excitement, and so he said nothing, instead leaning against the door and watching nothing happen across the airfield.

It didn't take long for the high of his morning's experience to wear off. In its stead came a jarring at the back of his mind, which soon grew into the frustration and disappointment he'd felt the previous evening. He wished someone would explain what he was supposed to be doing. Was he on duty or not? Were these pilots at readiness or were they simply passing the time of day? No one had said anything, and not wanting to isolate himself by making himself appear overeager, he did not like to ask anyone for the answers to a hundred questions. There was a spare deckchair outside, its green, red and white striped cloth flapping slightly on the breeze, and so he went and sat down on it. High above, the skylarks were still twittering busily, while nearby, a large bumble-bee toured the daisies. A quiet summer's morning. Joss closed his eyes. At least Peter Benson had eventually showed up, arriving the previous evening after spending much of the afternoon stuck on a railway siding. Together with Tommy, Peter had goaded Joss out of his dark mood. Drink revitalized the older members of the squadron too. Whatever scars they may have carried from the previous weeks, they had done their best during supper and in the mess afterwards to welcome their new colleagues. With the songs, drinking games, and indoor rugger, Joss had felt more like a Fresher at Cambridge than in a front-line fighter squadron. And now the new CO had arrived. Joss wondered what he would be like,

331

and hoped he would instil a sense of purpose into this squadron.

* * *

For a day, the new CO merely observed his new charges. The first Joss saw of him was when he turned up at the dispersal hut a few hours after his arrival, all ready to fly. Stocky, with dark brown eyes, wide nose and wearing an expression of ill-disguised impatience, he pointed at Peter and said, 'You. We're going up on a half-hour flight. You first, then you,' he added, turning to Joss. 'Be ready to take off as soon as I get back with this one.' Peter looked dubiously at Tommy and Joss, and went into the dispersal hut to pick up his parachute and flying helmet. By the time he came out again, the CO was already halfway towards one of the Spitfires lined up a short distance away.

Joss was sitting in the cockpit, ready as ordered, when Peter and the CO touched down again.

'All right Lambert,' said the CO, 'I'm Red One and you're Red Two. But don't speak unless I tell you to. Otherwise just stick on my tail, and do what I do.' They took off, climbed to eight thousand feet then the CO began a series of tight turns and dives, and in no time Joss lost him completely. The wings of the Spitfire were so large it was hard to see anything beneath and so for a while he circled about the sky hoping the CO would miraculously reappear. When he did, it was from out of the sun and with breathtaking suddenness.

'Rat-a-tat-a-tat-a-tat,' he said over the R/T, 'you're dead, Red Two.'

The CO shot up in front of him again, then dived

once more. Joss followed as the aircraft in front swayed from side to side and up and down, and he was just beginning to think he was keeping up quite well when they flew into cloud. When they reappeared, the Spitfire in front had vanished.

'Rat-a-tat-a-tat-a-tat,' said the CO again. 'Try looking behind you, Red Two.' Joss looked round over his shoulder saw the CO's plane less than a hundred yards behind. *How the hell did he get there?* He'd neither seen nor heard him coming.

Trudging back to the dispersal hut a short while later, Joss realized, with a mounting sense of panic, that had they been firing their guns, he would probably have been killed three times in almost as many minutes. *No wonder the others think we're finished,* he thought to himself. He found Peter no less dejected. Their inadequacy for the task that faced them could not have been clearer.

Later, they went up again, this time in two flights of six, and with some of the older members of the squadron. Everyone kept formation beautifully, but as soon as the CO broke off, or disappeared into cloud, their cohesion vanished. 'Rat-a-tat-a-tat-a-tat,' came the voice over their headsets, the CO's Spitfire once again looming large behind them.

That night he appeared for a quick drink in the mess then disappeared. None of the others seemed to have much idea of what to make of him.

'I hope he's going to say something other than rat-a-tat,' said Pip Winters.

'He's making a very clear point, though, isn't he?' said Colin Bishop.

No one answered him. Pip blew four perfect smoke rings.

The new CO was a New Zealander. Squadron Leader Stephen MacIntyre. The only person who seemed to know anything about him was Reynolds, the adjutant, so when he took up station at the bar, everyone stopped to listen.

'Learnt to fly on his parents' farm, apparently,' said the adj. 'Applied to Cranwell and was accepted. Passed out in '34, then almost immediately went out to Aden. Couple of years there, then back here where he became an instructor.'

'What did I tell you?' said Pip. A few wry smiles.

'And a bloody good instructor, by all accounts. But that's not all. He was in France.'

'France?' said Mike.

'Yes. Shot down three enemy planes and got a DFC to boot. So he knows his stuff all right.'

Joss retreated to a table with Peter and Tommy.

'This morning I thought I'd be in a better mood than this,' said Tommy, 'but this afternoon's little foray has left a bad aftertaste.'

'He made a complete fool of me too,' said Peter. 'And I think he rather enjoyed it, too. Probably gave him a sense of power or something.'

'Still, I suppose he knows his stuff,' continued Tommy. 'If he can pass that on ...' He paused to light a cigarette.

Joss nodded then said, 'What d'you make of the others?' So far, he'd kept his anxieties about the squadron to himself.

'Seem all right,' said Tommy. 'Bit subdued, I suppose.'

'Very subdued,' said Peter, leaning in towards them.

'Why, what do you think, Joss?' asked Tommy.

'I agree with Peter. They're all acting as though they've given up already. It's not at all what I expected.'

Tommy exhaled a line of smoke, then said, 'Peter and I were talking to Colin Bishop this morning. Those upturned glasses on the mantelpiece are in honour of the four men who were killed over Dunkirk. It's hit them very hard. The Squadron's been together a long time—and since the outbreak of war, they've really been living on top of each other.' He looked around to see if anyone was listening then said, 'Pip Winters had a particularly close friend—Paddy Something-or-other. Known each other since they were kids. According to Colin, these two were the life and soul of the party, two of the oldest members from the pre-war days. Anyway, on their first sortie over Dunkirk, Paddy gets it from a 109 and Pip has to watch his bosom friend fall out of the sky in flames. He's been a bit stand-offish ever since. Understandable, really.'

Joss whistled silently. 'Jesus,' he said, 'doesn't bear thinking about.'

'No,' said Tommy, and for a moment no one spoke.

Peter suddenly grinned. 'Come on,' he said, slapping Joss on the shoulder, 'there's no point letting it even cross our minds. We'll be all right. I'm going to get some more drinks and when I get back I want us to talk about something else. Like how we're going to get to meet some of those lovely girls in uniform I've seen wandering about the place.'

*   *   *

Squadron Leader MacIntyre called the pilots together the following day, along with all the ground crew. He sat on the bar twirling a snooker cue between his fingers while he waited for everyone to arrive. His cap had been laid down beside him, but as soon as everyone appeared to be there, he stood up and took off his jacket, very deliberately rolling up each of his shirtsleeves in turn. The massed gathering—some fourteen pilots and over thirty ground crew—watched this procedure in curious silence.

Then, still twirling the cue, he began. 'I don't think I've ever come across a group of men so inadequately placed to be a front-line fighter squadron,' he told them. 'You're a miserable, ignorant bunch. I wanted all of you in here because bad morale seeps down from the very top to the very bottom, and let's face it, you lot have hit rock bottom. Seven of you here are, according to what I've been told, experienced pilots, but you could have fooled me. You lost nearly half your number over Dunkirk, but you don't seem to have learnt anything. Instead you're moping about feeling sorry for your mates who got the chop and waiting to be killed yourselves. As for the new pilots, I don't know what you've been taught, but you are quite simply not ready to fly in combat. If I sent you up against the Jerries today, I'd put a lot of money on not one of you coming back.'

There was a slight murmur from the back and one of the pilots coughed.

'Sorry what was that?' said MacIntyre. 'Did someone say something?' Silence. 'If you've got anything to say,' he said, 'say it now, and we can go outside and fight it out. This is your last chance.' He looked around the room, staring at each of the pilots in turn. 'No? No one want to challenge me?' He was not a tall man, but his eyes were glaring brightly. His forearms flexed as he tightly gripped the cue with both hands. The room remained deathly quiet.

'Good,' he said. 'Right, first of all, let's talk about what's gone wrong and if you want to say something, put up your hand. This is—was—an auxiliary squadron. Most of you know each other, you come from the same part of the world and your mummies and daddies left you with enough money so you could indulge in a little bit of weekend flying. All jolly good fun, and you felt a bit superior and a bit elite and a bit above everyone else. Then war comes along, so of course you want to do your bit and you sign on the dotted line and become full-time pilots. Everything carries on much as normal until Jerry decides it's time to liven things up a bit and you are suddenly a part of the action. But although you've all learnt your six methods of attack, the reality is very different from the training. For starters, there's rarely one target, but lots, so which do you go for? Secondly, the target does not fly straight and level, but darts all over the place, so your perfect formation flying is suddenly completely useless. So you panic a bit and end up shooting at the nearest thing you see, following it as it dives out of your way and forgetting there might be any number of enemy planes behind you. In fact, I would also put money on the fact that none of those shot down over Dunkirk ever saw the plane that hit them.' He paused looking round the room. 'How many of you who flew over Dunkirk,

337

followed a plane down?' A pause, the pilots looking at each other guilty, then a reluctant show of hands.

'And why did you do that?' No one answered. 'Come on. Drummond. You tell me.'

'Because I wanted to make sure I hit him.'

'And did you?'

'Not certain. We flew into cloud.'

'Then what?'

'I was hit across my port wing and so I took evasive action. When I emerged from the cloud I couldn't see another plane in sight, so I flew home.'

'And by that time you'd lost the crucial advantage of height and speed and were no longer any use in that particular sortie. Did it ever occur to you that might not have been the best tactic?' Mike shrugged. 'Did it ever occur to any of you to sit down and talk about what happened over Dunkirk?' No answer. 'No,' said MacIntyre, 'I didn't think so.' He paced up and down the length of the bar, his cue still in his hands. 'Clearly most of you know how to handle an aeroplane, but being a reasonable pilot does not make you a reasonable *fighter* pilot. You have to do that by making sure you don't get hit yourself. If you *don't* get hit, you've got more time to hit other people instead. And every time you come back without a bullet hole, the better your chances will be the next time. So. How do you protect yourself? Firstly, you must have eyes in the back of your head. You need to look behind you by turning your neck every other second, and I mean literally. You never know when someone might get on your tail. Nor must you ever fly straight and level in the combat area for more than a couple of seconds. Anyone can shoot down an aircraft that's only

338

moving on one plane, i.e., forward, but very few can shoot a target that's constantly moving up, down and from side to side. And if you do spot a Jerry behind you, turn in towards them immediately. Our planes can out-turn anything they've got, so eventually you'll catch him up. And never, and I mean never, follow a plane down. A quick burst of your guns, then get out of there. Another target will come along, believe me.

'So far, the Germans don't seem to want to come out and play, which is very fortunate for you. God knows how long we've got, but we need to work bloody hard right now. I don't care what anyone in the air ministry says, but the standard command attacks are useless and a complete waste of time. I know the theory: the more of you that attack in one go, the bigger the punch—but it doesn't work like that. Surprise is everything in air fighting, so I want you all to forget you ever knew them. We're going to train all day, every day, in flights and individually and you're all going to learn very quickly, or else, I'm afraid, you're going to get yourselves killed. I'm sorry about your friends, but you must put their deaths to one side now. Feeling miserable about it won't help them and it certainly won't help you. And you, Winters, I don't want to see you wearing your Irvin again, all right? You can't possible see behind yourself properly with that bloody great collar of fur. It's better to freeze your bollocks off than get a cannon shell up your arse.' Pip, picking a loose strand of tobacco from his mouth, glared back at the CO.

'Right,' said MacIntyre, whacking the cue on top of the bar, 'I want to see you lot liven up a bit. Where's your fucking fighting spirit? Let's start thinking about avenging those dead colleagues, and making sure we can take on anything the Germans throw at us. Clear?' No one replied so he said again, 'Clear?'

'Yes,' came the mumbled reply.

Yes, thought Joss, *yes, absolutely.* He felt buoyed, lifted by a renewed sense of rightness about what they had to do. Then a voice at the back of his mind reminded him about his father, and he looked around anxiously, convinced that any minute his deception would be discovered. *Please don't let that happen,* he thought to himself—not now, when he believed more than ever that he was doing something important with his life.

With his speech over, MacIntyre quickly divided the pilots into two flights. Peter and Joss were put in 'B' Flight under Pip Winters, Tommy with Mike Drummond in 'A'. MacIntyre then ordered 'A' to go up with him to practise beam attacks, while 'B' were to divide into pairs and to practise dog-fighting with their partner. The room began to clear, and although several of the older pilots next to Joss were muttering and cursing, he did not join in. Instead, he made his way outside and began walking briskly towards dispersal. At least with MacIntyre they might have a chance after all.

Southern England—July, 1940

Still the Germans did not come. Two days after MacIntyre's arrival the squadron had been posted to Middle Wallop, an RAF station in 10 Group of Fighter Command based twelve miles' north-east of Salisbury. As the CO had promised, they trained hard. Taking off, they would fly to between ten and fifteen thousand feet, then in turns make attacks, head on, from the side, from beneath, from above, from out of the sun—all against their squadron leader, who valiantly braved the erratic performance of the rest of his pilots. They loosened their ties when they flew so that it was easier to twist their necks from side to side. 'Your neck should ache like hell,' MacIntyre told them. 'If it doesn't, you haven't been watching hard enough.' Nor was it just the pilots who needed working on. The RAF may have been out-done in France, but MacIntyre had learned a few lessons that the Air Ministry had not, and so ordered the ground crew to re-equip all their Spitfires with armour- plating behind each of the pilots' seats and to find a load of rear-view car mirrors which were to be bolted on to the outside of the canopy. 'Where are we supposed to get those from?' one of the mechanics had asked him. 'Use your imagination,' MacIntyre replied. 'A scrapyard for the armour-plating, and steal the mirrors.' Reynolds enjoyed retelling that story in the mess.

The quite open dislike of the new CO, especially among the older members of the Squadron, soon gave way to grudging respect. It was clear he didn't give a damn what anyone thought of him; he just cared about making the squadron a success. Pip Winters or Colin Bishop may have cursed him, but they never for a moment doubted what MacIntyre was telling them because it made such perfect sense. 'Whenever possible, try to use the twin advantages of sun and height,' he told them. Of course, it was obvious now they knew, but they'd never been told that before and nor had they ever

341

paused to think about it. Joss certainly hadn't.

A strange thing happened during that time while they waited for the Germans to attack: the squadron shed its old pre-war skin. It ceased to be an auxiliary squadron, made up of part-time gentleman fliers, and became a regular wartime squadron instead. When two sergeant pilots arrived—ordinary NCOs—the transition was almost complete. 'It's just as well,' Mike Drummond confided to Joss one night in the mess. 'because this war's not for amateurs. And I'll say one thing for MacIntyre: he's made me realize how little I knew about being a fighter pilot.' *Absolutely*, thought Joss. He'd finished his flying training believing the role of the fighter pilot in combat was to keep tight formation—with wingtips often just feet apart—and to follow the RAF standard attack procedures. Higher people with far greater experience than he had devised such plans and who was he to question it? Tommy and Peter, he knew, had thought much the same. And until he'd joined 629, Joss had never once practised dog-fighting. Not once! Barely fired his guns either. Now he and Peter, since they were both in 'B' Flight, were chasing each other about the sky every day. Thank *God* the Luftwaffe hadn't come; to think he might have gone straight into combat the moment he joined the squadron. The thought made him shudder. MacIntyre had been right: they wouldn't have stood a chance.

Moreover, as each day passed, the gulf between the older and newer members of the squadron lessened. By day they worked together, and by night they drank together, so that by the end of his second week with the squadron, Joss felt he'd known these people half his life.

But the moment was drawing ever nearer when Joss would see a German aircraft in the sky and he would have to kill or be killed. The thought had continued to grow in him like a malignant tumour—there, getting larger and ultimately unavoidable. He worried that when the moment came, he simply wouldn't be up to it—wouldn't be able to press his finger down on the gun button and purposefully try to kill his father's countrymen, or worse, members of his own family.

And as the squadron took a tighter hold of him, so did his fear of being caught out. If his new friends knew the truth, he would surely be thrown out, sent packing, rejected for being shown to be the person he really was. Yes, Tommy knew—and it hadn't affected anything—but that had been at Cambridge; they weren't at war then, weren't fighter pilots engaged in shooting down the enemy. Every time someone joked about the Germans, or worse, talked about what they would do to a German if they ever met one, Joss winced inside.

One evening he'd been careless. He'd left his trunk open while he went for a bath and when he came back Peter had been in the room and was looking at the Iron Cross.

'Where did you get this?' he asked.

Joss had frozen, then said, 'My mother gave it to me. My father found it in the last war. I'm afraid she wasn't prepared to let me have his own medals.'

Peter had nodded and put it back in the trunk, but then later, over dinner in the mess, he'd said, 'Did you know Joss here has got an Iron Cross?' and everyone had looked at him. For a moment,

343

he'd felt himself begin to panic, but then Peter added, 'His old man swiped it in the last war.'

'It's my ambition to try and win another,' said Joss, and everyone had laughed.

In the bar afterwards, Tommy said, 'You never told me your father won an Iron Cross.'

'Shh,' Joss whispered. 'Well he did. In France in 1916, but don't ever breathe a word. You must swear, Tommy, on all you hold dear never to mention my father to anyone in the squadron. Not even Peter.'

Tommy laughed. 'Oh come off it Joss, you're not still worrying about that? Don't be so bloody silly.'

'I mean it Tommy. Swear it. It might be very amusing to you, but it isn't to me.'

'Of course I swear. I just think you should put it to one side now. Really Joss, I thought you'd got over this.'

'Well, obviously not.'

Tommy had smiled—*all right, I'll tolerate this nonsense*—but he didn't understand. His argument rested on logic, but this was not about that. No matter how much Joss reasoned with himself, inside he *felt* different. And this made him an outsider. He might wish he'd been born English through and through, rooted to one place for hundreds of years like the Liddells—and God only knew how much he did—but he hadn't, and nothing anyone said or did could change that. His badge of identity might be invisible, but it was still something that had to be borne. And because of it, he believed he was not only fundamentally different from most of the people around him, but also a fraud, a charlatan ashamed of wearing his true colours.

*　　　　*　　　　*

On 5th July, the CO gathered all his pilots together. Earlier that day, he told them, German aircraft had attacked shipping in the Channel and bombed the naval base at Portland. The Germans, it seemed, were at last making a move. At dawn the following morning, the whole of 629 were to fly to Warmwell, a small airfield south-east of Dorchester. From there, they would patrol the south coast.

So, this is it, Joss thought.

On the twenty-minute flight to Warmwell he kept thinking: *In an hour's time I might have seen combat. I might have fired my guns at a German plane. I might have shot down a German plane. I might have been shot down myself.* He wondered what he would do if he was hit. Would it hurt? Would he panic? And what if he crashed into another plane? It was one thing practising dog-fighting with one another, but in the mêlée of battle, presumably there would be aircraft all over the place. He wasn't afraid of death exactly, but feared suffering; feared *burning*.

He still had no answers three days later, despite having flown four patrols the first day, three the next and one the day before. He began to relax again, and to think that perhaps the Germans would never appear after all, that the occasional attack on shipping was nothing more than a feint.

*　　　　*　　　　*

4 a.m., Tuesday 9th July. Joss was woken by Whiting, the batman he shared with Peter. A shake

345

of the shoulder, 'Time to get up, sir,' and a cup of tea in an old enamel mug. He sat up immediately, rubbed his eyes, yawned and thanked Whiting. He'd never found getting up difficult: once he was awake, he was awake, even when he'd only had five hours' sleep for four days on the trot. Not so Peter, who pulled the sheets up tight around his shoulder, then turned over. Joss had gone to bed before him the previous evening. Hadn't even heard him come in.

Joss went over and shook him again. 'Come on you lazy bastard, wake up.'

Peter groaned then rolled over and looked up at Joss through squinting eyes. 'Can't be morning already,' he said, 'I swear I only went to bed five minutes ago.'

'Maybe you did.'

'I kissed Felicity last night.' He'd closed his eyes again, but was grinning. 'She's crazy about me.'

'Of course she is.'

'And tonight we're going out together. As soon as she's finished her shift.' He stretched, then took a sip of his tea. 'Good old Whiting.' He continued talking while Joss shaved. 'Felicity only arrived here a few days before us. She's a plotter. While we're buzzing around up there, she's marking where we are and where the enemy are too. I never realized quite what an amazing system it all is. Radio Direction Finding, observer blokes. Almost foolproof.'

'They haven't found us much yet, have they?'

'That's because the Germans haven't been coming our way, but when they do we'll know about it all right. I tell you, Joss they work those WAAFs pretty hard, you know.'

346

'I suppose they have to. Still, as long as there's time in her busy schedule for you.'

'Exactly. She is an *amazing* kisser.' He sighed. 'Why have we got to fly today? I think it's very selfish of them to make me waste a day pointlessly patrolling up and down the coast when I could be making love to Felicity instead. And I bet we don't see anything.' He went over to the window and drew back the curtains. 'Christ, look at the weather. It's pissing down. Perhaps we won't be going after all.'

'Don't count on it.'

By twenty past four, they were washed, shaved and dressed. Peter splashed his face one more time with cold water, then flung his damp towel onto his bed.

'Ready?' said Joss.

'Ready. Come on, let's get it over with, then I can get back to my girl.'

*　　　*　　　*

Breakfast—toast, boiled eggs and coffee—then the flight down to Warmwell. The forecast was for better weather MacIntyre told them cheerily, but strong winds and total cloud cover meant the journey took more than twice the normal length. Joss was relieved when he safely touched down again.

The winds died down but not the rain. There were few facilities at Warmwell and the pilots had to make do with a couple of bell tents for a dispersal hut. With hunched shoulders, they sat on an assortment of chairs smoking and listening to the rain beating against the canvas.

'This is a bloody waste of time,' said Peter after they'd been sitting there for a couple of hours. 'No Germans are going to fly in this weather.' Then the field telephone rang.

'Yes?' said Calder, their new intelligence officer. The pilots all looked at him, listening, waiting. 'All right. Yes.' He put the receiver down. 'Reports of a German bomber attacking ships off Portland,' he said.

'Well, obviously you're just the man for the job, Peter,' said MacIntyre. 'Pip, take Peter and Joss and go and have a look will you?'

Minutes later they were airborne. 'This is Blue One,' Pip called to Peter and Joss. 'If we're going to have any hope of finding them we're going to have to fly low, so keep tight on my tail.' In fact the cloud was so low, even the line of hills between Warmwell and the coast were hidden. Then Pip spotted a gap where the valley road ran through towards the coast and so they roared through that, just a hundred feet from the ground, and out over the sea. But there was nothing. Just the grey-green English Channel and a leaden sky.

*   *   *

The squadron made several more patrols that day, but Joss did not fly again until the evening. The weather had improved, as MacIntyre had promised, although there were large banks of cloud in between the blue sky. Joss glanced across at Denis Tweed, one of the new sergeant pilots, some fifty yards to his right, then at Peter, on this occasion leading them and slightly ahead, their machines bowing gently but essentially flying

348

straight and level. Eight thousand feet beneath him, the curve of Weymouth Bay, the long finger of Chesil Beach and the outcrop of Portland Bill. Beyond that, the serrated coastline continued into the distance before disappearing into grey. Forty-five minutes they'd been flying this line: up as far as Lyme Regis, then a wide curving turn and back again to Lulworth. Back and forth, back and forth, and as usual, nothing. He thought about his leave. Both he and Peter had the following day off, their first since joining 629. Joss had arranged to borrow Tommy's car and was going to drive over to Alvesdon Farm. It seemed like ages since he'd last seen Guy—or Stella for that matter—and was looking forward to a day away from flying and the rest of the squadron. And Peter had his girl to get back to and lunch in London the next day with his father.

Peter was clearly as impatient as Joss to have the day finished. 'Hello Tartan, this is Nimbus Leader,' came his voice through the headphones. 'Can't see a thing. Can we have permission to turn back to base?' *Good idea,* thought Joss, *before I lose concentration altogether.*

Then from the sector control back at Middle Wallop: 'Hello Nimbus Leader, this is Tartan. Continue patrolling Weymouth Bay angels eight.'

'Roger Tartan,' said Peter, but Joss heard the click of frustration.

Concentrate, Joss told himself; his mind had been wandering. Once more he began twisting his head round one way, then the other. A shape flickered in the corner of his eye. He swung his head round and glimpsed an aircraft dart into cloud then reappear the other side, followed by two more. His heart quickened and it was with something like panic that he said, 'Bandits over there!' then, remembering protocol, added, 'at nine o'clock, three of them, about two miles, angels six.'

'Roger,' said Peter, and swung round towards them. Denis Tweed fell in behind him and Joss followed, his fingers fumbling to switch on the reflector sights, and turning the gun button on to 'fire' for the first time. They were catching them fast and from the gull-wing shape Joss recognized them as German dive-bombers, the already infamous Stukas. Just half a mile away now, and Joss saw the black swastika on the tail-fin of the rear aircraft, somehow more menacing now than when he'd seen them on the banners and flags in Munich. Nor had he had been expecting the vivid colour of the mottled grey-green fuselage. Enemy aircraft were always black on the identification charts.

Remembering to look round, Joss twisted his neck and to his horror saw at least half a dozen German fighters above them just beginning their dive. Now it was they who had the advantage of speed and height. *Twin-engines. Messerschmitts.* '110s behind us, look out!' shouted Joss over the R/T. He turned again. The leading 110 was now almost in range. 'Messerschmitts!' shouted Joss again, but both Denis and Peter kept flying straight towards the Stukas as though they hadn't heard his warnings. Then a dull rattle from behind and Joss saw tracer streak across his wing and more above his head. *Jesus, that was close.* Panic, his rapid breathing amplified into his rubber oxygen mask. *Think, Joss, think.* Peter and Denis were still closing and now opening fire. More tracer and a jolt as bullets tore into his fuselage, so that he felt the control column shudder in his hand. His proximity to death cleared his panicked mind. Turning the Spitfire into as tight a left turn as he could manage, he dived into cloud, his body pressed into his seat. His vision began to blur, and he grimaced as his ears popped and a stab of pain shot through his eardrums. Emerging through the other side of the cloud and out into blue sky once more, his vision cleared, and there, in front of him was a Stuka.

Joss was not conscious of any noise as he opened fire. The Spitfire shuddered as several hundred bullets spat from his machine guns. His senses had dulled but his mind felt clear and sharp as though he were in a kind of vacuum. In a trice the Stuka had gone, flying across his line of bullets, and Joss wasn't sure whether he'd hit the machine or not; when he turned to follow it, the plane had vanished into more cloud.

The roar of his Spitfire filled his ears once more and he remembered: *Peter and Denis.* He'd left them with the 110s right on their tails and so climbed back up to try and find them. Emerging through more cloud he saw no sign of the Spitfires, but another 110 was crossing the sky above and ahead of him. A sharp turn and climb, and again Joss pressed down his thumb on the firing button. Immediately the Messerschmitt turned away and Joss lost it as he flew into another bank of cumulus. White solitude enveloped him, whisping across his wings, then a spectral figure gradually emerged directly ahead of him. The shape was unclear, so for a moment Joss stalked it, closing behind until the cloud thinned and the two of them emerged into a large patch of clear sky. *A Stuka*—and no more than two hundred yards away. Its rather helpless form filled his gun-sights.

The sound of his Merlin receded to silence. His thumb hovered above the gun-button, no longer shaking, but in total control. 'Now,' he mouthed to himself, and bullets ripped out from his wings. Several seconds of fire, several hundred bullets, tearing into the soft metal of the aircraft ahead of him. Pieces of the Stuka flew off the fuselage and cockpit, then flames and smoke erupted from the engine. The plane appeared to hang motionless for a moment then exploded into nothing more than a ball of flame. A piece of hurtling white metal clattered into his windscreen, shaking Joss from his vacuum. The mass of flames was now falling, seemingly quite lazily towards the sea. Joss circled, looked above and behind, then down, just as the Stuka disappeared beneath the waves, gone forever.

My God, he thought, *I've killed two men.* He felt his chest tighten and he gulped, shocked by how easy it had been, but also excited. 'No!' he said out loud, disgusted. But he couldn't help himself. It was as though their deaths had made him feel more alive.

He looked around but could see no sign of any other aircraft, and so he turned back towards the coast. He began calling up again on the R/T, but heard nothing, not from Peter nor Denis. He glanced around him. The patchy cloud was high above him, but the sky looked empty, until he noticed away to his right another Spitfire weaving about from side to side. As he flew closer, he recognized Denis, with a large chunk missing from his rudder. So where was Peter? Hopefully already

352

back at Warmwell. He followed Denis all the way home.

A poor landing. He bounced three times and only just managed to pull up before hitting the perimeter hedge at the edge of the airfield. When he finally came to a stop, his fingers were shaking so badly he struggled not only to undo his leads, but even to pull back the canopy. Gingerly, he eased himself out, but his legs were weak and he found it difficult jumping from the wing root back onto the grass. His hands were still shaking as he approached Denis. When he tried to shut his mouth, his teeth began to chatter, so he opened it again.

'Jesus Christ,' said Denis. 'Jesus Christ.' He looked pale, his eyes wide.

'What happened to Peter, where is he?' said Joss, voice unsteady.

'I left my R/T on transmit,' said Denis. 'Only switched it back on just in time. Heard you say, "Messerschmitts", then dived out of the way, but I don't think Peter ever saw them.' Some of the other pilots had run over, asking what had happened.

Tommy was by Joss, an arm on his shoulder. 'Where's Peter?'

Joss could only shake his head. 'I don't know. I tried to warn him, but he didn't hear.' He glanced at his watch. Ten to seven. Just twenty minutes since he'd spotted the first Stuka.

*   *   *

As soon as Joss's Spitfire was refuelled and rearmed, he flew off with Tommy and four others to search for Peter. For an hour they hunted for

353

signs of a parachute or a lone pilot bobbing about on the surface, but the sea offered nothing but the flat empty surface of a calm summer's evening. It was as though the frenetic action of the hour before had never happened at all.

It was dusk by the time they eventually reached Middle Wallop. When Joss walked back into his room, he saw it was exactly as they had left it that morning. Peter's striped pyjamas were lying in a crumpled heap on the chair by his bed; his towel, hurriedly flung over the end of his bed, still damp. So much of him still there, but he was not. He was lying in the wreckage of his Spitfire, somewhere at the bottom of the English Channel. On the seabed along with two German aircrew.

He leant against the door for a moment and breathed in deeply, then went to the bathroom and ran a hot bath. He'd felt quite numb ever since taking off to search for Peter, but now, as he soaped himself, he could not stop thinking about what had happened; about how unfair it was that he should be alive while his friend was not. Only hours before, they'd been chatting happily, Peter bragging about Felicity. It was impossible to believe that such a lively, happy person was no more. *What have we got ourselves into?* he thought. First David, then Roger and now Peter. He had become a killer too. Somewhere, across the Channel, friends would be mourning the two men he had shot down just as he was mourning Peter. His complicity—his guilty thrill at their destruction—ate away at his heart. How pointless it all was. So futile, so tragic, and he felt ashamed too, for now he understood war for what it really was.

Joss began to weep, quietly at first, and then in

354

unconstrained sobs, crying harder than he had ever done before or would ever do again.

England—July, 1940

When Joss awoke the following morning, the rest of the squadron had long since departed for Warmwell. His mouth was dry and his head throbbed and when he tried to sit up and take the cup of tea offered by Whiting, he realized he was still a bit drunk. His first thought was, *poor Tommy*; he hoped his friend had been all right flying down to Warmwell some three hours earlier. Then glancing over at Peter's empty bed, he remembered why they'd got themselves drunk in the first place. At dinner in the mess the previous evening, he'd told Tommy he couldn't sleep in his room that night with Peter not there any more. 'Well, in that case, you have two options: either you sleep on the floor in my room—which I don't recommend—or you get plastered and then you won't know Peter's not there.'

'I think I'd rather get plastered.'

'Hoped you'd say that. Come on, let's get out of here and go to the Five Bells.' It had been nearly midnight by the time they made it back to the Officers' Quarters. Joss had been barely able to stand. Tommy was not much better. What was it Tommy had said? 'I've driven drunk many a time, so I'm sure I can fly drunk too.' Joss hoped he was right.

He dressed quickly, anxious to get out of his room and be away from Middle Wallop. Away from the war and the RAF. That empty bed was giving him a sickening feeling, heavy like a lead weight. He might still be a little drunk, but not drunk enough; eight hours of blissful amnesia had worn off.

*　　　*　　　*

Soon after he was driving out through the main gates of Middle Wallop and turning left on to the Salisbury road. There was little other traffic— petrol rationing had put pay to that—but this was just as well as Joss was barely concentrating on the road. What was he going to tell Guy? But then, of course, Guy had barely known Peter. Which in a way was strange, because Guy was his oldest and best friend and for so long they'd shared everything together, even other friends like Tommy.

His left eyelid had begun to twitch, and he rubbed it, hoping to wipe away his fatigue and hangover. The headache had grown worse too, not helped by the smell of the car: metal, rubber and the stale odour of a mountain of cigarette butts crammed into the ashtray. Not even an open window helped much. It was the first time he'd driven this journey, and although Middle Wallop was closer to Andover than Salisbury and Marleycombe ten miles beyond that, it was no great distance. Still, he was impatient to reach the farm. Only Guy would provide the necessary distraction to stop him thinking about the events of the previous day.

For now, however, he still had another twenty-five minutes of his own company. He thought about Peter's parents and younger sister and how they must be taking the news. MacIntyre had insisted on phoning Peter's father himself, even though Joss and Tommy had offered. 'It's neither your responsibility nor part of your remit,' the CO had told them, then added, 'but thanks anyway.' Instead they'd both gone to see Felicity. A small, dark-haired girl with a kind face and large brown eyes, she had been understandably upset and shocked. 'He was such a sweet boy,' she told them, 'it's so unfair.'

The others, slightly subdued, otherwise carried on as normal. They were careful to give Tommy and Joss a wide berth, although Pip had clasped Joss's shoulder and said, 'Sorry about Peter. He was a good bloke.' And yet now, strangely, as he drove towards Salisbury, he felt closer to those other members of the squadron. It was as though he could now meet them on an even footing because he, too, had seen action, and had lost a dear friend.

Through Wilton. No signposts now, and most of the windows he passed were criss-crossed with anti-blast tape, but otherwise the place was looking much as it had nearly two years before when he and Guy, along with Sam Hicks, had taken the truck to pick up five hundred gas masks. Past the market square and out on to the Shaftesbury road until at last, he turned off and drove up over the downs. The familiarity of every line and curve, each clump of trees and wooded slope acted like a drug that instantly calmed him. *We're still here,* they seemed to be saying.

Down the long hill, past the church at the bottom and round a bend until he reached the main valley road. Serene sunlight bathed the houses on either

357

side, giving the thatched roofs a renewed freshness, and casting pools of brightness through the trees and onto the road. Little sign of war here, he thought. Then up ahead he saw a barricade running across the road—large pieces of wood, a few barrels and some haphazardly strewn wire. Two men wearing armbands and carrying shotguns held up their hands and motioned him to stop. Stopping twenty yards in front, Joss watched the men wander cautiously towards him. The first approached his window while the second waited a few steps behind, shotgun half-ready.

'Let's be seeing your papers,' said the first. White hair sprouted from underneath his cap, framing a walnut face deep brown from a life spent outdoors. Joss was sure he recognized him.

'Really?' said Joss. 'I'm only going to Marleycombe.'

'You might be a spy for all we know,' said the man. White stubble sprouted underneath his jawline, missed by the morning's razor. Most of his teeth were gone, so that he spoke with something of a lisp, his watery tongue rolling across each of the words.

'All right, but I can't quite see what I could possibly be spying on around here.'

'We're looking for parachutists,' said the second man, his gun now lowered. Suddenly a Hurricane roared overhead, no more than a few hundred feet above the ground. They all turned to look, then Joss handed over his identity card.

'You flying them, then?' asked the first man.

Joss nodded. 'But Spitfires.'

The man nodded. 'You're all right,' he said handing back his card. 'Keep up the good work.'

358

The second waved Joss through the gap in the barricade. Joss couldn't help smiling—fat lot of good they'd be if they ever did spot a parachutist.

Five minutes later he reached the farm. As he pulled up the car outside the house, the door opened and Celia walked out. She still wore the same brooch as she always had, and still kept her hair in that slightly dishevelled way of hers, but Joss wasn't used to how much frailer she looked these days. Thinner too.

'Joss, how lovely!' she exclaimed as he stepped out of the car.

He smiled and kissed her on the cheek. 'Hello Celia. How are you coping?'

'Oh, you know, I think we're muddling through.' As was her way, she looped an arm through his and led him into the hallway. But she looked drained of life. Joss had never appreciated before how much personal contentment could enhance a face. The glow of her skin, the vibrancy of her eyes—the very joy of living—had vanished, leaving a rather plain, unremarkable-looking lady in her mid fifties.

'You look well, though,' he lied.

'Thank you, Joss. You look tired, if you don't mind me saying so.'

'Nothing a day here can't sort out.'

'Good,' she said, smiling.

It was a warm day, bright and fresh after the rain. In the drawing room it was light and clear. A wood pigeon was cooing throatily from the horse chestnut, its call carrying clearly through the open windows.

'Will you have some coffee, Joss?' asked Celia once they'd sat down on the sofas. 'Or a cold drink? I think we've still got both on offer. Fortunately, we've been buying those sorts of things in bulk for years, so we're not feeling the pinch too badly yet.'

'Coffee, if it's no trouble. Thank you, Celia.' His head still throbbed.

Celia rang a bell, then said, 'We only have poor Anna now, so I'm afraid we're doing most of the cooking ourselves. It's made me realize just how lucky we were. Still, it's good for me to keep busy. Keep's one's mind off things.' She smiled at him wistfully, then began telling him about just how much there was to do. The two evacuees took quite a lot of looking after. 'They eat earlier than us— not long after they get back from school. It's quite a performance, I assure you.' She asked him about how he was getting on. Fine, he told her. 'Been pretty quiet, actually. I know all the talk is of parachutists and an invasion any minute but we've barely seen a thing.' *I can't tell her,* he thought, then said, 'Where's Guy?'

'Oh, out about the farm somewhere. I never see him from dawn until dusk.'

A flash of disappointment, but Joss tried not to show it. When he'd rung three days before, Guy had said cheerily, 'That would be terrific Joss, come whenever you can,' and Joss had assumed that because *he* had the day off, Guy would stop working as well and that the two of them would have the day together, walking about the farm, talking and drinking in the Blue Lion just like they always used to. But of course Guy was out working. He realized now he'd been stupid to think otherwise.

'Poor Guy has had to learn a lot about farming very quickly,' Celia continued, 'and on top of that there's all these new orders and directives.

360

Sometimes I think it's just as well that David isn't here. He so loved every bit of this farm and the farming way of life. I don't think he'd recognize it now—ploughing up downland with tractors, many of the men gone. We've even had to kill most of the sheep. It would have broken his heart to see them go. But they don't want proper mixed farms any more. It's all crops and milk.' She sighed. 'And then there's the Local Defence Volunteers. Guy's joined that too. Says he has to do his bit like everyone else and so spends half the night manning roadblocks and searching the woods for Germans. The very thought—Germans here! In Marleycombe! It's utter madness, but then the world has gone mad, hasn't it?'

'They nearly had me,' said Joss, and immediately Celia put a hand to her mouth and said, 'Oh, I'm so sorry Joss, I didn't mean to imply—'

For a moment, Joss didn't know what she was talking about, then suddenly realized her misunderstanding. He felt his cheeks flush, more through shame than embarrassment. 'I mean, I was stopped at a roadblock. Checking for Fifth Columnists or something.'

Celia looked mortified. 'When I said Germans,' she said slowly, 'I of course meant Nazis. Parachutists.'

'I know,' said Joss. 'Don't worry. No offence taken, I assure you.' He didn't want to upset Celia, and of course he knew she had not meant to be rude, but at the same time, he *did* feel hurt, and that flustered him because he knew she would see that. He wished he could be more like Tommy. *He* would have found it hilarious, laughed out loud and made a joke about how he really *was* a Fifth

Columnist and please would Celia not let on to anyone. But he wasn't and so there was an awkward moment while he tried to think of something to say.

But it was Celia who spoke first. 'Perhaps after coffee we could go and look for Guy?'

'All right,' he said, brightening. 'Do you know where he might be?'

'He's up on Prescombe seeing to more fencing.' Joss turned round to see Stella standing in the doorway. She was wearing dark blue denim overalls with a thick leather belt round her waist and a red spotted scarf over her head, knotted at the front.

'Stella, darling, do you have to come in here wearing that awful clobber?' asked Celia.

'Oh Mum, don't go on.' She rolled her eyes at Joss, then said, 'Well this is a nice surprise. How are you Joss?'

'Fine. But more to the point, how are you?'

'You mean this?' she said looking down at her garb. 'I told you I was going to do my bit and I am. I'm an unofficial land girl working for Guy.'

'Your father would turn in his grave,' said Celia. 'All that money sending you to finishing school just for this.'

'Mum, don't start that again. We are at war, you know.'

Celia nodded sadly. Stella turned back to Joss. 'Actually, I'm a pretty good farmer. Just finished the morning's milking.'

'I'm impressed,' said Joss.

'Oh, it's quite easy once you know how.'

'Joss and I are just about to have a coffee,' said Celia.

'Good. I'll join you, then we'll go and find Guy

and see what else needs doing.'

* * *

They drank their coffee quickly. Perhaps Celia
sensed Joss was eager to find Guy; perhaps she
knew Stella would be better company.

'It's difficult for Mum,' said Stella, once they
were out of earshot and walking through the yard.
'For so long she's lived her life the same way, and
now everything's turned on its head.'

And she's lost a son and husband, thought Joss.
He glanced at the steps leading up to David's old
office. Cobwebs between the handrail sparkled in
the sunlight. 'I suppose so. But it's a difficult time
for everyone. None of us know what's going to
happen,' he said. Even without any make-up at all,
and wearing old workman's clothes, Joss still
thought Stella looked beautiful. Her face had
browned slightly in the early summer sun, so that
the light freckles that ran across her nose and
cheeks were subtly accentuated. Her eyelashes and
narrow eyebrows were naturally dark, like her hair,
and her pale eyes seemed to him to burn even
more brightly.

'And how about you, Joss? Seen any Nazis yet?'
In her directness, she was so like Guy. 'There's no
point in being rude,' Guy had once said, 'but I do
so hate the way people skirt round an issue.
Frankness is much better.' It was the kind of thing
David might have said; probably *was* something
David had said.

'Yes, actually I have.' He'd meant to tell Guy
all—desperately *wanted* to tell Guy all—so why not
Stella now that she was asking?

'Really?' she said, opening a wooden gate the far end of the yard. 'So you've actually flown against them?'

'Yes—only yesterday, as a matter of fact. I was beginning to wonder if we ever would. There's been days of patrolling the coast and not a thing, but then yesterday—' He stopped a minute, but Stella was looking at him, waiting for the rest. 'Well, yesterday, we saw quite a few.' He told her about spotting the Stukas then, just in the nick of time, the Messerschmitts hurtling down towards them. About shouting to Peter and Denis, but them not hearing him and the frantic few minutes darting in and out of the clouds.

'And were you very frightened?' They were walking up a chalk track now, that much-trod path that led up to the top of the downs and towards the Herepath.

'I don't know really,' said Joss. 'I'd thought about it so much beforehand. Felt more nervous and apprehensive than I'd ever felt in my life during my first operational trip. But then that wore off the more patrols we did and the more we never saw anything. And then when I saw the Messerschmitts behind me, I nearly jumped out of my skin and for a moment I was definitely panicking.'

'I'm not surprised.'

'But then I somehow took a hold of myself. It's difficult to explain, but a different part of myself took over. I was no longer conscious of any sound or smell or anything other than what I had to do.' He looked at her. 'This must sound ridiculous.' He glanced at her again for encouragement, but she was just looking ahead, deep in thought. Then he added, 'I was definitely not frightened then.'

He hadn't meant to tell her about shooting down the Stuka, but he couldn't help himself.

'And the fact that they were Germans?' she asked.

'It bothers me that I killed two men, whoever they were. I certainly think about them differently from the others. They *are* real people to me.' He thought for a moment, then said, 'Does it bother you? That I've done this, I mean?'

'No, of course not. Think of it this way: if you hadn't shot them down, they'd probably have killed some of us.'

'I suppose so. But I still have to live with what I've done.' Then he told her about Peter. Suddenly he couldn't stop talking. Words were spurting out of his mouth—the shock of the loss, returning to the room he'd shared, sobbing in the bath, visiting Felicity. Getting drunk with Tommy.

'I do understand, Joss,' Stella told him. They'd reached the Herepath, and although she briefly glanced around to look for Guy, they carried on walking along it, the chalk already dry and dusting their boots. 'I think we've got to get used to grief. After Dover I just felt numb. It was too incomprehensible. I do know he's dead—I've accepted that—but I can't *imagine* him dead. And I can't imagine never seeing my darling Roger ever again. I'm going to miss him all my life.' Like Joss, there was that sense of guilt too. Why him, she'd wondered over and over. It was so unfair that Roger had been sacrificed when so many had been saved. And why had she been born a girl? Shouldn't she be off fighting too? There were tears in her eyes now and she let them run down her cheek without shame or apology. She prayed he hadn't suffered, but then he must have done if he'd been wounded. 'The thought of him out there alone, bleeding and in pain tears me apart,' she told him. 'I'd have done anything to help him. Anything, but for all I know I was laughing and dancing with Philip. Having a good time while Roger was fighting for his life. But I can't talk to anyone about that. Neither Mum nor Guy will barely mention his name. My adored older brother has become a taboo subject, and it's horrible. I can't even talk to Guy about him and he's my twin. We're supposed to be able to talk about everything. Instead he works all hours on the farm and then goes out playing at soldiers with the old men of the village.' Her cheeks were flushed as she stopped and turned to face Joss. 'I'm sorry Joss—I don't mean to rant at you.'

'They're just trying to cope,' said Joss. 'Guy probably feels that as long as he's busy doing other things he won't have time to think about what has happened. And your mother—well, she wants to appear to you both as though she's coping. And this is her way of doing so.'

'Yes,' she said, 'I think you're probably right.' She smiled at him sheepishly. 'I never knew you were so wise, Joss.'

He felt himself reddening again. 'I don't know about that,' he said and turned to look out across the valley. Either side of the Herepath, where only a year before, and for hundreds of years before that, sheep had grazed, barley now rustled gently in the wind. The crop was already turning, the long whiskery ears a carpet of gold and green like brushed velvet in the breeze. 'Still no sign of Guy,' he said eventually.

'He'll be further along up here,' she said pointing, 'beyond the trees.' Ahead were a line of beech that straddled the track, a narrow wood running along the top of the downs. 'He's been clearing the rough land beyond the wood,' she told him. 'There were about eight acres of brambles, hawthorn and other bushes. Good for nothing but pheasants and rabbits, so he's had it cleared and ploughed and is now trying to get it fenced.'

But Guy wasn't there. A few new posts stood hammered into the ground, but he was nowhere to be seen. Only when they'd walked back down and were approaching the farm did they see him coming through the gate, leading one of the old horses and carts.

'Sorry,' he said, pausing and wiping his brow. 'Had to go to Shaftesbury to get more wire. Going to come and give me a hand, then?' he asked Joss.

Joss nodded and then looked at Stella. 'All right. Why not?'

'Did you know we've still got a whole load of wire in the shed next to the office?' said Stella.

'No. Have we? Damn.'

'I do wish you'd ask me about things sometimes,' said Stella. 'Might save you a bit of time. Anyway, what do you want me to do now? There's plenty of paperwork. Why don't I get on with that until milking?'

'Yes,' said Guy. 'Yes, you do that.'

Stella began walking on down the hill. 'Bye Joss,' she said, 'will you still be around for dinner?'

'You will won't you?' said Guy.

'I'd love to.'

'See you later, then.' Stella waved an arm in the air as she continued towards the gate.

'Bloody sister,' said Guy. 'Thinks she runs the place.' He wiped his brow again, looked morosely at the gleaming new wire coiled up in the cart and said, 'Oh well. Anyway, how are you keeping? How's the RAF and how's Tommy?'

Fine, all fine, Joss told him. He no longer wanted to talk of planes and sky battles and Peter. That need had been exorcised.

'A bloody great Hurricane flew over this morning,' said Guy, 'so low you could almost touch it.'

'I think I saw it. I was being held up by your LDV pals at the time on suspicion of being a spy.'

Guy laughed. 'Good old Laurie. No one gets past his barricade in a hurry. Did you know Goebbels has announced we're all to be considered "francs-tireurs". I don't know the literal translation but apparently it means that once they've successfully invaded we're all going to be shot. Makes your blood run cold just thinking about it.'

Joss thought: *I nearly* was *shot yesterday. Just yesterday!* Not even 24 hours ago.

They continued back up the hill. Guy seemed happy to accept Joss's reluctance to talk shop and so told him about the farm instead. 'I'm really pleased with this bit of reclamation,' he told him. 'Reckon we'll be seeding it in the autumn. Ministry of Ag sent down this bloody great gyro-tiller and the worst of it was cleared in a day.' What about labour, Joss asked. 'We're coping right now, but what I'm going to do in a month or so when the harvest's ready, God only knows. Probably have to take on a couple more land girls to work with Stella. Get the two evacuees to put their backs into it too.' Farming might have been a reserved occupation but even more of the workers had now gone to join up. There'd been eighteen full-time labourers in David's day, but now Guy had just five. The Fordson and other new machinery was cancelling out some of those losses in manpower, but even so Guy was worried. 'Dad had a lifetime learning about farming. I've had less than a year. Never paid the slightest bit of attention to it when I was growing up. Childhood folly coming back to haunt me.' He smiled ruefully.

'D'you remember when we let the cows out?' said Joss.

Guy laughed. 'God, yes. A night of underage drinking in the Blue Lion and then staggering home and leaving all the gates open. Never seen Dad so furious.'

'I thought I was going to be banished forever, never to set foot inside Alvesdon Farm again. And you kept saying, "It's only a few cows, I don't see what you're getting so upset about." '

'Did I really say that? Surely I couldn't have been that brattish.' They were both laughing now. 'Happy days indeed,' said Guy.

*   *   *

They returned to the house late in the afternoon. Joss had taken off his tunic and loosened his tie, and held up fence posts while Guy banged them into the ground with a large mallet, then helped with the wiring. He'd enjoyed it: enjoyed feeling the sun on his back, the time alone with Guy up on the downs. And it had been good to reminisce too. But something nagged at the back of his mind, like an itch that wouldn't go away no matter how hard he tried to ignore it. Ever since he'd known Guy, they'd done everything together—school, university, holidays—years of shared experiences. They'd been inseparable. But since the war, their lives had taken divergent paths and they no longer lived by the same creed. There was plenty to say about the past, but little about the present. Then at dinner Stella said, 'Did Joss tell you he shot down his first plane yesterday?' and Joss had looked up at Guy and seen the hurt in his eyes.

'You never said.'

'No,' said Joss. 'It's not something I feel terribly proud about, to be honest.' *But you told Stella.* Joss wanted to explain to Guy, to tell him that he'd been desperate to talk to him about it that morning but he hadn't been there, and so instead he'd confessed all to Stella. But they were having dinner and the conversation soon moved on to other things. Nor did he have a chance to speak to Guy alone later; as soon as the meal was over, Joss had to hurry back to Middle Wallop.

As he drove back through the fading summer light, Joss replayed the conversation with Guy in his mind. Perhaps he was being oversensitive. Next time he had a day off, he would come over again and make sure that if he needed to talk he would do so to Guy and no one else. Then guiltily he thought of Stella. He barely wanted to admit it to himself, but he'd been glad Guy had been away that morning. She'd listened and understood, given him comfort in a way he knew Guy would not have done. It was thanks to her, more than his afternoon with Guy, that he felt so much better and ready to face the squadron once more.

A quarter to ten, and in the villages he passed,

people were still out in their gardens and on the roads. He saw two men out cutting their lawns—a perfectly normal sight in summer, and yet 'normal' now looked odd, askew, because everything else had been turned on its head.

Past the checkpoint at Middle Wallop and through the gates, the outside world replaced in an instant by the microcosmic existence to which he now belonged. A quick glance through the window of the mess, but it looked quiet and so he went on over to his barrack block and up to his room.

Tommy was lying reading on Peter's bed. 'You're back,' he said. 'Hope you don't mind, but I decided to move in with you.'

'Of course not.'

'Rather like you, I didn't want to sleep on my own and since you weren't here to get drunk with . . .'

'Norman?'

Tommy nodded. 'And Colin. Three in two days. It's not good Joss. Not good at all.'

England—July, 1940

Fifteen thousand feet to just twelve in a matter of moments at a speed of nearly 400 miles an hour, but as the Spitfire plunged into cloud and the light changed from clear brightness into that strange milky glow, the sense of rapid speed stopped. Then the sky thinned, the power of the aircraft evident once more as the knife-like wings scythed through wisps of white. For once they had the advantage over the 110s; the German fighters were

371

comparatively low, protecting the Stukas who swirled beneath them as they prepared to attack the shipping steaming at a snail's pace along the English Channel. Stacked in layers like a set of stairs—ships then Stukas, then 110s, then Spitfires. And there was his target, dark mottled green like a grotesque giant insect, a hundred feet below and around a thousand yards ahead. Flicking off the gun safety catch, Joss held his thumb poised. *Wait, wait,* he told himself. *Let him fill the gunsight.* Eight hundred yards now and closing, six hundred, and then the rear gunner opened fire and Joss saw orange sparks of tracer flicking past his nose. *You're way off,* thought Joss, but the 110 was beginning to turn, heading for another patch of cloud. *Now!* Thumb down on the tiny red button. A long burst of his guns and the Spitfire shuddered from the recoil, jolting Joss in his seat. The return fire ceased immediately and he saw from his own tracer that his shots had raked the fuselage. *I've killed another man,* he thought. One last burst—the remaining rounds of his ammunition—and a trail of smoke from the port engine. The 110 disappeared, cloaked by thick cloud.

A deafening crack and Joss was pushed up out of his seat. The choking smell of cordite filled the cockpit, as more cannon shells exploded behind him. *Christ,* he'd been hit, but where? His backside was hot, but no pain. He thrust the stick over to one side and then back into the stomach. He glanced behind. A Messerschmitt 109 tight on him, an angry wasp, large and far too close—so close he could see flashes of orange and puffs of smoke from its wings and nose. He felt no sense of calm vacuum now, just nausea and a tightness the length

372

of his throat. Where had he been hit? Was the aircraft OK? *Please let the Spitfire fly all right.* The stick was still in his stomach, the plane on its side, almost beyond the vertical, turning and turning. His vision blurred again—*lean forward*—vision still greying, the drum of machine-gun fire from behind, the 109 still on his tail. Joss strained forward to ease the gravity loading. Sweat ran under his helmet and down his face, and he grimaced with the strain as they went round and round and round. His eyes felt as though they were being pushed into his skull. *Where was all the cloud when you needed it?* Another glance in the mirror—the 109 was still there. He saw the face of the German pilot— goggles down, leaning forward like him, face set with determination. Determination to kill. *I'm going to die,* thought Joss. He cursed again—for being so bloody stupid. For being so *fucking careless.* Over and over they'd been told to keep an eye out behind, but he'd been so set on catching the 110, he'd forgotten the most basic rule. It had killed Peter, and now it was about to kill him. His flicked his eyes to the mirror, then glanced over his shoulder. Joss was exhausted already, but he saw a glimmer of hope, for he was slowly gaining ground. So it was true—a Spitfire *could* out-turn a 109!

He tried to think calmly: the plane was still flying perfectly, gauges a bit high, but OK. And he was gaining ground, the stick still rooted into his stomach. He looked behind again and saw the 109 at last pull out of the turn. *What's he doing?* Gaining height, the 109 made another steep turn, trying to cut back across him from above. Joss glimpsed another dark shape in the corner of his eye—*shit, there's another one*—and in seconds it would be two against one—and he was out of ammunition. But the first had given him a chance to break and so with a gasp, Joss turned the Spitfire onto its back to prevent the engine from cutting, and pushed the stick far over to the side. The machine rolled and as he centred the control column once more, began a vertical dive. With the throttle still open, the engine began to scream. Joss clutched the stick with both hands and desperately tried to swallow as his ears throbbed and popped with the sudden change of pressure. He was falling at over five hundred miles an hour and the wings were visibly straining, actually *bending* backwards. Any faster and they would snap. The noise was deafening. The green-blue sea hurtled towards him. His arms ached and his ears hurt like hell, but he *had* to pull himself out of this dive. *My God these controls are heavy,* he thought. He yanked back the stick, heavy like a block of lead, straining as he lugged it into his stomach. The sea was still rushing towards him. *Christ, this will be close.* He thought of Peter. Thought of death. *I don't want to die. Concentrate Joss. One last effort.* He yelled out aloud. His entire body felt crushed. Sweat had soaked his shirt so that it clung to his body. The Spitfire, too, seemed to be howling with the pain and strain. But then, as Joss thought the plane must surely be about to break up, the Spitfire began to level. At just 150 feet above the water. The sea looked close enough to touch.

Joss scanned the sky but it was empty. Nothing, not even a contrail high above. He closed his eyes for a moment, breathing heavily, his arms weak and shaky. So now he knew what sheer terror was like. He looked at his dials—oil and glycol a bit high—

but otherwise his Spitfire was flying steadily, the Merlin thrumming rhythmically once more. His machine had not let him down. His eyes swept one more time across the sky above, and then he dropped to fifty feet and hurried back to the coast and to the safety of Warmwell.

*   *   *

Griffiths and Dowling, his fitter and rigger, were waiting for him as he came into land and taxied across the grass. He knew they regarded the Spitfire as their own. They called her 'Nessie' for the single 'N' painted either side of the fuselage. To begin with Joss's lack of experience or knowledge of the plane ensured he'd felt their junior despite his rank; all three knew perfectly well that the 'sir' they latched onto every comment meant nothing. But he'd soon learnt the idiosyncrasies of his aircraft and become accustomed to its power, and with every successful flight, his confidence in his ability had grown. Ever since he'd shot down the Stuka, Griffiths and Dowling had become less proprietorial too—more *sharing.* Theirs had become a three-way partnership.

As soon as he came to a halt, Joss pulled off his flying helmet and closed his eyes for a moment. *I'm still alive,* he thought.

'You all right, sir?' asked Griffiths, jumping onto the wing beside him. Joss nodded, then slowly pushed himself up until he was standing on the bucket seat. He lowered the half-door, then gingerly eased himself onto the wing root and leapt down. Just a few minutes before, he'd felt as though a ten-ton weight were pushing down on him; now his body seemed surreally light, and he

375

fell to the ground, his face pressing against the earth. The sweet smell of grass filled his nose, followed by a sharp wave of nausea. His mouth contracted. A moment later he was sick.

'Bloody hell, look at your 'chute, sir,' said Griffiths, jumping down beside him.

Joss wiped his mouth then spat. He had no energy left at all.

'Christ almighty,' said Dowling, squatting down next to Griffiths.

'Hold still, sir,' said Dowling, then triumphantly held up a piece of squashed metal. 'Look,' he said, holding it just inches from Joss's face, 'it's a fucking cannon shell—'scuse my French.' Denis was running over towards him, as was the CO. 'Look, a piece of bloody cannon shell stuck in his 'chute!' exclaimed Dowling again, now standing and holding it up into the air for all to see.

'What happened?' said MacIntyre, an arm on Joss's shoulder. Joss looked up at him, mouth open, face drained of colour. His brain was no longer working properly. He struggled to speak. 'I—' he began. 'I–I—'

'All right,' said MacIntyre, 'take it easy. A few deep breaths.'

Joss tried to gulp. He was still on his hands and knees and, for a moment, rooted to the spot, his mind unable to tell his body what to do. Stella suddenly came into his mind—he thought of her tears, tears shed for her brother and father, and because of her sense of frustration.

Someone was talking to him, close to his ear. MacIntyre. 'Come on,' he was saying, 'let's get you up. Denis, give me a hand will you?' Hands grabbed him under the arms and hauled him up onto his feet. His head spun for a moment, then suddenly he felt better again, as though his brain had once again reconnected.

'Thanks,' he mumbled. 'I could do with some water.' He freed his arms and began taking off his parachute.

'You had the luck of the devil, sir,' said Griffiths and Joss undid the straps and looked at the pack where there was a hole, singed black.

'Fuck me,' said Denis, whistling.

'Straight through the seat,' said Griffiths standing on the wing root. 'Don't get much closer than that. And looks like you've sprung a few rivets too.'

'Here, sir,' said Dowling, handing him the remains of the cannon shell. 'Think this is yours.'

Joss stared at him. 'Thanks,' he said, then held the crushed metal between his finger and thumb. He wondered why he'd been spared. The shell was flattened and jagged. Had it entered his body, it would have ripped through his flesh and torn his insides apart. Even closer to death than he'd thought.

'What happened Joss?' asked MacIntyre again. 'Joss?'

'Happened?' he turned to the CO, his eyes hollow. *Pull yourself together,* he told himself. He clenched his fist over the shell, and tried to think. 'We must have been bounced,' he said, now finding his voice. 'I hit a 110. I think it went down because I saw the port engine catch fire, but lost it in cloud. Then I had a couple of 109s after me.' Everything was clear now. He could barely get the words out fast enough. 'The first hit me before I saw him then I went into a tight turn. It's true what they say, you know, because a Spitfire really can out-turn a 109. I

377

just did—nearly blacked out—but I did it. Then I'd just got the edge over him and another one turned up, another 109'—he was gabbling and gesticulating wildly—'and of course, I was out of ammo, so I flipped over and headed for the deck. It was some dive, I can tell you. I've never been so fast in my life—saw the clock go over 500. Are the other two back? Where are they? I lost them after I went for my 110 and when I came out of my dive there wasn't a soul in sight.'

'No,' said MacIntyre, 'they're not. Pip told Control he was baling out, but we haven't heard a word from Karl.' His brows were pinched.

Joss's heart sank, energy spent once more. *We're being slaughtered,* he thought. Reaching dispersal, he briefly glanced at the others, but no one said much. With two more pilots missing there was little positive that could be said, so it was best to say nothing. Joss walked straight on into the dispersal tent. At one end stood a trestle-table with a number of telephones. Joss nodded to the orderly, who was picking his fingers while he awaited instructions. Wires ran down one side and away underneath the canvas. Either side of the tent were lines of camp beds, littered with clothes and various personal belongings; Johnnie Reeves was asleep on one, a line of dribble hanging like a rope between his mouth and the tea-stained pillow. Johnnie could sleep anywhere, lucky bastard. Joss had felt exhausted just a short while before, but now, with the nausea and shock worn off, he knew he would be unable to catnap. Who had he killed this time? He hoped the man hadn't suffered.

It was hot in there. Hot and sweetly damp; a smell of grass and canvas and rope, and Joss wanted to get back outside to the cooling breeze. But first he needed something to drink. There didn't appear to be any water, just a tray of old tea. *Bloody useless airfield,* he thought. It was about a mile back up to the main offices, yet the NAAFI van rarely came round, and the station commander was a stickler for insisting all meals should be eaten in the mess. *Well, a cup of cold tea then.* He poured himself a mug, adding sugar with a tablespoon—there was no teaspoon in sight. Nor was there any milk left in the bottle.

'Joss?' It was Tommy. 'A' Flight back from lunch. 'Are you all right?'

Joss nodded. 'Fine. Really.'

'Come on,' said Tommy. 'Let's go for an amble.' Seeing Joss look at his watch he added, 'Not far. Come on, just to clear your head.'

Outside the airfield was quiet, the sun warm. A bumble-bee hovered around some daisies. A couple of sparrows flitted past. Griffiths and Dowling were still standing by Joss's Spitfire with Chiefy, the head mechanic, their voices carrying softly across the field.

'So you never saw what happened to Pip or Karl, then?'

Joss shook his head. 'I was too busy trying to keep the 109s off my arse.'

Tommy nodded. Several pilots from 'A' Flight were standing chatting quietly, while most of the others were still rooted to their assortment of chairs. Soon it would be 'B' Flight's turn to trundle up to the mess, but for the moment a quiet pause had settled over Warmwell. Two scrambles that morning, but right now the war appeared to have stopped.

The two of them began walking slowly away, alongside the perimeter track. It was almost noon and getting warmer. Joss could feel the sun on his face and bare arms.

'It's hard to know what's really going on, isn't it?' said Tommy. 'I mean, one can't really believe what's being said in the papers, because of course they're going to put a gloss on everything. We're so isolated here. Sometimes it feels as though it's just you, me, the rest of the squadron, that no one else is involved. I don't know what I'd been expecting really.'

'I remember David Liddell once told me that in the last war he didn't have a clue what was going on half the time. He said he could, generally speaking, say what was happening thirty yards either side of him, but that that was about it.'

'Hm,' said Tommy. 'Perhaps it's just as well.'

They were silent a moment and then Joss said, 'I wonder whether in a thousand years people will be digging up aircraft with the same enthusiasm that we attack Anglo-Saxon graves.'

Tommy chuckled. 'I'm not sure about that. After all, we dig up Anglo-Saxon graves because we know so little about them. Future generations are going to know plenty about us, aren't they?'

'Yes, I suppose you're right.'

Tommy pulled out a cigarette, then said, 'I wonder what old Sleeman's up to. Whether he's still trying to ram that Norman bullshit down people's throats. My one real regret about leaving Cambridge is that we never had the chance to convert him.'

'We could always go back after.'

Tommy smiled. 'Yes, we could. In fact, I think I will. Definitely. Good idea. At least Noel will probably still be there. I doubt he's ever going to leave.' Tommy began talking about Noel, whom he'd seen recently in London. Cambridge was apparently very quiet, but Joss soon stopped listening, his mind wandering. He thought of Peter, then chided himself, but then began thinking about that Messerschmitt 110. Had it crashed, or made it back to France? Perhaps he'd killed the pilot as well. He wondered whether they'd had any foreboding that morning or whether, like him, they'd woken and had breakfast with their colleagues, just like any normal day. A few nerves, of course—that was to be expected. He wondered what they'd been thinking when he appeared, spitting bullets. What had gone through the gunner's mind as Joss's bullets tore into his flesh? In that instant, twenty or so years of life, learning and memories had been erased, 12,000 feet above the English Channel.

'Joss?'

He turned suddenly to Tommy. 'Sorry, I—'

'Are you sure you're all right?'

'Sorry, Tommy,' said Joss again. 'No, I'm fine, honestly.'

'You'd tell me if you were really worried about something?'

'I'd tell you.'

The Spitfires dispersed around the edge of the field gleamed in the midday sun. They ambled between them, the smell of oil and aviation fuel heavy on the air, then noticed the CO sitting under the wing of his own, in the shade where he couldn't be seen from dispersal.

'Hello, you two,' he called.

'Sorry, Mac,' said Tommy. 'Didn't mean to

381

disturb you.'

'You're not,' but he looked slightly embarrassed all the same. 'I just fancied a bit of time—well, peace and quiet, I suppose.' He was smoking a cigarette and offered one to Tommy then Joss. 'Here,' he said, holding out the packet.

'Thanks, but I won't,' said Joss.

'Oh, of course, you're one of those rare breeds who doesn't. Should've remembered.'

Joss smiled. He wasn't sure whether he and Tommy should walk on or stay and talk. But MacIntyre, it seemed, was only too happy to chat, and said to Joss, 'How are you feeling now?'

'Fine, thanks. Just a bit close for comfort up there.'

'And knackering.'

Joss nodded.

'Have you rung through to Calder yet with your report?'

'Not yet.'

'Make sure you do. It'll only be a probable, I'm afraid, but we must keep a count of everything.'

'Oh absolutely,' said Tommy. 'Show those bastards at Air Ministry we're worth our pay.'

The CO smiled ruefully at Tommy, then pulled out a piece of loose tobacco from his mouth and said, 'You know, it's absolutely bloody hopeless us operating like this—one flight on, one off, half the squadron down here, half up in Middle Wallop. Being sent up in flights of threes and fours. There's simply not enough of us. Those bastards in Air Ministry, Tommy, need their heads examining. Oh, I'm sure that on paper small manoeuvrable numbers makes sound tactical sense, but they're not the ones up there are they? No advantage outweighs the problem of being so totally outnumbered. And, you know what—we're a bloody good bunch of pilots now. I mean, for Christ's sake, another two gone this afternoon.' He looked at Joss. 'Almost three, from the sounds of it.'

'We've got to work in squadron strength, then,' said Tommy.

'Too bloody right we have. If we're allowed to do that, we might start getting somewhere.' He got up, emerging into the sunlight. 'And another thing— this fucking station is getting to me. I shouldn't be saying this, but that idiot running this place doesn't know his arse from his tit. What the hell he thinks we are, insisting we eat every meal in the mess, I really have no idea. This morning I told him that if he could get a message to Luftwaffe headquarters and ask them not to come over during breakfast or lunch, I'd happily go along with his little rules.'

'What did he say?' Joss asked.

Mimicking the station commander, MacIntyre said, ' "For God's sake man, what's wrong with sending one flight up to the mess at a time?" That's the sort of person we're dealing with. I told him we needed sandwiches brought down to dispersal, but I'm certain that won't happen. No doubt I'll have to go up in the car with one of the orderlies, as per usual. One of these days I'm just going to belt him one and be done with it.'

They laughed. 'I'd love to see that,' said Tommy.

'I dare say.' He grinned, and slapped them both gently on the back. 'Yes, it might bring some light relief. And I think we could all do with that.'

*　　　*　　　*

But some cheer came not from any showdown with the station commander, but from the arrival firstly of Pip, and then Karl. Back from the dead. Pip had showed up first, deposited at dispersal from an Army staff car. He was so casual in the way he patted the roof of the car and called out his thanks, that Joss and the other pilots around dispersal barely glanced up to begin with. Then Mike said, 'Bloody hell, it's Pip!' and everyone suddenly leapt from their chairs and rushed to crowd round him like overexcited schoolboys.

'I never knew you felt this way,' he grinned. 'I'm so touched.' Like Joss, he'd been hit by the 109s. With smoke trailing from his engine, his attackers had let him plummet to the ground on his own. He'd tried to bale out, but the canopy had jammed and so with what control he had left, he'd crash-landed onto Studland beach, coming to a stop in just a few inches of water. 'Just as well,' he told them, 'because the sea water stopped her from blowing up.' Once on the ground, the canopy had miraculously unjammed itself, so that Pip merely slid it back on its runners and hopped out onto the wing. He'd jumped, unscathed, onto the shingle when he heard a hollering from the cliffs above. It was the army, waving and shouting at him not to move. 'Of course the bloody beach was mined,' he said, 'so I thought, "Great, crash-land OK and now I'm going to be blown up by our own mines." But shortly after some sappers arrived and led me safely off the beach. Bloody glad I'm not a sapper, though—it was terrifying.' He'd then been taken back to their company HQ in Swanage, given lunch, and afterwards driven back to Warmwell.

'Charming people, you know,' said Pip. 'Couldn't have been nicer.'

Karl didn't reappear until later. The squadron had been stood down for the day and MacIntyre had insisted they all get off base rather than stay in the mess. No one questioned the decision. Commandeering a 15cwt truck, they'd piled in—officers and NCOs together—and driven over to the New Inn at West Knighton. Having gathered around the beamed bar, they were into their second pint when the door flung open and there was Karl, triumphant grin across his face.

From the moment of Karl's arrival a month before, Pip had maintained an air of thinly veiled indifference, but now, seeing him standing in the doorway, he quite spontaneously rushed over and clasped his hand. The others soon crowded round him, firing questions. What had happened? Where had he been? *Is it really you?*

Karl had not been hit by a 109, but by a rear-gunner of the 110 he'd gone after. 'A total fluke shot,' he assured them, 'got me fair and square in the glycol tank.' He'd managed to bale out all right, and had watched his Spitfire spiral down into the sea, a long tail of white smoke following behind. 'It was kind of peaceful up there,' he admitted. He landed not in the sea, but in a wheat field near the coast. A pair of ageing farmers had watched him drift down, and so had hurried over through the ripening wheat to where he was collecting up his parachute. They'd absolutely insisted he come back with them to the house for some refreshment. The two men had been amazed to discover he was an American. 'It was educational I can tell you,' said Karl. 'The farmhouse was a million years old, narrow and thatched.' He'd never seen such low ceilings before. 'Or so dusty—I couldn't stop sneezing, which was a bit embarrassing.' He also had some trouble understanding the local patois, while they were equally unfamiliar with some of the language he was using. They'd understood enough of each other to get along, however. A large woman—'I guess she must have been one of their wives'—sat him down and plied him with bread and cold chicken, and a large glass of scrumpy. 'Is that right?' Karl asked, 'a kind of highly alcoholic apple drink?' At any rate, he'd loved it and had drunk a gallon-full. They'd sat chatting for ages, and then he'd thanked them and told them he really ought to be going. By this time his head was swimming. Neither of the men had a car, but the doctor did, and so they fetched him and Karl was given a lift to Wareham. The local Home Guard couldn't find anyone to take him back, so he was given tea and some more to eat. Then he fell asleep. When he awoke, it was evening, and he was about to suggest he ring Warmwell for someone to pick him up, when a young lad turned up with a motorbike and drove him back to the airfield. When he discovered they'd all gone to the pub, he persuaded Chiefy to give him his third lift of the day. 'And here I am and I definitely need to drink some more.'

They'd all laughed, Joss included. Karl told his tale well. *The Street-Smart Californian and the Dorset Farmers: A Comedy of Two Cultures.* Joss watched him talking animatedly in the dim light of the pub. Karl had barely set foot out of California, let alone America, before he joined the RAF, yet here he was, perfectly at home in this alien environment. What would the station commander make of Americans flying from his airfield, Joss wondered?

Fifteen faces were now laughing, smiling, shouting, the cigarette smoke so thick it made your eyes smart. Joss thought about the squadron. It was evolving rapidly, no longer the cream of England, but a mish-mash of nationalities and classes. It occurred to him he had stopped fretting about them discovering the truth about his father. The matter hadn't crossed his mind for days. Another pint was thrust into his hand.

Perhaps things weren't so bad after all. The despair, so palpable just a few hours before, had evaporated. There was something almost manic about their jollity, and when MacIntyre announced he was introducing a squadron rule for those who were shot down and survived to tell the tale, everyone cheered and stamped their feet. 'A pint in one,' he told them, 'half beer, half cider, in honour of Karl's efforts this afternoon fraternizing with the locals, then a verse of *Blue Skies.*'

'Sure—I know that one all right,' said Karl. The concoction was handed over, dripping onto the stone floor as he brought the glass to his lips. While he drank, the others counted the seconds out loud. When he'd finished, he belched, then put the glass upside down on his head.

'Now the song, if you'd be so kind,' said Mac.

'All right,' said Karl. Theatrically clutching one hand to his chest, and with the other outstretched, he began. 'Blue skies,' he sang tunelessly, 'all of them gone, nothing but blue days, from now on.'

Everyone cheered again, and then it was Pip's turn. The pint, he complained, was 'too cold' for really speedy drinking, but his rendition of the song was surprisingly tuneful. 'Used to be a chorister as a boy,' he admitted. More laughter. Not long after he came over to Joss and said, 'We're the lucky three, you know. If we all survived that this morning, someone must have been smiling on us. I've been thinking that perhaps we're blessed.'

*   *   *

The truck—or tumbrel, as they called it—was there to meet them as they stumbled, laughing and shouting, out of the pub some time after half-past eleven. For the past fortnight, they'd been spending every third night at Warmwell, instead of returning to Middle Wallop, and although visiting squadrons were supposed to sleep in the sergeants' quarters, by general consensus it had been agreed that it was more practical to bed down in the camp beds in the dispersal tents, despite the lack of sanitation or running water. After all, they rarely went to bed much before midnight and had to be at readiness by four-thirty. It was better to be dirty and get an extra half-an-hour's rest.

Their exuberance had died down by the time they reached dispersal. Joss had fallen asleep in the truck and was barely awake as he clambered down and staggered across the dew-sodden grass. He joined the others already peeing into the hedge, then shuffled to the tent. Fully clothed, he collapsed onto the hard canvas bed, pulled an old and coffee-stained blanket tight over his shoulders, and fell immediately into a deep sleep.

When he awoke, it was just after four the following morning. MacIntyre, along with a handful of groundcrew, was shaking everyone in turn, and saying, 'Come on, wakey-wakey. Shift your arses.' Joss sat up on his elbows. He felt a bit light-headed still, his mouth dry and sour. His eyes stung through lack of sleep. He glanced across at Tommy who was sitting up and smoothing down his hair.

'Bacon,' said Tommy, sniffing. 'I can definitely smell bacon.'

Joss sniffed too. 'Yes,' he said, 'and I want some.'

Still yawning, they made their way outside to where there were several trays of sandwiches and mugs of tea. The dawn air was shrouded and cool.

'Where did this lot come from?' Mike Drummond asked one of the groundcrew.

'Don't look at me, sir, it was the boss.'

Good old Mac, thought Joss.

'Is this true?' asked Pip.

Mac looked almost sheepish. 'Don't say I don't look after you miserable bunch.' Murmurs of appreciation as hungry hands stretched towards the trays. 'The thought of another morning without breakfast was weighing badly on my mind,' he told them, 'so I thought, well, if the bloody cooks won't get up and make us some tucker, I'd better do it myself. Nearly set fire to the place, but otherwise it was straightforward enough.'

Joss munched through the thick bread in silence. Tomorrow he would be on leave—for six whole days. *Just get through today,* he thought to himself. A gulp of hot tea and then he wandered over to his Spitfire, his boots soon dripping with dew. A thin mist lay still across the field, shrouding the aircraft so that they looked sinister, deadly. An engine suddenly started up, tearing apart the silence with a thunderous roar. Others soon joined in as the pilots carried out their pre-flight checks.

Griffiths was standing by beneath the engine cowling with a metal box of tools, while Dowling, perched on the wing root, had his upper half immersed in the cockpit.

'Is she going to be all right?' said Joss, walking up to Griffiths.

'Should be. We started her up again last night and there didn't seem to be any problems. And we've had the wing looked at. Norm's just checking the seat and everything one last time—making sure we didn't miss anything.'

'As good as new, eh?'

'Not far off.' Griffiths grinned and patted the Spitfire.

*   *   *

Just after nine, 'A' Flight returned from convoy patrol. They'd seen nothing, all pilots safely back. The whole squadron was now sitting outside the tents. The morning mist had been burned off by the rising sun, which beat down with steadily mounting warmth.

The phone rang. Several of the pilots jolted nervously in their seats. Joss and Tommy, who had just begun discussing what Joss would do during his leave, immediately stopped talking, listening to the orderly inside the tent instead.

It was for Mac. A collective sigh. Shoulders dropped back into their seats. *Chance for a bit more rest.*

'Yes,' barked Mac into the phone. Tommy winked at Joss; the others, too, were listening in. 'Yes,' said Mac again. 'I'm sorry, but I can't do that,

390

sir. I'm at dispersal. We might be scrambled at any moment.' A loud sigh. 'All right then. If you insist.' He reappeared, glared at the others then jumped into a car and sped off towards the station buildings.

After ten minutes of fevered speculation at dispersal, the CO was back. Slamming the car door, he marched over to the rest of the squadron, and flipped a cigarette into his mouth.

'Problem up at the ranch?' asked Pip.

'Arsehole,' muttered Mac. 'It's the fucking limit. The cooks have complained that we didn't leave the kitchen properly cleaned and tidied this morning. Can you believe it?'

'So what did you say?' said Pip.

'I told him that if his fucking bone-idle cooks had bothered to get off their arses in the first place, I wouldn't have had to use his sodding kitchen. Well, of course, that didn't wash with him, so he's now banned us from ever using it again.' He dropped his cigarette and stamped it into the ground. 'I'm going to ring the AOC.' But no sooner had he turned towards the tent than the phone rang again. Another patrol needed over a convoy now passing south-west of the Needles.

'All right,' said Mac, 'I'll lead. "B" Flight, let's go. But when I get back I'm going to sort this out once and for all.'

*　　　*　　　*

They climbed to 15,000 feet, the great divide between land and sea stretching away beneath them. Joss was surprised, despite his experience the previous day, that he felt no more apprehensive than normal. His heart, of course, was racing, and his stomach churning, but he was able to think clearly. He was in control.

'Tartan this is Nimbus Leader.' Mac's voice crackled through Joss's headphones. 'We're at Angels fifteen and proceeding one-fifteen.'

'Nimbus Leader this is Tartan. No reported bandits, but patrol line as planned, over.'

Far below, Joss saw the convoy—four ships steaming clear of the Isle of Wight, heading, he assumed to London, a small creamy wake behind each one. He looked around at the others, wavering slightly as they continued to sweep across the sky. Then a momentary judder. *What was that?* It sounded like the engine faltering—nothing dramatic, but something not *quite right.* Joss tensed, straining to listen, but now all seemed well; perhaps he'd imagined it. Oil slightly high perhaps, but nothing to worry about. Then another jolt and a wisp of smoke. *No imagining that.* The oil gauge was rising. *Boost pressure rising too.* He glanced up at the others, but they were already moving away from him as his speed began to drop.

Christ, he cursed. His chest grew tight, and the now familiar sensation of nausea rose from his stomach.

He switched his radio to 'talk'. 'Nimbus Leader this is Blue One, I've got engine trouble.' He hoped he sounded calm.

'Blue One this is Nimbus Leader. Can you make it to base?'

The Spitfire coughed again, producing a larger puff of smoke. 'Nimbus Leader, this is Blue One. I'll try, over.'

He glanced around the sky then left the formation for good, turning back towards the coast.

No reported bandits, but after yesterday—well, it had taught him a lesson. Thick black smoke was now pouring from the engine, making forward vision difficult. The engine began juddering and clanking. Jesus, but he was going to have to bale out. Griffiths and Dowling would never forgive him. *And I'm supposed to be on leave tomorrow*, he thought.

But what was the procedure? For a moment, he couldn't think, his mind frozen by the panic of being ten thousand feet high in a Spitfire with a dying engine. *Come on*, he told himself, *think, Joss.* Smoke had crept into the cockpit, the dials in front of him flickering madly. He'd already dropped four thousand feet, and in a matter of moments the engine would die altogether, or worse, with more than three-quarters of his fuel tank full and sluicing about just above his legs, explode. 'Help me!' he shouted out loud. 'Please God, help!'

As though in answer to his prayer, the fog that filled his brain suddenly cleared as the smoke thickened. He checked his speed—*yes, under 300 miles an hour—260, in fact.* Now over the coast, he turned the plane so that it was pointing back towards the sea, then pushed back the canopy, thinking briefly of Pip's difficulties the day before. But the hood slid back and stayed there, just as it was supposed to. With fumbling fingers, he frantically pulled out his oxygen and radio leads, released his harness and with one last deep breath, flipped the plane onto her back.

He was tumbling through the air, the sky, sea and ground twisting and pirouetting around him. For a moment he couldn't find the parachute cord, then having shaken off his glove, his fingers clenched round the ring and he pulled. A flutter of silk and with a lurch he was no longer falling, but drifting slowly downwards.

Calm at last. There was his Spitfire, disappearing down towards the sea, already tiny, like a toy. And there below, and once more as it should be, was the soft, patchwork of Dorset, not quite so green as it had been just a couple of weeks before: many of the fields had turned a soft dusty gold. Perhaps he would make his leave after all. He yawned—actually yawned—despite floating down from 10,000 feet. Six whole days. Exhaustion coursed through his body and mind. So much had happened over the past few days, and yet everyone said the Germans had hardly begun. He wondered how he would possibly cope if and when the German onslaught started. How any of them would cope. At least Tommy seemed to be all right. *Where would I be without him?* Sleep—the thought of a proper bed and sleep. His room at Alvesdon, that distinctive *smell*. He hoped Guy would have some spare time. Hoped Stella would too—spare time to spend with him. Now that *would* be good.

Almost there. He was drifting down across a small wood and then over fields, one lushly green and full of cows, one with golden corn. The ground now hurried towards him. Then he was below the tree line, drifting over the hedge and gliding into the gently waving wheat.

Land at last, and safe.

* * *

When Joss reappeared at Warmwell later on that day, no one was able to decide whether he was the luckiest or unluckiest man in the squadron. Pip still insisted Joss was blessed and therefore lucky not just personally but for all of them. 'I know I was drunk last night,' he told Joss, 'but I stand by what I said. How we all survived that fight, I have no idea. And now you go and bale out safely again today. So you must be blessed.'

'My pilots keep returning,' said Mac, grinning. 'This is good news.'

'Sorry about the Spit, though,' said Joss.

'Don't worry yourself about that. Better to happen when it did than in the middle of a bloody great dogfight. Planes are expendable Joss, but not pilots.' The CO had been mollified since his argument with the station commander earlier that morning. He'd spoken to Brand, the commander of 10 Group, and had achieved something of a compromise. They would not use the kitchens again, but in future they would be supplied with a couple of Primus stoves and a few bits and pieces of crockery to use at dispersal. Moreover, Brand had also promised to try and get some latrines erected nearby. 'Soon we won't have to go anywhere near that son of a bitch,' Mac told Joss.

*   *   *

11 p.m. No replacement Spitfire could be arranged for Joss that day, so he had driven back with some of the groundcrew. Only 50-odd miles, but it had still taken well over two hours, and it had been dark by the time they'd reached Middle Wallop. Joss had paused in the mess for a couple of drinks, then headed off to bed.

'You scared me today,' said Tommy as they

walked across the road that led to their barracks.

'I scared myself.'

They were quiet for a moment, then Tommy said, 'I'm sure we'll be all right, you know. I mean, we've come this far, haven't we, and we're still standing.'

'You certainly are,' said Joss. 'You seem to be immune.'

Tommy thrust his hands deep into his pockets, just like he had that day Joss had first met him at Cambridge. 'Yes,' he said, 'I have a feeling you and I will be just fine.'

Southern England—July, 1940

Despite his exhaustion, Joss woke when Whiting came in to wake Tommy, and although he was now officially on leave and able to lie in for as long as he liked, sleep had deserted him. He wished he could stop thinking about the Germans he'd killed, but their deaths were haunting him. He felt he'd become tarnished, as though his own blood had somehow been infected; that he was now a different person as a result. Tommy didn't understand. It was all very well him saying it was the machine not the man, but Joss simply didn't see it like that. The others were the same: they all talked about 'Huns' and 'Bosch' and 'Nazi bastards', as though they were all one and the same, a sub-species of man that the world could do without. The death of German aircrew was treated with relish. Only the day before, Gordon had read out loud an article in the paper about the number of dead German airmen being washed up onto the beaches and left strewn across the English countryside. Mike had said, 'Good—the more the merrier. Let 'em fry,' and everyone had chuckled and nodded agreement. Peter had once said to him, 'Who do these people think they are, coming over here with their jackboots and swastikas? How dare they?' But Joss was unable to tar all Germans with the same brush. 'It's war, Joss,' Tommy had said. 'Total war, and that, by definition, is non-personal. Unless, of course, you're someone like Antonin—his sister raped and butchered, his parents God knows where. Family home burnt to the ground. And he's not an isolated case. You think he gives a damn about the distress he's caused some Bavarian frau?'

'But you and I don't have any cause to hate. Not yet, at any rate,' Joss had replied. For every ardent Nazi and rapist thug, he knew there must be men like Willie von Thadden, reluctant combatants caught up in something that was beyond their control. People whose blood he shared.

Nor could he simply forget about Peter. His friend was still much in his thoughts, especially at times like this when he was alone, in bed, his mind unoccupied. He wondered how Peter's parents were coping. Putting on a brave face, no doubt. Tommy had told him he'd developed a way of pretending good friends like Peter hadn't died, but had merely gone on a very long holiday and then decided never to come back. 'Peter was addicted to having a good time,' said Tommy, 'so I think he'd have gone to Hawaii. Now, every time I have bad visions of Peter in his Spitfire sinking to the bottom of the Channel, I immediately push it to one side and imagine him instead sitting under a palm tree, wearing one of those floral garlands round his neck

397

and sipping a cocktail.'

'And chatting up all the local talent.'

'But of course. It quite cheers me up.'

Joss turned over onto his side and closed his eyes. He tried to think as Tommy did, but the same images kept returning—the Stuka exploding mid-air, the lines of tracer arcing from the 110, then ceasing abruptly. He used to be so good at burying his head in the sand, and blocking out unpleasant thoughts. This war seemed to be changing everything. Even people like Pip—the one person who always seemed so controlled, so laconic, but who was now treating Joss like some untouchable talisman. Or maybe it was just that different sides of their characters were being revealed, another consequence of war.

He turned his pillow to find a cool patch of cotton. Perhaps he was just overtired. His leave would do him good. In six days' time, everything might look very different once again.

*　　　*　　　*

Tommy had generously offered his car again, but Joss was loath to take it for such a long time. Furthermore, petrol was increasingly hard to come by. The week before, Tommy had filled up with high-octane fuel from one of the bowsers, but it was a high-risk game to play, and even then they'd nearly been caught. Mac might look the other way, but the station commander wouldn't. It only needed some erk to give the game away, and he could face a court martial. Aviation fuel wasn't especially good for the engine, either.

Instead, Joss had borrowed a bicycle.

398

Marleycombe wasn't so very far—twenty-odd miles. The ride would do him good.

With his knapsack on his back, Joss set off after breakfast. He hadn't cycled anywhere for years; he'd forgotten how enjoyable it could be. There was little else on the road, the day promised to be another warm one, and although some of the hills made him hot and short of breath, the pedal-free run on the other side more than made up for it. As the cool breeze ruffled his hair, he relished the renewed sense of isolation his journey offered. The surrounding countryside was bursting with life into another summer's day. The air was cool and crisp, and scented sweetly with dry wheat. Birdsong sang out from the trees and hedgerows. Men and women were already out in the fields harvesting, carrying on despite the peril lining up on the other side of the Channel.

Ah, this is good, thought Joss.

*   *   *

The front door at Alvesdon Farm was open, so having propped up his bicycle against the wall, Joss walked on in. One of the dogs shuffled out to greet him, but otherwise the place seemed deserted. There was no sign of Celia or even the two evacuee children.

'Hello!' called Joss, then again, more loudly. 'Anyone about?' The grandfather clock chimed the half-hour, but otherwise the place was still. Joss squatted to tickle the dog then noticed the note scrawled by Guy on the round table. *'Harvesting. Come and find us on Prescombe—afraid will need to press-gang you into helping.'*

Joss smiled, but first went upstairs to change. As ever, he'd been put in his usual room. Despite the long ride, despite the lack of sleep, he felt reinvigorated already. He'd never been more eager to change out of his uniform. Blue trousers and shirt were slung on the bed, a fresh shirt and slacks snatched out from his knapsack. *Yes,* he felt much better.

By the time he reached Prescombe, Joss was hot from the climb and from the sun, which now glared down brightly from high in the sky. The early freshness had gone, replaced by warm, cloying air that would make gathering the harvest even harder work than normal. As he walked through the open gate and onto a path of trodden-down wheat, butterflies flitted lazily and Joss paused to wipe his brow. Half the field was already covered by row upon row of wheat sheaves. An assorted line of men, women and children were gathering the freshly-cut corn into more sheaves, while the tractor and its reaping machine methodically swathed through the remaining wheat, a small cloud of dust following in its wake. He spotted Guy and hurried over.

'Joss—you got my note then?' He grimaced as he straightened his back. His face glistened with sweat. 'Bloody good to see you. You don't mind helping out do you?'

'Course not. But it hardly looks as though you need my help. Who *are* all these people?'

Guy grinned. 'You remember how against evacuees I was? Well, I've changed my mind. Plus a few of the ladies from the village and I think we'll be all right. At least, so long as this spell of weather lasts.'

'What about the land girls?'

'Not yet. Shame really.' He smiled, then dabbed his face with a handkerchief. 'Muggy today, though. Supposed to cloud over later. Might even be rain. Maybe even thunder—this humidity's going to have to clear at some point.' He looked up at the sky, but there was not a cloud in sight—nothing but blue brightness.

'You're beginning to sound like your mother—obsessing about the weather. Where is she anyway? The house was deserted.'

'Gone to see my aunt in Exeter. So it's just us—and Stella and the two children, of course.'

Joss glanced around the field. 'Where is Stella?' He was longing to see her and had hoped she might have been at the house when he arrived.

'Driving the tractor.' He shook his head. 'Don't ask. She's suddenly the world's expert on farming. It's driving me up the wall. She's taken to driving the tractor whenever she can because she says it's less physically demanding than gathering hiles of corn, and that as my sister it's her prerogative.'

Joss took up position next to Guy, his arms soon red from where the ends of the brittle corn stalks chafed his skin. The temperature was still rising, a sticky humidity heavy across the downs. How was everything going? Guy asked. Had he seen much action? A bit, Joss replied. 'I had to bale out yesterday,' he said. He'd sworn after he'd last seen Guy that he'd tell him everything if he ever asked again; but right now, only hours after escaping Middle Wallop, he wanted to talk about normal life, not flying.

'Really? Bloody hell, Joss. What happened?'

'Oh it was all very unglamorous. My engine

401

packed up and so I had to ditch it.'

'Christ, must have been terrifying, wasn't it?'

'You wouldn't have liked it, that's for sure. I was feeling a bit panicky until the 'chute opened, but afterwards it was quite peaceful floating down like that. Great view.'

Guy did not probe further. Instead he said, 'And Tommy?'

Fine, Joss told him. 'Hugely liked by the rest of the squadron, and still cultivating his image of the glamorous, sophisticated man of the world. We've got a Pole in the squadron,' Joss explained. 'Antonin. His English is terrible, but he speaks French and Italian so Tommy has a field day talking in a loud voice in French one minute, Italian the next.'

Guy laughed. 'I can imagine. Good for Tommy.'

'He seems to be well-suited to life as a fighter pilot. I mean, I suppose he gets a bit scared, like anyone would, but you'd never know it. Life and soul, really.'

Guy smiled. 'I can't imagine him being anything else.'

'Oh, and he's seen Noel,' said Joss. 'He had a forty-eight-hour leave last weekend and met up with Noel in London.'

'I'd love to see Noel. Feels like ages since we were all together.'

'It's over a year.'

Guy sighed. 'Yes, I suppose it is.'

'He's still at Cambridge, of course. Tommy thinks he's working for the SIS or something, but I suspect that's just Tommy.'

'It's possible, I suppose.'

Two boys started fighting. 'Not again,' said Guy.

'Hey, cut that out!' he yelled, and hurried over to them. Joss watched him prise the two apart, clip one over the head and grab the other by the arm and lead him away. 'For God's sake,' he said, 'what's the matter with you?'

The boy looked sulky. 'He started it,' he said. He was, Joss guessed, nine or ten. 'Taking the piss out of my sister.'

'Watch your language,' said Guy. 'What was he saying about her?' The boy looked down and said nothing. 'Come on, Francis, what did he say? I can't help if you don't tell me.'

Still looking down, Francis mumbled, 'Said she was showing the boys her bits.'

Guy looked at Joss, trying not to laugh. 'He's probably just trying to get a rise,' said Guy, 'and the best way to get round that is to simply ignore it. Now go and work over there, well away from Richard Weekes.' The boy trundled off. 'It's an almost daily occurrence,' said Guy.

'Is she showing them her bits?' said Joss.

'Probably. She's a right little hussy. Perhaps I take back what I said earlier about evacuees.'

They paused for lunch, gathering in the corner of the field to eat thick sandwiches and drink beer from the clay flagons. Thunderflies clung to their skin. Everyone looked red-faced and hot, their brows glistening, shirts clinging to their backs. Stella wandered over. *At last,* thought Joss.

'Hello Joss,' she said, smiling, and kissed him lightly on each cheek, the edge of her lips fleetingly moist on his skin. She kept her hand on his shoulder for a moment so that Joss could feel the warmth of her palm through the cotton of his shirt. 'Sorry I didn't stop to say hello earlier.'

'That's all right. You've been busy.' He glanced across at the tractor.

'Yes, very.' She moved her hand away, smiled at him again, then puffed, and with her hands on her hips, glanced round the field. She wore trousers and a scarf on her head that knotted at the front. She appeared to be the only one not dripping with sweat. 'Nearly done,' she said with satisfaction. 'Then on to Middle Down.'

'Yes,' said Guy, 'although I want to get this lot loaded up and down to the farm as soon as possible. We need to get a move on and start building the ricks. I think it looks like it might rain later.'

'Well, you get on with that and I'll keep going with the reaping. As long as there's enough people to collect up what I cut we'll be fine.'

Guy nodded. 'All right. Just make sure you don't get too far ahead of yourself.'

'Yes, yes,' said Stella and rolled her eyes at Joss. *As if I don't know.* 'Hadn't you better start getting the carts up?'

'I'm just going.' He turned to Joss. 'You can keep me company.'

Guy talked about the harvest as they began walking down the track. It was the second one he'd done now, but although much had changed in the last year, he did at least have a better idea of what he was doing this time round. 'The bloody carter's gone and joined up,' he said, 'so we're all having to take it in turns with the wagons this time. Thank God Sam's still here, that's all I can say,' said Guy. Then he looked pensive and said, 'I wonder if we'll ever get back to Cambridge.'

'Tommy and I were talking about this just the

other day. If we make it through the war, I suppose I might. It's hard to look ahead though. Right now I find it difficult to think much beyond next week.'

Guy looked thoughtful. 'Yes, I know what you mean. Still, it would be good one day.'

'What about the farm?' said Joss. 'Isn't this your life now?'

'Oh, I expect it could do without me for a while. I could always get Stella to run things.' He chuckled, then glanced back up the hill. *It does bother him,* thought Joss.

They reached the farm and shackled the horses to two of the carts. It was still sticky and close, and flies buzzed around the horses.

'It *is* hot,' said Guy, wiping his brow again. 'Look Joss, you really don't have to do this, you know. Why don't you go and read inside or something?'

Joss would hear none of it. 'I'm perfectly happy, I assure you,' he said.

'I suppose it does mean we get to see a bit of each other, doesn't it?' said Guy as they led the horses through the yard. 'Because I'm afraid I'm on duty again tonight. It'll be just you and Stella for dinner once the two brats have gone to bed. But if she's annoying, say you've got a headache and leave her to it.'

Joss felt a flutter of excitement. *Stella all to myself—hooray.* 'I'm sure I'll be fine,' he said, 'and don't worry, it can't be helped. Anyway, it's not as though we still get long summer holidays any more, is it?'

Guy smiled ruefully. 'You can say that again.'

'So how are you getting on with the LDV?'

'Home Guard. Churchill changed the name the other day.'

'Home Guard then.'

'Fine. I mean, we drill, we discuss tactics, we spend time building roadblocks, then half the night manning them. If German parachutists suddenly pitch up, I'm sure we'll give it everything we've got, but to be honest, it isn't much. We've still got no uniforms and only a handful of rifles and shotguns. Half the people I'm with are over sixty.' He whisked away a fly, stroked the horse's nose, then said, 'I know you lot seem to be the golden boys at the moment, and it may not be as glamorous as flying a Spitfire, but I am trying to do my bit here. And even if we do have only a few cartridges between us, I know we'd all fight to the last man if we have to.'

Joss looked at Guy to see if he was smiling, but he wasn't. He felt a flush of irritation. For a moment he wondered whether to snap back, tell him to stop sounding defensive, but his exhaustion was beginning to catch up with him once more. He was too tired to argue. Life was too short. Instead he bit his lip and said, 'Well, I think you're a braver man than I, Guy. And it must be a huge responsibility running this place, too.'

Guy looked a bit sheepish. 'I don't mean to sound like I'm complaining. I just hope we're all here in a year's time for the next harvest.'

They had reached Prescombe. There was still no sign of a cloud and the heat continued to bear down oppressively. Stella had gone, the field now cut. A few people were left at the top by the Herepath, collecting together the last sheaves. Now it was Guy and Joss's job to start collecting them up, bundling the wheat into huge hayricks on the wagons that would then be taken down to the farm to be

406

threshed.

'Next year—all being well—I'll have a combine harvester,' said Guy, then grimacing, slung the first sheaf of wheat onto the back of the cart. There were no more questions about flying or the war. In one respect, Joss was glad; in another, disappointed.

*   *   *

Joss awoke with a start, and for a moment could not think where he was.

'Oh, I'm sorry Joss—did I wake you?'

He blinked and looked about him, then saw Stella standing by the sideboard pouring herself a drink. Her overalls were gone, replaced by a light summer dress, her shoulder-length dark hair straighter than when he'd last seen her, and no longer encumbered by her headscarf. She looked so lovely, Joss wanted to reach out and touch her.

'No, I—I'm sorry, I must have nodded off.'

Stella laughed. 'You've been asleep well over an hour. Perfect timing, I'd say—you've completely missed out on putting the brats to bed.'

Joss pushed himself up in his chair. 'That *is* a shame.' He smiled, then said, 'Guy gone out has he?'

'Yes, I'm afraid so. Do you think you can put up with me for a whole evening?' Her eyes seemed to sparkle.

'It would be a great pleasure.' He felt emboldened, and was slightly surprised at himself.

'Good. Then help me with the blackout and then we can go into the kitchen. But help yourself to a drink first.'

Joss went over to the sideboard and poured himself a generous measure of Scotch and soda, while Stella carried on talking. 'Most of upstairs is done already. I can't tell you the nightmare it was putting up these horrendous things. Mum was having kittens, as you can imagine.' Both the dining room and drawing room downstairs had long, heavy silk curtains, but behind those, thick, black wool blinds had been added. 'The two together seems to do the trick,' said Stella, 'although we hardly ever use these rooms after dark any more anyway. The ARP man insisted. He came round one day with his clipboard to check we'd done as we were told.' Joss followed her into the dining room. 'Anyway,' she continued, 'we've decided to virtually camp out in the kitchen. It's all very cosy.'

They went around the rest of the ground floor, ending up in the kitchen. There was a range against one wall, old flagstones on the floor and a worn rug, and under the windows, a series of wide ceramic sinks. A drying frame on a pulley hung suspended above the range. The centrepiece was a long, narrow, kitchen table with an assortment of chairs either side. On the opposite wall, next to an enormous dresser, a clock ticked gently. The spaniel snored rhythmically at the foot of the range.

'It's funny,' said Joss, 'but I don't really know this room at all.'

'No, well, you wouldn't. I mean, we never had much cause to come in here. It was always cook's domain. But actually, I rather like it. I'm even quite enjoying cooking.'

'Can I do anything?' he said, suddenly conscious he'd sat himself down at the table with his drink

408

without offering to help.

'You are sweet. No, no, you sit still. I think I can cope.' She placed an open bottle of wine on the table. 'We're rather ploughing through Dad's reserves at the moment, but still, it's there for drinking.' She flashed him another smile and Joss felt himself melt a little more. 'Anyway, it's only bangers and mash. I'm afraid that on a hot, sticky day like today I can't be doing with making a proper full-blown meal. Do you mind terribly?'

'Bangers and mash sounds perfect. Your own sausages, I suppose?'

'Of course. Most probably even hand-made by me.' Nearly everything they ate these days was home grown. They were very lucky, she said, living on a farm. There were always chickens they could eat and Guy had insisted on keeping the pigs as well. They grew most of their own vegetables and there were plenty of apples left over from last year. They still made their own butter and cheese. Stella had had to learn how to do that too. 'My friend Charlotte is having a terrible time in London,' she told him. 'Rationing is a nightmare for them. Honestly, Francis and Ruby have fallen on their feet coming here.'

'They don't seem to be too much trouble—no more than any other children their age,' said Joss.

'No, they're not really. Francis has stopped wetting his bed, thank God, but it's still a bit odd having them here, living in our family home. Ruby's discovering boys and getting a name for herself and so poor Francis keeps finding himself having to defend her honour.' She laughed. 'It keeps us all entertained at any rate. But Joss, I want to hear about how you are. Are you and Tommy being careful? You look exhausted.'

'I am a bit,' he confessed. 'We tend to go to the pub quite a lot, or stay up drinking in the mess. Then we're up at dawn the following morning. There are times during the day when we all get to catnap, but it's never really enough. At least, not for me. I suppose it catches up on you. And anyway, I've been harvesting all day today too.'

'Yes, well you mustn't let Guy bully you into helping. This is your leave, your chance to recuperate.'

'I know, but I enjoy it. I've had a lovely day. It's good to keep busy. Keeps your mind off things.'

'Have you much on your mind, then?'

Without really meaning to, Joss realized he'd set himself up to tell her about the previous days' events. Why did he feel he could open up to her and not Guy? *She understands,* he thought to himself, in a way that no one else outside the squadron was able to do. Once he began, he was unable to stop. Stella listened patiently throughout. At one point, she even squeezed his hand. Joss told her about the night in the New Inn too, and how he had felt such an overwhelming sense of belonging to the squadron. 'To begin with,' he told her, 'I was certain we must be resented by the others. It was still very much an auxiliary squadron, and we had joined them only because colleagues of theirs, friends they'd flown with and known half their lives, had already been killed and wounded. They were perfectly friendly, but they were all in a terrible way after Dunkirk. It was bad enough not coming from Suffolk, but the fact that I had German blood—well, I really worried about being found out. Tommy always says I'm overreacting,

410

but I didn't feel as though I was that first week.

'Then MacIntyre turned up and he seems to have turned everything around. He's given us all confidence, despite the losses. And, of course, he's a New Zealander. Then we've got an American, a Pole, a half-American in Tommy, me, a few other replacement pilots who come from all over. It's a real mixture. I feel a part of it now. I'd do absolutely anything for that lot.' He'd hardly touched the plate of food that had been put in front of him. 'Sorry,' he said, 'I've been talking too much.'

'It doesn't matter,' she said, 'there's no rush.'

Joss swallowed a mouthful then said, 'I had to sing the new squadron song last night.'

Stella, her chin resting on her hand, raised an eyebrow.

'*Blue Skies*,' said Joss. 'It's one of Mac's new rules. Anyone who safely bales out and makes it back to base has to down a drink then sing *Blue Skies* in front of everyone else. Pip and Karl had to the other evening. Last night it was my turn.'

Stella laughed. 'You see, every time I think you've grown up my hopes are dashed. You're still just a big kid—it sounds like you all are.'

'I'm learning the hard way that it's best not to get too serious,' Joss grinned.

'Hm,' said Stella, 'but it's hardly the *squadron* song. I know *Blue Skies*. Irving Berlin. She began singing softly, 'Blue Skies, shining above me, nothing but blue skies, do I see.'

'Right words,' laughed Joss, 'but tune *all* wrong, I'm afraid.'

'Is it? I'm sure that's how it's supposed to go.' She shrugged. 'Oh well, it's a good song anyway. I

411

like it.'

When he finished eating, Joss pushed back his chair against the stone floor and stood up to clear away the plates. 'That was delicious Stella—thank you.' She looked up at him, her face relaxed and contented, and she smiled. Joss felt a flush of pleasure.

Another wave of tiredness suddenly swamped him, and he paused a moment by the wooden draining board. He had to fight it—he didn't want the evening to end. He had to hold onto times like these.

'Are you all right?' said Stella.

Joss rubbed an eye. 'Yes, fine.'

'I mustn't keep you up.'

'No, really,' he said, sitting back down at the table, 'I really don't want to go to bed yet.'

'Good,' said Stella. She was smiling again, 'I don't really want you to either.'

Joss poured them each another glass of wine. 'I'm sorry,' he said, 'I seemed to have done nothing but talk about myself. Tell me how you are, Stella. Are you all right here?'

'Much better than the last time you saw me. I think it must be all to do with keeping busy. I've become quite the mechanic as well, you know. You should see me change the plugs on the tractor—there's nobody quicker.' She ran her hands through her hair. 'This war. Some say it's only just begun. But I'm glad I'm not in London any more. Glad I'm not that person any more.'

'And Philip?' He'd promised himself he wouldn't ask her about him, but now he wanted to know.

'To tell you the truth, Joss, I began to get a bit bored of Philip.' *Good—tell me more,* thought

412

Joss. 'He'll make someone a very good husband, I'm sure. He has money, and charm, and he's very sensible. But ...' She left the sentence hanging, twirling a lock of hair around her finger. 'Well, I suppose there's not much *substance* there. Or passion—call it what you will.' She laughed. 'I must sound dreadful. But I realized I needed to do something. Something useful. I can do that here. Philip keeps threatening to come down, but I think he knows the game's up really.'

'Well, you've certainly become very involved with the farm.'

'Yes,' she said, 'I suppose I have.' She paused for a moment.

'But what?'

'Nothing really. I just wonder what Dad would say if he could see Guy and me now. Me especially.'

'He'd probably be very proud, wouldn't he?'

'Maybe. But also rather horrified.' She paused again. 'You look surprised.'

'David always seemed rather progressive to me. And pretty liberal.'

'He loved us very much and spoilt us rotten, and for the most part he was a soft touch when it came to discipline, but he wasn't progressive. He *hated* what was happening to the world. You know how much he loved the house and its history. It's one of the reasons he was so fond of you—you were one of the few people to show an interest in his great passion.'

'But because it's so interesting. I have none of that—no past I can claim.'

'Yes, but Dad saw himself as a guardian of that past. He saw it as his duty to preserve it. He'd have

413

been terribly upset to know that most of the sheep had now gone, or that those copses up on the downs had been bulldozed, or that centuries of wild flowers and grasses on Middle Down and all the wildlife that went with it had been ploughed up and replaced by corn. I sometimes think he sensed what was coming. He gave in to his cancer, you know.'

Outside came a low rumble of thunder. They both looked up, ears turned towards the open window.

'At last,' said Stella. 'Not good for the harvest, but I'll be glad if it washes away this awful mugginess.'

Another rumble, closer this time, and then rain began beating down against the window panes. 'Come on,' she said, suddenly standing up. 'Let's go out and watch the storm.'

Joss followed her down a step and through into the pantry. It was dark, the only light coming from the kitchen, but it was enough for Stella to see the back door. She opened it as another loud crack of thunder rumbled above them.

'Listen to that!' she said. The rain was falling hard now, pounding the path outside and the tiles of the low-roofed pantry. Stella clutched her arms and leant against the doorframe, a sliver of light from the kitchen lighting her face.

Joss breathed in deeply, intoxicated.

Stella copied him. 'Hm,' she said, 'damp earth. I love the smell of rain on the ground after a dry spell.'

Lightning, and for a split-second the garden and the large elms were lit by a white glow.

'One, two, three,' Stella counted, then another deafening peel of thunder.

'Very close,' said Joss. He could feel her bare

414

arms just inches away from his. If he leant down, he could kiss her without even moving his feet. *If only*, he thought. Stella looked up at him, and he felt crippled by his desire. For that moment, nothing else existed.

'Joss?' she said, her face searching his. 'I wonder—'

A door slammed. Stella started, then said, 'Guy. He's home early.' She hurried back to the kitchen. *Damn him*, thought Joss, hastily following.

Guy was soaked. 'I had a feeling this damn storm would come,' he said, taking off his jacket and hanging it on the back of a chair in front of the range.

'I wasn't expecting you back so soon,' said Stella.

'Well, I think the major felt sorry for me. He's knows we're harvesting. Anyway, I don't suppose the Germans will be parachuting in this weather.' He took off his jacket and looked at them both genially. 'Had a good evening? I thought you'd have gone to bed hours ago, Joss.'

'We didn't have dinner until quite late and then we were watching the storm,' said Stella.

Guy looked at them both and said, 'Oh. Well, anyone fancy a drink? I definitely need one. Joss, you'll have a Scotch won't you?'

Joss nodded, miserable.

Soon after Stella sidled away. 'I'll leave you two boys to it,' she said. 'Good night.'

'Night,' said Joss, but Stella had already left the room.

Cairo—October, 1942

The first morning Joss had been at the Villa Jacaranda, his footless room-mate, Dobbo, had hobbled out on his crutches after breakfast to one of the wicker chairs in the garden, where he had then remained for much of the morning. Seeing him do the same the following day, Joss recognized he was being presented with an opportunity to be alone without anyone watching him, and so said to Binny, 'I'm just going to lie down on the bed for a while,' and went back to his room. He had no intention of sleeping, however; instead he surreptitiously opened his trunk and began re-reading through his bundles of letters and fingering his few belongings: the wooden lion, the remains of the scarf Stella had once given him, now faded and frayed through sweat and age; the small silver christening cup and Iron Cross that had once belonged to his father.

In the three days that had passed, this post-breakfast period alone had become an important daily ritual. He would wait for Dobbo and the others to make their way outside, then quietly slip back into his room, as he had again some quarter of an hour before.

Joss sat on the bed, the trunk stood open before him. In one hand he clutched a letter, while the other soothed his forehead. Physically, he felt much better, but, if anything, his headaches were getting worse. He'd been thoroughly examined when he'd first reached hospital and there'd been no sign of a fracture. 'I'm afraid,' said one of the

416

doctors, 'people do get migraines and headaches, and there's very little one can do except, perhaps, keep taking regular doses of aspirin whenever they get particularly uncomfortable.' That was back in August, and since then, Joss had become resigned to living with it. Just one of those curses he had to put up with.

The room was cool, and, with the shutters still drawn, filled with only a dim light. The letter was from Stella, written almost two years before to the day, but about events a couple of months before. Events that had happened during his leave that July.

'Do you remember the German plane crashing over Middle Down? I was thinking about those poor men this morning as I ploughed over the ground. And then that reminded me of something you once said about how the enemy were mostly young men like you or Tommy or Guy, people who all had families and friends back home who loved them just like anyone else. At the time I didn't see it like that. They were still the enemy, I thought, part of the Nazi machine that had already taken away my older brother. They were flying over our country and they deserved everything they got. But seeing them that day, scarred, bloodied and so very dead, I understood what you'd meant.'

What now? Did he still feel that way? *Yes,* he thought, *but I'm not sure I care any more.* As Tommy had said, people die in wars. It was an unfortunate but necessary by-product.

He remembered the crash. Remembered it very well. It was the day after the storm, and the sun had shone down relentlessly once more, so that the dampness from the night before had risen into a shimmering haze that saturated the valley. They'd

417

spent the morning in the yard, building huge ricks behind the barns, and getting covered in dust and shards of wheat.

By noon, with the ground hard and dry once more, they were back on Middle Down. Joss had barely spoken to Stella that morning and when he had, she'd been friendly but not overly so. It pained him that the intimacy of the previous evening had vanished, and as he heaved the sheaves onto a waiting cart, he could think of little else. He yearned to be near her, and was wondering about ways in which he might engineer more opportunities for them to be alone. But then came the doubts. Perhaps she had never wanted him to kiss her. Perhaps he'd just imagined it; wishful thinking, nothing more.

These thoughts were still churning around his mind when Guy came over and suggested it was soon time for some lunch.

'I feel unbelievably hungry today,' he said, then stopped. Joss had heard it too. A faint rumble and splutter. A bit louder, and some of the others were pausing to look.

'Someone's in trouble,' said Joss. Then he saw it, just as one of the boys shouted, 'Look! Over there!'

A twin-engine bomber, engine misfiring and unsteady. Having cleared the ridge of chalk downs the far side of the valley, it was now swooping over the village, trailing a long plume of smoke. The engine strained and coughed as the pilot desperately tried to gain some height, but it was hopeless. One of the engines had died, the other was about to follow.

Joss glanced, horrified, at Guy. 'It's going to crash.'

As the second engine died, the plane dropped height again. It was so close, the swastika of the tail fins and black cross along the fuselage were clearly visible. Moments later, a loud crash, and the agonizing sound of tearing metal as the aircraft began to break up across the stubble of Prescombe field. An eerie silence followed as smoke and dust began billowing into the air.

'Oh my God,' said Guy. Everyone had watched the crash in stunned silence, but now the boys dropped everything and were running as fast as they could towards the scene.

'Hey!' shouted Joss, 'Get back! All of you, get back!' He turned to Guy, 'For God's sake, Guy, we mustn't let them go near,' and began running after them. Then Sam Hicks began yelling at them too, and only then did they stop. Catching up, Joss said, 'There could be unexploded bombs, or she might even blow. Everyone must keep back.'

'Do you think there'll be any dead bodies?' said one of the boys, a London evacuee. 'I've never seen a dead body before.'

'And nor do you ever want to,' said Sam. He eyed them all, and pointing his finger at each in turn said, 'Now if I see one of you move one step beyond this fence, I'll give you the hiding of your life. You've been warned.'

'I'll go and check,' said Joss. 'There might be survivors.'

Sam nodded. 'If you're sure.'

Joss jumped over the fence and ran across the stubble towards to the stricken aircraft. He recognized it from his identification charts as a Dornier 17, although he'd not seen a real one before. As he drew near, he slowed. The air was rich with the smell of oil and fuel. One of the wings had been wrenched off and the fuselage ripped and bent. There was blood on the shattered Perspex of the nose of the plane. The pilot was still in his seat above, head back and mouth open, his skin waxy white. Joss approached cautiously. He couldn't see any bombs and nor was there any sign of flames; but you never knew—he'd heard tales of planes exploding long after the crash. Where were the others? There should be four, he reckoned, unless one or more had baled out already.

Then he saw two more bodies. They'd both been thrown through the nose and out onto the stubble. The first looked untouched, and Joss squatted to feel his pulse. Nothing. Beneath the flying helmet, a strangely peaceful face, and young, too, barely old enough to shave. The other lay on his front, and so Joss carefully turned him over, then recoiled. The front of the face had been sliced off, leaving nothing but a mess of bloody pulp.

'Oh, Jesus,' said a voice behind him. *Guy.* Joss swallowed hard, then calmly turned the dead man back over and stood up.

'Keep back Guy,' he said. 'There's no point both of us taking a risk.'

Guy appeared not to have heard. With an expression of appalled horror, he walked unsteadily towards the two dead men on the grass.

'Guy, come on,' said Joss.

'But—but they're *dead*,' said Guy, dropping onto his knees by the bodies.

'Guy, please.' Joss put a hand on Guy's shoulder. 'Come away.'

'Jesus,' said Guy again, 'oh my God.' He stood up and looked at Joss. His face was ashen, his eyes

420

wild. Moments later he vomited.

Stella was walking towards them. She looked frightened, Joss thought.

'Quickly. Take Guy, will you?' Joss called to her.

Stella nodded and quickened her pace. 'All dead?' she asked.

'Three certainly.'

She glanced at the two men on the ground then spotted the pilot. 'Poor them,' she said. 'How horrible.' Guy was still bent double, his hands on his knees. Stella put an arm around his shoulder and without saying anything more, led him away.

The smell of fuel and hydraulic fluid was still strong, but the aircraft had stopped smoking, so Joss cautiously approached the nose again. It was then that he saw the fourth man slumped off his seat and wedged against the metal. He'd been shot, a line of bloody bullet holes across his back. Joss swallowed hard again. The terror they must have felt. The panic, knowing one of them was dead, that they would crash and almost certainly die. He suddenly shivered.

He was about to turn away, when something caught his eye, nestling amongst the stubble. Reaching down, he saw it was a wooden lion, hand carved, and painted yellow. A mascot, a talisman, but one that had failed its owner that day. He picked it up, examining it, feeling the smooth wood in his hands. That it should be a lion seemed propitious somehow. Walking away from the wreckage and broken bodies, he put it in his pocket, hoping it might bring him better fortune in the weeks ahead.

*   *   *

Joss held it again now. It had served him well all this time. Then he thought of how, as a boy, he'd made his father the greatest lion-slayer in all Africa. He felt overcome with remorse; he wished he could hold that photograph once more, look at his father's image, an image that was fading from his memory. He understood so much more now. It took courage to walk away from a war. 'I'm sorry,' he said, quietly mouthing the words.

A knock on the door broke his reverie. Joss hurriedly put the lion back in the trunk, shut the lid and swung his legs onto his bed.

'Joss? Are you there?' Binny put her head around the door. 'Sorry to disturb you,' she said, and Joss followed her gaze to his trunk, still by the side of his bed, 'but I'm planning a trip to the Pyramids. A tour round the sites, then lunch at Mena House. Would you like to come?'

'Yes, all right. Thank you,' said Joss without really thinking.

'Wonderful. We'll be off in about half an hour.' She smiled, clasped her hands together then glanced at his trunk again. 'I'm so glad we were able to get that back for you.' Joss nodded. 'Well then,' she said, then added, 'oh, and there's a letter for you.'

A letter? A letter, but who from? Joss sat up immediately, his mind racing. From Stella, perhaps. Or his mother? He hoped so. *Prayed* so.

But it wasn't. Joss tore open the typed, Cairo-stamped envelope, aware that Binny, who was hovering nearby, could see his disappointment. Wafer-thin paper, typed and formal, but with an 'o' that was hammered slightly higher than the rest,

422

and headed 'RAF Middle East HQ'. Nothing personal about it at all. Not even 'Dear Flight Lieutenant Lambert,' but rather, 'For the attention of . . .' He was to report there at 0900 on 22nd October, 1942.

'Not bad news, I hope?' said Binny.

Joss shook his head. 'No news at all, really. I expect they want me to do some work again—my days as a stay-at-home are clearly numbered.'

'Even more reason to go to the Pyramids, then.'

'Yes,' said Joss, and with his hand tightly gripping his stick, he walked with Binny out to the veranda and the bright blue October sunshine.

England—August, 1940

Joss cycled back to Middle Wallop with mixed feelings. It depressed him that his relationship with Guy had, at times, seemed strained. They'd used to talk to each other about everything; now there were areas of their lives into which neither could intrude. Perhaps Stella was right; perhaps Guy *was* envious of him and Tommy, but he did not believe it was as simple as that. Over a pint in the Blue Lion, Joss had asked him whether anything was particularly troubling him, but Guy had shrugged and said, 'Apart from the fact I now have to work like a demon, I can't think of anything especially,' and that had been that.

There was also the bomber crash. Guy had acted peculiarly about it. Afterwards he'd initially tried to play down his reaction. He'd been tired, he said, overwrought by the long hours on the farm and the late nights with the Home Guard. But he didn't want Joss thinking he couldn't deal with seeing a dead body or two. Joss had shrugged and said, 'I shouldn't worry—I think a lot of people would have reacted the same way.'

After that Guy had barely mentioned it again, despite it being the biggest event that had happened to Marleycombe since war had begun. When the salvage team had finally taken it away two days later, all he'd said was, 'At least it crashed on stubble. I'd have been livid if it had ruined a whole field of wheat.' Then, just as Joss was leaving, Guy had said, 'Listen Joss, you won't tell Tommy or anyone about how I made a fool of myself the other day, will you?'

'No, of course not. But Guy, it's really nothing to be ashamed of.'

Guy had visibly winced. 'It is to me.'

And then there was Stella. They had not had another chance to spend an evening together. Guy had been there the following night and after that Celia had returned. It was hopeless anyway. What on earth would Guy say? He would consider it a betrayal, of that Joss was certain, as though he had been deliberately sidelined by his oldest friend and the twin sister he adored. Then their friendship really would be tested, although with each passing day, Joss had felt increasingly certain he'd imagined the whole thing anyway; Stella could not possibly have feelings for him beyond that of friendship. By the end of his leave, he was very relieved he hadn't tried to kiss her. Rejection would have been too much to bear; her friendship, however tantalizing, was better than banishment from Alvesdon Farm.

And yet, and yet. When he'd left, she'd kissed him goodbye and said, 'I'll miss you. Please be careful and come back to us alive.' He'd cycled off down the drive more in love than ever before, his heart aching from a mixture of pleasure and misery.

As he pedalled through the gates of RAF Middle Wallop, he was filled with mounting apprehension. *I'm a fool,* he thought: it was futile, he realized, worrying about a hypothetical scenario where he *might* jeopardize his relationship with the Liddells, when every time he flew a plane he was placing his life at risk.

Over the past few days he'd tried to keep thoughts of the battle ahead out of mind as much as possible, but it was often unavoidable—snippets of a radio broadcast about the aerial conflict, an overheard conversation, or something as startling as the bomber crash, brought the reality of his circumstances into stark focus, and reminded him that his few days at Alvesdon Farm were nothing more than a respite, a stay of execution. At such times, he would be struck by a nausea-inducing anxiety that weighed down upon him with aching heaviness. Only when sufficiently distracted would this overwhelming sense of dread go away. It was one of the main reasons he was so eager to help on the farm: work provided a necessary distraction.

Two Spitfires roared past overhead. To his surprise, this made him feel better. At least he still loved flying. The thought of flying—just *flying,* alone, high in that vast sky—lifted his spirits. And Tommy—*good old Tommy!*—it would be good to see him, and the others too, for that matter. Despite the battle that lay ahead, there was something unique about being part of a unit like

629. Unlike school, or even training, where one actively avoided certain people, there was no one he disliked within the squadron. Foibles or particular quirks of character which, under normal circumstances, might have proved irritating, were happily tolerated. It was as though no one could be bothered to work themselves into a lather over petty niggles. If only Guy could understand that.

A warm welcome was waiting for him when he walked into the mess a short while later, lifting his spirits further. 'My lucky charm returns to the fold,' said Pip, and stopped his game of snooker to come over and shake his hand.

'Looks like you've survived without me.'

Pip grinned, cigarette stuck between his teeth. He was in shirtsleeves, his collar and tie loosened. 'Been a lot of very anxious moments, though. Very testing times. Anyway, you're looking horribly healthy, Joss. You should go on leave more often.'

'I've been harvesting. Bloody hard work, I can tell you.'

'Well don't look at me for sympathy. Now go and get a drink while I finish off thrashing Antonin here.'

Antonin, who was about to take a shot, peered up at them both, then winked at Joss and potted another ball. 'Pip's not so hot shot,' he said.

'All right—that's it. Time to clear the table, I think.'

It was funny, Joss thought, but he'd been intimidated by Pip to begin with. He'd wanted Pip to like him. Then again, everyone wanted to be liked by Pip; he was that sort of person. However it wasn't until they'd been in that fight with the 109s that they'd become friends. Of course, suggesting

Joss was somehow lucky was nonsense—he certainly didn't *feel* particularly lucky—but he rather liked the tag.

He joined Mike and the CO at the bar.

'Pint?' said Mike.

Joss nodded. 'Thanks. So, what's the news?' He glanced around the room again. No Tommy. *No Tommy*—he couldn't believe he'd only just noticed. 'Where the hell's Tommy?'

Mac patted him on the shoulder. 'No need to sound so worried. He's on leave too—back tomorrow night.' *Thank God.* 'It's been so bloody quiet we've had several people take some time off.'

'Pip's been winding me up.' He looked around. 'A few new faces too.'

'I'm afraid Gordon and Dicky Leigh are in hospital,' said Mac.

'What happened?'

'Collided on take-off. Bloody lucky neither of them were killed. Dicky's in a very bad way and probably won't fly again, but Gordon's only broken both his legs and fractured his skull.'

'Only. Jesus.'

'Well, he'll be all right eventually. Anyway, we've got a number of new people. Another Pole—Jerzy—hates Germans even more than Antonin.'

'*Really* hates 'em,' said Mike. 'I certainly wouldn't want to be a German when Jerzy's around. Can fly a bit too.'

Joss shifted his feet and took a drink of his pint.

'And we've got another American,' said Mike.

'Another Yank, yes,' said Mac. 'From Texas. And a Jock NCO pilot, and a boy Pilot Officer. George Robbins, over there.' Mac pointed to a short fair-haired youth in an ill-fitting tunic sitting at one of the tables near the bar and said, 'Hey George, come over here a moment.' He turned back to Joss. 'Swears he's nineteen, but he looks about fourteen to me. Or maybe it's just that I'm getting older.'

George shuffled over and introduced himself. He looked bashful, uncertain of this new environment.

'Joss has been with the squadron—how long is it?' said Mac.

'Must be six weeks, I suppose.'

'Six weeks, so that makes him an old hand now. He's with you in "B" Flight. Stick with Joss, George, and you should be all right.' George smiled uncertainly. He looked like the new boy on the first day of term.

'When did you get here?' asked Joss.

George swallowed and said, 'Um, yesterday.' *They can't let him fight yet,* thought Joss.

'Been up in a Spit yet?' Joss asked him.

'Not yet,' said George. 'But I'm very much looking forward to it.'

'Maybe you could take him up tomorrow, Joss,' suggested Mac. 'Talk him through it.'

'All right,' nodded Joss. He smiled at George. 'It'd be a pleasure. You've a treat in store.' At this, George finally broke into a full smile of crooked teeth.

'All right, George, you can go back to your drink now,' said Mac, then once George had gone, turned to Joss and Mike. 'See, he really does look fourteen doesn't he? Makes me shudder to think I've got to send lads like him up against the 109s.'

'Good job there's something of a respite then, isn't it?' said Mike. 'Gives him a chance.'

Pip joined them. 'Another round? What about a

chaser to go with them?' Without waiting for their reply, he ordered four pints and four Scotches.

'So, did you win?' asked Joss.

'Nearly.'

'How much did you have on it?' asked Mike.

'Michael—I'm horrified that you should even suggest such a thing.'

'A couple of shillings?'

Pip lit another cigarette and held up a finger. 'Just the one.'

'I'm glad you can afford to throw money away,' said Mac.

'Fourteen shillings a day goes a long way when there's nothing to spend it on but a few rounds of booze,' said Pip. 'But still, I've learnt my lesson not to take on the Poles. In future, I think I'll target the new boys instead. More susceptible.'

'Well, there's a few of those,' said Joss.

'Yes,' said Pip. 'A week's a long time in the RAF these days.' He punched Mike lightly on the arm. 'D'you realize, Mike, that you, Johnnie, Tony and I are the only originals left? Four from fifteen.'

*   *   *

By the time they left the mess that night, they were drunk again—even Mac—and sang songs all the way back to their billets.

Joss collapsed on his bed with his head spinning. 'I don't want to die,' he said out loud, 'I really don't want to die, but I do like being with these people.' Then he closed his eyes and slept, his mind too dulled by alcohol to dream about the days that lay ahead.

429

England—August, 1940

The entire squadron sat outside the olive-green dispersal tents at Warmwell, the sky above them vast, blue and empty of clouds. Away to their right, their Spitfires were haphazardly lined up, ready to leave at a moment's notice. The pilots were quiet; the airfield was quiet. A few flies buzzed about in the hot morning sun. A blackbird occasionally sang from the hedge away behind them.

Joss squinted and glanced across at the others. Tommy in the deckchair next to him, smoking and reading a paperback, occasionally flicking back his dark hair. George Robbins, picking his fingernails and staring blankly towards the middle distance. Pip and Johnnie dozing on the grass, their tunics folded for pillows. The Poles in hushed voices testing each other's English vocabulary. Mac smoking a pipe and scribbling in a notebook. Karl and Buck Neill playing cards.

Joss went back to his letter. *Sorry about the scrawl,* he wrote, *but I'm writing this leaning on a book, which in turn is resting on my knee. It's now sometime after 11 o'clock in the morning and already fearfully hot. We've had a quiet week, practising our dog-fighting and occasionally chasing after German reconnaissance planes, although we never managed to catch one. These planes are up to something, though, and we're all expecting the balloon to go up any minute. We all thought we might see some action first scramble this morning, but we didn't see a thing, even though it's just the sort of day the Luftwaffe loves, honing in on us from a terrific height and with*

430

the sun behind them, so that it's almost impossible to see them until they're almost on top of you. It's funny, but we all pray for cloud and rain each day. It's the first time I've ever done so in summer! How are you getting on in London? I'd like to come up and see you next time I've got leave. I think I've got 24 hours on the 17ᵗʰ. Perhaps you could let me know if that's all right. He paused a moment, and sucked the end of his pen, then wrote, *What does Anthony think of the current situation? Is he as confident as Churchill? Please write to me and tell me all your news. It's a great help having Tommy here—you remember Tommy, don't you?—although did I tell you that Peter was killed? It was quite a blow.* He hadn't seen his mother since joining 629 back in mid-June. She'd written to him twice and sent one telegram— *'Don't forget your mother. Come and see me soon.'* This was only his second letter to her, long overdue. He'd stopped worrying about her for the time being; she had her life, as always, in London. She was probably still spending most of her evenings with Anthony. How he'd feel if the Germans *did* ever start bombing the capital, he wasn't sure, but as things stood, that seemed unlikely. The reconnaissance planes they'd been chasing the past few days had clearly only been interested in airfields and other military targets.

Suddenly the telephone rang and everyone sat up, waiting for the verdict.

' "B" Flight scramble!' shouted the orderly from within the tent.

'I'll lead,' said Mac, flinging his notebook onto his chair. The others all followed him, running towards their aircraft.

'All right, sir?' said Dowling as Joss reached his

plane.

Joss nodded, grabbed the parachute from his wing, quickly stepped into it and brought the straps round into the clip, then sprang onto the wing root, and hopped into the cockpit. In moments he had strapped himself in and given the thumbs up to Griffiths, who was waiting ready with the starter trolley. Joss pressed the starter button and with a lick of flame and smoke, the Merlin roared into life. He felt his pocket for the wooden lion, then released the brakes and rolled forward, joining Buck Neill and Denis Tweed at the start of their take-off. Ahead of them, Pip, Mac, Johnnie and Jerzy were already roaring down the grass field. Joss gunned the throttle as the four aircraft in front left the ground, their shadows growing smaller and smaller as they rose higher into the air.

Less than four minutes from the moment they'd left their seats to the last man lifting into the air.

'Tartan, this is Nimbus leader. All seven airborne.'

'Roger Nimbus. Proceed one-one-five, angels fifteen. Bandits twenty-plus attacking convoy.'

'OK, keep it tight,' said Mac. He was leading Green Section, now five hundred yards ahead. Below, the south of England rushed past and then they were out over the sea, scouting for the convoy.

Denis called out over the R/T; he was having oxygen trouble and was turning back. Joss glanced to his left and watched Denis peel off and head for home. Buck, to his right, waved. *I'm still here.*

Joss felt his heart quicken. The sky was particularly bright, the sun high above them as they continued to climb, and glaring off the metal cowling and Perspex canopy. Now there was one

432

less of them. He craned his neck and tried to scan the big blue above him, but it was almost impossible, even with his goggles. *Please don't let them attack us out of that,* he thought. Then up ahead, a small layer of cloud. He watched Green Section fly into it, and he and Buck soon followed but when they emerged the other side, there was no sign of the others. They were now some ten miles south of Bournemouth and away below, Joss saw the convoy. Tiny dark puffs of smoke littered the sky above the ships. The attack had clearly already started. A bit more height, that was what he needed, so he looked across at Buck and motioned upwards. Climbing into the sun so that they could attack with that natural advantage behind them, Joss prayed they had not already been spotted. Of the others, there was no sign—they had completely vanished.

At 16,000 feet, he levelled off, now only four miles north of the convoy. The scene below was much clearer now. Yes, there were the dive-bombers hurtling down towards the ships. Twenty at least. Huge columns of white spray erupted into the air. One of the ships was already on fire, livid orange flames spewing from the bows and black smoke billowing upwards. Above the Stukas, two circles of fighters—110s then 109s—swarming round and round like wasps over a jar of honey. Even more of them—closer to thirty.

A deep breath, a shiver, and Joss prepared to dive into the mêlée. Just then he spotted a squadron of Hurricanes some 3,000 feet below fly straight into the circle of 109s. Immediately, the German fighters split up as a large number of individual battles began. Aircraft swirled all over the sky as Joss and Buck hovered several thousand

433

feet above waiting for their chance to pounce. One plane—he couldn't tell what—plunged towards the sea trailing smoke. Another exploded mid-air.

Joss flipped his plane over and dived. Away to his right, slightly separated from the rest of the fight, he saw a lone 109. *OK, let's do it.*

Three hundred, three-fifty, three seven-five, four hundred. *Four hundred miles per hour.* The 109 loomed ever closer, gradually filling his gun sight. His thumb hovered above the gun button.

Vacuum.

His mind had become closed to noise—closed to everything but the destruction of the aircraft ahead. Four hundred yards now, and still the 109 hadn't seen him. *Come on, come on.*

A Hurricane suddenly swept in front, guns spitting. A second later, the 109—*Joss's 109*—had turned on its back, and, with a burst of flame and smoke, was plunging towards the sea.

Joss cursed. It should have been his. He turned to see if he could find another target, but the fight was over. The remaining enemy planes were already nothing but tiny specks as they streamed back towards France. Below, the ship on fire billowed smoke, stuck in the water and helpless, while the rest of the convoy slowly steamed onwards.

It was just after noon when he landed back at Warmwell.

'No joy then, sir?' said Griffiths as Joss clambered down onto the wing root. He was looking at the fresh red canvas patches that protected the guns from dirt and grit.

' 'Fraid not,' admitted Joss. 'Had a 109 all lined up but a Hurricane slipped in front of me and had it instead.'

'Ah well, next time, eh?'

Joss nodded and trundled back towards dispersal.

Everyone else had made it back safely. The CO, Pip and Jerzy had all shot down a 110, while Johnnie claimed a Stuka. It was Jerzy's first kill and he was cock-a-hoop, reliving the moment of its demise with sweeping arm movements and imitating the rat-a-tat of his machine-guns. Buck had lined up a 110 in his sights, but when he'd pressed his thumb down, nothing had happened; he'd already used up all his ammunition prematurely as he'd dived.

'If ever there was one for the taking,' said Joss as he slumped into the chair next to Tommy. 'Bloody annoying.'

Tommy looked at him. 'What's this I'm hearing?' he said. 'The reluctant combatant actually bemoaning a missed opportunity to shoot down a fellow man?'

Joss smiled sheepishly. 'Well, I didn't get him. That bloody Hurri did, so my conscience is clear.'

'Hm,' said Tommy, picking up his book once more.

'What do you mean, "Hm"?' Joss felt in his pocket, fingering the little wooden lion.

'Nothing.' Tommy put down his book again. 'Look, forget it. Finish your letter.'

Joss sighed. 'It was just that I'd never been in a better position to fire before, and to lose the opportunity was annoying. But of course I'm glad I didn't have to hurt anyone.'

Jerzy came and sat down next to them. He ran his hands through his hair, then looked at both Joss and Tommy. 'At last I kill one,' he said.

'Yes, well done,' said Tommy. 'Joss had his

435

chance taken by a Hurricane.'

Jerzy looked blank for a moment then said, 'Did the Hurricane kill him?'

Joss nodded. 'I think so.'

Jerzy shrugged. 'As long as Germans dead who cares who kills them? If I could I'd kill all Germans. After what they do in Poland.'

Joss glanced at Jerzy, then at Tommy, saw Tommy was eyeing him. He pretended to continue with his letter.

'Oh, I don't know,' said Tommy. 'Not *all* Germans are Nazi rapist bastards. Are they Joss?'

Joss felt himself freeze. What the hell was Tommy playing at? Glaring at him, he said, 'No, Tommy, I don't suppose they are.'

'After all, we met some lovely Germans in Munich before the war, didn't we?'

Joss cringed. His old anxiety about his background was rapidly returning. *Damn Tommy,* he thought. 'Look, I'm trying to write my letter,' he said.

Jerzy said, 'Well, I hate them all. Nothing will make me change my mind,' then stood up again and wandered back into one of the tents.

Later, after they had been stood down for the day, Joss found himself walking alone with Tommy back up to the mess. 'What was all that about with Jerzy earlier?' Joss asked. 'Trying to make me squirm on purpose?'

But Tommy just laughed. 'Oh come off it, Joss,' he said, 'don't you think there's slightly more to worry about at the moment than your origins? Simply getting through the day is quite hard enough.' He patted him on the shoulder. 'Look, don't worry, I'm not going to tell anyone.'

Joss felt suddenly ashamed; he'd been worrying too much about himself, not pausing to consider how Tommy might be feeling. 'Sorry,' he said. 'You're right of course.' He picked up a stone and hurled it over the hedge that ran behind their dispersal. 'But you *are* all right aren't you? I mean, we're coping with it all, aren't we?'

'I suppose we are Joss, yes.' He sounded tired; then, as though realizing this, added brightly, 'Anyway, enough of this talk. Doesn't do to get maudlin. Let's have a few drinks after dinner and worry about everything else tomorrow.'

Tommy's not infallible, thought Joss. The realization quite shocked him. He offered a silent prayer: *please don't let anything happen to him.* In the past, he'd always depended so much on Guy; but it was Tommy who was there to help him now. He didn't know where he would have been these past weeks without Tommy. As if sensing this, his friend put an arm on his shoulder. 'We're lucky, you know, Joss,' he said. 'To have each other right now.'

Joss nodded. 'I know. We are.'

England—mid-August, 1940

Second scramble of the day, fourth in 24 hours. Joss had thought the raid on Portland the day before had been big enough, but this was something else entirely. Up ahead, stretching in staggered layers off the east end of the Isle of Wight, hundreds of enemy aircraft approached Portsmouth.

'My God,' muttered Joss. He glanced either side of him: Denis to his left, Buck on his right. Up ahead, about half a mile, Red and Yellow sections, with Mac once again leading. The Spitfires looked tiny, innocuous. Joss craned his neck. *Yes*, there was Green section, behind him. Thirteen Spitfires—the entire squadron—pounding their way towards this black swarm.

There'd been mist earlier, but that had gone. Another day of dazzling hot sunlight. Mac turned the squadron into the sun, climbed towards it then, at 25,000 feet, levelled off. The CO might have drummed into them the enormous advantage of having height and the sun behind them, but right now, looking at the mass of enemy aircraft, Joss felt they were like minnows attacking sharks. They turned once more, facing the stacks of enemy formations, the sun now behind them. Down below, the familiar jagged coastline, hazy through a filtered light; behind, the sweep of southern England disappearing to a faint green curve along the distant horizon.

Silent explosions erupted beneath them, flashes of orange flame and dark smoke as the first bombs detonated. Above were the Stukas and Junkers, and above them, tier after tier of 110s and 109s, all going round and round, head to tail, in their defensive circle.

Mac's voice crackled over the R/T. He sounded calm and steady: ' "A" Flight and Green section will fly straight through the middle tier of 110s, Blue section stay behind us and protect our arses, then attack individually as the circle scatters. But don't hang around for the 109s.' *Good*, thought Joss. He swept the sky in front; the 109s were still higher

438

than them, several thousand feet higher. The odds were not good, but if they flew through the 110s quickly enough and without being seen as they dived, they might be able to hit a number of aircraft before the 109s had a chance to dive on top of them in turn.

Joss felt for the wooden lion in his pocket, then lifted his goggles, and pushed his helmet back off his brow. He glanced in the mirror, but the sun flashed off the glass and he squinted. Turning his head, he saw Buck and Denis fall in line astern behind him.

A couple of deep breaths. *Here goes.* Joss pushed the stick forward and the nose dropped as he began his dive. His ears popped with the sudden drop in height, but the engine whined happily as they hurtled towards their target. The 110s were no more than six miles away—less than two minutes. A glance at the dials—*oil pressure OK, air speed indicator rising.*

Ahead of him, the rest of the squadron was almost there. Nearly 400 miles per hour, and the airframe had begun to rattle and shake; *throttle back slightly.*

A Hurricane squadron arrived, tearing into the bombers; immediately the first tier of 110s peeled off and dived towards them. 'A' Flight opened fire, ripping through the circle. 110s scattered, one, then two, dropped in flames, the battle looming rapidly larger. *Just seconds away now.* Joss braced himself. *Find a target.* He frantically scanned across the swirling and turning aircraft, then spotted a lone 110 crossing a few hundred yards ahead. He pressed his thumb down on the red button and the Spitfire rocked as the eight Brownings opened fire—but with not enough deflection, and his bullets drifted harmlessly wide. *Shit!* Joss cursed. Pulling his plane into a tight turn, he gasped as the negative force of gravity slammed him back into his seat. His vision faded momentarily, then cleared as he came out of the turn. *Yes, there she is.* The Messerschmitt dead ahead and only a hundred yards away—a sitting duck. Orange flashes of tracer arced towards him but the rear-gunner's aim was high. Joss pressed down his thumb again. One three-second burst, then another. Black smoke poured from his port engine and the Messerschmitt banked to the right and stalled, and for a split, heart-stopping second, Joss thought he was going to collide. Instinctively, he ducked his head—not that it would do him any good—as his Spitfire flashed past a large grey wing, missing it by what seemed like inches.

Jesus, that was close. Joss gasped heavily into the rubber oxygen mask, his chest pounding. By the time he'd recovered, just seconds later, he could no longer see the Messerschmitt, nor anyone else in the squadron. He looked around and above, craning his neck once more. Sure enough, 109s were diving to join the fray. Aircraft were tumbling and rolling all over the place; there was no time to see what has happened to his 110. One last glance beneath him—*any good targets there? No, then let's head home.*

Joss dived, fast and quick, and away from the battle above. 'Don't stick around,' Mac had repeatedly warned them. 'Once you've made your initial attack, if you find yourself alone and with no obvious target, head for home. Much better to live and fight another day.' *Yes,* thought Joss, *it is.*

He crossed the coast at Swanage, just 300 feet off the ground, and craned his neck once more. Nothing. The sky was empty, save for a few contrails high, high behind him.

Pulling off his oxygen mask and pushing back the canopy, the rush of fresh, cool air soothed him. He'd been flying in only his shirtsleeves, but even so, his back was still sticky with sweat. He wiped a gloved hand across his brow then held it in front of his face for a moment; it was shaking. 'Come on,' he said out loud, 'stop that. Calm down Joss. You're all right.' *Deep breaths.*

An idea came to him. It was only a short flight back along the coast to Warmwell, but after a quick glance at his fuel gauges, he changed course and headed inland, through the gap in the Purbeck Hills. Almost at once he felt better. Down below, the fields and villages of Dorset spread away before him, an image of serene peace that seemed scarcely credible after the mayhem he had left just minutes before.

For a brief moment, he lost his bearings, then spotted Shaftesbury and the hilltop of Wingreen. *Nearly there.* He grinned, then turned down the valley: yes, there was Berwick and then Marleycombe, utterly familiar despite having never seen it from the air before. *Where are they? Aha—* people out in the fields, continuing with the harvest now the rain had gone and good weather returned. He dived down until he was just fifty feet off the ground, roared past the workers, then climbed and rolled his Spitfire. Joss whooped, then turned again. To his great joy, the workers below had all stopped to wave. As he swooped past he rolled the aircraft again, and laughed out loud as he did so.

441

What a good idea this had been! The horizon swivelled as he banked and prepared for one last fly-by. Someone was running up to the top of the field. Joss watched, hoping, and dropped height again as the hill rushed beneath him. Whoever it was now stood on the gate, waving their arms. Over the workers, across the half-cut field and—*Yes!* It *was* her! Joss raised his arm and waved, then climbed away and turned back up the valley, unable to stop himself from smiling.

England—August, 1940

Everyone had made it back safely from the fight over Portsmouth. It was, Pip had said, another miracle. Mac had been crowing. 'Pissing about in penny packets of twos and threes—waste of bloody time! I've been trying to tell their airships for bloody ages that attacking in squadron strength was the way forward, and I was bloody well right!' They'd shot down another five, which made nine in two days. Nine enemy aircraft without a single loss of their own, and that figure didn't include several probables like the Messerschmitt 110 Joss had hit. A palpable sense of excitement and growing confidence had swept through the squadron; despite the growing numbers of enemy raids, the CO's improved tactics were working. If anyone was the lucky mascot, Joss had thought, it was Mac. It was he, and he alone, who had turned the squadron's fortunes around.

They'd flown back to Middle Wallop, then Mac had insisted the whole squadron go for a night out in Andover. The pilots were still talking excitedly about the day's events as they'd sat crammed into the back of the tumbrel. First stop had been the Angel Inn, and then onto Pinkies, a nightclub, where there was a particularly attractive barmaid called Goldie. Once more they'd got drunk. Karl kissed Goldie and everyone else had whistled and cheered. He had been made to sing another rendition of 'Blue Skies' for that; the rules had changed, Mac told them—from now on it would be sung at his discretion. Then everyone had yelled out the song several times over. Tommy, who'd shot down his second plane that day, had put his arm around Joss and said, 'See. I told you this was the way to fight a war, didn't I? Damn sight more exciting than number crunching like Noel, and,' he said, wagging his finger in front of Joss's face, '*and, we get to go out and get drunk every night and sleep in a nice bed. Who could ask for more?*'

But going to bed with the room spinning and waking up four hours later was taking its toll. By five o'clock the following morning, they had all been sitting slumped inside the dispersal hut bungalow at Middle Wallop, most still drunk. By 7 a.m., the first hangovers were appearing. 'Time for some oxygen,' Tommy had said, and led Joss across the dew-sodden grass to his plane. Gingerly, they both clambered onto the wing root, and pressing the oxygen mask to their faces, breathed in deep lungfuls of the gas.

'Ah—that's better,' said Tommy.

'But it doesn't help with the exhaustion. Tommy, I barely have the energy to move.'

'Well, hopefully we'll have a quiet morning and then we can sleep a bit more.'

They were in luck. Slumbering on the camp beds

443

and armchairs at dispersal, the pilots were not scrambled once all morning. Only at noon were they ordered back down to Warmwell. The other Spitfire squadron there had been involved in heavy fighting twice that morning, once just after six when Portsmouth and the radar stations on the Isle of Wight were attacked, and then again at noon as another enemy raid had descended on Portland. 629 were to relieve them.

Joss had swapped a battered armchair at Middle Wallop for a green and white striped deckchair at Warmwell, and by 3.30 he had largely caught up on his sleep. The morning cloud had all but gone, and he was now sitting outside in the sun, wide awake and idly toying with a strap on his Mae West.

Tommy, next to him, paused from his reading to light a cigarette, then said, 'Come on Joss, spit it out.'

'What?'

'You've got that pensive expression on your face. What's the matter?'

'Nothing really. I was just thinking about how much booze I've consumed in the past week. It's certainly more than we ever drank at Cambridge, and we were drunk quite a lot then. I mean, I can barely remember the last time I went to bed sober. And now the Germans have begun in earnest— well, we've been bloody lucky the past couple of days, but what if we'd been down here this morning? Don't know how much use *I'd* have been at six.'

'Honestly, Joss, stop worrying. Adrenalin and oxygen will kick-start anyone into life. It's not as though you'd ever fall asleep in the middle of a dogfight is it? I think it's much better to drink and have a bit of fun with everyone—stops one from brooding.'

Joss looked doubtful, 'Maybe,' he said, then glanced at Tommy. He looked exhausted, his eyes, grey and sullen.

'I agree, Tommy,' said Karl, who was lying on the grass a few yards in front. 'I think we should get drunk *every* night.'

Buck, who was sitting in a deckchair nearby with his eyes still closed, said, 'That's easy enough for you. You're just like all Californians: can't hold your drink for any money.'

Karl laughed. 'That's just the kind of predictable comment I'd expect from a redneck Texan like you, Buck.'

Then the telephone rang. It was a scramble—a large formation of enemy planes appeared to be heading towards Portland once more. Everyone sprang to their feet, hastily fastening their helmets as they ran.

'I'll challenge you later, then,' shouted Buck.

'What?' said Karl.

'A drinking contest.'

'Stupid Texan,' yelled Karl. 'You're on.'

*   *   *

They climbed through cloud, grey, thick cloud. The aircraft in front and to the side of him looked pale and ghostly. Then they were through, into the blue. Once again, Joss, in Blue section—with Denis and Buck—was acting as top cover over the rest of the squadron. Mac had levelled them off at 22,000 feet with the rest of the squadron a couple of thousand feet below, when Joss heard a German voice

445

coming through his headphones, faintly at first, then becoming louder. It was a strange, guttural sound, but unmistakably that of the German controller vectoring his formation across the Channel. By a fluke, they were operating on the same radio wavelength.

'I can hear Krauts, but where the hell are they?' muttered Mac. Ten minutes later, Joss saw them. 'Here they come,' said Mac. A swarm of Stukas, with 109s above. Some two miles behind, a number of 110s, a force of around seventy machines in all.

'All right, wait for it,' said Mac. They had been patrolling inland with the sun behind them; it looked as though the German formation had still not spotted them. Away to their left, Hurricanes appeared and attacked the 110s as soon as the enemy planes had crossed the coast, while below, the Stukas and their fighter escort continued onwards.

Come on, thought Joss, *let's get it over with,* but only once the enemy formation had passed them did Mac shout 'Tally-ho,' and lead the squadron into a dive. They had clearly still not been spotted when five 109s flew underneath Joss's Blue section. Like an automaton, Joss broke away from the other two and dived down behind the last Messerschmitt. The pilot never saw him coming. Bullets poured from his wings. Immediately, bits of the 109's airframe flew off into the sky. The machine appeared to jolt before bursting into flames, and turning onto its back and spinning down towards the ground, a thick plume of brown smoke trailing behind.

He felt a renewed sense of exhilaration, and, unable to pull out of his dive before reaching

446

the cloud level, found himself following the plummeting Messerschmitt down as it spiralled through the sky. Emerging through the cloud, Joss saw he was just a few miles north of Weymouth. Beneath him, a column of smoke was pitching into the sky. *My 109*, thought Joss, and turned to have a look. There was little left but mashed wreckage and one wing—some twenty yards from the rest of the remains—its black cross still clearly visible. From the nearby village, people were rushing out across the field towards the burning remains, and some looked up at Joss in his Spitfire and waved. He banked and flew past again, waggling his wings as he did so, as though he were a gallant knight of old, bravely protecting the villagers from the mighty dragon.

Later, Joss discovered what he'd already known: that the pilot had not baled out, but had fallen from the sky with his machine, his smashed remains burning with his aircraft on that Dorset hillside; to his surprise, he'd felt little sense of remorse. The anxiety—the terrible guilt—about killing people whose nationality he shared, had silently slipped away without his even knowing it. Joss's Messerschmitt 109 was one of thirteen enemy aircraft destroyed by 629 Squadron that afternoon, the day the Luftwaffe called *Adler Tag*—Eagle Day. 'Thirteen on the thirteenth,' said Mac. 'Unlucky for some, but quite definitely lucky for us.' Tommy had shot down two, doubling his total in one four-minute flurry. Once more, every pilot had made it home, ensuring thirteen became a decidedly lucky number for the squadron. And once more, they'd returned to Middle Wallop only to spend the rest of the night drinking—after all, they could hardly let the most successful day in the squadron's brief history pass without celebration. Moreover, there was also the small matter of Buck and Karl's challenge, something neither was allowed to forget.

*   *   *

Much later, when the long days of summer had given in to winter, and when so much had changed, Joss was thankful he'd joined arms with the other pilots and drunk and sung his heart out that night. Whenever he thought about the squadron, it was as it was on that day, when thirteen pilots had been united by an unshakeable bond. He would not have missed it for the world.

Cairo—October, 1942

Dobbo had preferred to remain behind, but the other 'stay-at-homes'—Joss, Brian and Mark—had all joined Binny on the expedition to the Pyramids. Joss was glad he'd gone. It had done him some good to get out for a bit, and although he'd been several times before during his time in North Africa and was well-versed in the history of the sight, his appreciation of those monuments had in no way diminished since his last visit. He was also mindful, since Binny's request on his arrival at the Villa Jacaranda, to talk to Mark as much as he could.

'F-funny to think about how I used to read about the Pyramids when I was younger, and now here we are,' said Mark, as they slowly made their way along the sandy path that led them past the Sphinx. He had a slight stammer now, but like all of them, distraction was everything.

'Yes, and much bigger than I'd imagined,' said Joss. 'Bloody huge in fact.'

They laughed. 'My dad would love to see them,' said Mark. 'He has always been f-fascinated by all this ancient stuff.'

'What does he do?'

'He's a farmer. In Devon.'

'Really? I used to spend a lot of time on a farm in Wiltshire.' They talked of sheep, and cattle and harvests, and then Joss said, 'Maybe you should bring him here one day, when this is all over.'

'No,' said Mark. 'Once I get home, I'm staying there. Nothing will tear me away again. Nothing.'

Joss smiled. 'Actually, to tell the truth, I feel rather the same way.'

Afterwards, as planned, they went to Mena House, nearby at Giza. They had only just settled down to a table when Joss felt a hand on his shoulder. 'My lucky mascot,' said a familiar voice, 'I *knew* you'd still be all right.' Joss swivelled round and to his astonishment, there was Pip Winters—a bit leaner and with a few more lines etched into his face, but unmistakable all the same.

'Good God,' said Joss, pushing back his chair and clasping Pip's hand. 'Pip, it's so good to see you.'

Having been introduced, Binny said, 'Joss, why don't you and Pip go off for a bit and catch up on your own?'

Joss looked at Pip, then back at Binny. 'Well, if you really don't mind.'

'Of course not. You don't mind do you?' she said to Brian and Mark. They shook their heads. 'Go on,' she said. 'We'll come and grab you later.'

Taking their leave, Pip led them to the bar. 'I knew it was you,' he grinned. 'No one else with blond hair like that.'

Joss laughed. 'Well, you haven't changed much. It really *is* wonderful bumping into you like this.' Then noticing the extra stripe on Pip's shoulder tabs, he said, 'You've got your own squadron, then.'

'Over a year now,' said Pip. 'After the stint instructing, I was given a squadron up in Norfolk. Sweeps over the Channel, that sort of thing. Then in May, we were posted to Malta. We've just been moved here for a rest and refit.'

'Heard Malta was pretty tough.'

Pip rubbed his hands through his hair. 'Tough isn't the word. Made the Battle of Britain look like a picnic. The flying was the most intense and relentless I've ever experienced, and the conditions were appalling. No food, no booze—imagine that, no bloody grog!—collapsed buildings and bomb holes all over the bloody place. Dust everywhere. Raids almost every night—sleep was impossible. It was dismal. Honestly, Joss, there was nowhere to go, no way of getting there and nothing to do even if you did get there. I feel I've come to a holiday camp right now. It's bliss.' Having ordered a bottle of Scotch, Pip poured them two large measures and said, 'What about you? I like the stick, by the way. Your arms don't look too clever either.'

'Got shot down a while back. When was it? Christ, nearly three months ago now. Burnt arms, burnt legs. Bullet through my arm.'

Pip whistled.

'Crash-landed in the blue. Got picked up by some medics looking for a downed bomber crew.

Shouldn't be here really.'

'Well, you always were lucky. Some people just are. I reckon I can tell nine times out of ten who's going to make it and who isn't—sometimes it's because someone simply shouldn't be flying in the first place, but mostly it's just the look of them.' He chuckled. 'Perhaps I'm psychic.'

Joss smiled. 'Well, it's very good to see you, Pip. I haven't seen anyone from the old days for absolutely ages.'

'Good to see you, too.' Pip poured himself another Scotch. 'Saw Gordon Bowyer out in Malta. He was much the same, until he got himself killed crash-landing into a wall. Then again, he was always crashing wasn't he? Seem to remember he broke a leg or something during the Battle of Brit.' He smiled, then said, 'I often think about those times, though. In a funny sort of way, I think they were the best days of my life. Of course, bloody terrifying too, and a lot of lovely blokes dead as a result, but ... oh, I don't know. Well, cheers, anyway.'

Joss lifted his glass and nodded. 'Cheers,' he said.

*　　　*　　　*

They talked a lot about that summer. Mostly the good bits—funny incidents, or amusing things people had said. 'D'you remember when Tommy swiped that high-octane aviation fuel for his car?' said Pip at one point. 'And we were all so pleased with ourselves that we'd successfully made it off base without being caught.'

Joss laughed. 'God, yes. And those bloody bobbies stopping us.'

451

' "That's a very funny smell," ' Pip mimicked, ' "And your ve-hicle is making a very odd noise".'

'Yes! And Tommy said, "I'm sorry gentlemen, but my car's a little off-colour today. Would you mind terribly moving aside as I think it's about to be sick".'

'And they did as well!' They both laughed out loud. 'I remember one funny time with Tommy,' said Pip. 'Must have been after one of those August fights. I think we'd been over Portsmouth—at any rate, somewhere in 11 Group—and I'd run out of ammo and so had dropped into some nearby airfield to refuel and rearm. It was bloody hot and I was thirsty, so while the erks were sorting out my Spit, I grabbed a bicycle and pedalled up to the mess for a drink. When I got to the front door, I saw Tommy a few yards away, marching in the same direction. We both looked at each other— and I swear this is true—and without either of us saying a word, marched up to the bar and ordered a tall, iced, Pimms each. Most refreshing drink I've ever had. We'd both had exactly the same idea.'

'Then what?'

'I think we got back into our planes and flew back.'

'See anyone else?'

Pip shook his head. 'Mac's a Groupie now, though. Still in England.'

'Good for him. Mike?'

'Haven't heard a word about him for ages. Don't even know whether he's alive. You know Antonin got it?'

'No,' said Joss. 'I'm sorry.'

'Yes, he was all right wasn't he? Tough bastard. Apparently he got it over Dieppe a few months

452

back.'

All too soon, Binny came to collect him. Joss was sorry to have to leave, although he was already beginning to feel drunk. *Perhaps it's just as well,* he thought. He scrawled his address onto a bit of paper and said, 'Let's meet up soon. I've got to come into Cairo in a few days' time. Why don't we get together then?' and Pip had nodded, and said, 'All right, what day?' The 18th, Joss told him. Lunch at Shepheard's. 'I'll be there if I can,' Pip told him.

Pip had also mentioned the day the first bombs had landed on Middle Wallop. He even had something funny to say about that. 'It was just after tea, wasn't it? I remember I was sitting on the loo, having a crap, when suddenly there was this bloody great roar of engines followed by the most almighty explosion. Literally caught with my pants down.'

Yes, Joss nodded, the day after their great victory of the 13th. He remembered it very well. It was the day he'd received his first letter from Stella, and the day Tommy and he had shared their secrets of the heart. He might well have been killed that day too. He and Tommy had been walking back from the mess to dispersal across the airfield, Joss clutching his letter and Tommy quizzing him about who it was from. 'Come on Joss,' he'd said, 'surely you can tell *me*? I don't see why you have to be so damned secretive about everything.'

They were right in the very middle of the aerodrome, and they both stopped, as they heard, and then saw, the blue-bellied Junkers 88 swooping towards them.

'Shit!' said Tommy, and Joss began running towards the nearest hangar. 'No!' yelled Tommy,

'This way!' and they turned and ran away from the buildings as fast as they could. Even so, the explosions that followed knocked them off their feet. Joss could not say how long they lay there— probably less than a minute—but when they picked themselves up again, covered in white chalk dust, they saw a row of bomb craters leading up to the hangar, precisely where he had originally meant to run.

'Jesus Christ,' said Tommy.

'My God,' said Joss, 'thanks Tommy. I think you just saved our lives.'

'Look at my hands.' He held them up. They were shaking, quite visibly. Then he began to run. 'Come on,' he said, 'we'd better tear ourselves into the sky again.'

Spitfires were already taking off, roaring down the far side of the grass runway to avoid the craters, although by the time Tommy and Joss reached dispersal, the all-clear was being sounded.

'Christ,' said Tommy again. 'Jesus, that was too much.'

Four ground crew had been killed in the attack. Everyone had looked stunned. Tommy spent most of the afternoon staring into space and smoking cigarette after cigarette.

'Tommy,' said Joss, 'Tommy, are you all right?'

Tommy looked at him blankly, then nodded. 'Yes, I'll be fine,' he said, then closed his eyes and sighed. 'It's bad enough being under attack when you're in a fully-armed Spitfire, but quite another when you're defenceless and vulnerable on the ground.'

* * *

454

Joss thought that Tommy had forgotten all about the letter, but later that night, as they lay in their beds—and sober for once—he said, 'You're going to have to tell me now, you know. Surely that's a fair exchange for saving your life?'

'Tommy, why is it you always make me tell you things that I never mean to tell anybody?'

'It's good for you. If I wasn't around, you'd be even more bottled up than you already are.'

Joss sighed. 'It's from Stella.'

'Stella? My word.'

'It's not what you think.'

'Of course it isn't.'

'It isn't. We've become friends. Good friends, I suppose, ever since Dunkirk.'

'And Guy? He's always so protective of Stella. Protective of you, for that matter.'

'He's busy with the farm and his Home Guard duties.'

'Well, she's certainly very beautiful.'

'We're friends.'

'Hm,' said Tommy, 'but I bet you wish you were more than that. I'm right aren't I?'

Joss sighed again. 'Maybe you are. But that's irrelevant.'

'Of course it's not. Why would you say that?'

'Because firstly, I know she doesn't think of me in that way, and secondly, I hardly think Guy would be too pleased.'

'Joss, you really are impossible.'

'Why? What do you mean?'

'For God's sake. Life's too short—far too short at the moment. I can't see beyond tomorrow, let alone next week. We've got to make the most of life while we've got it. *Carpe diem* and all that. I bet

455

Stella feels the same way—she's hardly going to bother to write to you if she's not thinking about you is she? And I'm sorry, but sod Guy. He's a grown-up—he should be thrilled that his best friend is in love with his sister. All right, so maybe he'll be a bit put out to begin with, but he'll come round. Course he will.' He was quiet for a moment, then said, 'This war—it's made me see things differently. Suddenly anything seems possible now.' He paused again, then said, 'You see, I've met someone as well.'

Joss sat up. 'You have?'

'Yes.'

'You never said.'

'No, well—'

'And you call me secretive. Come on, Tommy, out with it!'

Tommy grinned. 'All right,' he said, 'her name's Ellen.' She was older than him, quite a bit older. 'Thirty-six if you really must know.' He still wasn't sure how he felt about her, except that she was more intelligent, more exciting than any other girl he'd met. The funny thing was, he'd met her at his parents' house during his last leave—the Haskells had held a tennis party, and some friends had brought her along with them. They hit it off immediately and before she left, they'd agreed to meet in London. He then spent two 'wonderful days' with her—walking around, visiting galleries, going to the movies. Talking. He'd been entranced.

'Where did you stay?' Joss asked.

'On her divan the first night and in her bed the second.'

'I can't believe it's taken all this time for you to tell me.'

'That, Joss, is a bit rich coming from you.' He sighed. 'I haven't told you because a large part of me thought I would never see her again. I had a feeling I should leave it as it was: two magical days. Anyway, what would people think? Me with someone like her? I know men frequently date girls much younger than themselves, but rarely the other way round. People would point. It would probably embarrass my parents.'

'But you don't give a damn about any of that stuff.'

'I don't want to upset people—my parents, or even Ellen for that matter. I wouldn't want to make her life difficult. But now. Well, now I see things differently. I've probably always been a bit selfish, but I feel I'm entitled to be even more so now. If I'm to die in this stupid war, don't I have a right to take what happiness comes my way while I can?'

Joss thought for a moment, and then said, 'Yes, Tommy. I believe you do.'

*　　　*　　　*

He still had that first letter from Stella. Arriving back at the Villa Jacaranda, he made sure Dobbo was still out on the veranda, then went into their room and pulled out his trunk from under his bed. It was at the top of the bundle—he'd kept them all in chronological order—dated, 12th August, 1940. The ink had faded, as it had on the others, but as his eyes glanced over the words again, he vividly remembered the thrill he'd felt the first time he'd read it, standing outside the mess that cloudy afternoon, the day the first bombs fell on Middle Wallop.

12ᵗʰ August, 1942

Dear Joss,

That was *you wasn't it? I* know *it was! How wonderful of you. I hope you saw me waving from the gate—I think you did. We've been talking about it non-stop all afternoon, and all the boys are proud to know a real fighter pilot. Guy, of course, is madly jealous, but I think even he was quite impressed by your fly-by. One of the boys said they'd seen dark streaks underneath your wings and said that was smoke caused from your guns firing. Is that so? Please be careful. We're all worrying about you terribly. I try and think what it must be like for you flying every day, meeting unknown numbers of enemy planes. For us down on the ground it is an unimaginable world you inhabit.*

You said it had been declared that all pilots were to have one day off in every seven, so please come and see us again next time. I can't tell you how much I have enjoyed our long chats these past months—and I loved our supper together the night of the storm. In these strange times they have been a great comfort to me. Mum is well, so is Guy, and Ruby is still kissing the village boys and causing her little brother no end of embarrassment.

Please be careful.
With love,
Stella.

Joss folded it and put it back with the others, retying the piece of string around the bundle. He rubbed his head: yet another *sodding* headache, a crippling pain that was impossible to ignore. In four days' time he would go to RAFME HQ, where, in all probability, he'd be given some part-time desk job and a date for his medical board. Then what? Physically, he was now well on the mend. His arms and legs were healing, at any rate. In another week he'd probably not even need the stick; only the scars would remain.

England—late August, 1940

Most of the pilots sat in the dispersal tent. Although it had been clear and sunny earlier in the day, cloud had appeared late in the morning over Warmwell, and, much to their delight, had not shifted all afternoon. There was beginning to be talk that they might not be scrambled once all day.

'No, they'll come over all right,' said Johnnie Reeves, 'just to piss us off.'

Denis looked out of the tent. 'I can see some blue up there.'

A few groans came from the others and Johnnie said, 'Well, they'll definitely come now.'

Joss and Tommy had been playing poker with Buck Neill, but he had pulled out and now sat opposite them on the edge of a camp-bed reading a letter.

'From home?' asked Denis, taking his seat inside once more.

'My dad,' said Buck. 'It arrived this morning but I

forgot about it until just now. Looks like my sister's getting married and my kid brother's fallen off a horse and broken his leg.'

'Do you know him?' asked Tommy. 'Your sister's fiancé?'

'Oh yeah, Billy, he's my best mate back home.'

'And is that OK with you?'

'Are you kidding? Course it is. I just never thought he'd ever have the nerve to ask. Been mad about her for years.' Tommy raised an eyebrow at Joss. Buck shook his head. 'Amazing what happens when you're away from home. I wish I could be there for the wedding.' He put the letter down for a moment and said, 'Billy and me used to get up to all sorts of crazy stuff when were kids. It was his old man who taught us to fly. He had this De Havilland that he used for crop-dusting, not just on his farm, but all round about too. Well, of course, us kids thought this was fantastic. Billy used to persuade him to take us up and bully him to show us how to fly. That's how we learnt. We used to bunk off school and help his dad do the crop-dusting. Billy's dad didn't really care too much about education. His mom used to go mad, but Billy's dad just used to say, "What's the point of education to a farming boy like Billy?" ' Buck chuckled. 'My mother had died, so my dad had to bring us up on his own. Course, he still had to go out and earn a living, so he never knew the half of what I'd been getting up to until the school started complaining. He'd no idea what I'd been up to, that I could fly a plane all on my own.'

'So what happened?' said Joss.

'Well, he was pretty mad, and told me I had to go to school and to stay at home the rest of the time, but I still sneaked out, and in the end he told me that if that was what I really wanted to do with my life, that was up to me. I don't think he had the energy to fight me about it. Probably reckoned his life would be a whole load easier if he let me have my way.'

'But you joined up and Billy didn't,' said Tommy.

'Well, as his dad said, he was a farming boy. Billy's old man died a couple of years back and so Billy took over and stayed where he was.'

'Maybe he didn't want to leave your sister,' said Tommy.

'Guess not,' said Buck. He scratched his head. 'Funny, but I almost wish they didn't write. It only makes me wish I could be back there.' He looked at the letter again, then said, 'My dad always signs off the same way: "Take care, son. We're all proud of you but worry like mad. Love from, Dad." I hate them worrying about me. Makes me feel bad.'

'I think that's rather touching,' said Tommy.

Joss thought: *At least your dad cares.* He still hadn't forgiven his mother for letting him down so badly on his latest 24-hour leave. He'd written to her and even sent a telegram the day before, but she still hadn't been there when he eventually reached the flat, and nor did she reappear in the evening. Instead, Joss had gone out to see a film on his own—a particularly bad one—and had ended up drinking with some locals at a pub in Pimlico. At closing time, he'd gone back to the flat, hungry and in a terrible mood only to find Diana still wasn't there. He was in bed when he heard the key turn in the lock. Stomping into the hallway in his pyjamas, he had given Diana a shock. Clutching her hand to her chest, she said, 'Joss,

461

darling, what on earth are you doing here? You gave me quite a fright.'

'I wrote to you *and* sent you a telegram,' he said.

'Yes, but for next week. Yes, I'm sure it was next week.' She hurried into the sitting room and to her desk. 'I know my diary's here somewhere. Where is it?' She gave up. 'Anyway, I had it written down as next week. I'm so sorry darling, really I am.' She went over to him and kissed him, but Joss turned away.

'Where are you going?'

'To bed. I'm tired. It's exhausting fighting daily battles in the sky which is why we're told to go and have a night off once a week.'

'I'm sorry, Joss. Of course if I'd known you were arriving today I'd have cleared the decks, but I honestly thought you were coming up next week. I would have been here today as well, but at the last minute Anthony had some time and—'

'I don't believe what I'm hearing,' he said. He felt his temper rising. *I could be at Alvesdon Farm now,* he thought.

'Joss, please, don't be like that.'

'Good night, mother,' he said, turning his back and walking back to his room.

They'd talked the following morning, and Diana had done her best to fuss over him. Was he being careful? She worried about him *constantly,* and, she told him, always listened to the reports on the wireless and read the papers. What were the rest of the squadron like? She even remembered to ask about Tommy. Even so, soon after breakfast he had to make his way back to Andover—his leave ended at noon. 'Will you come up next week? I *promise* I won't make the same mistake,' Diana had said. 'Please, Joss?'

'If I'm still alive,' Joss had told her. His parting shot, and perhaps a bit melodramatic, but it had served her right. Nor did he have any intention of going back to London for a while. Next leave he'd be going back to Alvesdon Farm. That was now due tomorrow. He could barely wait.

The telephone rang, much louder, now that they were in the tent. The pilots sat up immediately, as though they had been given a small electric shock. 'Scramble,' said the orderly. 'Fifty plus coming our way.'

'I *knew* it,' said Johnnie, jumping up off his bed. Cards were flung down, books tossed onto the camp-beds, and chairs knocked over in the rush to get out of the tent. Out on the airfield, engines were already being started up by groundcrews, twelve 1,000 horsepower engines drowning out the quiet afternoon calm.

It was, by now, a well-run routine, but that telephone ring still made the hairs on the back of Joss's neck stand on end. As he ran across the grass, his heart raced and the nausea returned. His movements became jerky, his fingers clumsy and fumbling. As he approached, Griffiths pushed himself up out of the cockpit and jumped down onto the wing. The Spitfire was already vibrating from the force of the Merlin, the propeller a vague whirr. Joss grabbed the parachute off the wing. He caught a leg in a strap. 'Shit! Come on, come on,' he muttered, then jumped onto the wing root, and swivelled himself into the bucket seat. Shaking fingers struggled to click his harness into place. He cursed again, took a deep breath, and then succeeded. *Good.* Feeling the wooden lion in his

463

pocket, he glanced at the dials in front of him, briefly checked his leads, and raised his thumb to Dowling, who removed the chocks from in front of the wheels. Joss gently opened the throttle and the Spitfire rumbled forward. Weaving from side to side so he could see enough not to crash into anyone else, he taxied the short distance to the beginning of the runway. Moments later, he tore down the grass strip along with eleven other Spitfires. From the moment the telephone rang to being airborne had taken just under three minutes.

*   *   *

Mac led them up to 15,000 feet. They were high above Swanage when they saw a large formation of German bombers approaching beneath them. Stacked in the usual layers above were hordes of Messerschmitt 109s.

Having warned them to keep a watch on the German fighters, Mac led them down to attack the bombers below. Forming up in Mac's favoured line astern, the Spitfires peeled off, one by one, sweeping and curling down through the sky. As Blue One, Joss was last but one in the line, and by the time he was within range, the formation of bombers was beginning to break up. Joss opened fire with a short burst at a Heinkel, but he was past before he had time to see whether he'd hit anything. Now below the mass of bombers, he climbed up underneath another and opened fire again. Smoke began pouring from the port engine. A shadow falling across him made him look up. Another bomber was hurtling towards him, a mass of flames and smoke. 'Jesus Christ!' muttered Joss, and threw the Spitfire onto its side. He missed the passing wingtip of the Heinkel by a few feet. Lines of tracer criss-crossed the sky. Everywhere he looked aircraft were turning and spiralling. Shouts and chatter from the other pilots filled his ears. *'Got one!' 'Look out behind you!' 'Shitting hell!'* Joss swung round ready to re-attack. A few seconds before he'd not been able to see any of the 109s diving on them, but suddenly orange flashes whipped past his cockpit and he heard machine-gun fire crackling in his ears. He glanced behind but there was nothing, then saw two 109s diving at him from the left, and more tracer curling across his Spitfire. He turned in towards them, and felt his harness cut into his shoulders and his goggles slip down from his helmet and partially cover his eyes. Frantically, he pushed them back up only to see another 109, this time attacking from the right. Again, he turned in towards it and found himself on the tail of another, who was in turn attacking a further Spitfire. Joss was about to fire when his view was completely blotted out by the underside of another Messerschmitt, streaked with oil, flashing past him. A split-second later it was gone and he was firing a long burst of machine-gun bullets into the 109 in front. The German aircraft began belching black smoke and toppled over on its side, but the Spitfire in front was struggling badly. Puffs of dark smoke were belching from the engine. *'Jesus, I'm on fire! I'm on fire! Jesus Christ help me!'* Buck—Joss felt his body freeze, then he shouted, 'Get out of there Buck, I'll cover you but get out of there now!' *'Oh my God! Oh my—'* The Spitfire exploded. The blast knocked Joss, jolting the control column in his hand. Debris smashed across his wings and above him, and his radio cut out. Where Buck had been just seconds before there was now nothing. Tumbling beneath him, a ball of flaming carnage.

Joss felt himself gag. An ear-splitting crack lurched him back to the reality of the battle. Frantically looking behind he saw another 109, this time on his tail. *Shit, shit, shit!* Another punch and smoke burst from the engine and flooded back into the cockpit. His Spitfire was knocked upside down, then he was spinning, the control column limp in his hands. He was falling out of the sky, his plane out of control and smoke billowing behind him. Desperately, he tried to pull off his oxygen mask and radio leads. His altimeter was spinning backwards too fast to read, as was the world below. He realized death was unavoidable, and with it came a moment of strange calm.

Suddenly, he felt the control column respond after all. He pushed the stick forward, applied hard left rudder and—*a miracle*—the Spitfire emerged from its spin. Joss glanced upwards. High above him aircraft were still circling and turning, but he could not see any more 109s. It was just as well, for with a splutter and cough his engine died, and he was left gliding. Silence, save the wind whistling through his open cockpit. Joss gasped—he'd been holding his breath again—and frantically tried to think about what he should do. His altimeter said he was now at just eight hundred feet, too low to bale out. Where was he? West of Swanage, inland somewhere, and there was blood streaming in tiny rivulets across his starboard wing. He recoiled, and brought his hand to his mouth. Not any old blood, but *Buck's blood. Jesus.*

The Spitfire was falling steadily. He would have to crash-land somewhere. His hands had begun to shake again. Lines of sweat ran down his back and cheeks. Joss cried out loud—frustration, fear; panic.

Just four hundred feet now. He could see people below watching, pointing. *Look! A Spitfire in trouble, trailing wafts of smoke*—waiting, hearts in their mouths, wondering whether they were about to witness an airman plunge to his death. 'A flat field that's all I ask,' he mumbled, craning his neck this way and that. He cursed Dorset and its hills. Then he saw a village and what looked like a cricket field—a fairly large cricket field. He banked the Spitfire and lowered the flaps, praying he'd judged it correctly; there would be no second chance. Just a hundred feet, the field approaching. Joss pressed down the undercarriage lever but nothing happened. *Damn it to hell.* Hydraulics shot to pieces. *Very well—a belly-landing then.* He checked the buckle again on his Sutton harness and braced himself. Perhaps he would die after all. Or perhaps he would be disfigured for life, his legs sheared by tearing metal wrenched apart by the impact. Over houses—so close he could touch them—and a long narrow garden. *Is this really it?* Over the hedge. *Seconds away now.* Joss closed his eyes.

The air was punched from his chest, the harness tore into his shoulders and his head was jerked forward onto the gunsight. The Spitfire groaned and slewed across the grass, ploughing up the turf and soil into a fountain in front of him, then stopped, thrusting Joss back into his seat and catching his elbow on a lever to his side. *I'm alive,*

467

he thought, but something was running into his eyes and half-blinding him. He lifted his hand to his brow and saw it was red. It didn't hurt at all; in fact, he felt almost completely numb. *I must get out of here,* he told himself and unbuckling his harness and wiping his face with his hand, lifted himself up out of the cockpit and onto the wing, and then jumped onto the grass. People were running towards him: children, men and women. A boy reached him. 'Are you all right?' he asked. He sounded breathless.

Joss nodded. 'I think so. Did I miss the cricket square?'

'Yes,' said the boy, 'but you've dug a big hole in the football pitch.'

Others had reached him, but Joss found it hard to focus. Strange voices peppered him from all around. His vision began to blur and he felt peculiar, not himself at all. Someone—something—dabbed at his face. His head began to spin, his legs buckled, and then he fell to the ground.

*   *   *

When he came to, he was at the local doctor's house having had four stitches sewn into his head. After talking to him at some length about cricket, the elderly doctor offered him a drink and the use of his telephone. Thanking him, Joss rang through to Warmwell.

'*Yes?*' said Mac.

'Mac, it's Joss.'

'*Joss!*' His voice softened. '*Where the hell are you? We thought you'd got the chop.*'

'I don't know. Not too far from Warmwell, I

think. I belly-landed on a cricket pitch. I saw Buck get it. Did everyone else make it back?'

'Yes. Johnnie baled out, but he's OK. Most of us got a few bullet holes.'

'Quite a fight.'

'Yes. We've put in claims for two Heinkels, a Dornier and a 109.'

'Think I got a 109. Saw smoke anyway.'

'Good. And are you sure you're all right?'

'I've got four stitches in my head and a sore elbow, but I'm fine, really.'

'I'll get someone to pick you up and get you back to Middle Wallop. And Joss?'

'Yes?'

'I'm beginning to believe what Pip says about you.'

*   *   *

When he eventually reached Middle Wallop later that evening, he felt exhausted. He walked into the mess but none of the squadron were there. Reynolds, the adjutant, was still about. 'They're in the pub, Joss. Come on, I'll give you a lift if you like.'

I've got to sleep, thought Joss, but he wanted to see the others too; perhaps a drink would do him good. 'All right, thanks,' he said.

Cheers greeted his arrival. 'The prodigal son returns!' said Mac. Joss grinned.

'Christ, you look like shit,' said Pip, looking him up and down. Joss shrugged. *So what?* He was still wearing his flying boots and his blood-stained life jacket. There were also flecks of blood on his shoulder and one arm sleeve of his tunic. His face had been cleaned but there was dried blood in his

469

blond hair. 'I didn't want to miss out on the fun,' Joss told him. Everyone laughed.

'You're just in time,' said Denis. He was standing in front of the others, clutching a full pint glass.

'I think Joss should do it too,' said Mike.

'But I didn't bale out,' Joss replied, 'I crashed. Not the same thing at all.'

'Mac?' said Pip.

'Let's not split hairs here. Baling out or crash landing—it comes to much the same thing: you lost your Spit. Joss, I'm sorry but you're going have to do it. Another cider and beer, please,' he called to the barman.

'All right, all right, but I do have a wound, you know.' He pushed back his hair and pointed to the blackening scar.

'Simply not big enough, I'm afraid,' said Mac.

Tommy came over and put an arm round Joss's shoulder. 'You have no idea the levels of anxiety you're causing me.' He looked strained—eyes bloodshot at the edges, his cheeks sallow.

'What happened to you?' Joss asked.

'I fired at all sorts of machines. A Dornier, a Heinkel. Didn't hang around to look. Got into a bit of a tumble with a 109, but he eventually gave up and headed for home. I was more worried about colliding than being hit.' Before he could say any more, Denis began to down his pint. 'One, two, three, four!' shouted the others in unison.

When it was Joss's turn, he spilt much of his pint down his front. After he'd finished, he put the empty glass upside down on his head, and he felt the cold dregs run down through his hair. 'Blood, sweat and beer,' he said. 'I'm sure that's what Churchill *meant* to say was on offer.' More

470

laughter. The pint sat heavy in his stomach. He'd been given a sandwich on the way back to Middle Wallop, but otherwise he hadn't eaten and as he began singing 'Blue Skies' he thought for a moment that he might be sick, especially as he kept seeing images of Buck's blood in his mind's eye.

No one had mentioned Buck. Nor did they, except Tommy, who later said, 'I'm sorry about Buck. Did you see it?'

Joss nodded. 'His plane just blew up in front of me. I tried to cover him but he didn't get out in time.'

'And then you were hit.'

'Yes.' They were silent for a moment, then Joss said, 'So where's he gone to then?'

'Buck? Oh, back to Texas definitely. He had to go to his sister's wedding. Billy asked him to be best man.'

'Yes,' said Joss. 'That's definitely what has happened.'

Tommy ruffled Joss's hair. 'Day off tomorrow—lucky you.'

'I need it after today.'

'I'm sure. Think you might see Stella?'

Joss grinned. 'Bloody well hope so.'

'I *am* right, you know, Joss. We've got to live like there's no tomorrow.' Then his expression changed; his face looked suddenly drained, the light gone from his eyes. He leant his head on his hand sighed deeply and said, 'Christ, I hope I make it to my next leave.'

Joss smiled, put an arm on his shoulder; there'd been too much of this kind of talk in recent days. It worried him. 'You're all right,' he said. 'You're only saying that because you're lovesick—and because you're tired and a bit drunk.' Tommy looked at him, and silently raised an eyebrow. 'Come on, Tommy,' said Joss, 'you've barely had a scratch all summer. Anyway, when are you off? Two days' time? You can look after yourself until then.'

He smiled wistfully. 'Yes, I expect so,' he said, then turned to the bar. 'Let's get another drink. The more time I spend drunk the quicker the time will pass.' Neither of them said anything for a moment. Joss felt crushed with fatigue. He could not tell whether Tommy was being serious or not. He watched him light a cigarette, as four shots of whisky arrived on the bar in front of him.

'Here,' said Tommy, passing him a glass. 'One to throw back, one to sip.' Joss hesitated. 'Come on Joss, drink up.' Tommy swallowed the first shot in one gulp. 'You know,' he said, banging the glass back down on the table, 'it's on days like these that I feel ashamed of myself. All that stuff about dying in a blaze of glory I used to spout. Noel was right: I *was* a vainglorious little prick.'

'I think you're being a bit hard on yourself.'

'Do you? Maybe I am. But I doubt poor Buck felt very glorious as he began to burn. I'm a little bit drunk—I admit it—and I'm sorry for sounding melodramatic, but I've just discovered that I'm actually rather scared of dying. I thought I wasn't, but I am. Joss, I don't want to die at all. And I'll still feel that way in the morning.'

England—late August, 1940

In the end, Joss didn't reach Marleycombe until mid-afternoon. They'd had a quiet morning—nothing had stirred—yet although Joss had bagged one of the proper iron beds set up at the Middle Wallop dispersal, he had struggled to sleep, dozing fitfully. Then just before noon—a tantalizing ten minutes before he was due to head off—they were scrambled for a patrol over Portsmouth. A new Spitfire had already arrived and so he'd had no excuse; he *had* to go. Mercifully, they saw nothing but the controller kept them up there ages. *Of course he would do,* thought Joss. It was nearly two hours later that they all touched back down again.

'I'm sorry about what I said last night,' Tommy said to him, as Joss was about to leave.

'As long as you're all right. You had me worried.'

'I'm fine. And please, you've no need to worry yourself on my account. I'm not going to become constantly maudlin and depressed. It's just that it's easy to think life's a bit grim when you lose good people like that. And for an hour or so, I thought you'd been killed too—it gets to be quite a strain preparing yourself for the worst, you know.'

'Don't suppose the drink helped too much either.'

'Oh I don't know—I think it helped a great deal.' He grinned.

'Well, just think, it's already Tuesday—only another day and you'll be able to see Ellen again.'

'Not so long, I suppose.'

'No. Come on, we're old hands now. We can take

473

care of ourselves.'

'Yes,' said Tommy, brightening, 'yes, you're right.'

Tommy had lent Joss his car again on the strict understanding that he would bring it back on time the following day. Joss had promised solemnly, then at last headed off for Marleycombe. He couldn't ever remember being so tired and had to stop twice on the way, just to clear his head and stop himself from falling asleep. *Why didn't I sleep properly this morning?* he thought to himself, and why was it that now he was away from the war for 24 hours and *wanted* to be awake, he felt so ready to sleep?

Celia had been visibly shaken by his appearance. He'd washed his hair before leaving, but the scar, high on his forehead, was big and dark enough for her to notice it immediately. He'd shaved too, but there was no hiding the grey rings around his eyes. 'My dear Joss,' she said, 'come in quick and sit down. Let me get you some tea. Have you eaten? Would you like something to eat? You must rest this afternoon—no gallivanting on the farm.'

Joss had allowed himself to be waited on, and, although he'd not meant to spend the afternoon on one of the sofas, he had succumbed to sleep, waking only at the sound of the two children clattering through the rest of the house some hours later. For a short while he just sat there, thinking about raising himself up and going out to find Guy and Stella, but the soft evening light pouring through the French windows, and the familiar smell of the room—polish, wood smoke, dog—were so comforting, so relaxing, he couldn't quite bring himself to move. He looked at some of the things around the room: the cluster of photographs on the grand piano—David, the boys, the infant Michael, Stella. David and Celia on their wedding day, smiling through the rain. The sideboard with its cluster of decanters, silver labels slung round the necks; the walnut bureau where Celia wrote her letters; the high wing-backed armchair where David had always sat; its accompanying side-table where he used to have his pipe-rack. Not one of these things had been moved or swapped around in all the years he'd been coming here. So much remained unchanged and yet it *was* different. People make the place, he realized. There had once been so much joy, so much *contentment,* here, a vitality that rushed out to greet him every time he walked in; now that was gone, replaced by a silent sadness that was almost oppressive.

'Hello,' said a voice. Joss instantly awoke from his reverie.

'Stella—sorry, I was miles away.'

She came over and kissed him on the cheek. 'How are you? Mum's terribly worried about you.'

'A lot better for that sleep.' He stretched and yawned, and Stella sat down beside him. She still wore her denim overalls, but had taken off her headscarf. A light smear of mud ran across one cheek.

'Your poor head,' she said. 'What on earth happened?'

'I crash-landed and hit it on the gunsight. I ended up right in the middle of a cricket pitch—it was the only flat place I could see for miles.'

She looked worried, her brow furrowed. 'But why did you have to crash-land in the first place? What happened to you, Joss?' She peered at his scar, then searched his eyes as though she were trying to imagine what it must have been like for him to have been in such a situation.

'I was hit by a German fighter. My engine packed up and the undercarriage wouldn't work, so I had to belly-land.'

'My God.' She held her hands to her mouth. 'I don't know how you can just sit here so calmly telling me that.'

'I'm fine now. Honestly.'

She forced a smile. 'You are a worry, you know Joss.'

'You sound like Tommy.' He grinned. 'I got your letter—thank you.'

'It was magical.' She smiled, remembering, and her face relaxed. Then she patted his leg and said, 'I'm afraid I've got to go and sort out the brats and clear up a bit. We'll talk later, though. Will you be all right?'

'Of course.'

Once she'd gone, Joss stretched again and wandered outside, around the garden and into the yard. There was no sign of Guy, so he began walking up the track to Prescombe, then stopped and turned around; he still felt heavy with fatigue—he would go for a walk in the morning instead.

*   *   *

Drinks at eight in the drawing room. Guy had appeared briefly, then disappeared to wash and to change into clean clothes, and was now organizing drinks from the sideboard. 'Mum said we should make an effort for you,' he said, 'although I'm glad she stopped short of making us dress up.'

'We hardly ever have dinner in the dining room any more,' said Celia. 'I thought it would be nice for a change, and since Joss is here, well—'

'But it's only Joss, mum,' cut in Guy. 'I hardly think he needs special treatment after all this time.'

'Well, I'm touched, Celia, thank you,' said Joss. He too had washed and changed, and felt better. Hungry too. 'Anyway,' he said, 'how's farming, Guy?'

'All right, I think.' He passed round the drinks then sat down in David's old chair. One of the spaniels came and sat at his feet. 'Harvest's all done. We've been lucky it's been so dry. Now we've got to start ploughing again.'

Stella came in. 'Sorry I'm late,' she said. Her work-clothes had also gone, replaced by cream culottes and a navy blue sweater. Joss tried hard not to stare as she went to pour herself a drink. 'Has Guy told you we've got another tractor, Joss?'

'Really?' said Joss.

'Yes,' said Guy, 'a Ferguson this time. It'll be a great help.'

'What happens to the horses? You can't get rid of them, surely?'

'Oh, good God, no,' said Guy. 'There's still plenty of work for them.'

They talked on: about the farm, people in the village, the two evacuees, until it was time to go through to the dining room.

'Anyway, you certainly set Ruby's heart a-flutter with that fly-by of yours,' said Guy as they went through to the kitchen to pick up the dishes.

'Oh yes,' said Celia, 'and a few others.'

Joss laughed. 'I thought she was only interested in the village boys.'

477

'Not any more,' said Guy. 'You are a bloody show-off.'

'Guy, please!' said Celia.

'Sorry mother, but honestly—'

'I thought you'd be pleased to see me,' said Joss.

'We *were*,' said Stella, then as Guy walked on through to the dining room, added, 'Ignore it—he's just jealous.'

As they all sat down at the table, Stella said, 'Joss had to crash-land on a cricket field yesterday.'

'Oh yes?' said Guy, 'Did you miss the square?'

'Actually, I did—bit of damage to the football pitch, though.'

'Must have been a bit hairy.'

'It was.' Joss felt his eyelid flicker and lifted a hand to rub it. 'Something in my eye,' he said.

'Tommy all right?' Guy asked.

'Fine. He sends his love.'

Guy put down his knife and fork for a moment and said, 'I'd love to see Tommy. Haven't seen him for ages. Can't you persuade him to come down with you one of these days?'

'I'm not sure about that. It's different for Tommy—his parents are only at Guildford now, so he's been going to see them whenever he's had leave. Or, at least, he was. He's just decided he's in love, and so he's heading up to London whenever he can.'

'What, *really* in love?' Guy looked incredulous.

'I think so. He says he's still not a hundred per cent sure, but she's definitely the most wonderful person he's ever met, and he's absolutely champing at the bit to get back up to town to see her.'

'Good for Tommy,' said Stella. 'Who is she?'

'She's called Ellen—she's thirty-six.'

Raised eyebrows from around the table. 'Goodness,' said Celia, 'quite a bit older then. And what about you, Joss? Have you taken a shine to any of the WAAFs?'

'Um, no,' he said. He glanced at Stella and saw she was watching him. 'A few of the chaps seem to have girlfriends on the station, though. And one of the American pilots is seeing a barmaid in Andover.' *One of the Americans—but there is only one.* He suddenly put down his knife and fork. For a moment he could only think of Buck's plane exploding, the burning debris fluttering down and the blood streaked across his own wing.

'Joss are you all right?' *Stella.* He looked up, trying to focus his thoughts once more. 'Sorry,' he said, 'yes, I'm fine.'

'You must still be tired, I expect,' said Celia.

'Surely not,' said Guy, 'I hear you've been kipping all afternoon while the rest of us have been valiantly toiling in the fields.'

'Guy!' said Stella, 'don't be so mean. It's Joss's day off. Anyway, he has to get up at the crack of dawn every day and yesterday crashed and was wounded. It's not surprising if he's feeling a bit whacked.'

Joss smiled at Guy—but these jibes were wearing thin. He could feel his anger rising. *Ignore it,* he told himself, *just ignore it.*

'But I have to get up at dawn every day too,' Guy continued, 'and I haven't had a day off in months.'

'Look, really, I'm fine,' said Joss, unable to keep the irritation from his voice. 'Anyway, this is hardly a competition to see who feels the most tired.'

'I'm not suggesting it is,' said Guy, 'I'm only pointing out that mum and Stella seem to cluck and fuss over you just because you've got the glamour job zooming about in aeroplanes while I get almost no thanks at all for busting a gut trying to run this place and keeping up my duties with the Home Guard.'

'Don't be so ridiculous Guy,' said Stella, exasperation in her voice. 'If we make a fuss of Joss, it's because he's risking his life every day so that you won't have to risk yours. You should be grateful.'

'Stella, please don't let's argue,' said Celia.

Guy sighed. 'Of course I'm grateful,' said Guy, 'and Joss, I'm sorry. I wasn't really being serious, just making a small point, that's all.'

'I know,' said Joss, relieved, 'it doesn't matter. Forget it.' There was a pause, and then he said, 'How are you getting on with the Home Guard anyway?'

Guy rubbed his chin, then said, 'Still don't have any uniforms although we've been given a handful of American rifles. The Major's in charge, and although he's given various guidelines from above, we're essentially left to our own devices. He's a survivor of the last war and a bit old fashioned—he likes us to drill and do lots of guard duty at roadblocks, but that seems a bit of a waste of time to me. We should be thinking about how we can best stand up to the Germans with what we've got—practising sniping and making the most of the fact that we know the surrounding country like the back of our hands. I *can* now make a home-made bomb, though.'

Joss smiled. 'Well, that's something.' He looked at Celia and said, 'I'm amazed how normal everything seems. Coming here today you'd hardly

480

know we were all threatened with invasion.'

'Well, we've all got to just get on with things, haven't we?' she said. 'I mean, it's not going to help if everyone flew into a mass panic. And the RAF seems to be doing tremendously well—the Nazis are losing a terrific number of planes, aren't they?'

'Thank God for the fighter boys, eh?' said Guy.

'Well, yes,' said Celia, not detecting the tone of irony. 'It really is the case that you pilots are our sole defenders now.' She glanced at Stella and Guy. 'Well, it's true isn't it?'

The conversation moved away from the war. Back to safer ground: past memories and happier times. Holidays in Cornwall; fights between Stella and Guy when they were children; childhood fads: Stella's passion for hunting, Guy's for railways, cars, then Africa. Celia told them stories from her own childhood in Kent, remembering the first car she ever saw, then the first aeroplane. 'And now look at us,' she said. 'Planes and cars everywhere.'

'Planes and cars—that would be a good theme for the summer party,' suggested Stella.

Celia smiled sadly. 'Yes. Of course this coming weekend would normally have been party weekend.'

'Yes, of course,' said Guy. 'The last weekend in August.'

'When the war's over, perhaps,' said Celia.

'Hm,' said Guy, 'although I expect everyone will be sick of planes by then.'

Joss shifted in his chair. What was the matter with Guy? Exhaustion swept over him as it always did at this time of night—in the pub or the mess he would overcome it, have another drink, and perk up—but right now his head felt heavy and the rims

481

of his eyes stung. He rubbed them, then yawned.

'Don't let us keep you up,' said Guy.

'No, no, you must go to bed whenever you want,' said Celia.

'I mean, we can't let our war hero go back tired.' It was said as a joke, but Joss could sense there was no humour there; could see that Guy was goading him, daring him to answer back in front of Celia and Stella. He felt his temper rise. 'I'm sorry,' said Joss, 'I think I will go up fairly soon.'

'And think of me at 5.30 tomorrow morning,' said Guy.

Joss felt frustration and hurt surge through him. It was this terrible fatigue, he knew—not just the lack of sleep, but the strain of the past few weeks, kept at bay for so long, but now chipping away at him, stretching his nerves and his patience. Was he overreacting? *Maybe,* but he could contain himself no longer, and he turned on his friend. 'Guy do you know what happened yesterday?' he snapped. 'Let me tell you. Twelve of us were sent to attack a German formation of over thirty bombers. The only trouble was, high above us, protecting these bombers were another thirty or forty German fighters. No sooner had we dived in among the bombers than the fighters dived in on us. It was a massive fight. Planes everywhere. One bomber nearly collided with me as it fell in flames. Then I was shot at by four different German fighters. Can you imagine what it's like having to fly for your life like that? Bullets zipping past your head, knowing that at any second you might be dead, or worse, burning? Can you even conceive how exhausting it is being flung about from side to side, up and down, the pressure so great you almost pass out?

482

And I had to listen to the screams of one of the men in the squadron—one of *my* friends—as he began to burn, and then I watched him and his plane explode up before my eyes. His blood was streaming across my wing. And then I was hit, and I honestly thought I was going to die, and all I could think about was how much I had been looking forward to seeing you and coming here the following day. I'm sorry you're tired, and I'm sorry you don't get enough thanks for what you do, but there's no need to sit there making snide comments as though I'm some over-indulged confidence trickster. I mean, for Christ's sake, Guy, what's the matter with you? I thought you were supposed to be my best friend. I thought you of all people would understand. But you haven't got a bloody clue.'

He was spent. There was silence around the table. Immediately Joss regretted every word he'd just said. He felt hot and light-headed, appalled at himself. He could no longer look any of them in the eye. Couldn't bear to see their faces. Pushing back his chair, he said quietly, 'I'm sorry—please forgive me. I don't know what came over me, but if you don't mind I think I'll go to bed.' Then he left the room.

What have I done? he thought to himself as he climbed the stairs. *Guy will never forgive me.* Close to tears, he sat on his bed and took off his clothes. Every limb in his body ached, and as he clambered beneath the sheets he wondered whether this would be the last time he slept there.

Downstairs, he heard muffled voices and the scrape of plates and dishes being cleared away. He wanted to shut out the world, to go away from everyone and everything; to be left alone. It was all too much: he no longer had the strength to keep going. *And Stella*: how lovely she had looked at dinner; if only she knew how much he *yearned* for her—and yet now she would probably turn her back on him too. Even Celia—what would she think of him now? After all her kindness, he had repaid her by ranting and raving uncontrollably—swearing even—when she had not once faltered herself. Joss bit his sheet. *How could I have been such a fool?* he thought. 'Oh God,' he mouthed, 'what's happening to me?'

*   *   *

Despite his exhaustion he was still awake over an hour later. He had heard the others come upstairs to bed and had been thinking of going to see Guy to apologize, when he heard the door handle turn. Sitting up he said, 'Guy?'

'Joss? It's me. Can I come in?'

'Stella. Of course, what is it?' He turned on the sidelight, his heart racing. She was wearing old stripy pyjamas, a size too big. Tucking a lock of hair behind her ear, she sat on the edge of his bed, and stretched out a hand to stroke his head.

'Are you all right?' she said, smiling. 'I was worried about you. Please don't worry about Guy.'

And at that moment Joss knew that Tommy had been right, and the despair that had weighed so heavily upon him vanished, replaced by an overwhelming desire and belief that what he was about to do was right. 'Stella,' he said, and reaching out, placed his hands on her cheeks, and kissed her.

484

Cairo—October, 1942

A cool, dark office: desk, filing cabinet, portrait of the King, and that most important piece of equipment, the fan, whirring at a subdued pace from the ceiling.

'Please, sit down,' said Group Captain Green. Mid-thirties, Joss guessed, with well-oiled hair and trim moustache. He inhaled deeply on a cigarette, the tip glowing brightly, and looked at some papers. 'Hm,' he said, scratched his chin, then said, 'Hm,' again. Joss, his walking stick resting between his legs, wondered if it would be impolite to light a cigarette himself: since arriving at the Villa Jacaranda he'd been smoking more than ever; it was something to do. He was about to ask, when the Group Captain spoke at last. 'Well, Flight Lieutenant Lambert, I have good news for you.'

Joss waited expectantly—*a ticket home perhaps?*

'You've been awarded a bar to your DFC. Congratulations.'

Oh, thought Joss, *is that all?* He must have looked disappointed, for Green said, 'Aren't you pleased? It's just been confirmed—it'll be in the *London Gazette* in the next day or so.'

'Thank you, sir.' Joss wondered whether his mother would spot it.

'Well,' said Green again, briefly glancing at the notes in front of him once more, 'you've a pretty impressive record. Six enemy planes confirmed destroyed, one shared and three probables since you reached the Desert. It's the least you deserve. How are you feeling? Sounds like you're lucky to

485

be alive.'

'Much better, thank you. I hardly need the stick any more.'

'Good, good. Feel up to helping the effort here, then?'

'Yes, sir, although I was hoping I might be able to go back to England soon.'

The Group Captain inhaled deeply again. 'Back home, eh? You do realize that there's about to be a major battle up in the blue? We need every Tom, Dick and Harry we can get our hands on.'

'Yes, sir, but I'm not passed fit for flying yet, and I've not much experience of clerical work, so I'm not sure how much use I can be to you here—'

Green smiled and lifted a hand to cut him off. 'Can tell you're a fighter pilot, Lambert. You're all the same—terrified of flying a desk.'

'It's not that so much, sir, but I have been out here since the beginning of last year. I thought most pilots were only doing a six-month tour these days.'

The Group Captain continued to smile—*I've heard all this before*—then said, 'According to my notes, Lambert, you came out in February '41, served with 465 Squadron for six months, then spent seven months instructing in Khartoum. You joined 713 Squadron in April as a supernumerary Flight Lieutenant until you were shot down and wounded in July. I'm afraid you can't count the three months you've just had off, so by my reckoning, you've another three months to go.'

Joss bit his cheek. *The bastard,* he thought, *he's playing with me.*

'Tell you what,' the Group Captain continued, 'let me see what I can do, eh? I'm not promising

486

anything, but there might be a chance I can pull a few strings.'

Joss visibly brightened. 'Thank you, sir. Thank you very much.'

'In the meantime, you can come and work for me. Your doctor says only half a day to begin with, but you can probably manage a bit more than that can't you?'

Joss nodded.

'Good man,' said the Group Captain. 'It's mainly a question of sorting through intelligence and reports filed from the front—and no clerical experience necessary. A bit of chivvying too—we get a lot of requests from the various squadrons, everything from new planes to bottles of beer, but of course, you'd know all about that. I know it's not the same as flying, but it's essential work—and without giving too much away, we're in for a very busy time at the moment.' He tapped his notes on the desk and said, 'Anything you'd like to ask me?'

Joss thought for a moment, then said, 'How are 713 getting on? Is Prior still in charge?'

'Yes, as a matter of fact he is.' Joss was glad. Prior had been a good man. 'We've taken far fewer losses in the past couple of weeks,' Green continued. 'You know Marseille's been killed?'

Hans-Joachim Marseille—the Germans called him the 'Star of Africa'. He'd been the scourge of the RAF for many months. 'No,' said Joss, 'no I didn't. What happened?'

'His plane let him down and he baled out too low. Killed instantly the moment he hit the ground. I don't know whether the German claims can be trusted, but we picked up intelligence that he'd shot down a hundred and fifty-one of our chaps out here.

487

A hundred and fifty-one! Phenomenal amount.'

'I expect most of those were fighters too.'

'Yes, I believe they were. Bad luck on you lot, but a blessing for our war effort as a whole. Our bombers have caused no end of havoc to the Jerries, largely because our friend Marseille and others were more interested in building up their personal scores than concentrating on the job in hand. We've got virtual air superiority now—the main danger to your old friends now is AA-fire rather than 109s. They're spending their days shooting up anything that moves the far side of the Alamein line.'

Times *had* changed, thought Joss. Enemy fighters had been a constant menace ever since he'd first come out, especially the German 109s. Their battered Hurricanes and Kittyhawks had been little match for the new 109Fs and Gs. They'd lost so many men—and machines; no wonder men like Marseille had built up such enormous personal scores. But now—well, perhaps they really had seen the worst in North Africa; maybe the confident accounts of the Allied military build-up relayed on a daily basis at the Villa Jacaranda were no fanciful exaggeration after all.

*   *   *

After leaving RAF Middle East HQ, Joss went to Shepheard's, where he had arranged to meet Pip Winters. He'd half expected him not to be there, but after briefly scanning the terrace, spotted Pip wave at him. As ever, the terrace was heaving, thick with officers in uniform, women in their brightly-printed frocks, and safragi scurrying around with trays held high above their heads. The mood was noticeably more upbeat than the last time he'd been there during his leave back in June—more laughter, more gesticulating, more *noise.* They all seemed to be saying the same thing: *We've turned the corner.*

'You made it, then,' said Joss, sitting down.

'Yes, we're still out at Heliopolis jack-arsing about.' He'd already bought a bottle of whisky and poured Joss a glass then himself another. Wearing tatty old khaki shorts and a sweat-stained light blue shirt, Pip looked somewhat dishevelled. His cap, frayed at the rim, lay on the table. 'I feel like something out of a Bateman cartoon,' he said, ' "The Man Who went to Shepheard's in old shorts." I've been glared at constantly by the stuffy staff officers in their winter-wear trousers.'

'I shouldn't worry,' Joss laughed, 'they're probably just jealous of your hard-won battle-experience.'

'Pen pushers the lot.' He grinned, then said, 'How did you get on?'

'All right. They want me working at HQ filtering reports.'

'When are you up to see the medical board.'

'In a week.'

'And if you're passed fit?'

Joss shrugged. 'I asked to be sent home.'

'What did he say to that?'

'Said I was needed here really, but he'd try and pull a few strings. Don't think he meant it though.'

'But you want to fly again.'

'Of course.'

Pip eyed him curiously, and blew three smoke rings in succession. Joss couldn't help smiling—Pip was the only person he'd ever known be able to do that.

'What?' said Joss. 'Why are you looking at me like that?'

'I've got a proposition for you,' he said. 'I'm being sent home. I've been promoted—Wing Commander, can you believe it?'

'Congratulations,' said Joss.

'I'm taking over a Wing up in Suffolk somewhere. And this is where you come in.' He leant forward on the table. 'How do you fancy taking on one of the squadrons? They're short of a CO at the moment—one of the flight commanders is care-taking.'

Joss took a gulp of his drink, the hot spirit searing his throat. 'But I haven't even been passed fit yet,' said Joss, 'how can you possibly wangle that?'

'But you will, won't you? You more or less feel all right don't you?'

Joss nodded. He felt his spirits rising, wanting to believe it might be true.

'It would mean a promotion too.'

'Christ, Pip,' said Joss. 'Are you sure? I mean, how?'

'Because I can pretty much hire and fire who I like—you know what it's like—and because I know people at Fighter Command. I'm off in a week or so.'

'Boat or plane?'

Pip grinned. 'Plane—Cairo, Malta, Gib, home. No three-month cruise round the Cape for me. You could come too.'

That soon. 'I can't believe it,' he said.

'It'll be like the old days. Pubs, green fields, decent digs.'

'Do you really think you could arrange it?'

'I don't see why not. Tell you what, leave it with me for a day or two, all right?'

Joss nodded. 'Thank you, Pip, that would be wonderful.'

After Pip left him, Joss remained at the table for a while longer, thinking. Here in Cairo were tantalizing tastes of home: tea and scones, Scrabble, spotted dick and custard, Binny's Lake District watercolour, cricket, the sheer number of English-speaking people. Yet there was no disguising that Cairo was an alien place and Egypt an alien land. Even from where he was sitting on the terrace at Shepheard's—and one could hardly find a more European spot in all Cairo—the stench of cooking, human refuse, dust and sweat permeated the air, always, inescapable; the cacophony of noise never-ending. He wanted to leave Africa—the place of his birth—leave it forever. If he could no longer love or be loved by a fellow being, then at least he had his love for a place. And if it should still be his fate to die in this war, *please God let it not be here.*

His head had begun to ache again—that familiar stabbing throb. He rubbed his temples, then lit a cigarette and closed his eyes, feeling the smoke fill his mouth and lungs. Would he try and see her on his return? He wasn't sure, although just the thought of being closer to her once more was making his chest beat harder. If only he hadn't been sent out here in the first place, perhaps then he would have hung on to her. Perhaps then their love would not have become corrupted. *Ah, that first kiss,* he thought. His hands on her cheeks, her lips parting, accepting, *wanting* to be kissed. 'I love you, Stella,' he'd told her

491

and she'd looked at him, smiling, her eyes shining, and said, 'Do you, Joss? Because I love you too.' He'd felt so happy he'd thought he might cry. But instead, they'd laughed and held each other, and he'd breathed in deeply the smell of her skin and hair, and run his hands across her narrow back. Then she had pulled back the sheets and lain alongside him, her arms across his chest, stroking his hair and face. 'I can't stay long, but please don't worry about Guy.'

'What on earth am I going to say to him?'

'He knows he was in the wrong, that he pushed you too far. We both told him so.'

'Both?'

'Mum understands, Joss. Dad was in the last war, remember.' She'd kissed him again, repeatedly all over his face. 'I'm so happy,' she'd told him, 'although I can't bear the thought of you going back to the war. It was bad enough worrying about you before, but now'—she looked at him, searching his eyes—'promise me you'll be careful?'

The following morning, Joss had found Guy ploughing in one of the lower fields. Guy stopped the tractor, cut the ignition and said, 'I'm sorry, Joss. I really am. Will you ever forgive me?'

'No, it's me who should be apologizing. I behaved appallingly. I'm sorry Guy, I should never have spoken to you like that. It's just the war. I think it's making us all feel a bit on edge.'

'Yes,' Guy had nodded sadly, 'I think you're right.' A make-up of sorts.

*   *   *

Loud laughter from the neighbouring table woke him from his thoughts. He flicked a fly away. It was

492

time to get back to the Villa Jacaranda where there would be tea on the lawn with the others, and a chance to catch up on the latest from the front. After months of stagnation, his life was at last on the move again, going forward, and with it, he glimpsed the first faint ray of hope.

England—early September, 1940

The last few days of August had been quiet for 629 Squadron. The Germans had turned their attention to the airfields of Sussex and Kent in an attempt to destroy the RAF on the ground, but those squadrons further west had been largely spared. Middle Wallop had been bombed again—even Warmwell had been hit—but despite all the stories in the newspapers and the excited reports relayed over the wireless, the battle seemed to have forgotten about 629 Squadron for the time being. Even when they were given the task of protecting the factories around Surrey and south-west London from low-level attack, they rarely saw a thing. The dogfights raging to their east were sometimes glimpsed but never reached them. 'Make the most of it,' Mac had warned them, 'we'll be seeing our fair share again before long,' and so between patrols, they had practised dog-fighting and caught up on their sleep. The days had begun to shorten too. In early July they had often been on stand-by until as late as ten at night; now, they rarely flew beyond 7.30. Joss had been able to think of little else but Stella, Tommy little else but Ellen. 'What a pair we are,' Tommy had joked, 'mooning about

493

like love-struck teenagers.' It was a source of amusement for the others in the squadron too. The sudden flurry of letters had been a give-away and for several days both had been the butt of jokes. 'Do you mind?' Tommy had asked Joss, 'I know how secretive you are.'

'Only about things I'm ashamed of,' Joss had told him. Letters arrived every day from Stella. *I long to see you again,* she had written. *If you are now coming off duty earlier, could I see you in Salisbury?'*

Let anyone try and stop me, Joss had replied.

They'd met at the White Hart. For much of the day—in between the two patrols he'd done over Brooklands and Kenley—he'd been wondering what the evening would be like, running through imaginary conversations in his mind, and hoping he would have the opportunity to kiss her again. He'd pictured walking hand in hand, then arm in arm, through the Cathedral Close or across the water-meadows. He longed to see her and had been counting the hours then the minutes, but as he parked Tommy's car and walked the short way towards the hotel, his heart began a fretful pounding, and he worried that he would clam up, his brain unable to cope with all the hundreds of thousands of words he wanted to say to her.

Pausing underneath the pillared portico, he took a deep breath, flattened his hair with his hands, and straightened his tunic, and walked on in. He glanced around the reception and then entered the lounge. He scanned the room. A number of army officers were already there, but then he spotted her, sitting at a small table in the far corner, and he thought his heart would melt.

'You made it,' she said. She looked radiant and

stood up to kiss him. 'Hmm,' she said as their lips met. 'I've been worried sick all day that something might happen and spoil it for us.'

'You needn't have,' said Joss. 'It's been quiet for us the past few days. Haven't seen an enemy plane at close quarters since I was shot down.'

'Long may it continue.' She wore a knee-length pale green belted dress and a cardigan draped over her shoulders. A dark shade of lipstick and a short row of pearls around her neck. Joss wondered why fortune had smiled upon him quite so sweetly.

She leant towards him and said in a whisper, 'I've booked us a room.'

Joss's eyes widened, then he grinned. 'Have you? Really?'

She nodded, smiling. 'Please say you can stay.'

'As long as I'm back by six.' He took her hand. Her skin was cool and soft. 'What name did you use?'

'Mr and Mrs Lambert of course.'

'And what about your mother and Guy?'

'I told Guy that I'd been working non-stop since the beginning of June and that I needed some leave. Even the land girls are allowed time off, so I don't see why I shouldn't. I'm going up to London tomorrow for a few days to see Charlotte and others, only they think I've gone up to town today. Aren't I clever?'

'Do you think I could see you in London?'

'Could you come up too?' Her face brightened.

'Tommy and I both have a twenty-four-hour leave in a couple of days' time. He wants me to come up to London with him to meet Ellen. We could all meet up.'

Stella clapped her hands together. 'Yes please, that

495

would be perfect. I'd love to meet the mysterious Ellen—and see Tommy, for that matter.'

'She lives in large flat in Hampstead. We could have another night together.'

'I want to make the most of every minute, Joss, I really do.'

They did not wander through the Cathedral Close, or the water-meadows. Instead, they ate a quick dinner then went upstairs to their room. Joss shut the door behind them and turned the key and for a moment they said nothing, looking at each other coyly. A window was open and it had become cooler, and Stella sat on the edge of the bed and clutched her arms around her. Joss sat down next to her and Stella said, 'I suddenly feel a bit shy. I've never done this before.' She glanced at the wall where there was a blackened portrait of an elderly lady. 'I don't think she's helping.'

'No, she definitely would not approve,' said Joss, 'Far too puritanical.' He stood up and took the picture down, leaning it face to the wall. He wished he'd never had that night with Joan, and was relieved that Stella had not asked him whether it was his first time too.

'I feel much better now,' she said. Her face twinkled, and, putting her arms around his neck, she brought her mouth to his. As he kissed her lips, then her face, then her neck and shoulders, his inhibitions melted away. Her breathing quickened and they began to undress. His jacket came off first, then his tie and shirt, her hands feeling their way across his chest. He kicked off his shoes and felt for the fastener at the back of her dress. Almost frantically, he fumbled for the clips, his hands clumsy, but one by one, they came undone, until Stella pulled the dress off her shoulders, unlooped her arms and dropped it to the floor, then pushed off his braces and began undoing his trouser buttons, while Joss kissed and caressed her arms and chest. Her skin was soft, slightly freckled, he noticed, her shoulders and collarbone slender and delicate. *Lovely.*

Now wearing nothing but their underwear, Joss felt a shiver, although from mounting excitement rather than cold. So much of Stella had been physically hidden from him all these years, but he was at last just moments away from knowing all of her. Still kissing her shoulders and neck, he gently eased the straps of her bra over her arms then moved his hands to her back and after a moment's fumbling—*yes!*—unclipped the silk strap and pulled it from her. Stella closed her eyes, and Joss brought his lips and hands to her chest. She gasped, then lifted his vest and clasped him to her, so that he felt her breasts pressed against his face. He wanted to kiss every inch of her body, to feel and touch all of her. Now that this moment had finally arrived, his happiness was so overwhelming he thought for a moment that he must be drunk, or even imagining things. How could he have been so lucky? What had *he* done to deserve this night? It was unbelievable good fortune; the other pleasures of his life paled in comparison.

Kicking off the last pieces of clothing, Stella said, 'Let's get into bed.' A moment of fumbling as they turned back the starched linen, and then she slid towards him, her warm, smooth body next to his. 'My love,' she whispered, and Joss moved on top of her and stared into her pale eyes, and her dark brown hair spread across the pillow. She smiled—

497

a smile of unmistakable love and trust—then wrapped her arms around him and pulled his face towards hers. He kissed her again, then moved his lips down her neck, and to her chest, and to her belly and beyond. He heard her gasp again, and she said, 'Please Joss, now.' Brushing his lips back up her body, he met her mouth, then carefully pushed apart her legs with his own and eased himself into her.

She winced. He stopped, alarmed.

'No,' she said, 'please, my love, don't stop.'

'Are you sure?' he breathed.

'Yes,' she said, 'please Joss.' He could feel her passion; the intensity surprised him. As he entered her once more, her hands stretched across his back, and she tensed. It bothered him that he might be hurting her, but she was urging him in deeper, until suddenly she seemed to relax, so that her murmuring was not from pain, but from pleasure.

His momentary anxiety over, his ecstasy returned. The two of them were now linked together; the moment could never be taken away. She had given herself to him, laid bare her body and soul. The sensations coursing through his body, causing him shivers of delight down his legs and up his spine were unlike anything he had ever felt before. Opening his eyes, he gazed at her once again: her eyes, now closed, her mouth parted; the pale smoothness of her skin and her breasts moving with his rhythm. He vowed that however long or short his life was, he would never, ever forget this most magical of moments.

*　　　*　　　*

Later, they lay side by side in bed, their eyes just inches apart. With her fingers she stroked his hair, while he ran a finger over her shoulders, along her arms and over her breasts. *Just imagine waking up to her every day!* thought Joss.

'Look at my arms,' she said, 'brown from the elbow down, white everywhere else. It looks so silly.'

'You've got beautiful skin.'

'It's too freckly. Dark-haired people aren't supposed to have freckles.'

'I love your freckles.'

She smiled and kissed him. 'And what about you? Not a freckle or mark in sight. Just your scar.' She gently ran her finger by the scar on his head where he'd crashed a few days before. 'You still look so young, you know. You may be wiser in there'—she ran a hand across his head—'but you still look young.'

'Good—I don't want to grow old.'

She looked anxious for a moment, as though she were about to say something important. Instead she said, 'Did you feel nervous at all—I mean, before we met tonight?' Her voice was soft, barely above a whisper. 'Because I was—a bit. I'd been longing to see you, but I so wanted everything to be perfect.'

'Yes—I don't know why. But as soon as I walked in and saw you, I forgot all about it.'

'Me too. It's funny. We've known each other for such a long time, but not really known each other at all.' She kissed him. 'When did you first decide you loved me?'

'I think I've always loved you,' he said. 'From afar for a long time, but I think I *really, properly* fell in

499

love with you when you took me up to see the derelict inn.'

'I remember that day, it was the first time we ever really talked, and I remember thinking there was a lot more to you than I'd realized. You'd always ignored me before.'

'You always ignored *me*! You seemed so much older, so much more mature than us. And you and Guy have always had this rather exclusive relationship—your own jokes and codes—to which no one else is a part.'

She smiled. 'I suppose we have. Being a twin is different from having an ordinary brother or sister. You know so much more about each other—I still feel I know him better than anyone. But do you know when I fell in love with you?' Joss shook his head. 'It was when we went to Dover. We'd just parked the car and I was walking away and you stopped me, grabbed my arm, and told me what we had to do. I realized you'd grown up since you'd been away. And you were kind and understanding, especially afterwards. We *do* understand one another, don't we?' She lifted her head and looked at him. 'I wished you'd kissed me during the storm.'

'I think I would have done if Guy hadn't turned up. I wanted to.' She put her head back on his chest, ran her hand down the length of his arm. 'Stella, what are we going to do about Guy? I don't want to be deceiving him. I don't want us to have to hide at all. I want everyone to know and be happy about it.'

Stella sighed. 'Oh, darling Joss, I wish I knew what to do for the best. He'll be upset—I know it's not logical—but he will. For so long he's been the most important person in the world to both of us, and now he's not to either. At least, that's how he'll feel, and I know he'll be terribly hurt.'

'He will be, won't he? Oh, damn it,' he said, 'why does anything have to spoil it for us? Or is that a selfish thing to say?'

She put a hand to his cheek. 'No, of course not. But it's not even just that. He already feels you've somehow moved on and left him behind. That you're no longer the young boy who waited on his every word, who let him rule the roost. You don't need him any more.'

'I do though. I'll always need a friend like him.'

'But not in the same way. It's why he behaved as he did last week. But you're right, we must tell him, and soon.' She moved herself onto her elbows and put a hand to his cheek. 'Let's have this time together now, and in London, and then we'll tell him. Right now I like it that no one knows. I feel I've got you all to myself, my lovely blond-haired Joss.'

'You are beautiful, you know.'

She laughed and wrapped her arms around him. 'Mine, all mine,' she said. 'I'm going to hold you captive and never let you go. If the RAF calls for you I'm going to tell them you're indisposed.'

'Perhaps I should break an arm or something. You'd have to nurse me though. I'd be a very demanding patient.'

Stella laughed, then her expression changed.

'What is it?' Joss asked.

'I was just thinking about tomorrow. I'm dreading it. Dreading having to leave you and let you go back to the war.'

He held her closely. Where her body was left untouched by the sun, her skin had an almost luminescent paleness. 'Try not to think too much about what might happen. We're together now, aren't we? Let's make the most of that.'

'I know. You're right, but now I've got you, I worry so much that I'll lose you again. I don't think I could bear it if anything happened to you now.' She turned and kissed him once more, her hair falling onto his face, and her pale grey eyes searching his, *devouring* him as she brushed her lips across his mouth and cheek. 'I love you,' she whispered. *The best words in the world,* thought Joss.

* * *

Two days later he saw her again in London, as arranged. Tommy had been delighted by the plan. 'A foursome!' he had exclaimed, 'Perfect! We can all have dinner together and then stay at Ellen's flat.'

After a morning patrol over Brooklands—once again uneventful—they set off in Tommy's car. Joss had never seen Tommy so excited. 'I do hope you like her Joss. She's longing to meet you—and Stella for that matter. I just couldn't get that patrol over with quick enough this morning. Ah, being in love, eh?' He laughed. 'I swear I never thought I'd ever feel this way about anyone.'

'What about that girl in Nice last summer? You were pretty keen on her when we were all at camp.'

'Doesn't even come close. Just you wait, Joss, she'll bowl you over too, I know it.'

Tommy had dropped Joss off in Kensington. 'See you at the flat at seven,' he told him, then drove off. Charlotte's mother had opened the door;

behind her stood Charlotte and Stella. It frustrated him that he could not immediately rush to her and take her in his arms, tell her how much he'd missed her, how much he loved her.

'You must be Joss,' said Charlotte's mother, 'Please do come in. I'm afraid I'm not going to let you go until you've at least stayed and had some tea.'

But I really don't want to, he thought. 'Thank you,' he said, 'that would be lovely.'

Stella and Charlotte sat together on the sofa opposite, tantalizingly far away, while Mrs Padfield bombarded him. 'We all think you're doing the most terribly brave job,' she said, 'we've been listening to the radio and reading the papers and one can only think, thank God for the RAF. My husband says that from the moment you get the signal you can be airborne in less than five minutes, is that so?'

'Yes—sometimes even less.'

She clasped her hands together. 'My word, isn't that *incredible*? No wonder you're giving the beastly Germans such hell.' She went on—had his airfield been bombed? Was it true they had to be up at first light and had to fly until it got dark? Weren't they all *absolutely* exhausted? Did he think they'd ever bomb London? Had he shot down any planes himself? Was the Spitfire the most marvellous plane he'd ever flown?

'Thank God,' said Joss, once they'd finally got away. 'For a moment, I thought she was going to lock us in and keep us there all afternoon.'

Stella laughed. 'She's very sweet really. Anyway, it's not every day you get to meet a real fighter pilot, and especially one straight from a hard morning's work defending the realm.'

They laughed, but then Stella suddenly turned to him and said, 'Do you really think Hitler will invade? What's happening up there, Joss? Do you think we're winning?'

Joss looked up at the sky. Innocuous puffs of white lolled gently across an otherwise deep blue. 'I don't know,' he told her. 'We hear little more than you. But I keep thinking, a year's passed and we're still here.'

'A year since Dad died.'

'Yes. I miss him.'

'Me too, more than he could know.' She tightened her grip on his arm. 'In a way I'm glad he's missing it—it would have depressed him terribly and I know he wouldn't believe what we're being told. He became an awful pessimist after the rise of Nazism, although I think he'd approve of Churchill. But should we believe all the reports we're given, Joss? Every night on the news they tell us we've shot down another large number of their planes but there doesn't seem to be any let-up. They still keep on coming don't they?'

'Tommy thinks Hitler wouldn't want to invade without total command of the air, and the Luftwaffe hasn't managed that just yet. 629's still going strong at any rate. And if our intelligence officer's anything to go by, I'd say our claims are pretty accurate. He's an absolute stickler. Actually, it's quite funny—we all land back down and start gabbling away about what's just happened and then when we talk to him and present our claims, he says things like, "So you're the third person to have shot down this Dornier." To be honest, I've almost stopped bothering making any claims. Unless you can be absolutely certain you've shot an aircraft down or have a witness who can verify it, Calder only gives you a 'probable' or even just a 'possible'. But look at it this way: we've got RDF, we've got Spitfires, and we've got a great big bit of water between us and them. I don't know how many fighters are being built or how many pilots we've got coming through, but I do know that when I lost my Spit last week I had a brand new one early the following morning—that's got to be a good sign, hasn't it?'

Stella nodded. 'I suppose so.'

'Anyway, let's not talk about the war any more. Pretend we're in one of those clubs where talking shop is forbidden.'

'All right,' said Stella. 'It's so lovely to see you safe.' They wandered through Kensington Gardens and Joss remembered how proud he'd been to walk through St James's Park with his mother, he in his uniform, she in her fur coat; he felt the same way now, although this time, he knew he would not end up feeling disappointed the following morning.

*   *   *

They took a bus to Hampstead. When Joss had held out his money, the conductor said, 'Don't worry sir. It's free to the likes of you. Keep up the good work.'

'Thank you,' said Joss. He noticed others on the bus look round, some nodding in agreement at the conductor's sentiment.

'You're blushing,' said Stella.

'I'm embarrassed. I had no idea people thought

505

that way.'

'Of course they do. You're the ones in the front line at the moment.'

'Not me. The Germans have forgotten all about us lot in 10 Group.'

'Suits me.' She squeezed his hand, then said, 'Tell me about Ellen. I'm dying to meet her.'

'Me too. Tommy's completely mad about her. According to him, she's the funniest, cleverest, most alluring person he's ever met.'

'The *most* alluring—my word!'

'Yes, the *absolute* most,' Joss grinned, 'and not only that, she also has the most perfect lips and cheekbones ever seen on a woman. Apart from you, of course.'

'Well, naturally.'

'Tommy says she's also a really *good* person, without a bad bone in her body. He says she makes him appear an appalling individual by comparison.'

Stella laughed. 'But if she's so perfect, why isn't she married? You'd have thought she'd have been snapped up years ago.'

'Ah, well, she was. Years ago. Apparently she was a society beauty—quite the talk of the town, so Tommy says—and married very young. I don't know what happened, but they divorced pretty soon after. Her family was very upset about it, but she took herself through art school and became an interior designer—a rather good one, by the sounds of it. Tommy says she's hugely in demand, even now.'

The flat was not in a new apartment block, but in an old six-storey town house that had been converted over three levels. Ellen lived on the top two floors. Having rung the bell, they stood outside at the top of the wide stone steps glancing up at the tall, fine windows and white stuccoed walls. 'Someone's coming,' whispered Stella and then the door opened.

'Joss, Stella, hello.' Ellen stood before them, smiling and ushering them in. She was tall, with deep, dark eyes and, as Tommy had promised, high cheekbones and wide, yet narrow lips. Her voice was soft and calm, her hair dark but already streaked with grey. Two faint lines edged either cheek and there were laughter lines stretching from the corners of her eyes; but it was more her air of mature intelligence that belied her age rather than any physical attribute.

They followed her up two flights of stairs and through an open door, into a narrow hallway with a large oval gilt-framed mirror, and on into the drawing room. Two sets of French windows looked out onto a narrow iron balcony and to London spread out beyond. Tommy sprang up from a divan. 'Isn't it the most incredible view?' he said, and for a moment they paused by the heavy silk drapes that hung either side of the windows and looked out.

'It's the main reason I bought it,' said Ellen. 'I've always loved London and one could hardly hope for a better view than this.'

'You can see for miles,' said Joss. Through the clouds, a beam of sunlight lit up the silver dome of St Paul's. Beyond, he could even see Tower Bridge and the cranes lining the docks and wharves along the Thames to the east. Interspersing the view, and hovering above the skyline, were hundreds of silvery-grey barrage balloons.

'Tommy, will you open that bottle of

champagne?' Ellen asked him, then turning to Joss and Stella, said, 'I've a case left over from way back which I delve into on special occasions.'

'Thank you,' said Stella, 'what a treat. I haven't had champagne in ages.'

'Tommy told me your flat was wonderful,' said Joss, 'and it truly is. You have some lovely things.'

'That's very good of you to say so,' said Ellen, 'although I've been lucky. I spend a lot of time scouring for clients and so am able to pick up the odd piece here and there.'

Tommy returned with a tray of drinks. 'Tell me, Joss,' said Ellen, 'do you drink as much as Tommy? He says all you pilots do, but I'm not sure I believe him.' She smiled then looked at Tommy.

'Course he does,' said Tommy.

'Maybe not *quite* as much,' said Joss, 'but almost.'

'But don't you all feel awful the following morning?'

'Well, sometimes. But if we're not flying we sit and sleep it off and if we are, there's nothing like being in the plane to wake you up.'

'I suppose not.' She sounded unconvinced, then stood up and went over to a table in the corner where there was a gramophone. Putting on a record, she said, 'I've always had such a crush on Ivor Novello.'

Not long after, they went out to dinner to a French restaurant on the High Street. 'I hope you don't mind going local,' said Ellen, 'but I thought this would be so much easier than going into town. The blackout makes travelling anywhere such a palaver.'

At the restaurant, the maitre d' made a great fuss of them, *delighted* to see Madame once more and,

508

of course, her distinguished friends. He ushered them to a dimly lit table near the back, then, nodding at Tommy and Joss's wings, assured them their aperitifs were on the house.

'You love this kind of attention, don't you darling?' said Ellen, running a hand across Tommy's cheek.

'It's nice to be appreciated,' said Tommy, smiling at her.

'What was it Churchill said the other day?' said Ellen. 'Something about the many owing so much to the few.'

'Actually, there's an amusing joke doing the rounds about that,' said Tommy. 'One pilot apparently heard it and thought the PM was talking about the fact that they hadn't paid their mess bill.' He grinned. Joss had heard that joke too. He thought Tommy seemed more animated than he'd seen him for ages. His eyes sparkled, and his face glowed in a way that he now realized they hadn't during the previous weeks. He'd lied to Ellen about Tommy's drinking: Tommy *did* drink more than him, much more.

Despite—or perhaps because of—the war, the place was busy. A large mirror filled the end wall, making the room seem bigger, while all along one side ran a long padded seat and a line of tables. Having swooped down a tray with their drinks, a black-waistcoated waiter thrust some menus in front of them, apologized that some of the dishes were now unavailable—'C'est la guerre'—and lit the candle that stood in a wax-drenched wine bottle in the middle of their table.

Tommy lifted his glass. 'Cheers,' he said, 'to us all.'

'I'll drink to that,' said Stella.

Joss and Ellen chinked their glasses too.

'I'm in such a good mood,' said Tommy. 'I think it's because we've had such an easy time of it the last ten days. I feel as though I've made it through the storm and the sun is shining once more. And now here I am having dinner with people I love.' He beamed at them.

'I never realized you were such a sentimentalist, Tommy,' said Joss. 'Imagine what Noel would say if he'd heard you say that.'

Tommy laughed, then turning to Ellen said, 'Noel's an old friend. He's the world's biggest curmudgeon.'

'And Tommy's the complete opposite,' said Joss.

'But a great friend all the same. He's stayed on at Cambridge, although I have a theory that he's working as a spy.'

'You have no evidence for that at all,' said Joss, 'apart from the fact that he's a mathematician and I don't see how that follows at all.'

'But I bet you I'm right, all the same.'

'Where were you flying this morning?' said Ellen suddenly.

'This morning?' said Tommy. 'Ages ago. Up over Guildford. Why?'

'I saw the most extraordinary sky battle. I was working at home,' she said, 'and then there was a siren at about nine. I went out onto the balcony and looked up and I couldn't see or hear any bombers, but then I noticed hundreds of white contrails curving and spiralling high above. You couldn't hear it—must have been too high—but it made the most beautiful pattern against the blue. I so hoped it wasn't you up there.'

'God no,' said Tommy. 'As I said, we haven't seen

an enemy plane for over a week now.'

Joss glanced at Stella, and felt for her hand. He wove his fingers briefly between hers, gave her a squeeze, then said, 'How is it in London, Ellen?'

'Oh, it's not so bad. We get a few alerts and of course the blackout makes life awkward at night, especially now the evenings are drawing in. But I think we're all trying to get on with life as best we can. It does feel as though the Germans are getting closer, though. There's a shelter in the garden behind us, although I hope to God we never have to use it.'

'They're more interested in military targets than bombing civilians,' said Tommy. 'I'm so glad we're not in 11 Group. It was horrible when Middle Wallop kept being bombed. I *hated* being bombed. We all felt so helpless—at least in a Spitfire you've something to fire back with.'

'I'd rather put all the sandbags and barrage balloons out of mind,' said Stella. 'Of course we get papers and listen to the radio but where we are it's the absence of certain people that reminds us of war. The countryside looks the same as ever.'

'Do you miss London?' asked Ellen.

'I'm more use on the farm,' Stella told her. 'Before the war, I never gave the farm much thought—it was home and that was all. Dad and the men looked after it and ran it, so there was no need to know anything about it. I wasn't curious to learn either. It's funny, but I rather regret it now, because it's been fascinating working there this summer. I milk cows, and cut the corn, I drive the tractor. I see how the land changes week by week. And I feel I'm doing something worthwhile. Guy would never admit this, but we pretty much run it together now.'

'I'm all for change when it's for the better,' said Ellen. 'There's not much good that can come from a war but I am glad some of our prejudices are breaking down. Already the world seems full of possibilities that would have been inconceivable a few years ago.'

They chose the *menu du jour*: a thin consommé, a small piece of haddock, some lamb cutlets and finally a paltry offering of cheese. And wine, plenty of wine. Under cover of the starched tablecloth, Joss and Stella rubbed legs and let their hands touch. Joss was enjoying himself—the company, the restaurant, the *relief* of being away for 24 hours—but while he did not wish any of his precious time away, he still longed to be alone with Stella in bed once more.

Ellen told Stella that she wished she had a bolt-hole in the country; Stella told her about the derelict inn, up on the old mail road on the downs above the village. 'I'm determined to buy it one day,' she said, 'renovate it and live there happily ever after.'

'If you ever do,' Ellen told her, 'I'll come and help you decorate.'

One day, one day, thought Joss, *after the war.* They all had plans for when that day came. Tommy wanted to move to the south of France and become the most celebrated novelist on the Riviera. 'And you could become one of the most fashionable interior designers in Provence,' he said to Ellen.

'I'd love that darling, just so long as I can keep my flat here in London.'

And what about Joss? 'I don't want to tempt fate by telling you,' he said, 'but if it ever came true, I'd be a very happy man.'

'He keeps his cards close to his chest,' said Tommy.

Joss felt Stella place a hand on his thigh.

'I think you're just an old romantic, Joss,' said Ellen, and she smiled at him in a way that made him warm to her even more.

*   *   *

Later, in bed. By the time they had closed the door and were alone once more, they had barely been able to undress quickly enough. Both a bit drunk, hands clumsy, they laughed and kissed as they flung their clothes recklessly about the room, and collapsed on the bed. Joss felt dizzy, partly from the wine, but more because he was so happy.

Afterwards, they lay side by side, entwined, her breasts crushed against his chest.

'Tell me what you want when the war is over?' Stella asked him.

'I'm not sure I should.' He smiled and kissed her. He'd become more superstitious of late—the one time he'd forgotten his wooden lion, he'd panicked throughout the entire patrol—and it worried him that he would somehow jinx his greatest wish if he told her now. 'Can't you guess?' he said.

'Does it involve me?'

Joss nodded.

'And an old derelict house?'

'I'm saying no more.'

She clasped him tighter. 'Tomorrow you'll be off and I won't know what's happening to you. Won't know when I'm next going to see you.'

'Soon,' he whispered, 'it'll be soon, my darling.'

*   *   *

Saturday, September 7th. Stella drove down with them as far as Andover. The town was quiet—barely a soul breathed. *Perhaps they're all at church, praying,* Joss thought.

At the station, she said, 'I almost forgot, I have something for you,' and gave him a small, narrow cardboard box. 'Open it,' she said. Joss pulled off the lid, unwrapped the tissue paper and lifted out a dark blue white-spotted silk scarf. 'It's perfect,' he told her. 'I've been meaning to get one for ages.'

'Warmer and more comfortable than wearing a tie.'

'Yes,' he grinned. 'I love it—thank you. The others will think I've become very flash.'

'Take care, Joss, take very great care.'

'Of course. You too. And Guy?'

'I'll talk to him.'

'Or maybe I should when I can next get away?'

'No—leave it to me.'

She kissed him, her arms around his neck. 'I'm going to miss you.'

Tommy had said less and less the further they travelled from London. Now that the two of them were on their own once more and drawing closer to Middle Wallop, Tommy looked even more pensive.

'Tommy, are you all right?' Joss asked him.

'I'm fine,' he said, lighting his fourth cigarette of the journey. 'I'd be absolutely bloody marvellous if only I hadn't had to leave Ellen and come back down here.'

'You'll see her again in a week.'

Tommy grunted. 'I've gone off flying. My

514

obsession with the aeroplane is officially at an end.'

'You're just saying that. You'll forget all about it once you're in the air again. It's like going back to school—you dread it, but once you're there it doesn't seem quite so bad.'

'Hm,' said Tommy. He sounded unconvinced.

Passing through the main gates they saw Reynolds. 'Better get yourselves down to dispersal right away,' said the adjutant, 'we're on invasion alert.'

'Christ,' said Tommy, slamming the car into gear and speeding on round the cluster of buildings.

'All right you two?' said Mac as they walked into the bungalow. 'Nice scarf, Joss. From your girl?'

Joss smiled sheepishly.

'Very snappy,' said Pip. They were all ready in their flying gear: fur-lined boots, Mae Wests, an assortment of scarves, loosened ties and roll-neck sweaters. Pip and Mac were playing cards with Denis and Karl. Others read newspapers and paperbacks. Antonin was bouncing a tennis ball against the wall. No one was asleep. The tension was palpable.

'When did this warning come through?' asked Tommy.

'This morning. "Attack Imminent".'

'Been up yet?' Joss asked.

'Just after nine,' said Mac. 'Small raid over Portland. Pip here got a 110.' Pip bowed.

'Good for you Pip,' said Joss.

'Anyway, stop yapping,' said Mac, 'and go and check your Spits sharpish. I've a feeling we're going to be out of here any second.'

*   *   *

515

Mac was wrong. The phone rang at dispersal four times that day and on each occasion the pilots all visibly tensed. 'Fucking phone,' muttered Johnnie after the third call. Only on the last, just after a quarter past four that afternoon, were they finally scrambled.

Another factory and airfield protection patrol. 10,000 feet above Brooklands and Windsor. As they reached their patrol line, Joss heard increased chatter over the R/T, and then, as Mac turned the squadron down sun, he saw them: wave, upon wave, upon wave of planes. 'Oh my God,' Joss said under his breath, 'God help us.' The sky was black with hundreds of enemy aircraft—bombers, then above them stacks of fighters. Around the lower level of bombers black dots of anti-aircraft gunfire peppered the sky. *My God,* thought Joss, *London. The Germans are bombing London.* He thought of his mother, then Ellen. Anger welled within him and as it did so his normal fear subsided. *Come on, Mac,* he thought, *let's go and get them.*

'This is Nimbus leader,' came Mac's voice through his headphones, 'we're going to climb to angels sixteen then attack as they withdraw.'

Other squadrons were already attacking. Contrails filled the sky, but even from where they were, some distance south-west of the capital, Joss saw clouds of smoke billowing into the sky from along the Thames. He thought about Tommy, hoped he was keeping calm.

Once again, Joss was leading Blue Section, with Denis and George Robbins either side of him. If only their Spitfires could climb faster; he worried they would be too late. By the time they reached

516

16,000 feet, they were still only a thousand above the nearest wave of bombers, already stretching away from them and back towards the Channel. Above and behind, hundreds of 109s. Sweat trickled down his back; his body tensed. Yes, he was angry, angry in a way he had never been before during combat, but the number of German fighters above, preparing to pounce, had made his chest tighten and pound once more. *See me through this,* he thought, touching his wooden lion in his pocket, *and Tommy too.* As Mac ordered them to attack, he lowered his goggles, and with Denis and George behind him, followed the rest of the squadron as they dived into battle.

The nearest formation was made up of Heinkels, and long before Joss was within range he saw lines of tracer arcing towards him. Behind, 109s were dropping like hornets. *Don't hang around,* he told himself. The silk of his new scarf was soft as he craned his neck. A bomber loomed towards him. Joss aimed at the fuselage, and watched the rear-gunner swivel round and shoot. Bullets hit his fuselage, and Joss cursed, but it made no noticeable difference. Now for a squirt of his own guns. The Spitfire jolted from the recoil, and a second later slid underneath the Heinkel, so close he instinctively ducked his head as he passed. Climbing up again, he fired at the underside of another, saw bits of metal flying into the air like wood shavings, and the plane tilt and begin to drop from the formation. *No time to see what happened to it.* He pulled into a tight turn, and felt himself being crushed into his seat, and his guts lurch. A black veil fell across his eyes. When it cleared once more, he saw two 109s almost upon him, flashes of

517

orange fire spitting from their wings. *Shit, shit,* he cursed, and, turning in towards them, fired as well. A line of bullets whipped across his starboard wing. The Spitfire jerked, then righted itself, just as a dark shadow flitted across him—one of the 109s, just a few feet above. Joss let out a deep breath, turning his neck left then right. Aircraft skidded and spiralled across the sky, but the main bomber formation was already slipping away from him. Then he spotted one struggling bomber lagging behind the rest. Joss dived below it to gain speed then climbed up underneath and fired a long burst. The Heinkel wobbled then dropped a wing and with a belch of smoke began to spiral frantically through the sky. Glancing behind him to check his tail, Joss followed it down—against Mac's rules, but he was short on fuel and ammunition and he needed to escape the fray. As he corkscrewed down he saw two of the crew jump out, their white parachutes billowing out shortly after. Then a third jumped too, but as he opened his pack, the silk and strings caught itself on the tail fin of the falling plane. As the Heinkel spiralled, so the man was helplessly swung round and round like a grotesque fairground ride. Joss watched, appalled. No one deserved to die like that. For a moment, he thought he might be sick. Perhaps he should shoot the man, put him out his misery, as one might a rabbit caught in a trap. But he couldn't—it wasn't an easy shot anyway. Instead he turned his Spitfire away. High above, the battle continued, scribbles of white across the blue September sky, but the 109s had vanished, their fuel spent.

What was his nearest airfield? he wondered. Probably Tangmere. And what of the others? He thought he'd seen one Spitfire falling from the sky, but he couldn't be sure. Up ahead he spotted a plane, drifting lazily. He opened his throttle, and as he drew behind it, saw that it was a Spitfire, heading west. A late afternoon haze had settled over the country. The sun was lowering and it wasn't until he was quite close to the plane that he saw the unfamiliar squadron identification letters. The canopy was slightly open and the pilot still in his seat at the controls. Joss drew alongside and waved, but the pilot did not notice him. Joss waved again, and only then did he see that the man's head was leaning against the Perspex. The propeller still whirred, and although the aircraft occasionally fluttered in the wind, it appeared to be flying almost perfectly straight and level.

Joss opened his throttle and dived away. He felt quite cold suddenly and when he glanced back he could see no trace of the Spitfire at all.

*   *   *

Two of the squadron were missing: John Allinson, one of the public schoolboy pilot officers Mac so worried about, and Antonin. The Pole had been seen swinging downwards in his parachute and later Biggin Hill rang through to say he'd been safely picked up and was uninjured despite being attacked by locals who had mistaken him for a German. Of John, there was no news. Several, like Joss, had had a vague impression of a Spitfire falling and trailing smoke, but no one could say more than that. Between them they claimed a further seven enemy aircraft destroyed. Joss didn't mention the first bomber but two crewmen from the Heinkel had been picked up and so he was given a confirmed kill. Calder never mentioned whether a body had been found strapped to the wreckage with parachute rope, and Joss never asked.

Tommy had returned safely. He'd been one of the first to make it back to Middle Wallop and had run from his Spitfire and over to dispersal to try and ring Ellen. Ignoring the orderly's protestations, he had snatched the telephone and put a call through to her flat. She was quite safe—no bombs had landed near her, although most of London, she told him, was now shrouded in smoke. From her balcony, she could see flames rising into the fading evening light.

*　　　*　　　*

Later on. Dinner in the mess, the pilots still subdued, stunned by the afternoon's events—by the sheer numbers of German aircraft, and by the sight of thick black smoke rising from the Thames. A year into the war and the capital was finally under attack. But no invasion. Not yet, at any rate.

Joss felt exhausted. Any kind of flying was tiring, but making it through the mêlée of a dogfight involving several hundred aircraft had drained him of energy, and he groaned inwardly when Mac announced that the tumbrel would be leaving for the Five Bells ten minutes after dinner.

In the back of the truck, Tommy sat opposite him. Joss thought he looked more cheerful again—he was whistling quietly and tapping his hands on his legs, as the lorry lurched over potholes and lumbered its way down the Salisbury Road and then turned into Nether Wallop. He suddenly looked up at Joss and said, 'What about a song?' then began chanting, 'Hitler has only got one ball.' Everyone else quickly joined in, causing an immediate and collective release of tension. *Perhaps he's right,* thought Joss. *Perhaps getting drunk is the best tonic.* If he'd stayed and tried to have an early night, he'd have only brooded, and brooding didn't do any good at all.

The drink calmed him further—a whisky chaser, then a pint of beer. And then another pint, and another. He told his story about the spectral Spitfire. Opinion was divided—some felt it *must* have been a ghost, others that it had been a strange anomaly of the air fighting.

'It was an omen, clear as day,' pronounced Tommy. 'Yeats wrote a poem about it.'

'Thanks, Tommy,' said Joss, 'I'd rather not think about it that way, if you don't mind.'

'What are you on about?' said Johnnie.

'Nothing,' said Joss. 'Ignore him.'

'I think we should all shut up about it,' said Mac. 'It was just some poor bastard who got himself killed. You probably didn't see him after you flew on, Joss, because he ran out of petrol and dived out of the sky. Or his body moved and flipped the stick. Any number of reasons. But you're all following a dangerous line if you start believing that kind of shit.'

The episode was soon forgotten. They sang 'Blue Skies' a couple of times, then those not chatting up girls moved to a corner of the pub where they pushed several tables together and played games. Karl said he had one they could try. He produced a pack of cards and placed them on the top of an

521

empty bottle. They had to take it in turns to blow some of the cards off the top. Anyone who failed to blow off a single card, or who blew the last one onto the table had to finish their pint. It was a great success, especially as the others made sure it was Karl who lost time and time again.

The landlord declared a lock-in. A local policeman banged on the door at a quarter to midnight, but when he saw who was there, he waved his hand and left them to it. At half-past twelve, they finally piled back into the tumbrel, and those who did not fall asleep sang all the way back to the aerodrome.

*　　*　　*

The following day they were up again at 4.30 a.m., Tommy still in his uniform from the night before. A cup of tea each from Whiting, then yawning and stretching—*is it really that time already?*—they staggered down the corridor for a cursory shave and wash. Tommy smelled—of distilled alcohol when he spoke and of the stale cigarettes that hung heavily on his clothes. Back in their room, Joss put his own shirt and trousers to his nose—*urgh, revolting.* A clean shirt but the rumpled trousers and tunic would have to do. His head hurt and his mouth tasted parched and sour. Shortly after, they stumbled out into the dark morning air. Dark and cold, not even a dawn chorus yet. Breakfast in the mess—coffee, toast, scrambled egg—back into the tumbrel, and down to the bungalow at dispersal. Grabbing his parachute, he tramped over the sodden grass, cursing when he felt the dew seep through his left flying boot. As he wandered round

522

his Spitfire, checking the outside, he heard the early birds begin their morning song. First light, strips of pink and turquoise spreading upwards from the far end of the airfield. He nearly slipped on condensation on the wing, then steadied himself and clambered into the cramped close confines of the cockpit.

By the time he had completed his checks and trudged back to dispersal, one of the orderlies had already stoked the stove, and the pilots came in one by one and sat huddled around it, clutching their sides, hardly speaking, and wondering why they'd stayed up so late. Reynolds appeared. London had been bombed again—heavily—during the night. The docks were still ablaze. Whatever respite there may have been for the squadron the past fortnight was now over.

Joss thought about his mother. Hoped she was safe. Hoped he would at last be able to persuade her to leave. He glanced at Tommy. His friend looked agitated, biting his nails, tapping his foot.

'What am I going to do, Joss?' he hissed. 'I've got to get Ellen out of there.' He stood up, began pacing up and down.

'Try not to worry, Tommy. It's the Thames they're after, not north London. She'll be all right.'

'Do you think so?'

'I'm certain.'

'I've got to persuade her to leave.'

The phone rang. Everyone flinched, all eyes on the orderly as he lifted the receiver. A small plot approaching Portland, probably a reconnaissance raid. 'All right, "A" Flight get cracking,' said Mac. Tommy grabbed his leather flying helmet and dashed with the others to the door.

Half an hour later, Joss watched the six returning planes drop in and land one by one. Tommy was last, but although Joss waited by the door for him, he did not reappear.

'Where's Tommy?' he asked, as Tony Simmonds brushed past.

'Still sitting in his plane, I think.'

Joss immediately got up and hurried over. Groundcrew were already busy refuelling. 'Tommy,' he called up, 'what's the matter?'

Tommy looked at him blankly, then said, 'Nothing,' and lifted himself up out of the cockpit and jumped down onto the wing. 'Come on,' he said, 'I need a walk.'

Joss glanced back at dispersal. 'Don't worry,' said Tommy, 'they can live without us for a bit.'

'What is it?' Joss asked again. 'Is it Ellen?'

Tommy lit a cigarette. 'I don't know Joss.' He sighed, then said, 'I'm just not sure how much more I can keep doing this.'

'What do you mean? Of course you can.'

'No, I'm really not sure that I can. I thought I didn't care. That old bravado—I meant it in a way. I was never afraid of dying because I thought at least then I wouldn't have to grow old. I've loved my life, but I did think that if I died I would do so without any regrets. I suppose I also never thought it would happen to me, that somehow, I'd be all right, pull through. But now—well, now I'm not so sure. You see, Joss, I've a reason to live now. I can see a future after all this is over, a future that I desperately want. I'm scared of losing it.' He turned and looked at him. A tear ran down his face.

'Tommy—' Joss began.

524

'Funny, isn't it?' he said. 'To begin with it was you I worried about. After every sortie you'd come back shaking as though you'd seen a ghost. And you seemed to struggle so much with your anxiety about killing Germans.'

'It still troubles me.'

'But not as much. You've become hardened to it. Look, I'm not judging you, Joss. We've all changed, and that's hardly surprising when you think of what we've been doing all summer. But when it started I believed I was well equipped to deal with it. I've never had much remorse about killing and I worried very little about death. And the flying was glorious, exciting and deadly. I admit it—I relished every second. Now I hate it.' He wiped his eyes, then began to laugh. 'Oh, Christ, look at me,' he said. 'I'm pathetic. But you know what? I curse the day I ever met Ellen. I love her to my very core and it's killing me.'

England—mid-September, 1940

A week passed. The fine cerulean skies that the pilots had so cursed at last gave way to cloud and rain, and with it the German raids lessened, although they still had to be at dispersal by first light, and they were still scrambled several times a day. On the 8th, a large raid had developed over Portland, and the squadron intercepted it and shot down two more. Antonin had returned, but they lost Bill Horton in the action. His plane was seen plummeting to ground just north of Weymouth; what was left of Bill—and that wasn't very much—

was imbedded some twenty feet into the hillside. His Spitfire, just under thirty feet in length before it hit the ground, was compressed to just six by the impact.

The next day, they were scrambled to intercept two separate plots of German reconnaissance, but both evaded them in the huge banks of cloud that hung over the country. Much the same happened the next day, although John Allinson, missing since the large battle over London on the 7th, was found. He'd baled out too low and had been found in a field near East Grinstead, his partially-opened parachute fluttering next to him. He'd broken almost every bone in his body. The men who'd found him had struggled to lift him.

On the 11th, the squadron was sent to patrol the south-west of London again, and attacked another giant formation as it returned south of the capital. After scything through the bomber formations, fierce dogfighting had once more quickly followed. Joss soon found himself weaving between huge skyscrapers of cloud trying to dodge the 109s. A cannon shell shattered the Perspex of his canopy, hit one of the metal struts the other side and ricocheted into his gunsight. It had all happened in an instant—a loud crack, then another and half his gunsight had vanished—and Joss had been concentrating so hard on shaking them off his tail that it was only once he was safely back on the ground with Dowling and Griffiths ruefully examining the damage, that he'd realized how close he'd come to losing his head. They'd all made it back safely that day. The squadron had now shot down eighty planes since the start of the war. To celebrate the achievement, they had the longest lock-in of the summer; the tumbrel didn't leave the pub until after two the following morning. No one had drunk more or sung louder than Tommy.

Joss had pleaded with Mac to give Tommy some immediate leave, but to no avail. 'Come on, Mac,' Joss told him, 'he's due a week off on the 16th, but he needs it now. Please.' But the CO was adamant. 'We all need it, Joss. I can't let Tommy jump the queue. You probably got him at a bad moment. Hungover, feeling a bit sorry for himself. I've seen really jumpy people before, Joss, and believe me, he's not one of them. If he starts coming back early every time with a faulty oil gauge or undercarriage, then I'll start to worry.' In the days that followed, Joss began to wonder whether the CO wasn't right after all. Tommy never once returned early from a patrol. During the fighting on the 11th, he even claimed another 109. Joss once watched him at dispersal reading a book. It was a squadron joke that Tommy could and would read anywhere, but after ten minutes, he hadn't turned a single page. 'Tommy?' Joss had called to him, and Tommy had looked round, startled. 'Are you all right?' His face had relaxed and creased into a smile. 'Yes, Joss, I'm fine,' and later, when they were alone, said, 'Look Joss, I meant what I said the other day, but you don't need to watch over me all the time. I want to survive this, remember, so I'm going to be even more careful.' Nor was he so visibly agitated about Ellen. He had been unable to persuade her to leave the capital, but after a night with her in London, he confessed to Joss that he felt less anxious than he had at first. 'Nothing's come near her and she showed me the shelter in the garden,' he told him. 'She's promised me she'll head for that as soon as

527

the sirens begin. I made her swear solemnly.'

Diana had also refused to budge from her flat in Pimlico. Joss had rung her—a three-minute call that had taken the best part of an hour to get through—then written, but she'd told him not to fuss. But she was closer to more obvious targets than Ellen: the power station at Battersea, the Thames, the Houses of Parliament. Joss had had a day off on the 12th. He'd intended to spend as much of it as possible with Stella, but had felt duty-bound to see his mother in person, to make one more effort to get her to safety. He soon wished he hadn't; Diana was as implacable as ever. 'I don't come down to your airfield and make a stand against you flying, do I?' she told him. 'Darling, it's sweet of you to care about your dear old mother, but I can look after myself.'

It had rained most of the day. Joss had been so angry, he'd taken the train back to Andover the same evening, staring out of the windows at the passing countryside, the rain streaming down the windows. He longed to be with Stella. They'd seen each other just once in the past week—meeting to see a film in Salisbury—and had kissed and held hands but had then gone their separate ways. She'd still not spoken to Guy. He had 'flu and had been in bed for three days. 'I can't tell him now,' she told him. 'But when he's better, I *promise*.'

*   *   *

It was now Saturday, September 14th. 'B' Flight had been stood down for an hour in the middle of the afternoon, and Joss went for a walk around the edge of the airfield. He came to a wooden gate, wrinkled and grey with age. Along the hedgerows on either side the grass was long and wild and the hedge thick with cow-parsley and brambles. The sun was out, shining down through a gap in the clouds. Joss leant against the gate, folding his arms along the rough warm wood, then rested his chin. Skylarks were singing somewhere high above, and he closed his eyes and listened, savouring the sense of peace that had descended over the aerodrome. He breathed in deeply—the smell of dried wheat in the stubble field in front of him, the grass at his feet, damp from the rain and so very much more pungent because of it. *Ah, this is good,* he thought. Both eyelids had been flickering all day and his hands had been shaking. No matter how hard he'd tried, he could not stop them. *Tommy was wrong,* he thought, *I'm not that hardened to it.* His lids twitched again, even though his eyes were closed. In two days' time, Tommy would have a whole week's leave; he wished his would come around sooner. He was exhausted again; they all were. That morning Johnnie Reeves had fallen asleep at the table in the mess. They'd been tucking into their scrambled eggs when suddenly there'd been a light thud and Johnnie had dropped his head into his plate. That had woken him with a start and everyone had laughed, but four hours' sleep a night was not enough, even if you catnapped through the day. Another eight days, and then it would be his turn for a week off. It seemed an eternity away. Stella had talked about them going away together, to a cottage somewhere in Devon or Cornwall. He couldn't think of anything he'd rather do—a whole week just the two of them!—and with any luck by then they might have Guy's blessing. He thought

529

about Guy, wondering whether he knew already. Tommy had reassured him of this. 'Of course Guy'll be all right about it. For Christ's sake, there's slightly more important things to worry about at the moment.' In many ways, Tommy had been right: with death so close, one looked at life in a different perspective. For his own part, Joss now believed he could forgive anyone anything. Even his stepfather, George. Even his mother for all the times she'd let him down. He'd been hard on her these past years—too hard, he realized now. He had much to thank the squadron for. Amid the killing and chaos there had evolved an indestructible spirit of human fellowship. To bear grudges was so futile, so utterly pointless. Love and friendship: there was nothing more important than that, and so it had to be protected and preserved, not frittered away over some petty dispute or disagreement. Guy had been his truest friend, and always would be. The strain that had tested that friendship in the past few months was an unnecessary corrosive; Joss saw that now, saw it all too clearly. He should have been supportive towards his friend. More understanding, and less intolerant. What they had was of greater importance than any difference of opinion. He wished he had understood this the last time they'd seen each other. If only he'd not shouted at him. Joss cringed inwardly, remembering. He should have talked to him, explained how he felt now. Guy would have understood.

A chill in the air. The sun had disappeared behind a cloud, and as he looked up at the sinister clouds rolling in from the west, he felt the first drop of rain.

Joss hurried back around the perimeter, but the rain soon gathered pace so he stopped underneath one of the curved, corrugated aircraft shelters dotted around the edge of the aerodrome to wait until the worst of the shower had passed. He saw another pilot running towards him and recognized him as Rupert Blackwell, one of the new faces.

'Urgh—that came down a bit suddenly,' said Rupert, bending over to catch his breath. He was tall, thin and looked unsure of himself. 'Just went off for a bit of a walk,' he said.

'Me too—needed to clear my head a bit.'

Rupert looked surprised. 'Did you? So did I.'

'How are you settling in?' Joss asked.

'Fine. Fine, I think.' He was silent for a moment, as though trying to decide whether to say more.

'You haven't gone operational yet, have you?'

'Er, no. I took a Spit up this morning, but—well, I nearly crashed. Forgot to lower my undercarriage, and only remembered just in time.' He grinned ruefully, then looked down at his feet. *Ah yes,* thought Joss. They'd all laughed and made jokes about greenhorns.

'Oh, I shouldn't worry about that,' he said. 'There's a lot to think about first time you take one up. I was hopeless to begin with.'

'Were you?' His face brightened.

'God yes. Takes a while to get used to everything. I'll take you up later if you like—as long as it clears up a bit. You'll soon get the hang of it, though, I'm sure.'

'Thank you—thank you very much.' He smiled but his eyes looked glazed. 'I'm not scared or anything, but I just don't know what to expect. I suppose I just don't want to let anyone down.'

'You won't.' Joss stepped from beneath the shelter and held out his hand. 'Still raining,' he said, 'but shall we make a dash for it?'

Rupert nodded. 'All right. I suppose we should be getting back anyway.'

The rain stopped shortly afterwards and Mac gave Joss permission to take Rupert up to practise dogfighting. Just as Mac had done over two months before, Joss found it all too easy to get himself on Rupert's tail. *He hasn't a hope,* he thought. It depressed him. No wonder Mac had been so hard on them to begin with. 'Red Two, let's try one more time,' said Joss, clamping his Spitfire into another turn. Even after dropping into a patch of sky clear of cloud and throttling back, Joss struggled to let Rupert catch him, but knew that he must. As soon as he spotted Rupert behind him, he weaved slightly so as not to make it look too obvious then, when Rupert was still some 600 yards behind heard him triumphantly shout, 'Rat-a-tat-a-tat-a-tat, Red One!'

'Argh—you've got me!' said Joss. 'But you might want to think about getting a bit closer in future— just to make sure you really knock me out. Come on—let's get back.'

Back at dispersal, Mac looked at Joss and said, 'How was he?'

'You can't send him up yet.'

'Shit,' said Mac. 'Then let's hope I don't have to.'

*   *   *

The rain returned and they were stood down early—at seven o'clock. Half an hour later, they were sitting down to dinner in the mess when an orderly appeared and came over to Joss.

'There's someone to see you, sir,' he said.

'Who?' said Joss. The others all looked at him.

'I don't know, sir. Wouldn't say his name. But said it was urgent, that he had to see you right away, sir.'

Joss looked at Mac, who nodded.

'All right.' He put down his napkin, and scraped back his chair. 'Sorry everyone. Won't be long.'

Joss followed the orderly through the rain, his hands deep in his pockets and his shoulders hunched. 'He's by the main gate, sir,' the orderly explained.

As Joss approached, he saw Guy get out of the car. His first thought was one of delight. 'Guy!' he shouted and raised a hand in a wave. 'How good to see you, but what on earth are you doing here?'

'You bastard!' said Guy. 'You bloody bastard!'

Joss's mind reeled. 'Guy? What is it? What do you mean?' He walked up to him. Guy's eyes looked wild. Spittle had caught at the edges of his mouth.

'Stella's told me. After everything I've done for you. I just can't believe you'd do this to me.'

'Guy,' said Joss, and tried to put a hand on his shoulder, but Guy pushed him away. 'Get off me,' he said. 'All summer you've been strutting about like you're God's gift, but I never dreamed you'd be this selfish. I mean, for Christ's sake, Joss, *Stella*.' He ran his hands through his hair. 'And behind my back too—it's, it's so *underhand*.'

'But I'm in love with her, Guy.'

'Don't say that! You can't be. You're supposed to be *my* friend.'

'And I still am. You're my best friend in the whole

world. Guy please—'

'No, no I'm not. Not any more. You should have thought about that before you started casting your little tricks on my sister. It's over Joss. Finished. I never want you to see me or my family again. Do you hear?'

'Guy, come on, please, don't be like this. I didn't mean to fall in love with Stella, but it just happened. I don't see why it should change anything.'

'It changes everything.' Guy turned, began walking back to the car. Grabbing his shoulder, Joss said, 'Guy, this is ridiculous, just hear me out—' The punch caught Joss completely off guard. Guy's fist was slammed into the side of his face with such force that Joss lost balance entirely and fell over backwards onto the rain-drenched tarmac.

For a moment, he lay there, the rain gently spattering his face. He was vaguely aware of the sound of a door slamming, and a motor starting. The car reversed, then sped away. He looked up and saw the orderly standing over him. 'Are you all right, sir?' he said.

Joss nodded, put a hand to his cheek, then said, 'Give me a hand up will you?'

'Been knocking off his girl have you, sir?' said the orderly as Joss got to his feet once more.

'Sister,' said Joss.

'Ah.'

'I think if you don't mind, I'll skip dinner and go to my room,' said Joss. 'Will you give my apologies to the others?'

*   *   *

534

Joss was lying on his bed, staring at the ceiling, when Tommy came in.

'What the hell's happened?' he said, then saw the bruise already rising on his face. 'For God's sake.'

'It was Guy,' said Joss. 'He says he never wants me to see him or any of his family again.'

'He's gone mad,' said Tommy. 'Jealousy and resentment clearly knows no bounds.'

'No, it's my fault. This has been brewing a while and I should have dealt with it earlier. I can't believe he'd say that, though. Christ, what a bloody mess. If I lose Stella and Guy,' he said, 'I just don't know what I'd do. My life really would not be worth living.'

Tommy sat on the bed beside him. 'Joss, my dear friend, it's not your fault. We can't plan our lives perfectly, nor can we spend our time wishing we'd said something differently three months before. It doesn't work like that. Guy feels humiliated because he knew nothing about it, and jealous because Stella's now more important to you than he is. He can't rant and rave at her, because he has to live and work with her—so he does it to you instead. But he'll come round, of course he will. In fact, his driving here tonight was probably the best thing he could have done in the circumstances—he needed to let off steam and that's what he's done. He'll probably be full of remorse tomorrow morning.' Joss looked at him doubtfully. 'Look, I tell you what,' said Tommy, 'tomorrow night, I'll drive over there and go and see him. I'll talk him round.'

Joss said quietly, 'Would you? Would you really?'

'For you, Joss, yes.'

'Thank you, Tommy. You're a good friend.'

'There's one condition. I'm not going to let you stay here staring at the ceiling. There's nothing you can do tonight, so I want you to come with us all to the pub and have a few drinks and try to put it out of your mind. All right?'

Joss nodded. For once he needed little persuasion.

*   *   *

Sunday, the 15th. Mid-morning. Joss sat in an armchair next to Tommy outside the front of the bungalow. A cool breeze wafted across the airfield, but the rain had long gone. Up above, just a few wisps of white streaked across an otherwise blue sky. A perfect late summer's day. Neither Joss nor Tommy had spoken for twenty minutes. Joss's head still pounded from the night before and he was in no mood for either reading or conversation. Instead he kept going over and over what he should say to Guy—composing letters, then imagining how the conversation would go when he next saw him. *If* he saw him. Every time he thought of the hatred in Guy's eyes as he'd stood there in the rain, he felt a renewed weight of gloom press down upon him.

The telephone rang inside. Tommy put down his book and listened.

'Yes,' they heard Mac saying. 'Yes. All right.'

'All right,' he said loudly, 'there's another big one developing. Get to your planes and wait for the signal to roll.'

Tommy looked at Joss. 'Come on,' he said, 'let's go and give them hell.'

536

They took off just before half-past eleven. By ten to twelve they had reached the Brooklands-Windsor line and at 15,000 feet were searching the sky for the enemy formations. Puffs of anti-aircraft fire began to pepper the sky away towards London. Through his headphones, Joss listened to Control vectoring them towards their target. 'Nimbus, this is Tartan. You should see a plot soon to your port.' And there they were—a formation of around thirty Dorniers flying in two formations over the centre of the city, escorted by many more fighters. As they turned towards them, Joss saw more and more anti-aircraft fire breaking further to the east. His head had stopped throbbing—the oxygen had helped—and now, despite his fatigue, his mind felt sharp and clear once more.

'This is Tartan Leader,' said Mac, ' "A" Flight attack first then "B" Flight follow once the 109s begin their dive.'

Hovering above, the sun behind, Joss watched 'A' Flight peel off and swoop down on the bomber formation from straight ahead. The leading formation of Dorniers split as seven Spitfires tore into them. Smoke gushed from one of the bombers and it began to dive as the 109s above dropped down to attack. 'Now!' said Pip and within seconds 'B' Flight had joined the fray. A minute before all the aircraft had been progressing in a calm and orderly manner; now there was nothing but swirling chaos, tracer criss-crossing the sky as each aircraft fought its own private battle. Joss spotted a 109 turning gently away from him. *He hasn't seen me.* Following him, Joss watched with satisfaction as the Messerschmitt gradually filled his gunsight. He felt the knob of his firing button beneath his thumb and pressed down, but then out of the corner of his eye, saw two more 109s coming towards him to his right. *Bastards!* thought Joss, breaking off, and turning towards them. Seconds later they passed above him, yellow noses and grey undersides streaked with oil. He breathed out again, and felt his stomach lurch. Tracer arced across his wing— *where the hell was that coming from?*—so he clamped it into another turn and saw a 109 slightly below him turning across him. Joss steadied himself, and watched him loom ever larger. Hand down on the button and his machine-guns clattered. Flashes of orange burst from the German's wings, but Joss was already turning and the fire from the 109 passed wide. Joss clamped the stick tight over to one side, and the horizon swivelled further. As his vision cleared he saw he was now on the German's tail. *Got you,* thought Joss, and opened fire once more.

'Break, Joss.' Tommy's voice startled him. 'Joss, BREAK!'

Joss pitched the plane sideways and despite the pressure looked back to see cannon shells and tracer flashing through the sky on a line where he'd been a split-second before. His plane lurched as something exploded behind him. The stick was almost knocked out of his hand and the aircraft rolled. 'Got it,' he heard Tommy say then, a second later, 'Oh Christ no, oh my God.'

'TOMMY!' screamed Joss, frantically turning his head. *Where is he? Where is he?* Leaning forward in straps, Joss desperately scanned the sky but could not see him. 'Come on Tommy!' he shouted again.

538

'Where are you?' But there was nothing—no sound or sign of him at all.

* * *

Only Tommy was missing—everyone else safely returned. Johnnie Reeves had seen what had happened. 'You hit that 109, Joss,' he said, 'but another came up on your tail. Tommy saved your arse, getting it from very short distance, but then he was attacked by two 109s in turn.' Johnnie had seen white smoke—burning glycol—and saw Tommy do a flick roll and fall into a spin, but he'd been watching his own back and so had lost sight of him. Joss could barely look the others in the eye. He slumped back into the same chair outside the bungalow and looked at the empty seat next to him, the pages of Tommy's paperback fluttering gently in the breeze.

'I'm sure he's all right,' said Pip. 'He'll probably pitch up later, totally rat-arsed.'

'Maybe,' muttered Joss.

* * *

They were scrambled again early in the afternoon. Another massive raid of several hundred enemy aircraft. 629 were almost too late, but caught up with the retreating bombers just before they reached the south coast on their return to France. The 109s had already gone, and so the squadron was able to pick off a further five planes. Joss, a glazed automaton, drew up close behind one Dornier, and gave it such a long burst that it began to disintegrate before his eyes. None of the crew

539

jumped out. 'That's for Tommy,' shouted Joss.

Just after half-past five, they took off again to deal with a raid headed for Southampton. They arrived too late—the 50-strong formation had already been driven off.

At 7.30 p.m. they were stood down. Mac came over and sat next to Joss. 'I've just rung through,' he said. 'I'm afraid they've heard nothing. Suppose I should call his parents.'

'You should have sent him on leave,' Joss hissed. Mac winced visibly. 'You could have saved him, Mac. Think of that when you're speaking to them.'

Mac looked down for a moment, then quietly said, 'All right, Joss, steady on. Listen, perhaps you could ring his girlfriend?'

'Ellen.'

'Yes. Would you do that for me?'

Joss nodded. 'Someone's got to.'

'Thanks.' Mac clasped his shoulder. 'It'll certainly be quiet around here without him.'

It took over an hour to get through to Ellen, during which Joss's frustration, grief and anger rose with every minute that passed. Then at last the line began to ring. Joss felt his chest pounding and his whole body seize as though in a rigid clamp. He dreaded her voice.

'Hello?'

'Ellen. It's Joss.'

'Joss?' Surprise—then comprehension. *'Oh God, what's happened?'*

Joss could barely say the words. He felt his throat catch. 'He's missing.'

'No.'

'I'm still hoping.'

She gasped and then said, *'No, Joss. He's gone. I*

know he has.'

'Christ, I'm so sorry,' said Joss, his voice cracking again. In the background he heard a siren begin to wail.

'I've got to go,' said Ellen. *'Thank you for telling me, Joss. It was kind of you to think of me.'*

'Ellen,' said Joss. 'He went down trying to save me. He saved my life. I'm so sorry—it should have been me, not him.'

'No, Joss. Tommy would never want you to think that.'

*   *   *

Afterwards, he walked back slowly to the mess. He wished he hadn't said those things to Mac. It wasn't the CO's fault. Pointing an angry finger would not help Tommy. Mac had had to carry the burden of all the squadron's deaths that summer; Joss knew how much it troubled him.

Mac was standing at the bar. 'Did you speak to her?' he asked as Joss came over to him.

'Yes.'

'I'm afraid his mother went to pieces.'

'Well, it's unimaginable isn't it? They're a very close family.' said Joss. 'Mac?'

'Yes?'

'I'm sorry about what I said earlier. It was unforgivable. I didn't mean it.'

'I know.' He smiled. 'It's all right. Have a drink. Calm you down.' He nodded to the steward, who poured a large Scotch and placed it on the bar. Joss thanked him, then drank it back in one. Then he drank two more. His mind became numb. At nine, Reynolds switched on the radio. Barely able to contain his excitement, the broadcaster announced that in massive air battles over London and south-east England, 185 enemy aircraft had been shot down, while the RAF had lost under 40, of which thirteen pilots were safe. A spontaneous cheer erupted around the mess, then quickly subsided.

When he eventually reached his room, Joss felt slightly drunk, but not as drunk as he'd wanted to be. Lying open on Tommy's bed was his friend's leather-bound journal. He'd always kept it, not as a diary, because Tommy had always claimed he wasn't self-disciplined enough to keep one, but for writing down various thoughts and musings as they came to him. Joss picked it up. A pen had been left in it, marking the last entry. *'I don't know where I'd have been the last few weeks without Joss,'* Tommy had written. *'He's been a great friend. Together we've helped each other along, shared our thoughts and worries. He's troubled by Guy's visit here yesterday. I can hardly blame him, but am determined to make Guy see what a bloody fool he's being. I wish I could stop thinking about Ellen, but I do so almost constantly. I miss her so much and live for the moment I will be with her again. I just hope I can keep myself going; getting into my Spitfire now is torture. Two days until my leave—I suppose it's not so very long.'*

Joss closed it again and placed it on the cabinet by Tommy's bed. Still fully clothed, he went over to his own bed, lay down, and turned off the light. He tried to imagine Tommy with Ellen on a Caribbean island, reading books on sunbeds overlooking the sea. Then he heard Tommy's last words and realized his friend's ruse for dealing with grief was never going to work. Not this time, at any rate. A terrible emptiness spread across him. It was as though half his heart had been eaten away.

*　　*　　*

Waking the following morning, he half expected to see the shape of Tommy underneath the bedcovers on the other side of the room, but the bed looked as neat and sanitized as it had the night before. Later, at dispersal, Joss tried to write both to Ellen and Tommy's parents. He struggled, however. What was a difficult task was made more so because Tommy was yet to be found; somehow it seemed wrong to be writing about him in the past tense already.

The not knowing—it was too much to bear. Where was he? What had happened? He was dead, Joss was certain. He'd known it the moment he'd heard his friend's last desperate words of shock and then resignation, some 15,000 feet up in the burning blue. How ironic it should be that Tommy had to die almost directly above his parents' home; he wondered whether they'd been watching the aerial battles going on silently above them.

'Where are the Krauts today?' said Pip; it was mid-morning and they'd not been scrambled once. For the first time, Joss found himself eagerly awaiting the telephone, longing for action that would distract him.

He stood up and wandered outside, wondering whether the German who had shot down Tommy had been as full of revenge as Joss had been when he'd opened fire on that Dornier; as full of hate. He felt ashamed of himself now. Tommy was right: he had become hardened, as though the humanity

543

with which he had begun the summer had been gradually kicked from within him. None of the deaths for which he had been responsible had troubled him as much as those first two back in July. One got used to killing other people. He had learnt to put it out of mind, to no longer think of them as people whose nationality he shared, or people who were loved and adored as Tommy was. But he'd not lied when he'd told Tommy that killing enemy airmen still troubled him—it did, although more because he could no longer lie to himself about his mounting indifference, rather than through any sense of personal sorrow or guilt. 'War is by its nature dehumanising', Tommy had once grandly claimed during their time at Cambridge: a statement designed to aggravate Noel, and one that had prompted another entertaining argument between the two of them. And then somehow or other the conversation had changed and the discussion had been forgotten, until now, on this September morning, Joss remembered it once more. Whether Tommy had been right had mattered very little at the time: war, and their involvement in it, had, even then, seemed impossibly far away. But Tommy *had* been right. *This is what has happened to me,* thought Joss, *I've become dehumanised.* And yet, paradoxically, when he was with Stella—when he felt her eyes search his face, or her breath close on his—he felt more alive, more aware of the vitality of life, than ever before.

Joss wondered again about the pilot who'd killed Tommy. He imagined a young man much like himself landing back in France the previous afternoon, cheerfully telling his aircrew that he had shot down another Spitfire, then recounting the moment again to his fellow pilots. Exaggerated arm movements, a laugh and a slap on the back, then off to his billet for a wash, or even a bath. There would have been no remorse as he ate his dinner; over drinks in the mess afterwards, the RAF pilot would probably have been put out of mind entirely. As Joss had come to understand in Munich eighteen months before, young Germans were not so very different from young Englishmen.

With heavy steps, he wandered back into the dispersal bungalow. Pip looked up at him through a cloud of cigarette smoke. 'It'll be easier when he turns up Joss,' he said. 'You'll see.'

*   *   *

'B' Flight was stood down at midday, and so Joss took the opportunity to telephone Alvesdon Farm to let them know what had happened. He was relieved to get through almost immediately. He hoped Guy would answer and that with the awfulness of the news, Guy might forget his ill-feeling towards him. But it was Celia's voice he heard at the other end of the line.

'Joss,' she said, 'how are you?' She sounded unsure of herself, somehow awkward.

'Er, not so good. It's Tommy—he's missing. Is Guy there?'

'Oh, I can't bear it,' she said, 'not another one. It's too awful. Joss, I'm so very sorry—he was a good friend of yours wasn't he?' She sounded distraught, even though she had barely known Tommy herself. 'Guy and Stella are both working,' she said. *Of course they are*—it was only just after midday. Joss cursed to himself. 'I'm so sorry, Joss,'

545

said Celia. 'Shall I tell them?'

'Or perhaps I should try and drive over?'

'No, no you mustn't do that,' she said quickly. 'The petrol—' The message was clear. Another wave of despair flooded over him.

'No, you're right. Well, if you don't mind. I'm sorry, it's a difficult thing to . . .' He trailed off.

A wire arrived the following morning from Stella. *Can you meet me White Hart tonight? Will be there 8.30. Love Stella.'*

*　　　*　　　*

'You made it,' said Stella as he walked over to her table. 'My poor darling.' She looked sad, her brows knotted with anxiety.

'Can we walk somewhere?' he said.

She nodded and stood up. 'Of course.' Holding her hand tightly, they walked out of the hotel, crossed the road and on through the gateway to the cathedral close, just as he'd imagined they would the first time they'd met there.

'I just wish they could find him,' Joss told her. 'We've already got another replacement—arrived yesterday morning—but because Tommy's still posted as missing, I have to wake up and see his bed and his clothes hanging up in the wardrobe. I keep having these moments when I forget what has happened, then the reality hits me square in the face.'

She said little, just clutched his arm and listened. Joss sighed heavily. 'And what about Guy? Stella what am I going to do? It wasn't supposed to be like this.'

'He won't speak to me either. Mum's tried

talking to him, but he won't listen. I still think he'll come round eventually, though. You know, there was a time once when he wouldn't speak to me for a whole week.'

'Really? When was that?'

'I think we must have been nine or ten at the time.'

'What happened?'

'I suppose it was a bit similar, really. He became friends with the doctor's daughter. They would go off and play together, but then he began to bring her back to the farm and I started to join in. Well, of course, we girls soon ganged up against him. He was terribly hurt about it and shouted at both of us and swore he would never talk to me ever again. After a few days I began to think he meant it, but then eventually we kissed and made up.'

'What about the girl?'

'I can't really remember. We both stopped being friends with her I suppose. And she moved away soon after anyway.'

They walked on in silence. It was a warm evening for the time of year, and although it was dark, a three-quarter moon lit the giant cathedral and the paths of the close with a pale creamy light.

'I tried to stop him driving off to see you,' said Stella.

'He hit me.'

'I know. Did it hurt?'

'Not physically. Not much anyway.'

'He thought I was joking to begin with.'

'When did you tell him?'

'In the kitchen, after we'd come back in for the evening. I should have probably told him first thing when he wasn't so tired. I've been such a coward.

547

But Mum had made me promise to tell him that day, and of course I'd been putting it off. She'd guessed already.'

'How?'

Stella shrugged. 'Female intuition? I think she saw one of your letters too—recognized the writing on the envelope. But she said I had to tell him right away.'

'I was going to drive over yesterday, but she didn't want me to. It was awful—first time ever I've not been wanted at Alvesdon.'

'It's just until Guy cools down. If it weren't for him she'd be delighted.'

'Do you think so?'

'Of course. She's so fond of you, Joss.'

'So what did Guy say?'

'Well, he looked incredulous. Asked me whether I was joking, then realized I wasn't. And then he said he had to go out. I asked him where, and he said to see you. I begged him not to, but I couldn't stop him. I'm afraid I did it all wrong. I should have waited for Mum to be there too.'

'Where was she?'

'Only out in the garden. She came hurrying in as soon as she heard Guy speed off down the drive. She was cross—cross with me, cross with Guy. "Such a waste of our precious fuel too," she kept saying.'

They were silent for a moment. Joss put his arm around her shoulder and looked up at the cathedral: solid, steadfast; unsullied by the passing centuries and the never-ending cycle of life, death and war. A wondrous edifice built for the glory of God. He thought about the level of faith and devotion needed to build such a thing—it was beyond his comprehension; and yet, surely, it had been so tragically misplaced. It had to have been— how could a truly benign God have allowed another war? And how could a God who loved every man have toyed with him so cruelly? To have been granted his greatest wish, but then to have had Tommy killed and Guy turned against him, was like some grotesque Faustian pact.

Stella stopped and turned his face towards hers. 'It does get easier, Joss. I promise. I still think about Roger and Dad every day, but the pain is less. And Guy will come round. I know he will. You'll see.'

'Yes, I'm sure you're right. I'm sorry.'

'Don't be.' She wrapped her arms around him and held him tightly, her head against his chest.

'You know, Tommy was going to drive over and see Guy. Try and talk him round. I just wish that— that things could be different. That it didn't feel as though everything was stacked against us. I don't see what we've done to deserve it.'

'You mustn't think that way. The world doesn't work like that.' She lifted her face to his. 'Darling Joss, I love you so much. I know everything seems very bleak at the moment, but it won't always be that way.'

They walked on slowly beside the houses that lined the close.

'I wish I could stay with you tonight,' said Stella as they turned back.

'I wish you could too.'

'But next week,' she said, 'we can still go away for your leave if you'd like to.'

'Could we? Could we really?' His mood brightened. 'But what about Guy and your mother?'

'It's probably a good thing if I was out of Guy's way for a few days. Would Cornwall be far enough from the war?'

Joss kissed her. 'It would be perfect. I'd love that more than anything.' A week away from flying, from the squadron, from Guy, from the whole world. Just the two of them, on their own. For a whole week, he could hide away with her and pretend that all was well with the world.

*　　　*　　　*

Tommy's Spitfire was found the following day in a wood near Epsom. Because the trees had absorbed much of the force of the falling aircraft, and because most of Tommy's fuel had already been spent, the cockpit—and Tommy's body—had survived almost intact.

'He was probably dead before he hit the ground, Joss,' Mac told him. Having been stood down for the day, they were now sitting in Mac's office.

'Where was he hit?'

Mac eyed him and then scratched his head. 'I don't think you need to know that sort of thing.'

'I do. Please Mac—tell me. It's important to me that I know.' Why? Why was it? Joss wasn't sure, only that he knew he had to learn the truth.

Mac sighed wearily. 'All right then, if you must. Stomach, chest. And he lost an arm.'

'Jesus.'

'Yes. Well, now you know.' Mac shuffled some paper and then coughed. 'One other thing Joss, before you go. You've been awarded a DFC. Congratulations.' He passed him the typed citation.

550

Joss looked blankly at the words. They meant nothing. 'Thanks,' he said, then stood up and left.

*   *   *

The funeral was two days later. Mac told Joss he was to go as the representative of the squadron. 'Take a plane if you like,' he suggested.

'No, thanks, I'll go in Tommy's car.' He supposed it was his now anyway—Tommy had promised it to him should anything happen. It was still parked where Tommy had last left it. One of his pullovers had been thrown onto the back seat. There were maps and a scarf in the glove compartment, an ashtray still full of his cigarette butts. Joss lifted the scarf to his face. A familiar smell: stale smoke and a faint, lingering whiff of aftershave, the one Tommy had had specially made for him by a perfumier in Cairo.

Joss had given himself two hours to travel the 60-odd miles, but had barely got as far as Basingstoke when he felt the steering veer and heard the tell-tale slapping of a flat tyre. *Of all the accursed luck.* Pulling over to the side of the road, he stopped and found the spare wheel and the jack, but it took him a while to work out how to use it; and his mounting panic that he would be late made him fumble and take longer over the task than he might otherwise have done. The spare tyre was almost flat as well, and so he had to find a garage in Overton and have it pumped up.

He kept glancing at his wristwatch, but the minutes were ticking by. Why did this have to happen now, of all days? He swore and shouted and banged his hands on the steering wheel, but

551

the Riley would go no faster. By the time the funeral was due to begin, he was still only at Farnham.

By the time he eventually reached the church, the funeral was over, and the last of the guests were out of the churchyard. As he hurried around the back of the church, he saw Guy and Noel disappearing through the lych-gate. For a moment he thought about running after them, but instead decided to walk over to the mass of flowers that marked Tommy's grave. It had yet to be filled, so he stood for a moment looking down at the wooden coffin and the brass inscription on its top. It seemed to him impossible that someone so bright, so *alive,* could be no more. How he missed him already.

Kneeling, he placed his own flowers and the wreath from the squadron beside the others, then began walking to the Haskells' house—slowly; the thought of seeing Tommy's parents and of what he would say to Guy filled him with dread. Stella had told him Guy would be there; she was staying behind to look after the farm. At first he'd welcomed the chance it would give him to speak to Guy, but now he feared another scene; feared his pleadings would once again be rejected.

He turned into the gravel driveway and past borders of limp flowers and fading cherry trees. He paused for a moment at the door, straightened his tie, then knocked. Tommy's mother opened the door to him. She looked ashen and strained. 'Joss,' she said, 'you made it. I'm so pleased.' Tears immediately began running down her cheeks, and clasping her hand to her mouth, she said, 'Oh, Joss, how are we going to survive without him?'

'I'm so sorry,' said Joss, aware of the inadequacy of his words. Seeing her had shaken him. Tommy's father hurried over. He looked crushed with grief. 'So glad you could make it,' he said. 'We wondered where you were.'

'I had a puncture. I—'

Mr Haskell laid a hand on his arm. 'Don't worry. We're just relieved you could make it at all. And thank you for your letters. They meant a great deal to us.' His wife, standing by his side, nodded. Joss could see she was struggling to keep herself from breaking down altogether.

'Come on in and get a drink,' said Tommy's father, then briefly turned back and whispered something to his wife.

'Thank you,' said Joss, his misery mounting. While Mrs Haskell hurried off out of sight and away from the throng of people, Joss was ushered into the crowded drawing room. He recognized few of the faces. Most of Tommy's friends were away with the war. Instead, the room was filled with middle-aged and elderly relatives and friends of Tommy's parents. Their eyes turned towards him, looking at his uniform, making the connection. He wondered whether they resented him being alive when Tommy was dead.

Spotting Ellen, he made his way towards her. She seemed dazed, a faraway expression in her eyes. Joss could see she wasn't listening to a word the man next to her was saying. *This is hell for her*, he thought.

'Joss—you made it.' She smiled as he lightly touched her arm. Her voice was soft, barely above a whisper. Joss apologized some more. 'Don't,' said Ellen, 'please Joss, stop it.'

553

He looked down, and checked himself from apologizing for apologizing. Then he said, 'Actually, I've got something for you, Ellen,' and from his pocket produced Tommy's small pocket-journal. 'It's probably not mine to give, but I think he'd have wanted you to have this.'

She smiled wistfully, and touching his arm, said, 'Thank you—I shall treasure it.' She put it away in her bag, then said, 'I hope you'll keep in touch Joss.'

'Yes, of course,' he said.

Someone interrupted them, an older man, wanting to know from Joss about life with the squadron, about the intensity of the air battles, about whether they were winning. Joss answered the questions patiently, but when he next looked round, Ellen had moved away. He spotted Guy, still talking with Noel on the far side of the room, so excusing himself, inched his way across.

'Joss,' said Noel, extending an arm. 'What happened?'

Joss glanced briefly at Guy, then said, 'Today? I had a puncture. It took a while to sort out. I can't believe I missed it ...' He saw Guy glance about him. 'Anyway, it's good to see you again, Noel.'

'You too, although I wish it might have been otherwise. I never really thought he would die in a blaze of glory, did you?'

'No. No, I thought he'd be all right somehow.' He thought about Tommy in the last few weeks of his life. About his friend's mounting anxiety, the increasing reliance on drink, his worry about Ellen. He'd been in torment. *I should have done more.*

'We're going to miss him, aren't we?'

Joss could only nod as his throat tightened again.

'Anyway how are you?' Noel asked. 'You look awful, if you don't mind me saying.'

Joss smiled, then recovering his composure, managed to say, 'Slight lack of sleep probably. But I'm all right—in the circumstances. And still alive. You look exactly the same.' Noel's hair was as dishevelled as ever. The collar on his shirt was worn and there was a faint but noticeable stain on his suit jacket. 'How's Cambridge?' Joss asked him. 'Tommy was convinced you're working for British Intelligence.'

Noel laughed, and Joss glanced again at Guy, but his face remained set.

'Nothing quite as exciting as that I'm afraid,' said Noel, then pointing at the purple and white ribbon on Joss's tunic said, 'I see you've got a gong then.'

'Yes.'

'Well done. I hate to admit it, but I'm rather proud of you Joss. I know I wouldn't have the guts to do what you and Tommy have been doing all summer. Have you seen this Guy?'

'Ah, yes,' said Guy disinterestedly.

Noel furrowed his brows, looked at the two of them in turn, then said, 'Am I imagining things or is there something going on between you two?'

Neither Joss nor Guy spoke.

'I thought as much,' said Noel. 'You haven't said a word to each other.' He looked at them both again, then said, 'Come on, out with it.'

'It's nothing, Noel,' said Guy.

'Well if it really is nothing, then you both need your heads examining. We could all be dead tomorrow—and Joss, you quite likely so from the sounds of things—so is this squabble of yours really worth it?' He glanced at his watch, then said,

'Look, I've got to head back fairly soon, so I'm going to go and have a quick word with Mr and Mrs Haskell, but please, whatever it is, sort it out, before it's too late.'

He left them and for a moment Guy and Joss stood awkwardly looking past each other. Then Guy said, 'Let's go outside. I could do with some fresh air.' They began squeezing past the other guests, although several tried to talk to Joss. Making his excuses, he hurried on behind Guy.

In the hallway Tommy's father said, 'Not leaving already, are you?'

'No—no, we're just going outside for a moment, if that's all right,' said Joss.

Mr Haskell said, 'Ah—yes, of course. I'm half-tempted to join you myself.' He smiled and opened the door for them.

'Not easy to escape,' said Joss, as they stepped out onto the gravel driveway. An attempted ice-breaker, but Guy said nothing, just reached into his pocket and then lit a cigarette.

'Guy—'

'It's all right Joss,' he said. He paused a moment, then said, 'I overreacted, I know. And I'm sorry I hit you.'

'It hurt.' He gave Guy a rueful grin.

'But you hurt me, Joss.'

'I didn't mean to. That's the last thing I wanted to do.'

'We never used to have any secrets, you and I. But since you started flying, you stopped telling me things.' They walked through an iron gate and down a box-hedged path.   Joss said, 'No, that's not true. I only didn't talk to you about flying because I didn't want to bore you.'

'But flying has become such a large part of your life—don't you see that? Can't you see that from the moment you started flying, we've been drifting apart?'

'No, Guy, it's not like that.' They had reached an area of lawn and Guy walked over towards a stone seat set against a high yew hedge that was out of view from the main part of the house.

'And now you and Stella only have eyes for each other, there's even less room for me,' he said. He brushed away a few red yew berries, then sat down.

'Guy, you're my greatest friend. Always will be.'

Guy drew on his cigarette and exhaled into the now grey, overcast sky.

'It was different when we were at school,' Joss continued, 'but even without a war there was going to be a time when we saw less of each other. We'd have ended up having different jobs, getting married. Living different lives.'

'It's not just that. The war's changed you Joss.'

Joss sat down beside him on the stone seat, and put his head in his hands. *Am I really so different?* he thought. He'd *seen* more of life, certainly—and death. His old self, he realized, had been impossibly naïve, and childish too. But inside— *inside I am the same.*

'I suppose it's inevitable,' Guy continued, 'after what you've been through these past months. I suppose you and Tommy must have thought I've got it so easy in comparison.'

'No of course not—'

'No one shooting at me. No people to try and kill. And I know farming is a reserved occupation, but you don't know how hard it is when you see the expression on people's faces. "Look—he's not in

557

uniform! He must be shirking his duty!" '

'Guy, really, I'm sure—'

'No, Joss, you don't see it because everybody thinks you fighter pilots are the most wonderful people on earth. But it's true—I get all these accusing stares as though I'm some sort of coward because I haven't gone and joined up too. There're no medals for trying to feed people—no courage needed for that. But what I'm doing *is* making a difference, Joss, it really is.'

'Of course it is. You don't need to persuade me on that.'

Guy sighed. 'This bloody war. It's ruined everything. Christ, I still can't believe Tommy's dead.'

'I know.'

'At least you've got your other friends in the squadron. And you have Stella hanging on your every word. But I feel as though I've no one to confide in any more. I know I'm sounding sorry for myself, but I can't help how I feel no matter what else is going on around the world. I can't even seem to get along with Stella, and that's not just because of what's happened this past week. Apart from you, she was the one person I used to talk to about *everything*.'

'Look, can't we put all this behind us Guy? Can't we agree to talk to one another again?'

'I don't know Joss. Maybe one day.' He stood up. 'Noel's right about one thing, though: I'd hate us to part on bad terms.' He held out his hand. No embrace, no bear-hug as of old, but a shake of the hands. 'Look after yourself, Joss, and look after Stella too, won't you?'

'Of course—but I'll see you soon.'

Guy looked at him; Joss could see the corner of his eyes beginning to fill. 'Look, Joss, I don't think I can face going back inside, so I'm going to head off now, all right?'

Joss nodded.

'Bye Joss,' said Guy, then he turned and started to walk away.

'We are still friends then?' Joss called out after him.

Guy stopped and smiled, then turned down the path and out of sight.

*   *   *

Later, as Joss drove back under a dark and ominous mass of gathering cloud, he found it hard to think clearly about the day's events. He couldn't shake the weight of sadness that consumed him. Images of Tommy's grief-stricken parents kept reappearing in his mind's eye; the awful finality of Tommy's death—that he had lost such a vital companion was so hard to bear; and then there was Guy.

Guy. There'd been forgiveness—or acceptance at any rate—but also a wistful admission that they would never be so close again. *He's ashamed,* thought Joss, then out loud said, 'The fool'. But their parting was troubling him too: so long as Joss managed to keep alive, they would probably see each other again in a couple of weeks' time, yet Guy had acted as though they would not be seeing each other for years.

Then it dawned on him. *Oh no,* he thought, then aloud said, 'No Guy, don't. Please don't.' His friend had *told* him in as many words, almost urging Joss

559

to understand, as though a part of him had wanted to be dissuaded. And yet Joss had failed to read the signals, failed to comprehend the expression of resignation on Guy's face. He cursed himself—if only he'd helped his friend more, as he could and should have done. Tommy and now Guy: he'd been so wrapped up in himself, he'd offered them too little too late, and lost them both.

But perhaps it wasn't too late. As soon as he reached Middle Wallop, he telephoned Alvesdon Farm.

'Darling, what is it?' Stella asked.

'Is Guy back yet?'

'No. Why, what's the matter?'

'Stella, I think Guy's joined up.'

*   *   *

But Guy had already gone. His letter arrived the following day. *'Dear Mum and Stella,'* he had written, *'I know this will come as a surprise, but I knew if I told you both, you'd only try and talk me out of it. Dad once made me promise never to join up, but to stay and fight any war by farming the land. But much though it pains me, I can't honour that vow. I'm not needed here—not really. Stella, you and Sam can manage the farm perfectly well without me. Roger, Tommy and Joss, and countless others have done their bit and now I must do mine. Deep down I've known this for some time, but I've been using my promise to Dad as an excuse. Well, I can't rely on excuses any more. I must face my fears like everyone else. But please don't worry about me. I assure you I'll take very great care of myself. I'll write as soon as I can. With all my love, Guy.*

It was not until March the following year that Joss and Stella finally spent a week together in Cornwall. Guy's departure had left Stella in sole charge of the farm—taking time off was out of the question. Five months later, however, life at Alvesdon Farm had settled down once more. The summer's crops had been sown, hay had been cut down from the ricks for the cows, and although Stella complained to Joss that there was always so much to do (there was still threshing to complete from the previous harvest), March was as good a time as any for her to leave the farm in the capable hands of Sam Hicks.

It was just as well, because this was going to be their last chance to be together for an unknown length of time. Joss had hoped, like Pip and Mike before him, that he might be posted somewhere in England as an instructor, but to his great dismay, Nick Mitchell, the new Canadian CO, had called him into his office one morning and told him he would be leaving the squadron in a week to be posted overseas.

'I'm sorry, Joss—I'm going to miss you. And I'm afraid I can't even tell you where you're headed or what squadron you're joining. All it says here is that you're to report to the seaplane base at Mountbatten, Plymouth on March 21st. I guess it's fair to assume it's the Middle East somewhere, though. And you get ten days' leave—that's something.'

Joss had felt the colour drain from him. *What*

561

about Stella? he thought. To leave her now was unthinkable; *unbearable.*

The CO looked at him. 'Are you all right, Joss?'

Joss rubbed his forehead. 'I'd assumed I'd be instructing next.'

'They need experienced pilots abroad, and you've been with 629 a long time.'

Ah, the squadron. Much changed in recent months. One could almost say it was hardly the same squadron at all. At Christmas Mac had moved on—promoted to Wing Commander and moved to 12 Group. Mike had been posted in October, Pip in December. Antonin and Jerzy had joined the Polish Squadrons, Karl the newly-formed Eagle Squadron. By March, Joss and Denis Tweed were the only two left from the previous July.

In January, 629 had been moved to Tangmere, near Chichester on the south coast, and had begun flying sweeps over to France looking for German planes to attack, or escorting British bombers. On the offensive at last, the threat of a German invasion over—for the time being at any rate. It had made midweek visits to Salisbury or Alvesdon Farm impossible, although Joss tried to see Stella on his weekly 24-hour pass, or whenever he was due more substantial leave. As rationing tightened, petrol was harder and harder to come by, but there were ways and means of filling the tank of Tommy's old Riley; a blind eye was usually turned when pilots siphoned fuel from the bowsers.

If Celia had ever felt that Joss was in some way to blame for Guy's departure, she never once let on. 'It's so nice to have some male company about the place,' she would say, and welcomed him during his regular visits just as she had always done. The light had gone from her eyes, however, and although she tried to keep busy looking after the house and the two evacuees, more than once, Joss caught her sitting alone in the drawing room, staring blankly at the photographs on the top of the piano. She once confessed to him, 'I don't know what I've done to deserve it quite, but all the men in my life seem to have been taken from me: my brother Alex, baby Michael, David, Roger and now even Guy.'

'Poor Mummy,' Stella said to Joss one night, 'her heart's been broken, you know. I wish I could help her, but I'm not one of her boys.'

At least Guy had written regularly, with detailed accounts of his training. He never mentioned which regiment he'd joined, or where he was, but the descriptions suggested Scotland. Celia's enquiries at the War Office proved fruitless. 'Could you make some enquiries, Joss? Perhaps being in the services already you might have greater luck than me . . .' But he'd been unable to discover anything more than her.

'Ah well,' said Celia. 'Thank you for trying, Joss.' After all her kindnesses towards him, he wished he'd been able to offer her some news at least, and keenly felt her look of disappointment.

It was then that Joss suggested to Stella that she ask Philip Mornay. 'He's in intelligence isn't he? Perhaps he could pull some strings.'

'I hadn't thought of him,' Stella said. 'All right, I will.' Within a week of her writing to him, Philip had replied. Guy had joined the Rifle Brigade, not on a commission, but in the rank and file. *There is one condition for this,'* Philip had written, *'you must allow me to take you out to dinner some time soon.'*

563

'Will you?' asked Joss. They were lying in Joss's bed, in the spare room in which he had always slept. Celia had accepted that the two of them had fallen in love, although whether she knew that at night Stella always tiptoed into his room and slipped into bed beside him—as she had that first night they'd kissed—Joss could only guess.

'Maybe one day,' Stella told him. 'Not for a long time, though. I wouldn't want to waste precious time with Philip when I could be spending it with you. Anyway, I don't have any time to go swanning up to London.'

'I'm glad with all those bombs falling. I just wish I could persuade Diana to move out.' Joss had still not given up trying—he asked her to do so every time he wrote or spoke to her, but the answer was always the same: he was not to fuss, she was fine; really, the chances of a bomb falling on her were very slight; he should spend his time worrying about his own safety, not his dear old mama's.

Although Guy and Tommy never strayed far from his mind, he had lived for Stella during those months. Every time he woke up he thought of her, as he did every time he strapped himself into his Spitfire, and he would pray that he would make it safely back so that he could once again enclose her in his arms. The moment he left her, he yearned for the time he would see her again. Of course he'd known that one day he would leave the squadron, but he had pushed out of his mind any thoughts of being posted abroad; such a total separation would be too much to bear. But now it was happening after all, and he was powerless to do anything about it.

Leaving the CO's office, his façade of outward

calm collapsed. He walked outside into the chill late-February wind, and, gulping several times, squatted down and put his hands to his face. Tears ran between his fingers. There was no one about; no aircraft taking off or landing; no groundcrew busying themselves. No one to hear his sobs, only the wind whistling against the hangars and rustling the hedgerow along the perimeter.

* * *

Two days later he drove over to Alvesdon Farm. All afternoon he waited for a chance to tell her, but convinced himself the moment was never quite right, and so while he helped her with paperwork in her father's old office and all through supper with Celia in the kitchen, he kept the news from her. Several times she said he seemed quiet, asking him if there was anything troubling him, and each time, he said, no, he was fine, perhaps a bit tired, that was all.

It was only once she had climbed into his bed and started kissing him that he knew he could keep back the news no longer.

'Darling,' he said, dragging the words out of himself, 'there's something I've got to tell you.'

Stella sat up immediately. 'What? What is it?'

'I'm leaving the squadron.'

'To be an instructor?' Hope in her voice.

'No. I've been posted overseas. I've got to leave on the 21st.'

'But that's less than three weeks' away. My God, is that all we've got left?' She rolled over, silent for a moment.

'Stella?'

'I knew it,' she said. 'I knew that this was too good to be true, that you'd be taken from me.'

'It won't be for ever.' But as he said that he knew their world had already irreversibly changed from just a minute before, just as he had known it would all day when he'd been battling to find the courage to tell her of his sentence.

In the darkness, he leaned over and found her face. He kissed her, and tasted the salty tears already running down her cheeks.

*   *   *

'At least I have ten days' leave before I go,' Joss had told her.

'But it will pass and then you'll be gone.'

'We could take that week in Cornwall. At least we could have some time together on our own.'

'Yes,' she conceded, 'yes, that would be lovely.'

His last week with the squadron passed quickly. There was little flying—the weather had been poor—although on his final morning he had flown on an uneventful sweep across the Channel. Later that evening, Mitchell, the new CO, ensured Joss was given a rousing send-off, then the following morning, with a pounding head and having passed on Tommy's old Riley to Denis Tweed, he caught a train to London to see his mother for one last time before his departure.

Over an insipid dinner at a restaurant in Victoria, Joss told her, 'I'm not sure where I'm being sent, but odds are it'll be North Africa.'

'Back to Africa,' she said. 'I'm almost envious of you—just think of all that sun and heat. God, I hate the English winters.'

'I'd happily live through a hundred English winters if it meant I could stay here.'

'Stella?' said Diana.

Joss nodded.

'My poor darling. I wish there was something I could say to cheer you up. Perhaps Anthony could speak to someone and get your posting cancelled.'

Joss smiled. 'Yes, maybe,' he told her. *If only he could.*

No sooner had they arrived back at the flat than the air-raid sirens began. Along with several hundred others, they trooped down to the shelter around the corner, and waited for the first bombs to drop. A few distant crashes, then it was over. Only a light attack that night.

In the morning, Diana accompanied Joss to Waterloo. On the platform, amidst the rush of people and soldiers and steam, he hugged her tightly and said, 'I wish you'd leave London.'

'No Joss. I'm being very careful, as you saw last night. Anyway, it's getting better. Apart from last night, we haven't had any raids for days.' She kissed him. 'Write to me won't you? And be careful. You are all I've got, you know.'

As the train slowly drew away, he leant out of the window and waved to her, feeling more fond of her than ever. He was glad she had said those words to him.

He met Stella at Salisbury. As arranged, they had travelled on to Exeter together, then changed onto a train for Bodmin, before changing again for the branch line to Newquay. The hotel was some way out of town, high on the cliffs overlooking the sea. It had been a long, cramped journey, and so wearily, they trudged the last few miles on foot.

Seven days. They passed too fast. They walked, talked and made love, only too aware of the preciousness of each moment. Seven days of grey skies and rain, so that although the budding daffodils and first flecks of green lining the hedgerows hinted that spring was on its way, the cold winds coming off the sea and rattling the windows of their cliff-top hotel reminded them that the bitter winter was not yet through.

When they ventured out, they held hands, hers sometimes clutching his in the depth of his greatcoat pocket, or they stumbled, his arm around her waist, as though he wished they might have been glued together; as though he might never have to let go.

The last night. Joss could hardly bring himself to go to bed, because he knew that when he did so, it would be for the last time with her. Watching her undress, he tried to imprint on his mind every curve: the shape of her breasts, the line of her shoulders, the small mole on her right-hand thigh. As she came to him, he thought about the feel of her skin on his, the way she smiled, *preened* almost, like a cat, her eyes closed, as he kissed her neck. These images he would take with him, would have to last for him, locked as a detailed memory, for as long as was necessary.

'I don't want to sleep,' she said after, 'but I feel so sleepy.'

'I don't want to sleep either.'

'Oh my darling,' she said, threading her fingers through his hair, 'I just don't know how I'm going to get through this. I'll try, but I don't know how I'm going to. I know thousands of others are in the same boat as me but that doesn't make it any easier.'

'Marry me,' he said. 'Marry me, Stella.'

She smiled. 'Yes, I will. I'd love to be married to you more than anything.'

'We can have it to look forward to. For when I get back. We can be married in the church at Marleycombe, and have children of our own, and wake up every morning together and live happily ever after.'

She was silent a moment, then said, 'Do such things ever happen, Joss?'

'I don't know. I never thought so before, but now—well, now I think we have to believe they can.'

'If only I knew where you were going and for how long. I won't be able to imagine you out there, won't be able to count the days. You don't know what it is to worry about someone *all* the time.'

'I'll write. I'll write very detailed letters about everything I see and do. I *will* come back for you, Stella. And I'll be thinking of you every moment of every day that I'm away.'

She sat up and brought her knees tight under her chin, her arms around them. 'Have I got the strength for this Joss? Oh, my love, how am I going to survive without you? I sometimes wish I'd never met you, so that I wouldn't have to put up with the torture stretching ahead of me.'

Joss put his arms around her and brought her slowly towards him. Silently, she stretched out her legs once more, and twined them within his. He clasped her head, his hands in her hair, and felt her tears on his chest, then some time after, the gentle breathing of her sleep.

'I love you,' he whispered into her hair, 'but please wait for me. Stella, please wait for me.'

Cairo—November, 1942

The mounting sense of jubilation reached a crescendo on the morning of November 5th. Rommel was now in full retreat, and it was widely expected that Montgomery would overtake the remainder of the Axis forces in a matter of days. This time, surely, there would be no counter-attack, no see-saw across the desert; this time, the Axis would be swept from North Africa for good. And this great victory was in no small part thanks to the efforts of the RAF, as Group Captain Green happily reminded them all at every turn. 'Done bloody well, really bloody well,' he said as he wandered through their offices, clutching a whisky and slapping people on the back.

Joss had noticed that not everyone at RAF Middle East Headquarters shared the buoyant mood and *bonhomie,* however. Jim Thorne, a desk-bound squadron leader, had been wearing a miserable expression all morning. Normally as easygoing and affable as anyone could be, Jim had barely looked up from the stack of papers on his desk.

'Jim—anything the matter?' Joss asked during a moment of quiet.

Jim sighed. 'No. No, I'm fine.' He sighed again. 'Well actually, no I'm not. It's my wife—the little

570

bitch!' Joss was surprised by his vehemence. Jim rubbed his forehead. 'She's only gone and bloody well left me. Says she's terribly sorry, but she's fallen in love with someone else.'

'I'm sorry,' said Joss. 'That's hard.'

'Yes, well, what can you do? You answer the call, risk life and limb and this is the thanks you get. I loved her very much you know. I sometimes think she was the only thing that kept me going.'

Yes, thought Joss, *I know*. Those 'Dear John' letters—as everyone called them—he'd watched men get those from the moment he'd arrived in the desert, although he'd never believed his turn would come. For nearly a year, she'd written almost every day. He'd receive nothing for weeks, then a whole bunch would suddenly arrive, and he would retreat to his tent and devour them hungrily. Unlike Diana's letters, which tended to be short and generally uninformative, Stella had poured out every detail of her life. She once wrote that she liked to pretend she was telling him things as they would when they were married and catching up on the day's events over dinner. She also sent him news of Guy: he had been posted to North Africa too, but by that time, Joss was instructing at Khartoum. Shortly after, another letter arrived telling him Guy had been captured during the British evacuation of Benghazi, and was now a prisoner of war. *At least he's safe*, wrote Stella. Joss hoped so. Short messages had occasionally reached Alvesdon Farm via the Red Cross—Guy had been taken to a camp in Italy. He was fine; the Italians were treating them well. *It's such a relief*, wrote Stella. *He says we're not to worry. Mum's happier than I've seen her in a long time.*

They were the only source of comfort in an otherwise miserable existence, the only real link to the life he had known back in England. He hated the desert. The others in the squadron were all right, but the camaraderie of the previous summer—the intense sense of fellowship—could not be replicated. How could it when there were so little means of letting off steam? There was no pub in the middle of the desert. No mess ward-room with snooker table and darts board. Nowhere to go but the stinking melting pot of Cairo when they were given leave. He had often wondered whether Stella had been right: perhaps it would have been better if they'd never met. He saw the young men still untainted by love, and how much better it was for them. He remembered asking Laurie Collins—poor Laurie Collins, who'd gone missing back in June—how he always seemed to keep so cheerful.

'Don't you mind being out here in this shit-pit?' Joss had asked.

Laurie had shrugged. 'I was in the Boy Scouts, you see,' he'd said, 'so I've always quite liked camping. And the flying's wizard.'

The flurry of letters had stopped abruptly. In three months, there'd not been one letter. Any day, he told himself, a sackful would arrive, but with each week that passed, his anxiety grew. Then at last; he'd been at breaking point. That day he'd received her letter—that day he'd crashed—he'd lain beside his smouldering aircraft, the sun bearing down on him, and knew that his will had been broken, his spirit annihilated. He'd been left stupefied with grief and despair.

That was then, thought Joss, as he walked out of MEHQ and hailed a taxi. Pip had rung him and told him he had good news and that he was to meet him at the Gezira Sporting Club at three.

A battered car drew up—the headlight and off-side fender badly smashed. Joss stepped in. She'd wondered whether he was the same person, after all this time. *Yes,* he thought to himself, *I am*—but someone very different too. Older, if not in years—he was still only 22—then definitely in experience. Someone who had been taken to the very edges of hell, but who had survived; someone who had spent his life not knowing who he was or where he belonged, but who now knew the answers. The thought of returning to England—and yes, it was *home*—had given him the first real tingles of excitement and hope he'd experienced in months. *I do not belong here,* he thought, *any more than I do in Germany.* There was not even a flicker of belonging, nor affiliation to their people. They were alien to him. Tommy had been right all along: nurture, not nature defined the man. He accepted that now. It was a fact, clear in his mind, something that would never again cause him anxiety.

*   *   *

Pip was already there, seated at the bar and blowing smoke rings.

'Good to see you,' he grinned, holding out his hand. 'What'll it be?'

'A beer, thanks.'

'Hm—think I'll join you.'

The safragi poured two beers, then Pip said, 'Well, d'you want the good news or the bad?'

'Er, bad, then good,' said Joss, his heart sinking.

Pip laughed. 'The bad news is: there is no bad

news. The good news is: we're leaving tomorrow.'

'Tomorrow?' Joss whistled and ran his hands through his hair.

'I thought you'd be pleased.'

'Pleased? I am Pip, truly I am. I just can't believe it's over.'

'What do you mean?'

'My time out here. Eighteen months—it feels like a lifetime. A large part of me thought I'd never ever get back.'

Pip took a draught of his beer then said, 'Well, you better get used to it quick, because we're out of here tomorrow morning. On a Wellington flying out of Heliopolis.'

Joss left Pip an hour later. The news was only very slowly sinking in. He picked up another taxi at the club and gave the driver the address of the Villa Jacaranda, then changed his mind. However fond he was of Binny—and the others for that matter—he felt a strong desire for some time alone.

'Sorry,' he said to the driver. 'Please take me to Groppi's instead.'

He realized how much he was looking forward to seeing his mother again. Even London, for all its people, smog and density, held an appeal he'd never appreciated before. He thought of cold afternoons, and crisp frosty mornings, of going to pubs and drinking proper beer once more. England would not be the same place—how could it when there was no Stella, no Alvesdon Farm, no Guy and no Tommy?—but it was still the place he wanted to be more than any other. At least when he returned from a sortie, he would be flying over friendly countryside and landing on a green field. At least

574

he could look up old acquaintances—Noel, maybe, if he was still at Cambridge. At least he'd be with Pip.

The car passed a group of American servicemen, their shirts pristine, and he suddenly remembered something Tommy had once said to him: 'You know, Joss, it's a pity that you weren't brought up in America, then this shame of yours would never exist.' Joss had looked perplexed. 'What do you mean?'

'Irish-Americans, Georgian-Americans, Lithuanian -Americans, Italian-Americans, Polish-Americans, Austrian-Americans, Japanese-Americans, *German* -Americans. A whole nation of immigrants yet every one proud to call themselves American, and why shouldn't they?' But Tommy had been a modern; at Cambridge he'd seemed so—well, *daring,* was probably the right word. Yet the breaking down of old barriers and constraints had been an obvious product of the war; they ceased to be quite so important when thousands of people were being killed every day. It was as though not only Joss, but the entire civilized world, had grown up. He'd met few people who really hated Germans. To most he had flown and fought beside, the enemy was someone to be ridiculed, but not despised; Antonin and Jerzy had been the exceptions, not the norm. Not all Germans were bad people, just as not all Englishmen were good; it was so obvious, but as a child Joss had firstly refused to believe it, then as a young man failed to see that others could view the world as anything other than black or white. What a fool he'd been! It was who you were inside that mattered; one fought for what one believed in, and for who and what one loved. Relief coursed

575

through him. 'I am going home,' he mouthed to himself, as the taxi trundled through the never-ending bustle of Cairo. 'I am going *home.*'

*   *   *

It was growing cool, sitting outside in the garden at Groppi's, the sun sinking ever lower in the sky. The brightly-coloured umbrellas that normally shielded every table had already been taken down, and now lay stacked in a corner. The smell of coffee and sweet pastry drifted across the walled garden. Joss lit a cigarette and watched the blue-grey smoke rise idly into the still late-afternoon air. He had picked up a newspaper left by a previous customer. 'ROMMEL ROUTED' ran the headline. The previous night at the Villa Jacaranda they had all sat around the wireless, and having heard the news that General von Thoma had been captured, had celebrated into the night. Even Dobbo had smiled at one point. 'We might not have won the war yet,' Walter had repeated over and over, 'but mark my words, it's a turning point all right.' *God, I hope so,* thought Joss.

He was about to leave when a group of three officers and two ladies came into the café. One, Joss recognized immediately. Tall, dark-haired, a fine pencil-thin moustache. Joss watched as his eyes swept around the walled garden, and stopped at him. He glanced away again, then back, saw that Joss had recognized him and, excusing himself from the others, took a few steps towards Joss's table. He narrowed his eyes, and smiled, then clicked his fingers—*I know you, it'll come back to me any second.*

576

'Hello, Philip,' said Joss, and stood up to shake his hand. 'It's Joss. Joss Lambert.'

'Of course it is. Good God, Joss Lambert. Barely recognized you. How the devil are you?'

'Fine, thank you. You?'

'Yes, very well. Even better now there's been this news from up in the blue.' They smiled at each other, each wondering what to say, so Joss said, 'Can you be spared for a drink?'

Philip looked at the others quickly, then said, 'Of course,' and sat down while Joss called over a safragi.

'So,' said Joss. 'Been over here long?'

'About three months.'

'Intelligence still?' said Joss.

Philip smiled, and put a finger to his mouth. *Hush hush.* 'Yes. But this is where it's all happening at the moment, so they posted me over here to MEHQ. Can't say I mind particularly—after London, this is the lap of luxury.'

Joss wondered. How could he have been glad to leave Stella behind? 'Well,' he said, 'I suppose there's no blackout here.'

'And plenty of booze and food too. London's been grim—honestly, we're far better off out here. Anyway,' he said, lifting his glass to his mouth, 'what are you doing now?'

'Just about to head back, actually. I was wounded back in July, but I've just made it past the Medical Board. Flying out tomorrow.'

'Good for you,' grinned Philip, 'good for you.'

They were silent for a moment, then Philip said, 'I'm just trying to think of the last time I saw you.'

'It was at a party in London,' said Joss. 'In the Albany building at Piccadilly before the war. You

577

came with Stella.'

Philip nodded. 'Y-es. Yes, that would be it.'

Joss watched him. He wanted to ask about Stella, but was afraid of what he'd tell him—that she was well, expecting their first child, that they were blissfully happy together.

He put a cigarette in his mouth, conscious his hands were shaking as he tried to light it. 'How's Stella?' he said at last. *There—I've said it.*

'Ah,' said Philip. 'I'd love to tell you, but I don't really know.'

'Bloody post,' said Joss.

'No, no, nothing like that. You see, I haven't seen her for nearly six months.'

Joss stared at him, his heart quickening.

'In fact, I've a bit of a bone to pick with you. We were engaged, as you obviously know, but she broke it off.'

'Broke it off?'

'Yes. And it's all due to you.'

'What do you mean?'

'In a nutshell: she was still too strung up on you, old thing.'

For a moment, Joss could say nothing. Then very slowly he said, 'Please Philip, tell me. Tell me exactly what you mean.'

Philip took out a cigarette from a shiny silver case and lit it. 'Very well, if you really want me to.' He drew on his cigarette, then exhaled through the side of his mouth. He looked much older, less debonair than Joss remembered. 'Well, I've known her quite a long while now. Got to know her when she first came to London,' he told Joss. 'She was a lovely girl—pretty, funny. I was a bit older so it was easy to turn her head, I suppose. Then she

578

disappeared—her brother went missing at Dunkirk and she said it changed everything. Well, I was busy in London and couldn't go chasing after her, but then she wrote to me out of the blue wanting me to look up her other brother for her. Anyway, I found out his battalion and told her that in return I wanted to take her out to dinner. I didn't hear anything for a while, but then I had to go down to her neck of the woods so I thought I'd look her up. Well, frankly, she was in a bad way. Looked tired—had lost that spark that made her stand out so when I first knew her. But still lovely. Beautiful really. "What is it?" I asked her. "It's not right for a girl like you to be so down." Well, she told me. There was this man she was in love with, and she was finding it hard to cope—not knowing where he was or whether he was alive or dead. So I told her that what she needed was have a bit of fun—to get out more. Well, eventually I got her up to London, and I made a few more trips down to see her and I noticed that she had stopped talking about this man of hers and so I thought she must have got over him and that the coast was clear, so I popped the question. But I'd barely got her the ring when she told me she was sorry but she couldn't marry me after all. "Why on earth not?" I asked her. "Because," she said, "I still think about Joss every minute of every day." So—there you have it. If I were you, I'd get straight to down to that farm of hers just as soon as you possibly can.'

Joss could say nothing. His mind reeled. It was impossible, incredible, to believe she could still love him. *After all.*

'Sorry if I've given you a shock,' said Philip. 'Look, are you all right?'

Joss stubbed out his cigarette. 'Yes, yes I'm fine. It's just so—Christ. Then why didn't she say?'

Philip shrugged. 'God knows. I've never been able to understand women. Are you sure you're all right. I didn't mean to alarm you—'

'No, I'm glad you did. Very glad.' Joss could barely contain himself—could certainly not sit there calmly chatting to Philip any longer. Looking at his watch, he said, 'Goodness, is that the time? I'm really sorry, Philip, but I must dash.'

'Really? Well, good to see you. Good luck.'

'Yes, you too. And *thank you.*' Leaving too much money on the table, he hurried out.

He stumbled through the streets, lit up with the garish lights of the city at night. The traffic rumbled by, hawkers shouted, drunken servicemen sang and chanted and children tugged at his tunic and pleaded for baksheesh. Joss saw none of it, nor heard the deafening cacophony of noise that filled the air, for his soul was dancing on a wave of exultation that grew with every step he took.

Historical Note and Acknowledgements

The major events in this book are all rooted in fact. The North African desert was notoriously grim for all those concerned, and for much of it, the RAF fighter pilots were flying battered Hurricanes and American P-40 Kittyhawks that were inferior to the German Messerschmitt 109Fs and Gs. There were no Spitfires in the desert until the summer of 1942, around the time that Joss was wounded. It is also true that the Luftwaffe in North Africa tended to concentrate on picking off fighters at the expense of the bombers, a tactic that would cost them dearly. Egypt, while not strictly part of the British Empire, was very much a colonial city, and throughout the war, was home to a vast number of servicemen and British civilians from around the globe. Most of the places mentioned did exist in Cairo—the 9th Scottish General Hospital, Shepheard's Hotel, the Gezira Sporting Club, Mena House and Groppi's.

For the flying training sequences, I have relied heavily on the memories of several former Battle of Britain fighter pilots, but particularly Maurice Mounsden, Geoffrey Wellum and Joe Leigh. In writing about the Battle of Britain, I tried as far as possible to follow actual events, purely in the interest of accuracy: the fictional 629 Squadron is based heavily on the very real 609 (West Riding) Squadron, a pre-war auxiliary squadron that was decimated during the fighting over Dunkirk. MacIntyre is unmistakably the former 609 CO,

Squadron Leader George Darley, while most of Joss's experiences are based on those of David Crook, a cheerful and intelligent former pilot who wrote a brilliant book about his experiences, *Spitfire Pilot*, in 1942. From his logbook and from the squadron's Operational Record Book, both housed at the Public Records Office in Kew, I was able to draw a detailed picture of how the squadron operated throughout that summer. Joss's leave, for example, follows Crook's. Darley himself was also interviewed on a number of occasions after the war, and his memories feature in a number of books on the subject. Both Warmwell and Middle Wallop were real fighter airfields, and the way in which the fictional 629 Squadron used the former, mirrors that of the real 609 Squadron. Warmwell is no more, but Middle Wallop remains, now used by the Army Air Corps. The wartime bungalow used by the pilots as their dispersal is still standing, as is the Five Bells pub at Nether Wallop and the New Inn at West Knighton. Warmwell was also, in 1940, notoriously short on amenities for visiting fighter squadrons, and pilots suffered particularly from the lack of conveniences at dispersal.

For the most part, weather conditions, and the size, timings and numbers of enemy raids are also true to real events, including the large attacks in September 1940, which in many ways decided the outcome of the battle. There are a vast number of archives, memoirs and other books relating to the Battle of Britain, but I was also fortunate to talk with a number of Battle of Britain veterans, who freely shared with me their memories of those days. A number of their anecdotes have been 'borrowed' for the book.

The intensification of farming as experienced at Alvesdon Farm is also based on fact. Flocks and herds were cut drastically and many thousands of acres of 'ripe but rugged' land turned over to the plough. It was also a time of rapidly increased mechanization, that hurried the end of mass-labour and the horse. The effects of the war changed British farming forever.

The University Air Squadron at Cambridge operated in much the same way as described, and a number of Oxbridge graduates joined the RAF Volunteer Reserve as a result, rather in the same manner as Joss, Peter and Tommy. However, the UAS was extremely popular and such were the waiting lists that in reality, by 1939, all three would have been very unlikely to have been given places. There was a Dr Sleeman at Queens' College, Cambridge, in the 1930s, although his character in the book is entirely fictional, and I certainly have no idea whether the real tutor was in favour of the Norman conquest. The rowing sequences at Cambridge, are not, however, realistic. The River Cam is generally too narrow for side-by-side racing. Instead, college teams were generally eight-men strong and racing came in the form of 'bumps' whereby boats set off at different times and tried to catch up with the ones in front. I hope any former Cambridge rowers will overlook my stretching of the truth.

I spoke to a number of people who lived through those times and would like to thank the following: Squadron Leader Geoffrey Wellum, DFC; Group Captain Allan Wright, DFC; the late Wing Commander Roland 'Bee' Beamont, CBE, DSO*, DFC*, Squadron Leader Joe Leigh, DFC; George

Williams; Les Collins; Wendy Maxwell; the late Dr Jim Bourne; Wing Commander Tom Neil, DFC, Bronze Star, AFC; Wing Commander Bob Doe, DFC*, DSO; and Tommy Thompson, DFC.

I would also like to thank the following: Ron Beard; Bill Bond of the Battle of Britain Historical Society; Giles Bourne; Cassie Chadderton; Bernice Davison; Lynne Drew; Harriet Evans; Kirtsy Fowkes; Emma Gardner; David Hindley; Lalla Hitchings; Sarah Hulse; Mark Lucas; Wendy Kyrle-Pope; Mark McCallum; Andy McKillop; Nicky Nevin and everyone else at Random House who helped with the book; Peta Nightingale; David Ross; Dilip Sarkar; Malcolm Smith and the Battle of Britain Fighter Association, and the Spitfire Society. Special thanks go to Georgina Hawtrey-Woore, Susan Sandon and Kate Parkin for all their enormous help, support and guidance. Finally, I would like to thank Patrick Walsh and Emma Parry, and also Rachel for her support and various suggestions.